DISNEY MASTERS

UNCLE SCROOGE: KING OF THE GOLDEN RIVER

by Giovan Battista Carpi

Publisher: GARY GROTH
Series Editor: J. MICHAEL CATRON
Editor: KEELI McCARTHY
Editorial Assistance: CONRAD GROTH
Archival Editor: DAVID GERSTEIN
Designer: KEELI MCCARTHY
Production: PAUL BARESH
Associate Publisher: ERIC REYNOLDS

Fantagraphics Books, Inc.
7563 Lake City Way NE
Seattle WA 98115
(800) 657-1100

Visit us at fantagraphics.com. Follow us on Twitter at @fantagraphics and on Facebook at facebook.com/fantagraphics.

Thanks to Luca Boschi, Arianna Marchione, and Anne Marie Mersing.
Front and back cover illustrations by Giovan Battista Carpi, color by Disney Italia.

First printing: March 2019
ISBN 978-1-68396-170-3
Printed in The Republic of Korea
Library of Congress Control Number: 2017956971

The stories in this volume were originally published in Italy and appear here in English for the first time. "King of the Golden River" ("Paperino e il re del fiume d'oro") in *Topolino* #270-272, January 29, February 5, and February 12, 1961 (I TL 270-AP); "Mickey the Kid and Six-Shot Goofy" ("Topolino Kid e Pippo sei-colpi") in *Topolino* #968-969, June 16 and June 23, 1974 (I TL 968-AP); Illustration on page 156 in *Tesori Disney* #6, April 2010 (IC TSD 6); "Me, Myself—And Why?" ("Zio Paperone e la triplicità progressiva") in *Topolino* #758, June 7, 1970 (I TL 758-A)

These stories were created during an earlier time and may include cartoon violence, historically dated content, or gags that depict smoking, drinking, gunplay, or ethnic stereotypes. We present them here with their original flaws with a caution to the reader that they reflect a bygone era.

TITLES IN THIS SERIES

Mickey Mouse: The Delta Dimension (Romano Scarpa) (*Disney Masters* Vol. 1)
Donald Duck: Uncle Scrooge's Money Rocket (Luciano Bottaro) (*Disney Masters* Vol. 2)
Mickey Mouse: The Case of the Vanishing Bandit (Paul Murry) (*Disney Masters* Vol. 3)
Donald Duck: The Great Survival Test (Daan Jippes and Freddy Milton) (*Disney Masters* Vol. 4)
Mickey Mouse: The Phantom Blot's Double Mystery (Romano Scarpa) (*Disney Masters* Vol. 5)
Uncle Scrooge: King of The Golden River (Giovan Battista Carpi) (*Disney Masters* Vol. 6)

COMING SOON

Mickey Mouse: The Pirates of Tabasco Bay (Paul Murry) (*Disney Masters* Vol. 7)

ALSO AVAILABLE

Mickey Mouse: The Greatest Adventures (Floyd Gottfredson)
Walt Disney's Uncle Scrooge: "The Mines of King Solomon" (Carl Barks)
The Complete Life and Times of Scrooge McDuck Volume 1 (Don Rosa)

Walt Disney UNCLE $CROOGE

King of the Golden River

FANTAGRAPHICS BOOKS

SEATTLE

CONTENTS

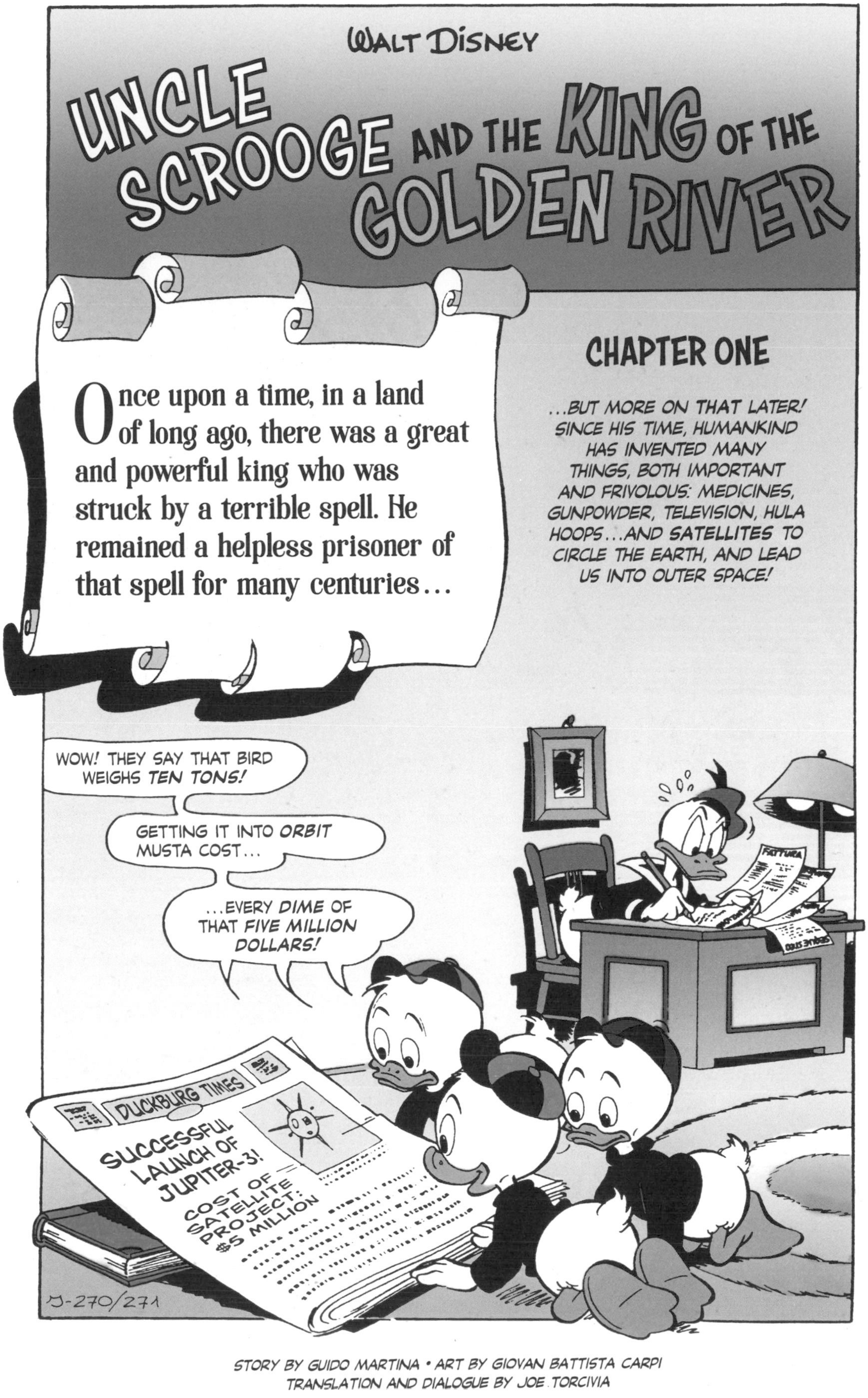
WALT DISNEY
UNCLE SCROOGE AND THE KING OF THE GOLDEN RIVER
Once upon a time, in a land of long ago, there was a great and powerful king who was struck by a terrible spell. He remained a helpless prisoner of that spell for many centuries...
CHAPTER ONE
...BUT MORE ON THAT LATER! SINCE HIS TIME, HUMANKIND HAS INVENTED MANY THINGS, BOTH IMPORTANT AND FRIVOLOUS: MEDICINES, GUNPOWDER, TELEVISION, HULA HOOPS...AND SATELLITES TO CIRCLE THE EARTH, AND LEAD US INTO OUTER SPACE!
WOW! THEY SAY THAT BIRD WEIGHS TEN TONS!
GETTING IT INTO ORBIT MUSTA COST...
...EVERY DIME OF THAT FIVE MILLION DOLLARS!
DUCKBURG TIMES
SUCCESSFUL LAUNCH OF JUPITER-3!
COST OF SATELLITE PROJECT: $5 MILLION
FATTURA

STORY BY GUIDO MARTINA • ART BY GIOVAN BATTISTA CARPI
TRANSLATION AND DIALOGUE BY JOE TORCIVIA

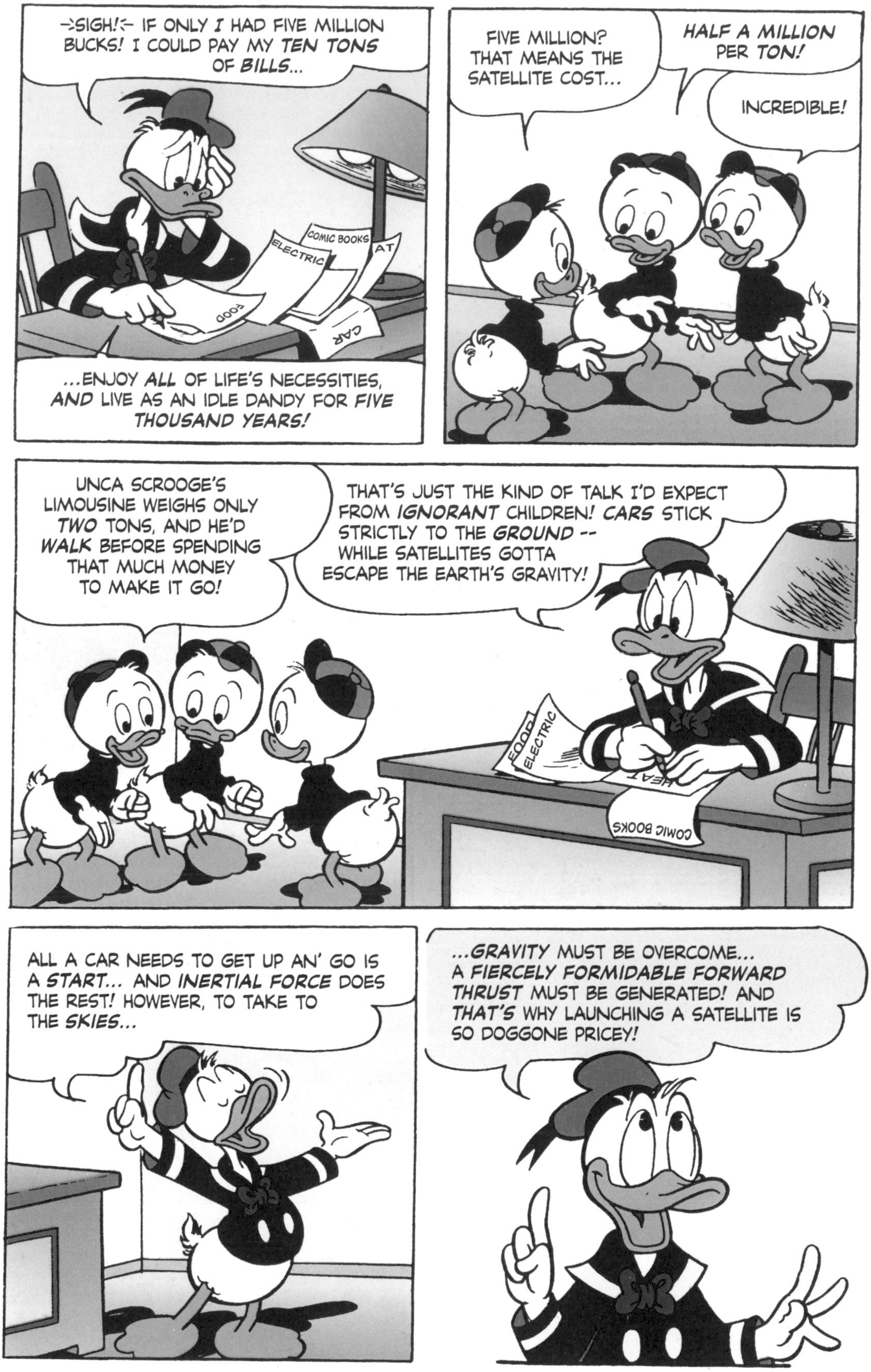

-SIGH!- IF ONLY I HAD FIVE MILLION BUCKS! I COULD PAY MY TEN TONS OF BILLS...
COMIC BOOKS
ELECTRIC
FOOD
CAR
...ENJOY ALL OF LIFE'S NECESSITIES, AND LIVE AS AN IDLE DANDY FOR FIVE THOUSAND YEARS!
FIVE MILLION? THAT MEANS THE SATELLITE COST...
HALF A MILLION PER TON!
INCREDIBLE!
UNCA SCROOGE'S LIMOUSINE WEIGHS ONLY TWO TONS, AND HE'D WALK BEFORE SPENDING THAT MUCH MONEY TO MAKE IT GO!
THAT'S JUST THE KIND OF TALK I'D EXPECT FROM IGNORANT CHILDREN! CARS STICK STRICTLY TO THE GROUND -- WHILE SATELLITES GOTTA ESCAPE THE EARTH'S GRAVITY!
ELECTRIC
HEAT
COMIC BOOKS
ALL A CAR NEEDS TO GET UP AN' GO IS A START... AND INERTIAL FORCE DOES THE REST! HOWEVER, TO TAKE TO THE SKIES...
...GRAVITY MUST BE OVERCOME... A FIERCELY FORMIDABLE FORWARD THRUST MUST BE GENERATED! AND THAT'S WHY LAUNCHING A SATELLITE IS SO DOGGONE PRICEY!

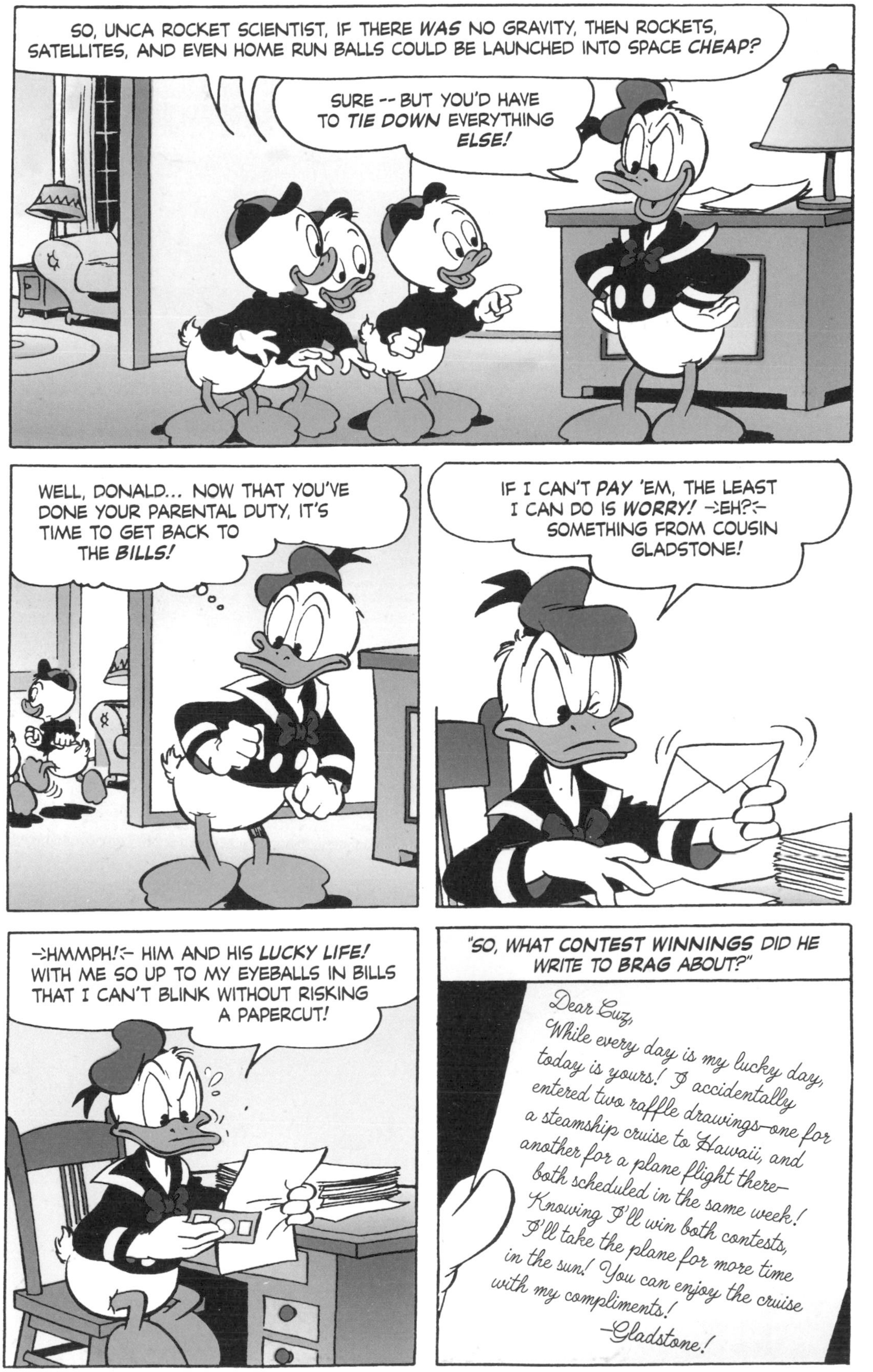
SO, UNCA ROCKET SCIENTIST, IF THERE WAS NO GRAVITY, THEN ROCKETS, SATELLITES, AND EVEN HOME RUN BALLS COULD BE LAUNCHED INTO SPACE CHEAP?
SURE -- BUT YOU'D HAVE TO TIE DOWN EVERYTHING ELSE!
WELL, DONALD... NOW THAT YOU'VE DONE YOUR PARENTAL DUTY, IT'S TIME TO GET BACK TO THE BILLS!
IF I CAN'T PAY 'EM, THE LEAST I CAN DO IS WORRY! -EH?- SOMETHING FROM COUSIN GLADSTONE!
-HMMPH!- HIM AND HIS LUCKY LIFE! WITH ME SO UP TO MY EYEBALLS IN BILLS THAT I CAN'T BLINK WITHOUT RISKING A PAPERCUT!
"SO, WHAT CONTEST WINNINGS DID HE WRITE TO BRAG ABOUT?"
Dear Cuz,
While every day is my lucky day, today is yours! I accidentally entered two raffle drawings—one for a steamship cruise to Hawaii, and another for a plane flight there—both scheduled in the same week! Knowing I'll win both contests, I'll take the plane for more time in the sun! You can enjoy the cruise with my compliments!
—Gladstone!

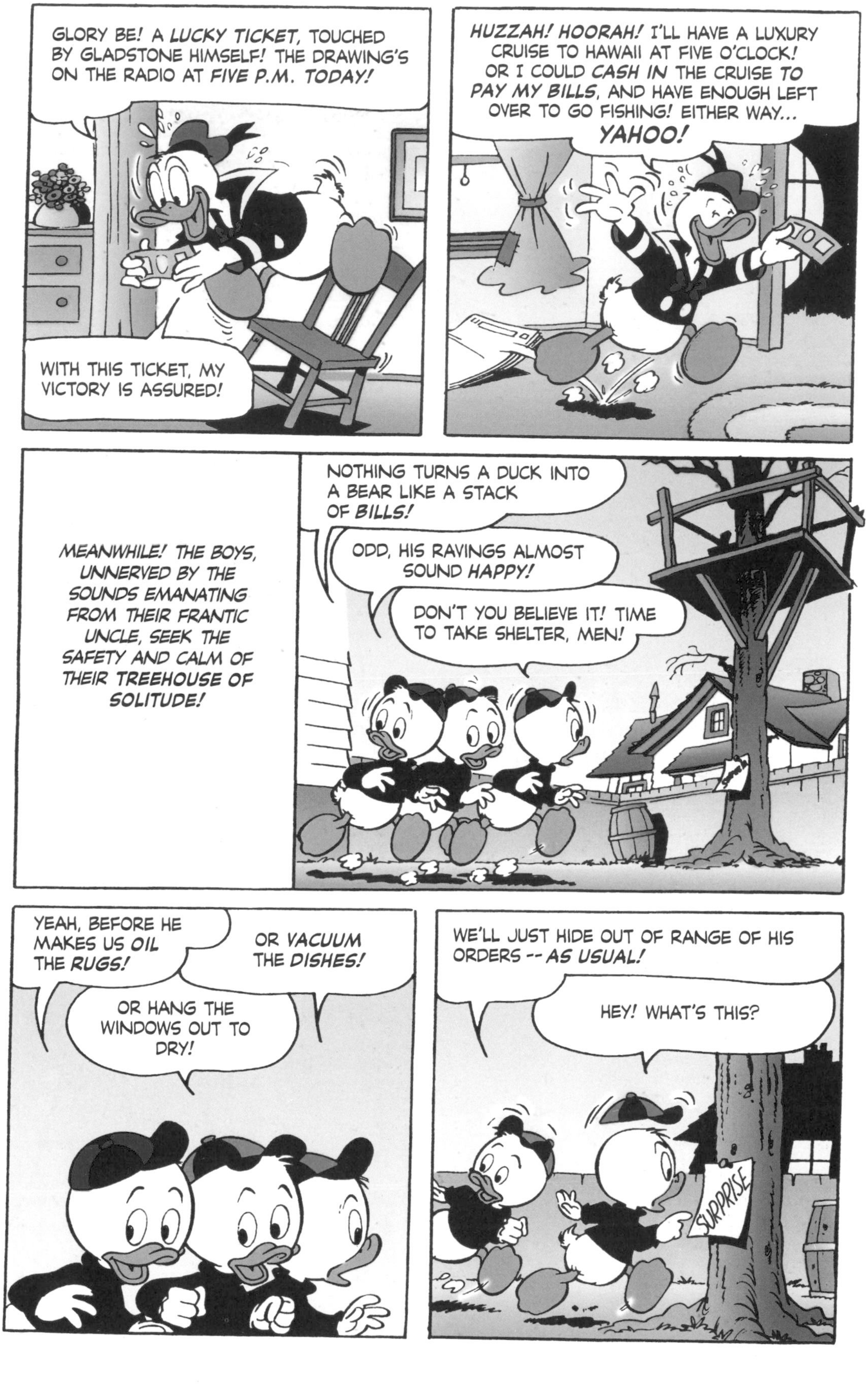
GLORY BE! A LUCKY TICKET, TOUCHED BY GLADSTONE HIMSELF! THE DRAWING'S ON THE RADIO AT FIVE P.M. TODAY!
WITH THIS TICKET, MY VICTORY IS ASSURED!
HUZZAH! HOORAH! I'LL HAVE A LUXURY CRUISE TO HAWAII AT FIVE O'CLOCK! OR I COULD CASH IN THE CRUISE TO PAY MY BILLS, AND HAVE ENOUGH LEFT OVER TO GO FISHING! EITHER WAY... YAHOO!
MEANWHILE! THE BOYS, UNNERVED BY THE SOUNDS EMANATING FROM THEIR FRANTIC UNCLE, SEEK THE SAFETY AND CALM OF THEIR TREEHOUSE OF SOLITUDE!
NOTHING TURNS A DUCK INTO A BEAR LIKE A STACK OF BILLS!
ODD, HIS RAVINGS ALMOST SOUND HAPPY!
DON'T YOU BELIEVE IT! TIME TO TAKE SHELTER, MEN!
YEAH, BEFORE HE MAKES US OIL THE RUGS!
OR VACUUM THE DISHES!
OR HANG THE WINDOWS OUT TO DRY!
WE'LL JUST HIDE OUT OF RANGE OF HIS ORDERS -- AS USUAL!
HEY! WHAT'S THIS?
SURPRISE

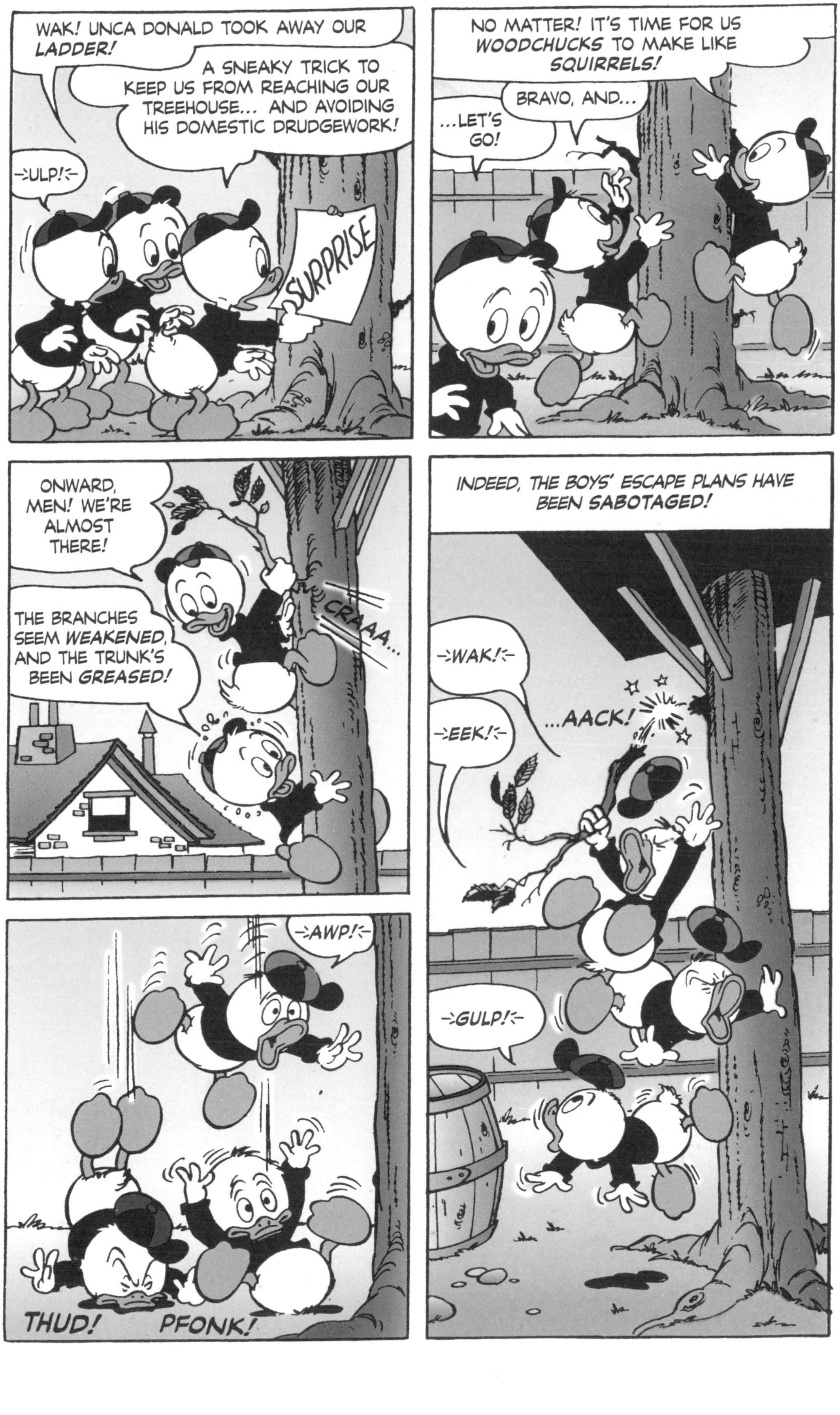

WAK! UNCA DONALD TOOK AWAY OUR LADDER!
A SNEAKY TRICK TO KEEP US FROM REACHING OUR TREEHOUSE... AND AVOIDING HIS DOMESTIC DRUDGEWORK!
-ULP!-
SURPRISE
NO MATTER! IT'S TIME FOR US WOODCHUCKS TO MAKE LIKE SQUIRRELS!
BRAVO, AND...
...LET'S GO!
ONWARD, MEN! WE'RE ALMOST THERE!
THE BRANCHES SEEM WEAKENED, AND THE TRUNK'S BEEN GREASED!
CRAAAA...
INDEED, THE BOYS' ESCAPE PLANS HAVE BEEN SABOTAGED!
-WAK!-
-EEK!-
...AACK!
-GULP!-
-AWP!-
THUD!
PFONK!

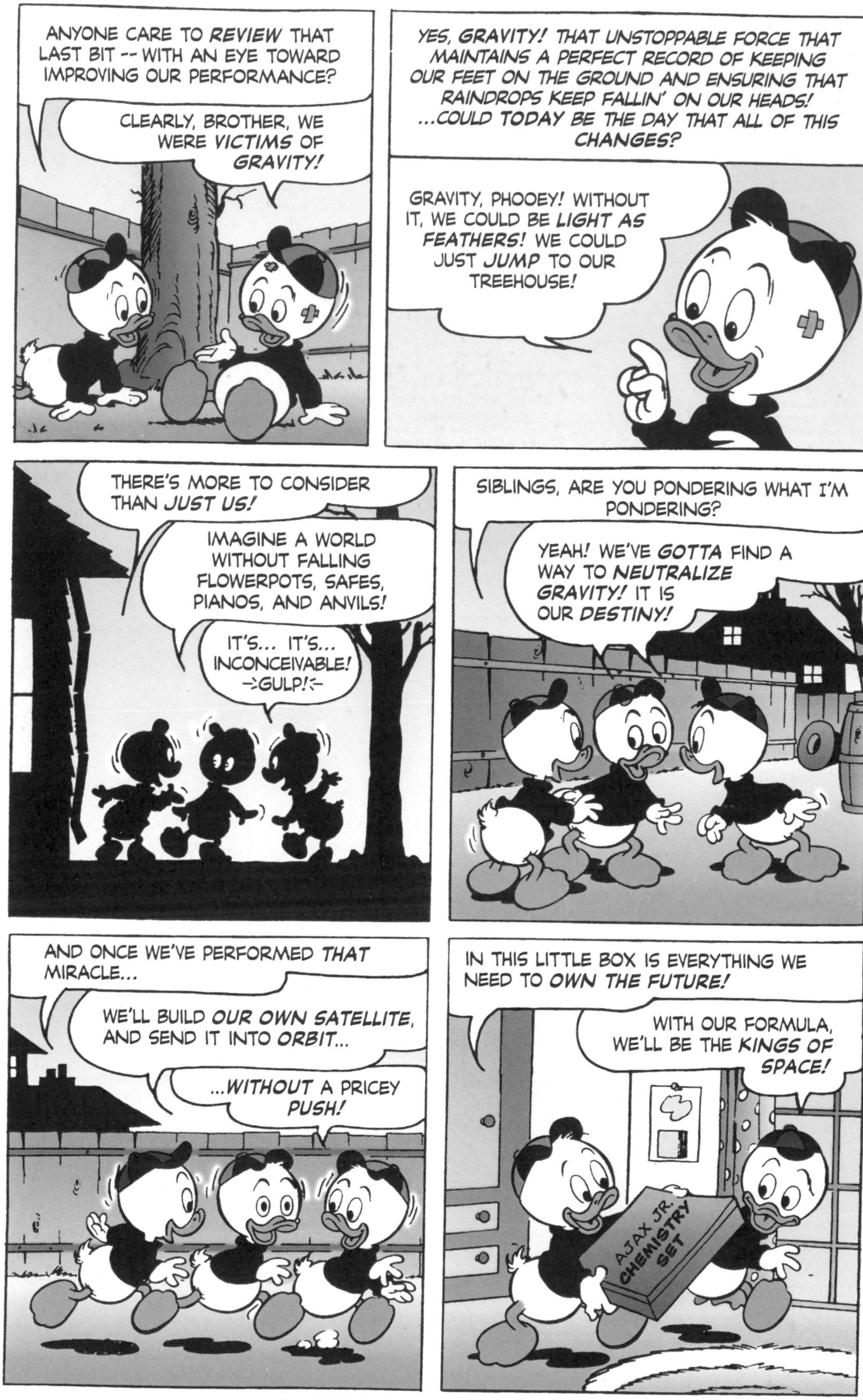
ANYONE CARE TO REVIEW THAT LAST BIT -- WITH AN EYE TOWARD IMPROVING OUR PERFORMANCE?
CLEARLY, BROTHER, WE WERE VICTIMS OF GRAVITY!
YES, GRAVITY! THAT UNSTOPPABLE FORCE THAT MAINTAINS A PERFECT RECORD OF KEEPING OUR FEET ON THE GROUND AND ENSURING THAT RAINDROPS KEEP FALLIN' ON OUR HEADS! ...COULD TODAY BE THE DAY THAT ALL OF THIS CHANGES?
GRAVITY, PHOOEY! WITHOUT IT, WE COULD BE LIGHT AS FEATHERS! WE COULD JUST JUMP TO OUR TREEHOUSE!
THERE'S MORE TO CONSIDER THAN JUST US!
IMAGINE A WORLD WITHOUT FALLING FLOWERPOTS, SAFES, PIANOS, AND ANVILS!
IT'S... IT'S... INCONCEIVABLE! -GULP!-
SIBLINGS, ARE YOU PONDERING WHAT I'M PONDERING?
YEAH! WE'VE GOTTA FIND A WAY TO NEUTRALIZE GRAVITY! IT IS OUR DESTINY!
AND ONCE WE'VE PERFORMED THAT MIRACLE...
WE'LL BUILD OUR OWN SATELLITE, AND SEND IT INTO ORBIT...
...WITHOUT A PRICEY PUSH!
IN THIS LITTLE BOX IS EVERYTHING WE NEED TO OWN THE FUTURE!
WITH OUR FORMULA, WE'LL BE THE KINGS OF SPACE!
AJAX JR. CHEMISTRY SET

ANYONE WANNA *SPITBALL* IDEAS?

I GOT MORE *SPITBALLS* THAN IDEAS!

I KNOW IT DEFIES WOODCHUCK RULES, BUT *FORGET* PLANNING!

SOME OF THE GREATEST INVENTIONS HAPPEN *BY* CHANCE!

SO, LET'S MAKE WITH THE CHANCE, VANCE!

SURE, BUT *I'M* DEWEY!

A PINCH OF THIS!

A DASH OF THAT!

AND A DOLLOP OF THE OTHER THING!

WHEN THE FORMULA COMES TO A BOIL, WE'LL DRIP SOME OFF INTO THIS CONTAINER, AND SEE WHAT HAPPENS!

I'M SO OPTIMISTIC, I ALREADY *SEE MYSELF* IN *ORBIT!*

STEP AWAY FROM THE VAPOR, BRO!

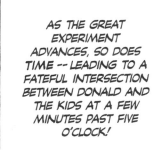

AS THE GREAT EXPERIMENT ADVANCES, SO DOES *TIME* -- LEADING TO A FATEFUL INTERSECTION BETWEEN DONALD AND THE KIDS AT A FEW MINUTES PAST FIVE O'CLOCK!

BOYS! →PUFF-PUFF!← ...RADIO! →GASP!← I HAVE THE WINNING TICKET!

RADIO?

WINNING TICKET?

YAHOO!

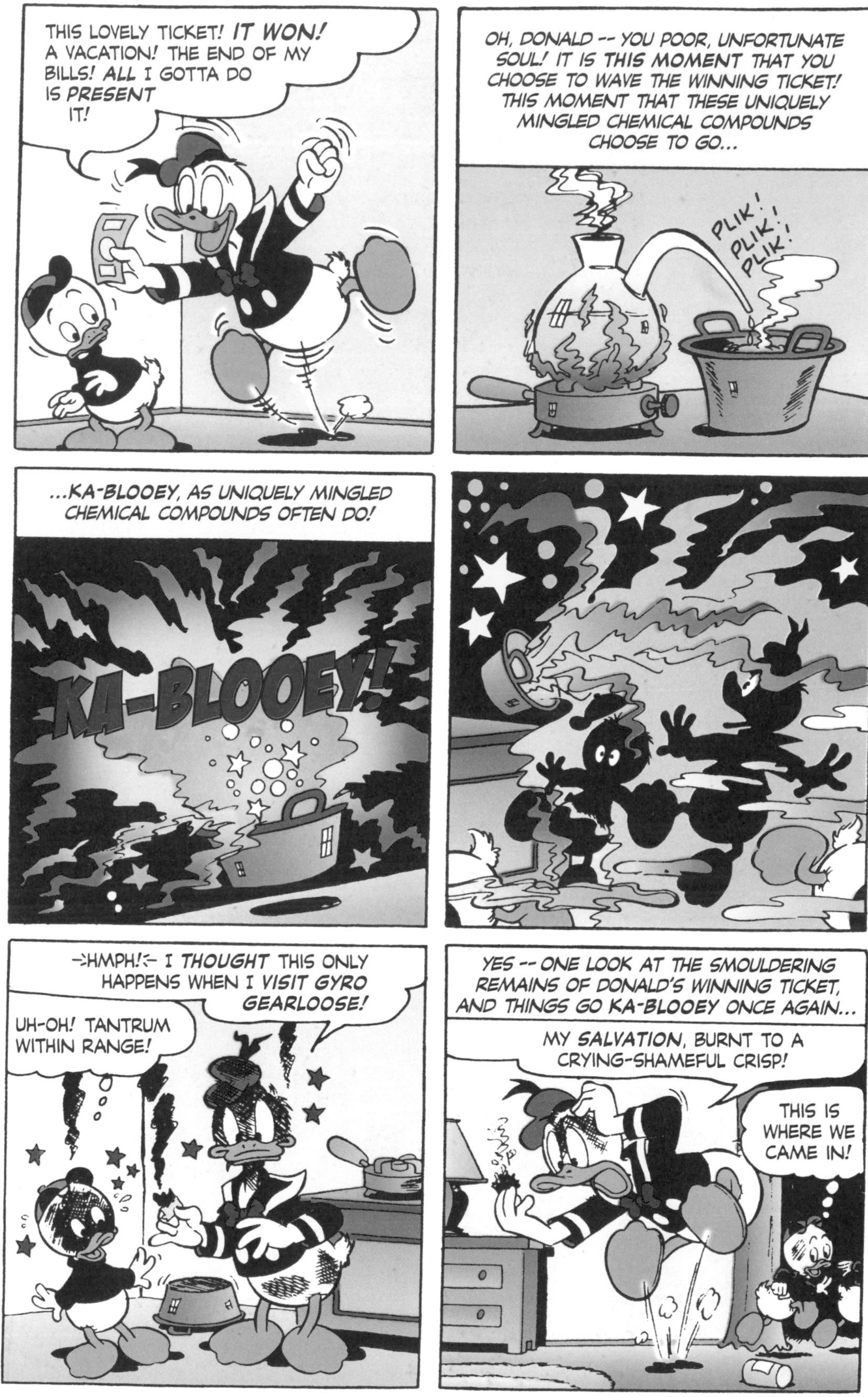
THIS LOVELY TICKET! IT WON! A VACATION! THE END OF MY BILLS! ALL I GOTTA DO IS PRESENT IT!
OH, DONALD -- YOU POOR, UNFORTUNATE SOUL! IT IS THIS MOMENT THAT YOU CHOOSE TO WAVE THE WINNING TICKET! THIS MOMENT THAT THESE UNIQUELY MINGLED CHEMICAL COMPOUNDS CHOOSE TO GO...
PLIK! PLIK! PLIK!
...KA-BLOOEY, AS UNIQUELY MINGLED CHEMICAL COMPOUNDS OFTEN DO!
KA-BLOOEY!
-HMPH!- I THOUGHT THIS ONLY HAPPENS WHEN I VISIT GYRO GEARLOOSE!
UH-OH! TANTRUM WITHIN RANGE!
YES -- ONE LOOK AT THE SMOULDERING REMAINS OF DONALD'S WINNING TICKET, AND THINGS GO KA-BLOOEY ONCE AGAIN...
MY SALVATION, BURNT TO A CRYING-SHAMEFUL CRISP!
THIS IS WHERE WE CAME IN!

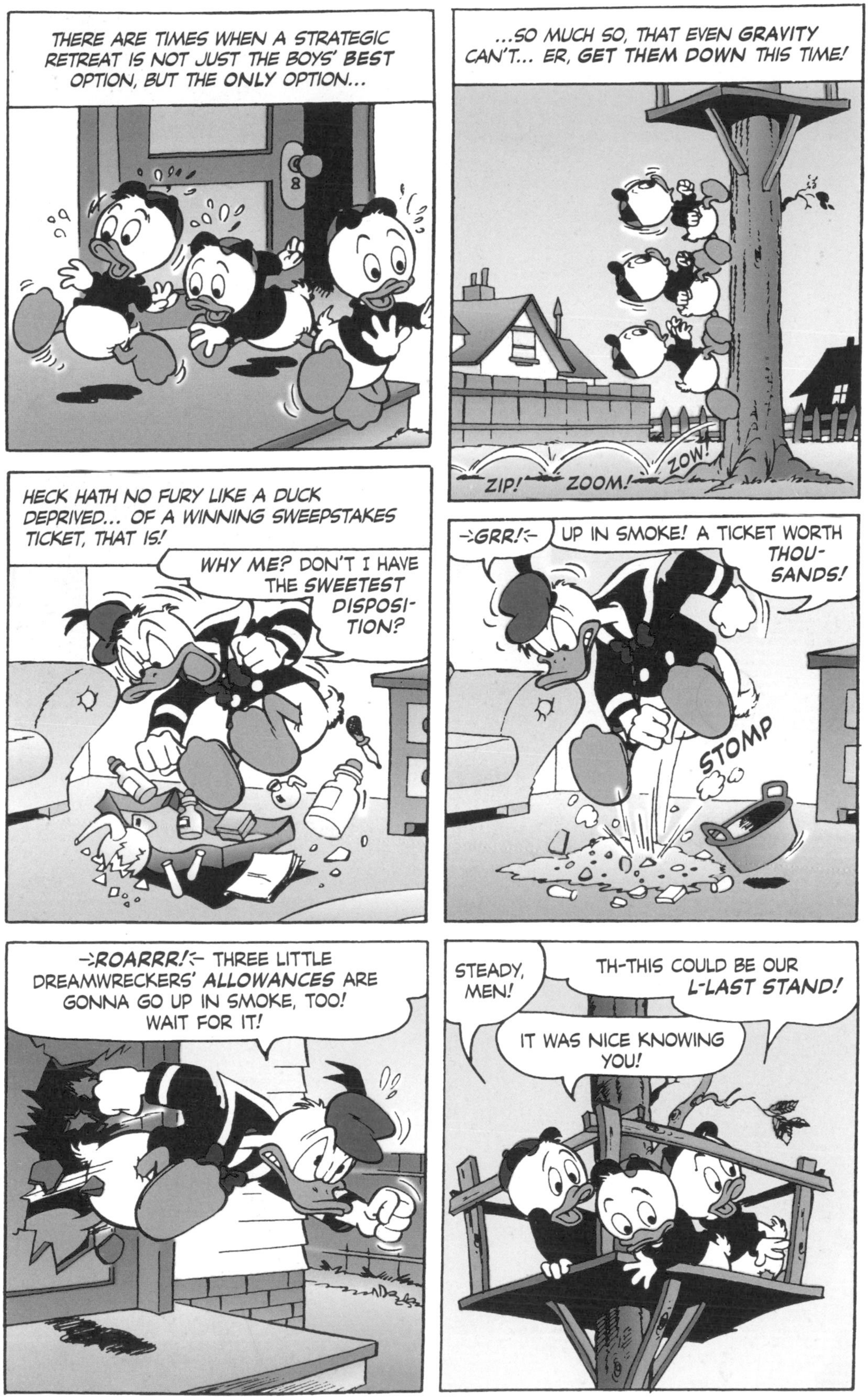
THERE ARE TIMES WHEN A STRATEGIC RETREAT IS NOT JUST THE BOYS' BEST OPTION, BUT THE ONLY OPTION...
...SO MUCH SO, THAT EVEN GRAVITY CAN'T... ER, GET THEM DOWN THIS TIME!
ZIP!
ZOOM!
ZOW!
HECK HATH NO FURY LIKE A DUCK DEPRIVED... OF A WINNING SWEEPSTAKES TICKET, THAT IS!
WHY ME? DON'T I HAVE THE SWEETEST DISPOSI-TION?
-GRR!-
UP IN SMOKE! A TICKET WORTH THOU-SANDS!
STOMP
-ROARRR!- THREE LITTLE DREAMWRECKERS' ALLOWANCES ARE GONNA GO UP IN SMOKE, TOO! WAIT FOR IT!
STEADY, MEN!
TH-THIS COULD BE OUR L-LAST STAND!
IT WAS NICE KNOWING YOU!

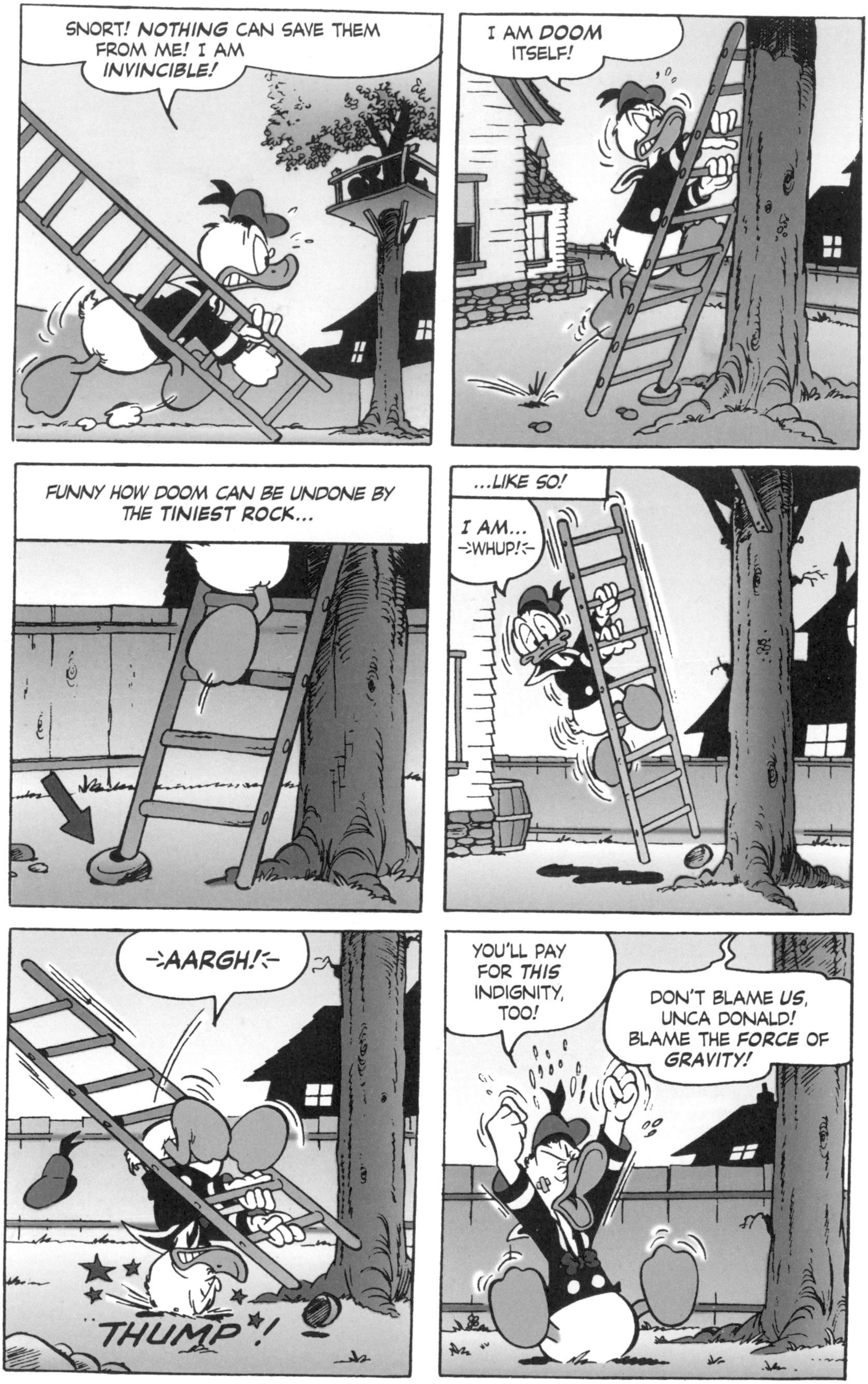
SNORT! NOTHING CAN SAVE THEM FROM ME! I AM INVINCIBLE!
I AM DOOM ITSELF!
FUNNY HOW DOOM CAN BE UNDONE BY THE TINIEST ROCK...
...LIKE SO!
I AM... WHUP!
AARGH!
THUMP!
YOU'LL PAY FOR THIS INDIGNITY, TOO!
DON'T BLAME US, UNCA DONALD! BLAME THE FORCE OF GRAVITY!

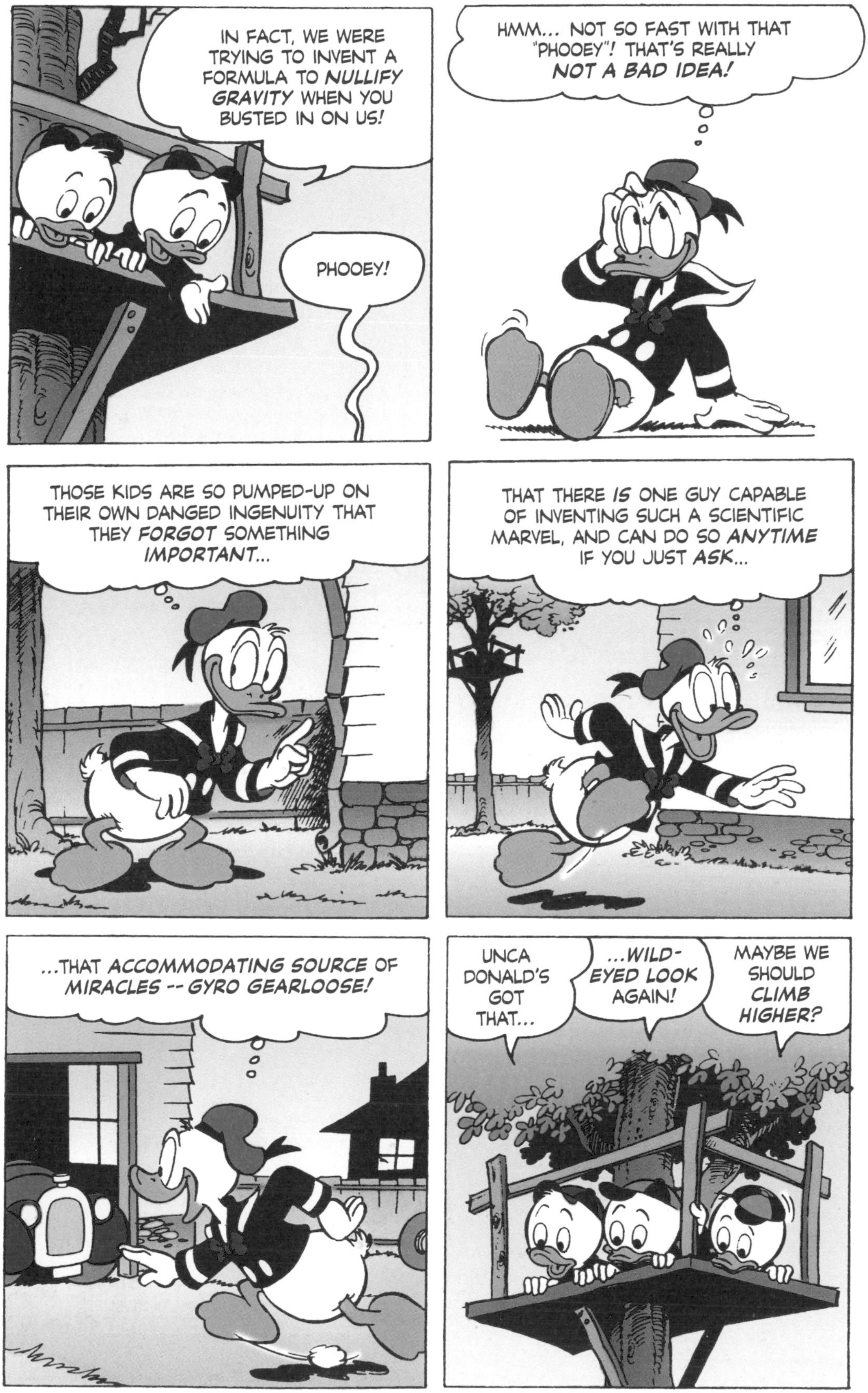
IN FACT, WE WERE TRYING TO INVENT A FORMULA TO NULLIFY GRAVITY WHEN YOU BUSTED IN ON US!
PHOOEY!
HMM... NOT SO FAST WITH THAT "PHOOEY"! THAT'S REALLY NOT A BAD IDEA!
THOSE KIDS ARE SO PUMPED-UP ON THEIR OWN DANGED INGENUITY THAT THEY FORGOT SOMETHING IMPORTANT...
THAT THERE IS ONE GUY CAPABLE OF INVENTING SUCH A SCIENTIFIC MARVEL, AND CAN DO SO ANYTIME IF YOU JUST ASK...
...THAT ACCOMMODATING SOURCE OF MIRACLES -- GYRO GEARLOOSE!
UNCA DONALD'S GOT THAT...
...WILD-EYED LOOK AGAIN!
MAYBE WE SHOULD CLIMB HIGHER?

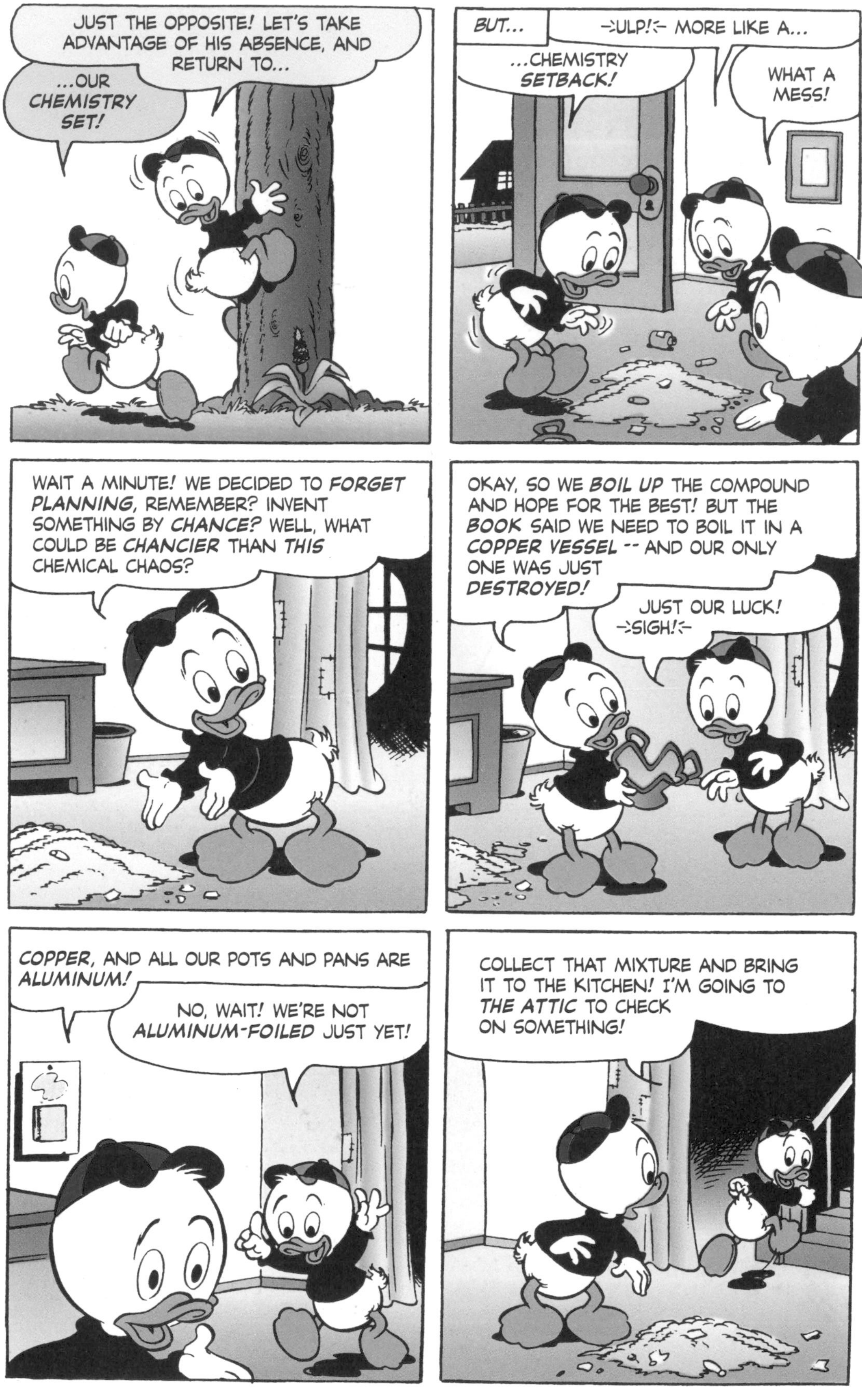
JUST THE OPPOSITE! LET'S TAKE ADVANTAGE OF HIS ABSENCE, AND RETURN TO...
...OUR CHEMISTRY SET!
BUT...
...CHEMISTRY SETBACK!
-ULP!- MORE LIKE A...
WHAT A MESS!
WAIT A MINUTE! WE DECIDED TO FORGET PLANNING, REMEMBER? INVENT SOMETHING BY CHANCE? WELL, WHAT COULD BE CHANCIER THAN THIS CHEMICAL CHAOS?
OKAY, SO WE BOIL UP THE COMPOUND AND HOPE FOR THE BEST! BUT THE BOOK SAID WE NEED TO BOIL IT IN A COPPER VESSEL -- AND OUR ONLY ONE WAS JUST DESTROYED!
JUST OUR LUCK! -SIGH!-
COPPER, AND ALL OUR POTS AND PANS ARE ALUMINUM!
NO, WAIT! WE'RE NOT ALUMINUM-FOILED JUST YET!
COLLECT THAT MIXTURE AND BRING IT TO THE KITCHEN! I'M GOING TO THE ATTIC TO CHECK ON SOMETHING!

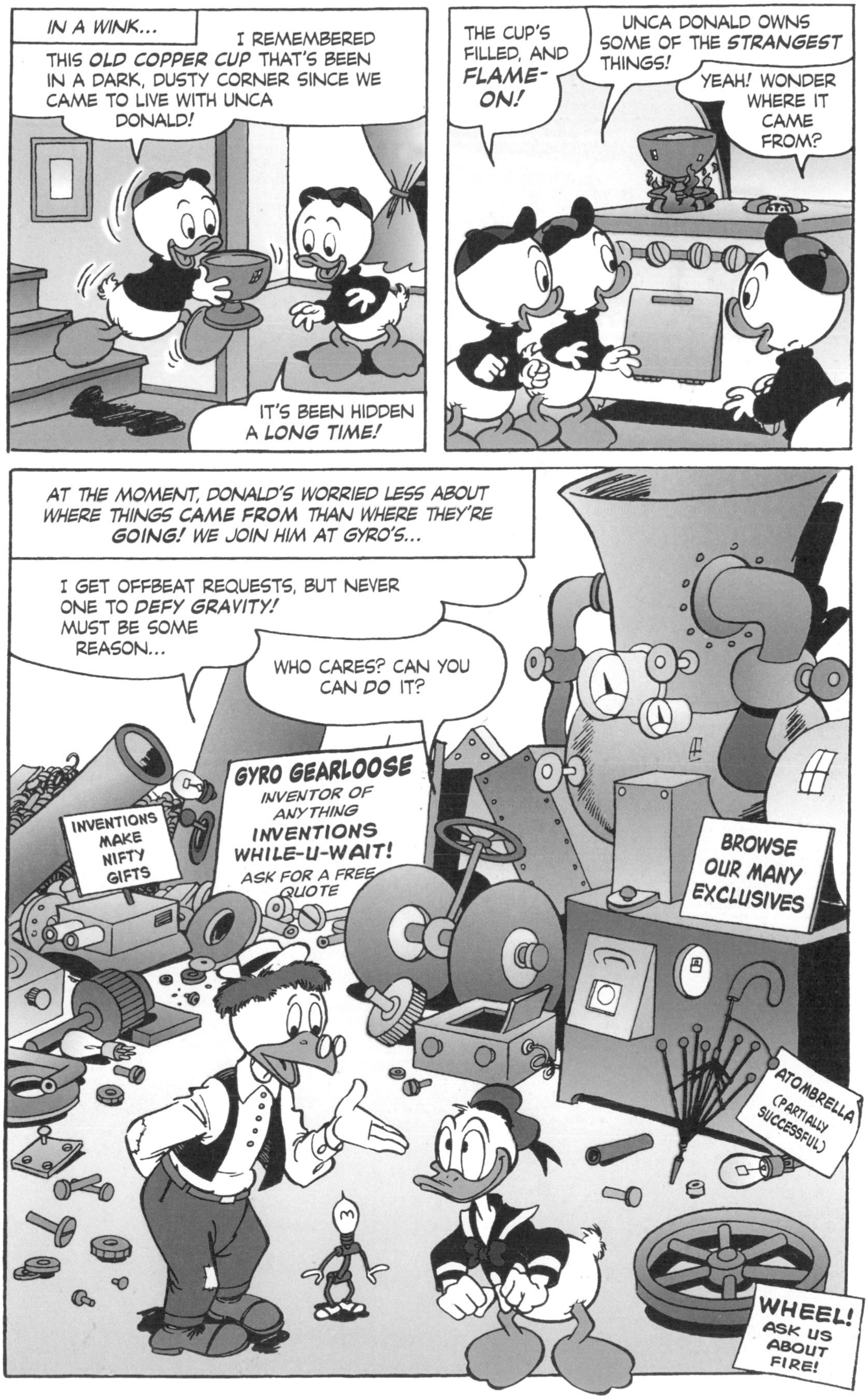

IN A WINK...
I REMEMBERED THIS OLD COPPER CUP THAT'S BEEN IN A DARK, DUSTY CORNER SINCE WE CAME TO LIVE WITH UNCA DONALD!
IT'S BEEN HIDDEN A LONG TIME!
THE CUP'S FILLED, AND FLAME-ON!
UNCA DONALD OWNS SOME OF THE STRANGEST THINGS!
YEAH! WONDER WHERE IT CAME FROM?
AT THE MOMENT, DONALD'S WORRIED LESS ABOUT WHERE THINGS CAME FROM THAN WHERE THEY'RE GOING! WE JOIN HIM AT GYRO'S...
I GET OFFBEAT REQUESTS, BUT NEVER ONE TO DEFY GRAVITY! MUST BE SOME REASON...
WHO CARES? CAN YOU CAN DO IT?
GYRO GEARLOOSE
INVENTOR OF ANYTHING
INVENTIONS WHILE-U-WAIT!
ASK FOR A FREE QUOTE
INVENTIONS MAKE NIFTY GIFTS
BROWSE OUR MANY EXCLUSIVES
ATOMBRELLA (PARTIALLY SUCCESSFUL)
WHEEL! ASK US ABOUT FIRE!

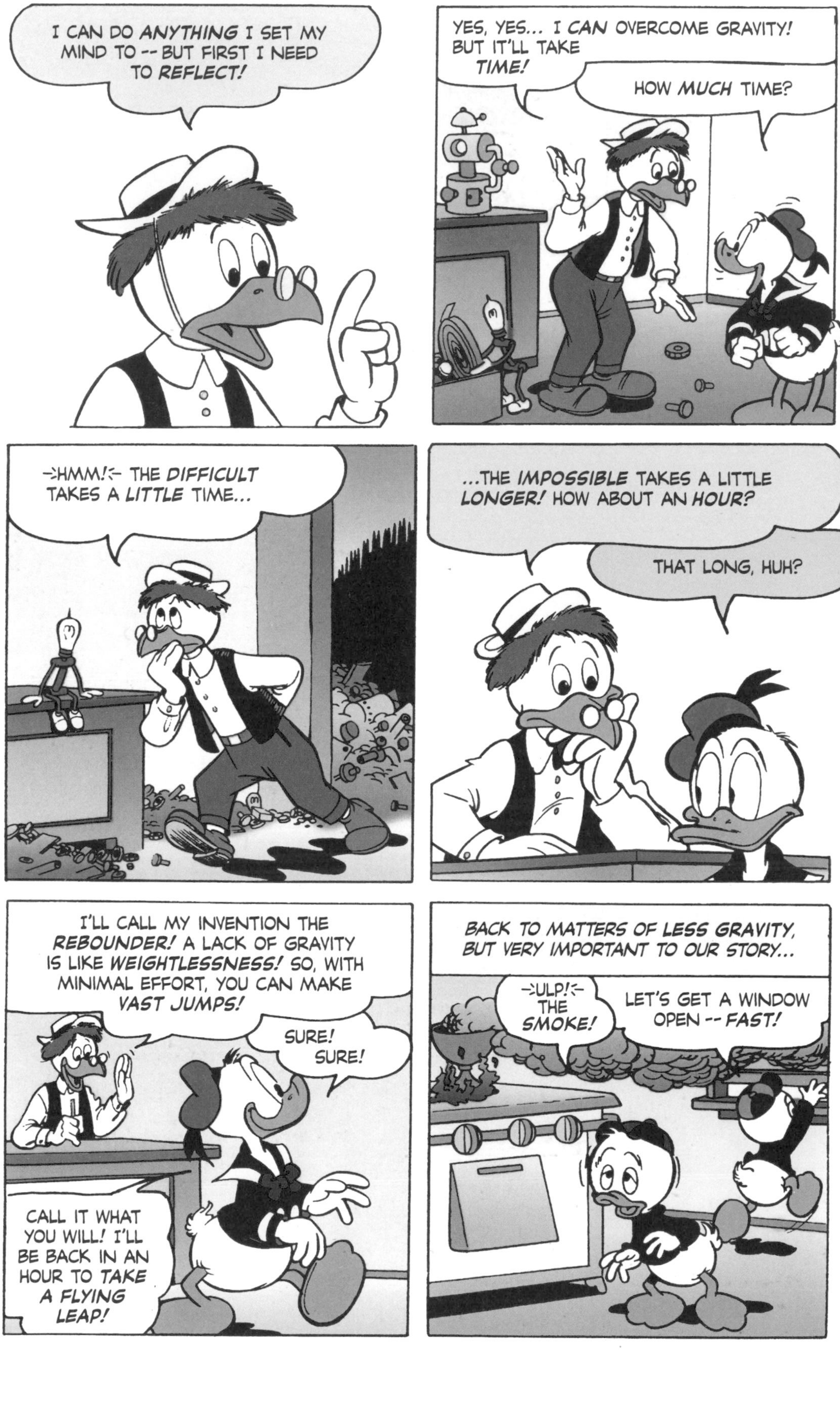
I CAN DO ANYTHING I SET MY MIND TO -- BUT FIRST I NEED TO REFLECT!
YES, YES... I CAN OVERCOME GRAVITY! BUT IT'LL TAKE TIME!
HOW MUCH TIME?
-HMM!- THE DIFFICULT TAKES A LITTLE TIME...
...THE IMPOSSIBLE TAKES A LITTLE LONGER! HOW ABOUT AN HOUR?
THAT LONG, HUH?
I'LL CALL MY INVENTION THE REBOUNDER! A LACK OF GRAVITY IS LIKE WEIGHTLESSNESS! SO, WITH MINIMAL EFFORT, YOU CAN MAKE VAST JUMPS!
SURE! SURE!
CALL IT WHAT YOU WILL! I'LL BE BACK IN AN HOUR TO TAKE A FLYING LEAP!
BACK TO MATTERS OF LESS GRAVITY, BUT VERY IMPORTANT TO OUR STORY...
-ULP!- THE SMOKE!
LET'S GET A WINDOW OPEN -- FAST!

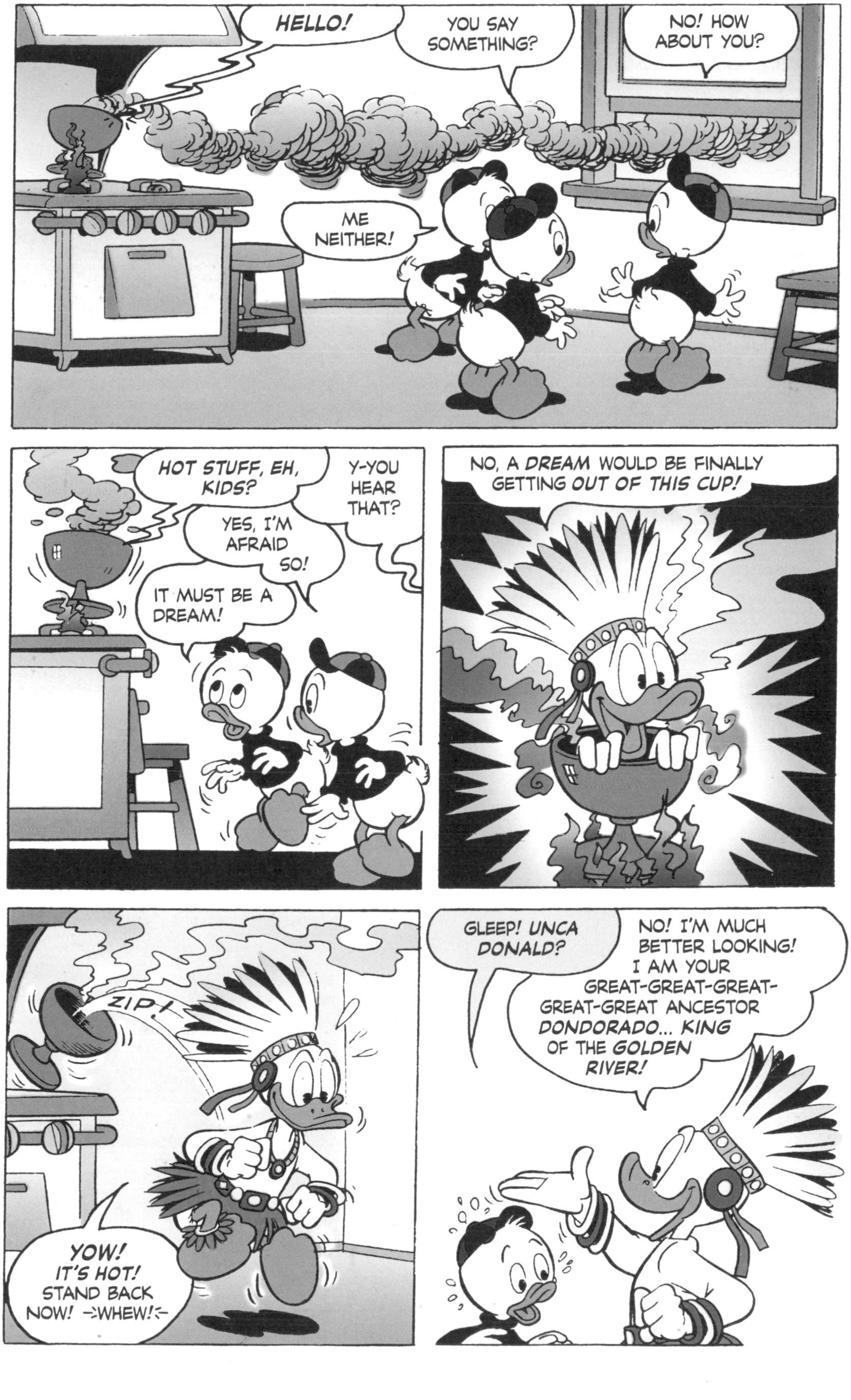
HELLO!
YOU SAY SOMETHING?
NO! HOW ABOUT YOU?
ME NEITHER!
HOT STUFF, EH, KIDS?
Y-YOU HEAR THAT?
YES, I'M AFRAID SO!
IT MUST BE A DREAM!
NO, A DREAM WOULD BE FINALLY GETTING OUT OF THIS CUP!
ZIP!
YOW! IT'S HOT! STAND BACK NOW! WHEW!
GLEEP! UNCA DONALD?
NO! I'M MUCH BETTER LOOKING! I AM YOUR GREAT-GREAT-GREAT-GREAT-GREAT ANCESTOR DONDORADO... KING OF THE GOLDEN RIVER!

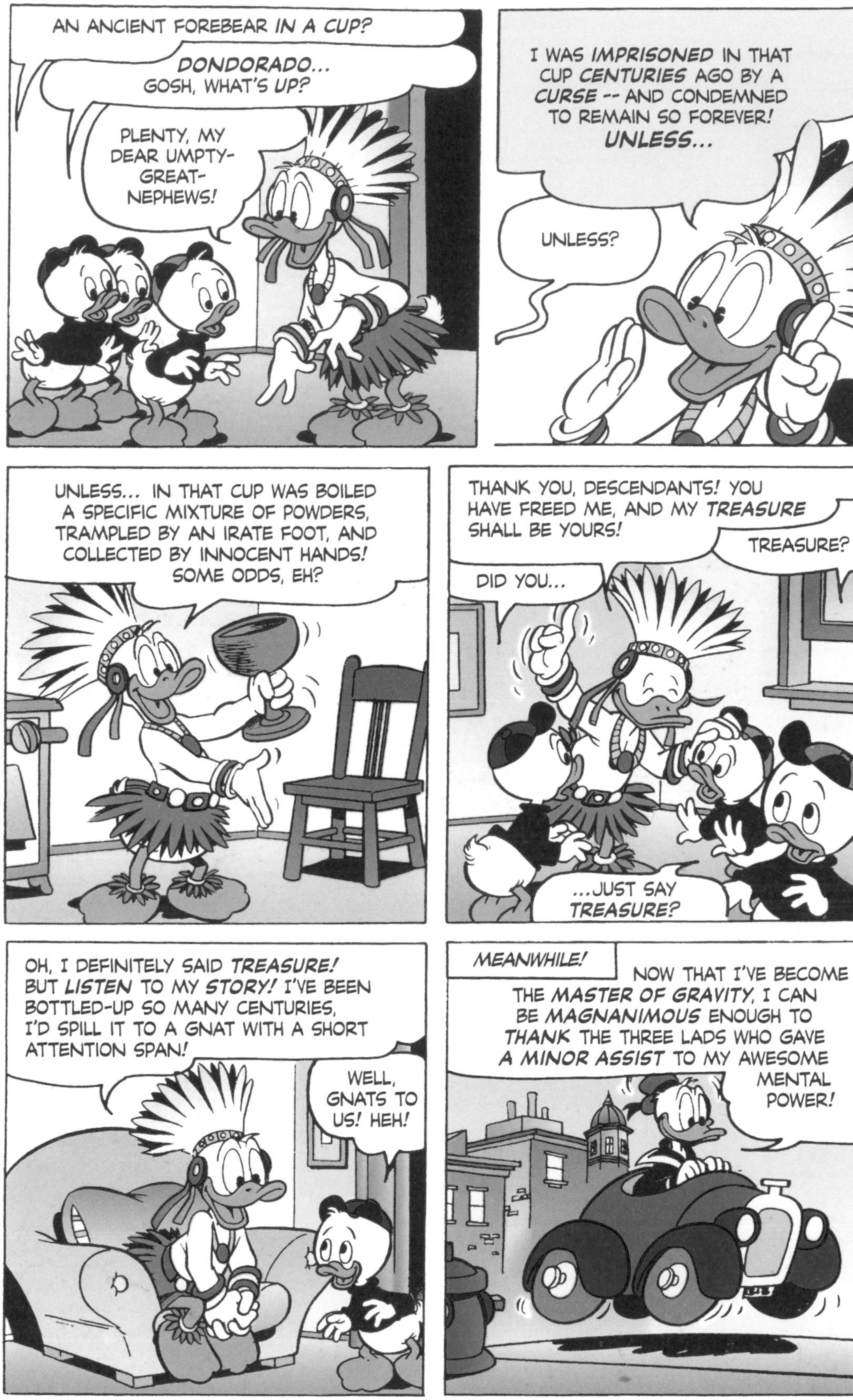
AN ANCIENT FOREBEAR IN A CUP?
DONDORADO... GOSH, WHAT'S UP?
PLENTY, MY DEAR UMPTY-GREAT-NEPHEWS!
I WAS IMPRISONED IN THAT CUP CENTURIES AGO BY A CURSE -- AND CONDEMNED TO REMAIN SO FOREVER! UNLESS...
UNLESS?
UNLESS... IN THAT CUP WAS BOILED A SPECIFIC MIXTURE OF POWDERS, TRAMPLED BY AN IRATE FOOT, AND COLLECTED BY INNOCENT HANDS! SOME ODDS, EH?
THANK YOU, DESCENDANTS! YOU HAVE FREED ME, AND MY TREASURE SHALL BE YOURS!
TREASURE?
DID YOU...
...JUST SAY TREASURE?
OH, I DEFINITELY SAID TREASURE! BUT LISTEN TO MY STORY! I'VE BEEN BOTTLED-UP SO MANY CENTURIES, I'D SPILL IT TO A GNAT WITH A SHORT ATTENTION SPAN!
WELL, GNATS TO US! HEH!
MEANWHILE!
NOW THAT I'VE BECOME THE MASTER OF GRAVITY, I CAN BE MAGNANIMOUS ENOUGH TO THANK THE THREE LADS WHO GAVE A MINOR ASSIST TO MY AWESOME MENTAL POWER!

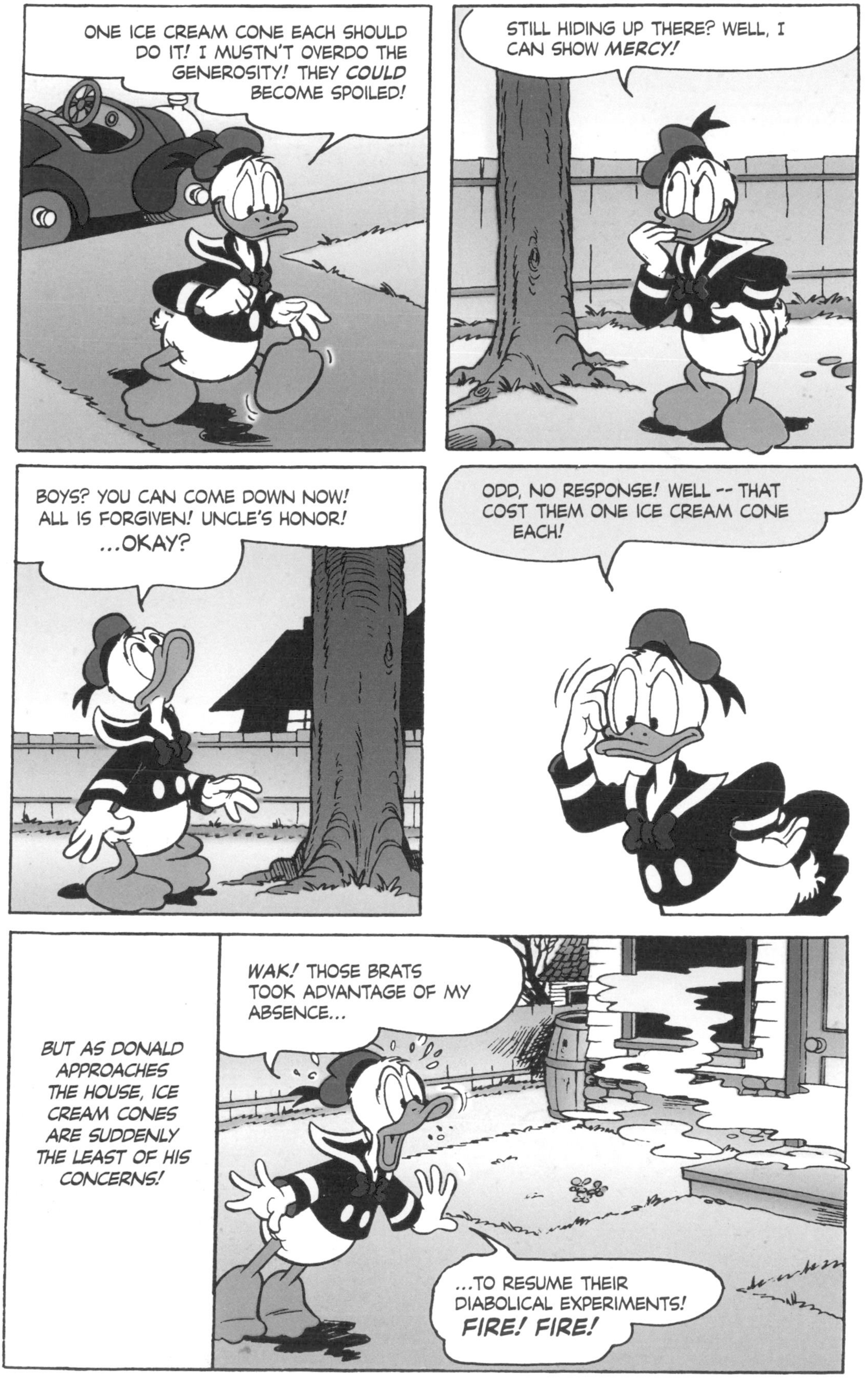
ONE ICE CREAM CONE EACH SHOULD DO IT! I MUSTN'T OVERDO THE GENEROSITY! THEY COULD BECOME SPOILED!
STILL HIDING UP THERE? WELL, I CAN SHOW MERCY!
BOYS? YOU CAN COME DOWN NOW! ALL IS FORGIVEN! UNCLE'S HONOR! ...OKAY?
ODD, NO RESPONSE! WELL -- THAT COST THEM ONE ICE CREAM CONE EACH!
BUT AS DONALD APPROACHES THE HOUSE, ICE CREAM CONES ARE SUDDENLY THE LEAST OF HIS CONCERNS!
WAK! THOSE BRATS TOOK ADVANTAGE OF MY ABSENCE...
...TO RESUME THEIR DIABOLICAL EXPERIMENTS! FIRE! FIRE!

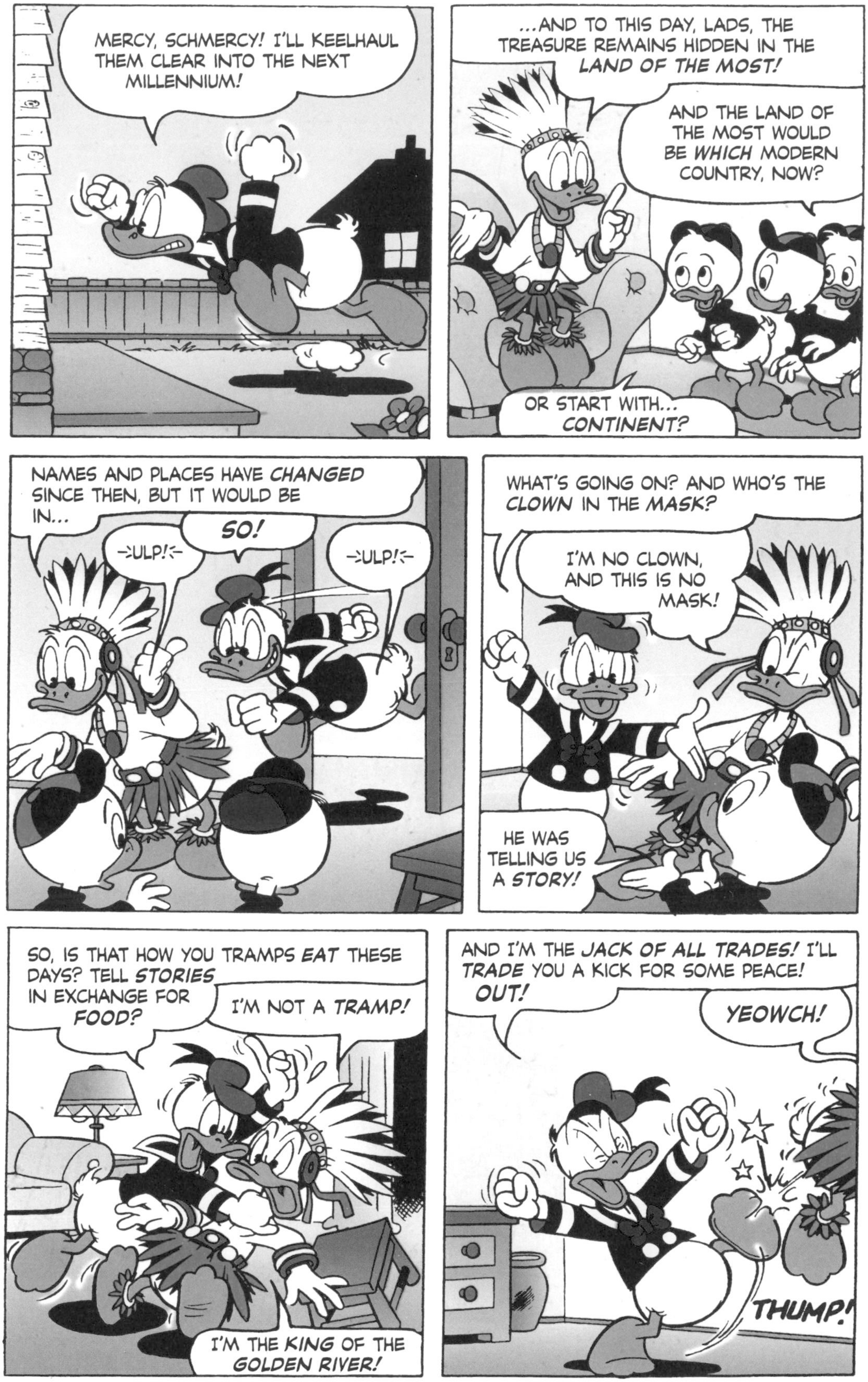
MERCY, SCHMERCY! I'LL KEELHAUL THEM CLEAR INTO THE NEXT MILLENNIUM!
...AND TO THIS DAY, LADS, THE TREASURE REMAINS HIDDEN IN THE LAND OF THE MOST!
AND THE LAND OF THE MOST WOULD BE WHICH MODERN COUNTRY, NOW?
OR START WITH... CONTINENT?
NAMES AND PLACES HAVE CHANGED SINCE THEN, BUT IT WOULD BE IN...
-ULP!-
SO!
-ULP!-
WHAT'S GOING ON? AND WHO'S THE CLOWN IN THE MASK?
I'M NO CLOWN, AND THIS IS NO MASK!
HE WAS TELLING US A STORY!
SO, IS THAT HOW YOU TRAMPS EAT THESE DAYS? TELL STORIES IN EXCHANGE FOR FOOD?
I'M NOT A TRAMP!
I'M THE KING OF THE GOLDEN RIVER!
AND I'M THE JACK OF ALL TRADES! I'LL TRADE YOU A KICK FOR SOME PEACE! OUT!
YEOWCH!
THUMP!

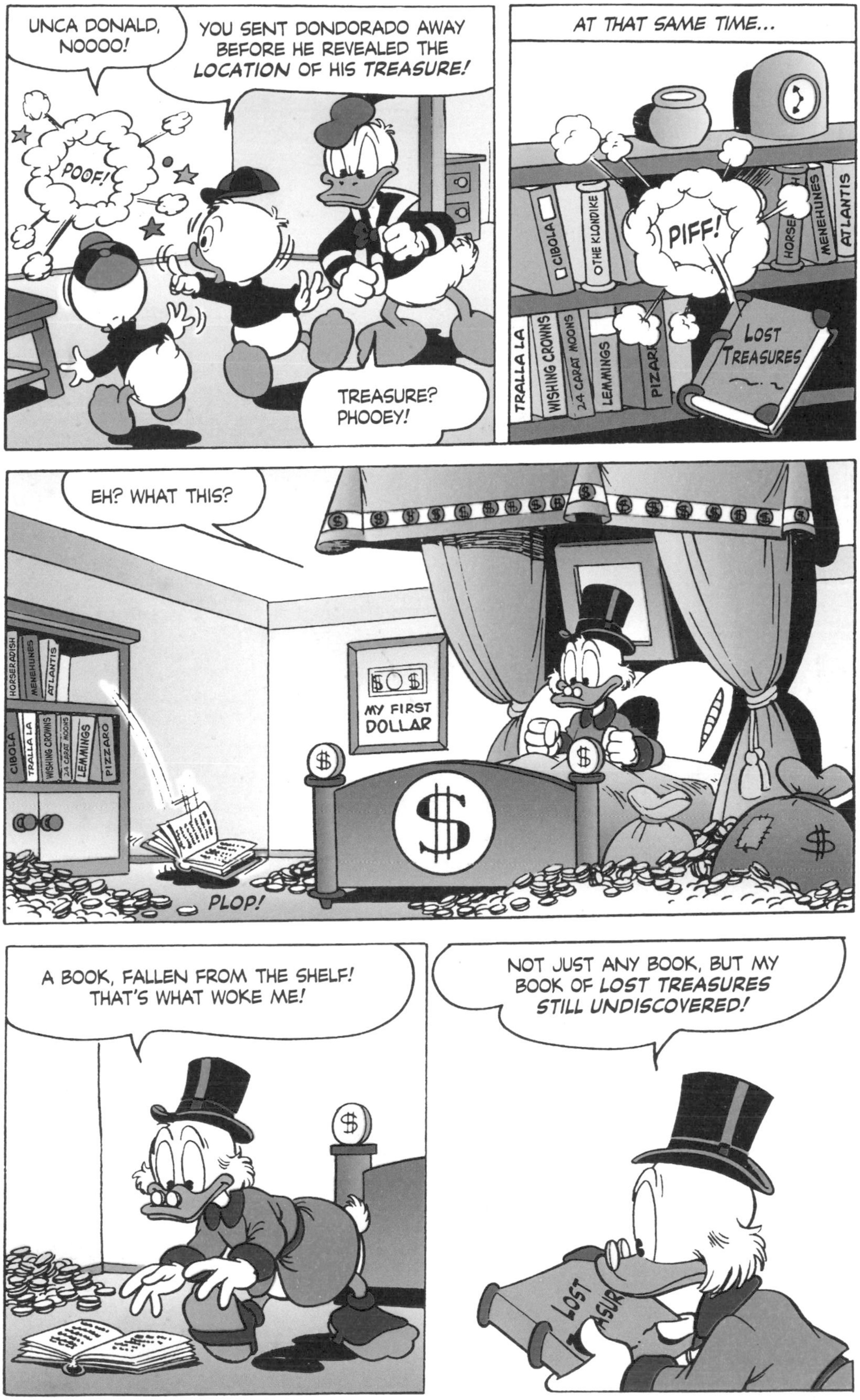
UNCA DONALD, NOOOO!
YOU SENT DONDORADO AWAY BEFORE HE REVEALED THE LOCATION OF HIS TREASURE!
POOF!
TREASURE? PHOOEY!
AT THAT SAME TIME...
CIBOLA
THE KLONDIKE
PIFF!
HORSE
MENEHUNES
ATLANTIS
TRALLA LA
WISHING CROWNS
24 CARAT MOONS
LEMMINGS
PIZAR
LOST TREASURES
EH? WHAT THIS?
HORSERADISH
MENEHUNES
ATLANTIS
CIBOLA
TRALLA LA
WISHING CROWNS
24 CARAT MOONS
LEMMINGS
PIZZARO
MY FIRST DOLLAR
PLOP!
A BOOK, FALLEN FROM THE SHELF! THAT'S WHAT WOKE ME!
NOT JUST ANY BOOK, BUT MY BOOK OF LOST TREASURES STILL UNDISCOVERED!

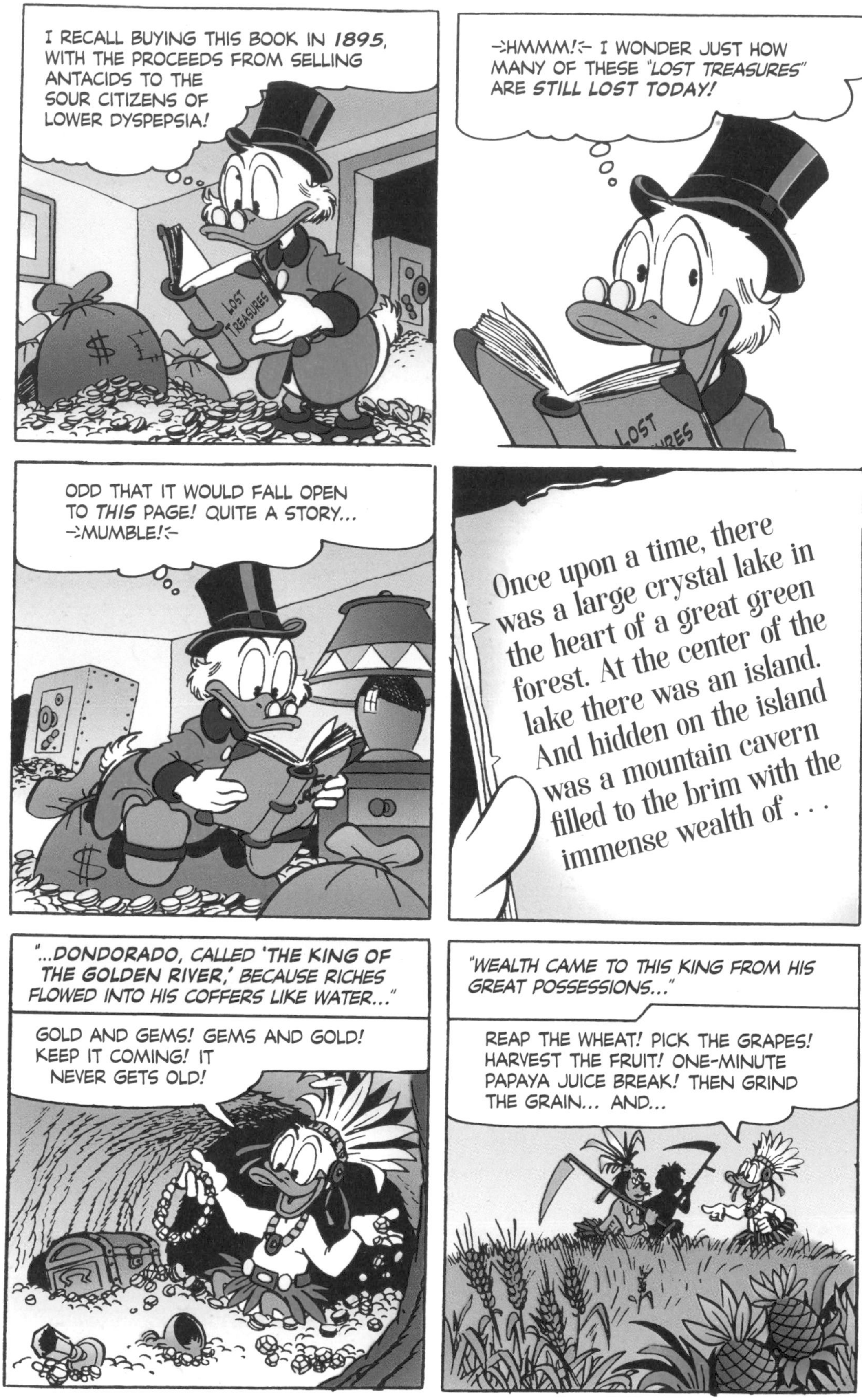

I RECALL BUYING THIS BOOK IN 1895, WITH THE PROCEEDS FROM SELLING ANTACIDS TO THE SOUR CITIZENS OF LOWER DYSPEPSIA!
LOST TREASURES
-HMMM!- I WONDER JUST HOW MANY OF THESE "LOST TREASURES" ARE STILL LOST TODAY!
ODD THAT IT WOULD FALL OPEN TO THIS PAGE! QUITE A STORY... -MUMBLE!-
Once upon a time, there was a large crystal lake in the heart of a great green forest. At the center of the lake there was an island. And hidden on the island was a mountain cavern filled to the brim with the immense wealth of . . .
"...DONDORADO, CALLED 'THE KING OF THE GOLDEN RIVER,' BECAUSE RICHES FLOWED INTO HIS COFFERS LIKE WATER..."
GOLD AND GEMS! GEMS AND GOLD! KEEP IT COMING! IT NEVER GETS OLD!
"WEALTH CAME TO THIS KING FROM HIS GREAT POSSESSIONS..."
REAP THE WHEAT! PICK THE GRAPES! HARVEST THE FRUIT! ONE-MINUTE PAPAYA JUICE BREAK! THEN GRIND THE GRAIN... AND...

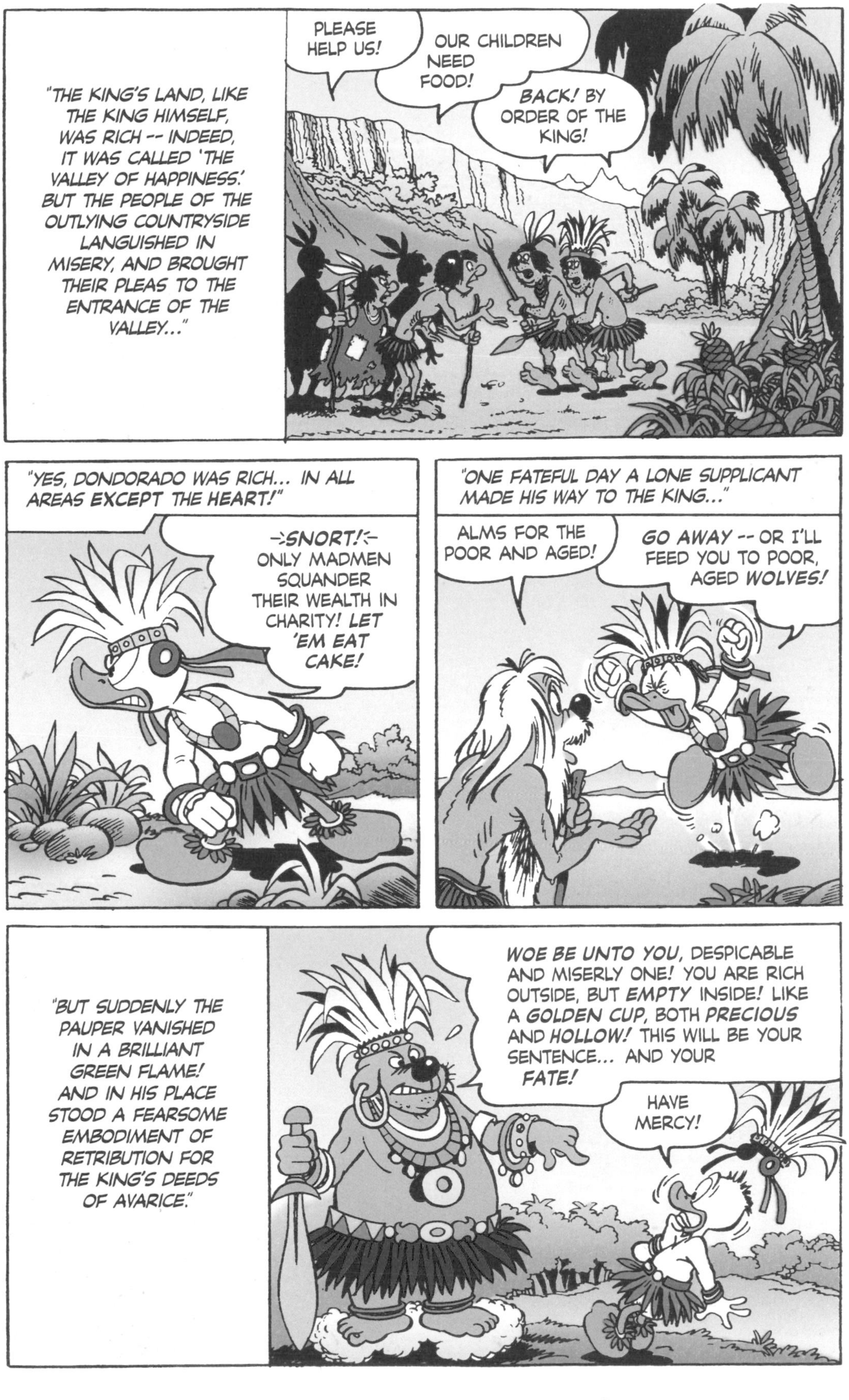
"THE KING'S LAND, LIKE THE KING HIMSELF, WAS RICH -- INDEED, IT WAS CALLED 'THE VALLEY OF HAPPINESS.' BUT THE PEOPLE OF THE OUTLYING COUNTRYSIDE LANGUISHED IN MISERY, AND BROUGHT THEIR PLEAS TO THE ENTRANCE OF THE VALLEY..."
PLEASE HELP US!
OUR CHILDREN NEED FOOD!
BACK! BY ORDER OF THE KING!
"YES, DONDORADO WAS RICH... IN ALL AREAS EXCEPT THE HEART!"
SNORT! ONLY MADMEN SQUANDER THEIR WEALTH IN CHARITY! LET 'EM EAT CAKE!
"ONE FATEFUL DAY A LONE SUPPLICANT MADE HIS WAY TO THE KING..."
ALMS FOR THE POOR AND AGED!
GO AWAY -- OR I'LL FEED YOU TO POOR, AGED WOLVES!
"BUT SUDDENLY THE PAUPER VANISHED IN A BRILLIANT GREEN FLAME! AND IN HIS PLACE STOOD A FEARSOME EMBODIMENT OF RETRIBUTION FOR THE KING'S DEEDS OF AVARICE."
WOE BE UNTO YOU, DESPICABLE AND MISERLY ONE! YOU ARE RICH OUTSIDE, BUT EMPTY INSIDE! LIKE A GOLDEN CUP, BOTH PRECIOUS AND HOLLOW! THIS WILL BE YOUR SENTENCE... AND YOUR FATE!
HAVE MERCY!

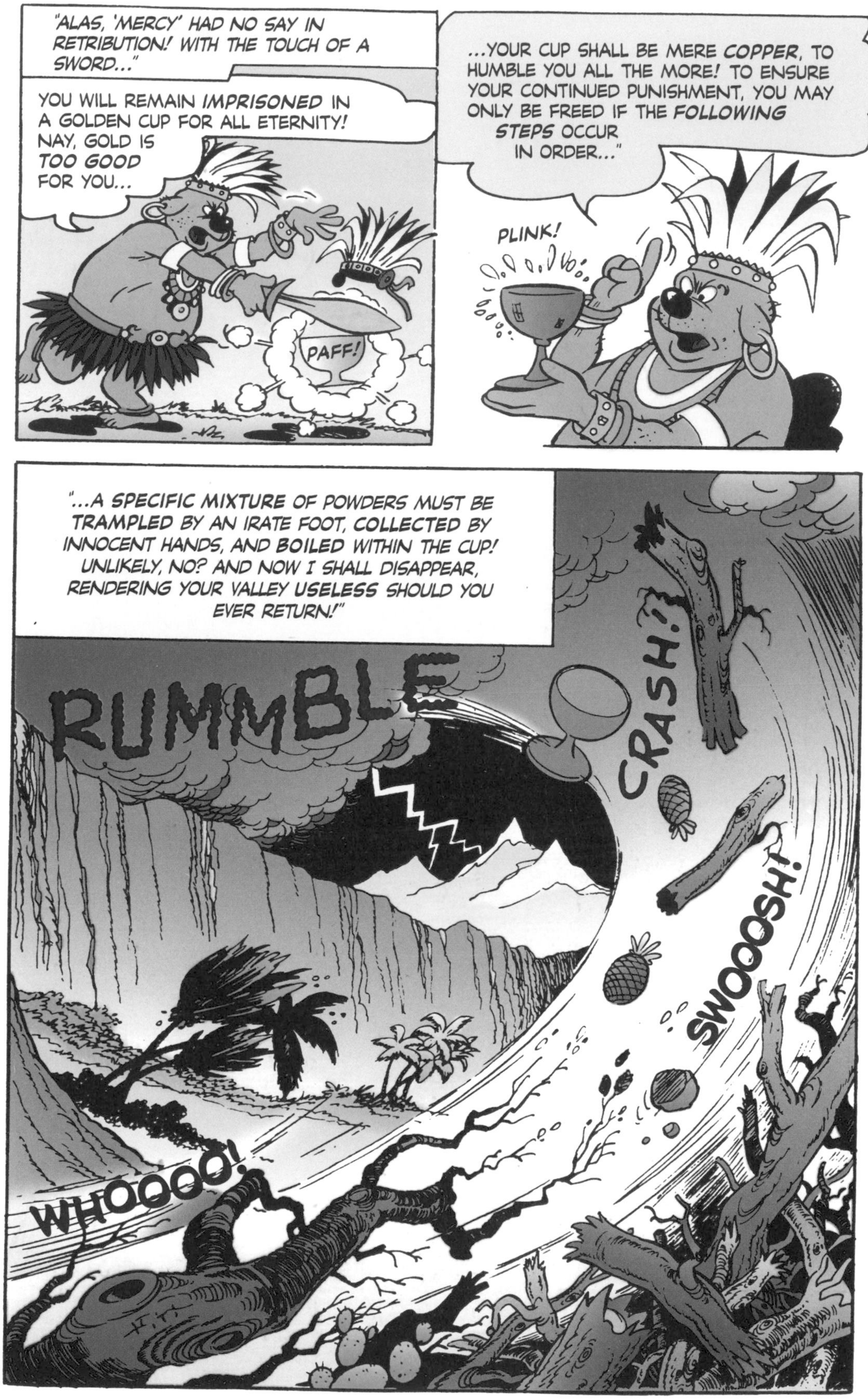
"ALAS, 'MERCY' HAD NO SAY IN RETRIBUTION! WITH THE TOUCH OF A SWORD..."
YOU WILL REMAIN *IMPRISONED* IN A GOLDEN CUP FOR ALL ETERNITY! NAY, GOLD IS *TOO GOOD* FOR YOU...
PAFF!
...YOUR CUP SHALL BE MERE *COPPER*, TO HUMBLE YOU ALL THE MORE! TO ENSURE YOUR CONTINUED PUNISHMENT, YOU MAY ONLY BE FREED IF THE *FOLLOWING STEPS* OCCUR IN ORDER..."
PLINK!
"...A *SPECIFIC MIXTURE* OF POWDERS MUST BE *TRAMPLED* BY AN *IRATE FOOT*, *COLLECTED* BY *INNOCENT HANDS*, AND *BOILED* WITHIN THE CUP! UNLIKELY, NO? AND NOW I SHALL DISAPPEAR, RENDERING YOUR VALLEY *USELESS* SHOULD YOU EVER RETURN!"
RUMMBLE
CRASH!
SWOOOSH!
WHOOOOO!

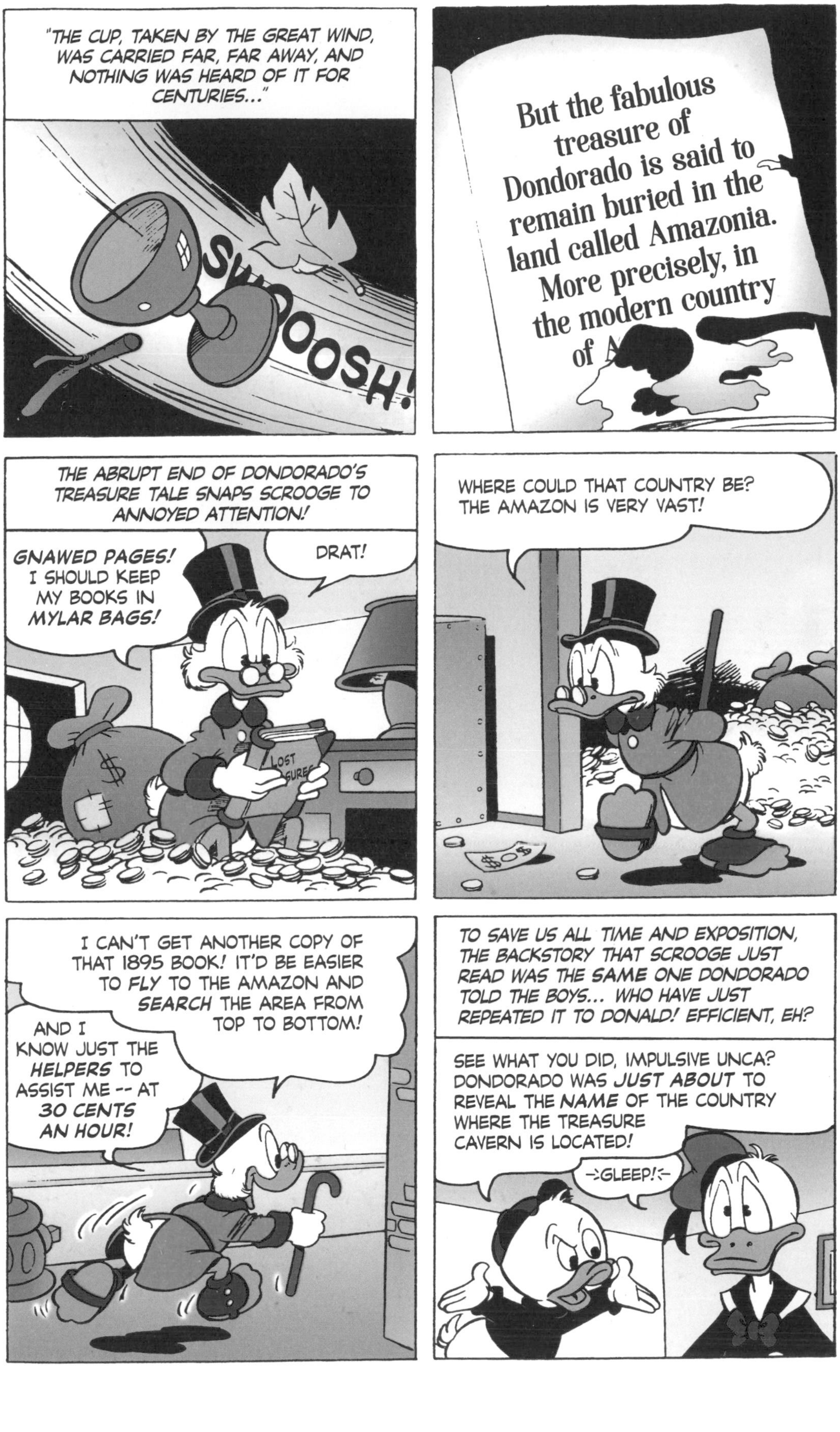
"THE CUP, TAKEN BY THE GREAT WIND, WAS CARRIED FAR, FAR AWAY, AND NOTHING WAS HEARD OF IT FOR CENTURIES..."
SWOOOSH!
But the fabulous treasure of Dondorado is said to remain buried in the land called Amazonia. More precisely, in the modern country of A
THE ABRUPT END OF DONDORADO'S TREASURE TALE SNAPS SCROOGE TO ANNOYED ATTENTION!
DRAT!
GNAWED PAGES! I SHOULD KEEP MY BOOKS IN MYLAR BAGS!
WHERE COULD THAT COUNTRY BE? THE AMAZON IS VERY VAST!
I CAN'T GET ANOTHER COPY OF THAT 1895 BOOK! IT'D BE EASIER TO FLY TO THE AMAZON AND SEARCH THE AREA FROM TOP TO BOTTOM!
AND I KNOW JUST THE HELPERS TO ASSIST ME -- AT 30 CENTS AN HOUR!
TO SAVE US ALL TIME AND EXPOSITION, THE BACKSTORY THAT SCROOGE JUST READ WAS THE SAME ONE DONDORADO TOLD THE BOYS... WHO HAVE JUST REPEATED IT TO DONALD! EFFICIENT, EH?
SEE WHAT YOU DID, IMPULSIVE UNCA? DONDORADO WAS JUST ABOUT TO REVEAL THE NAME OF THE COUNTRY WHERE THE TREASURE CAVERN IS LOCATED!
GLEEP!

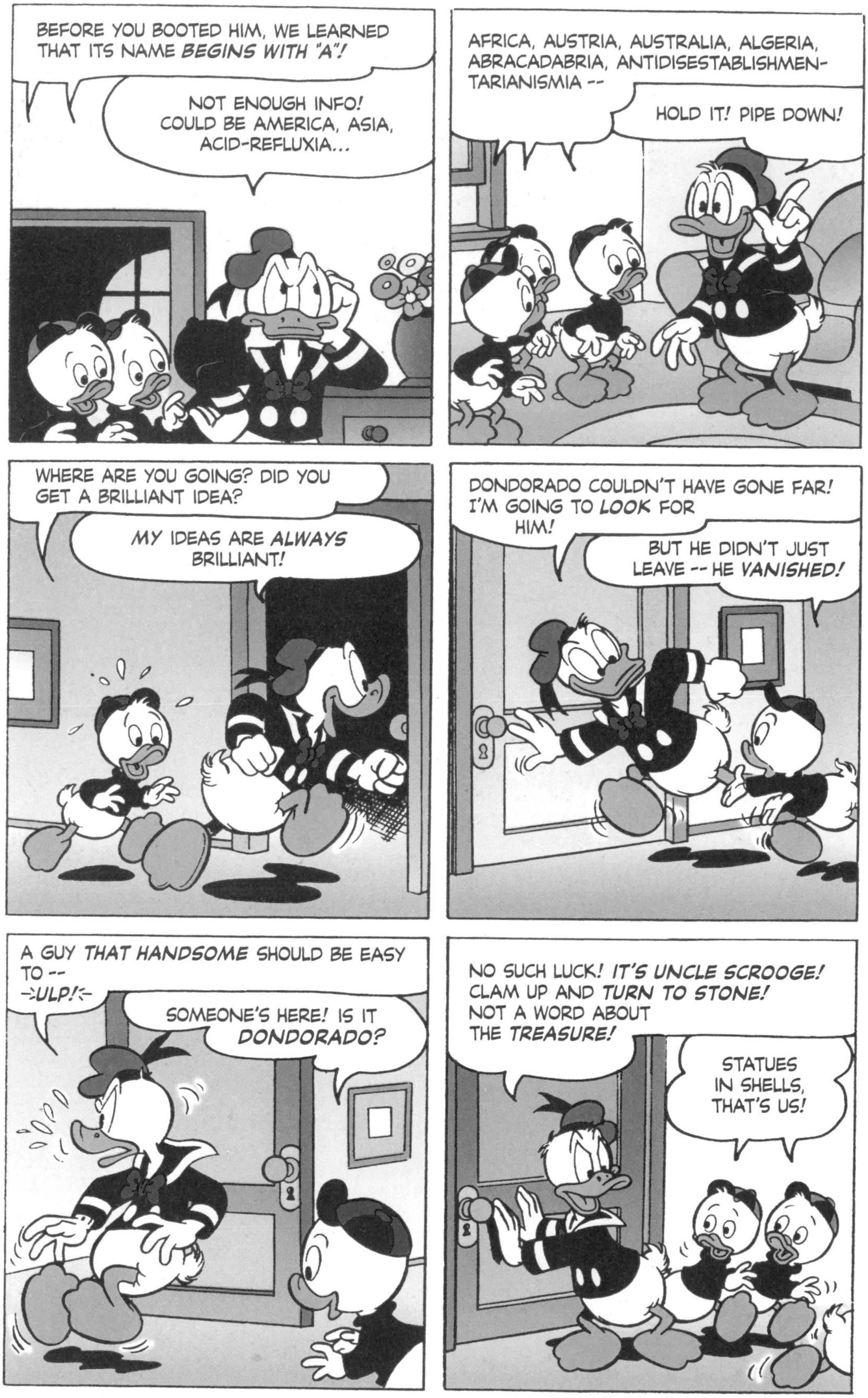

BEFORE YOU BOOTED HIM, WE LEARNED THAT ITS NAME BEGINS WITH "A"!
NOT ENOUGH INFO! COULD BE AMERICA, ASIA, ACID-REFLUXIA...
AFRICA, AUSTRIA, AUSTRALIA, ALGERIA, ABRACADABRIA, ANTIDISESTABLISHMENTARIANISMIA --
HOLD IT! PIPE DOWN!
WHERE ARE YOU GOING? DID YOU GET A BRILLIANT IDEA?
MY IDEAS ARE ALWAYS BRILLIANT!
DONDORADO COULDN'T HAVE GONE FAR! I'M GOING TO LOOK FOR HIM!
BUT HE DIDN'T JUST LEAVE -- HE VANISHED!
A GUY THAT HANDSOME SHOULD BE EASY TO -- ULP!
SOMEONE'S HERE! IS IT DONDORADO?
NO SUCH LUCK! IT'S UNCLE SCROOGE! CLAM UP AND TURN TO STONE! NOT A WORD ABOUT THE TREASURE!
STATUES IN SHELLS, THAT'S US!

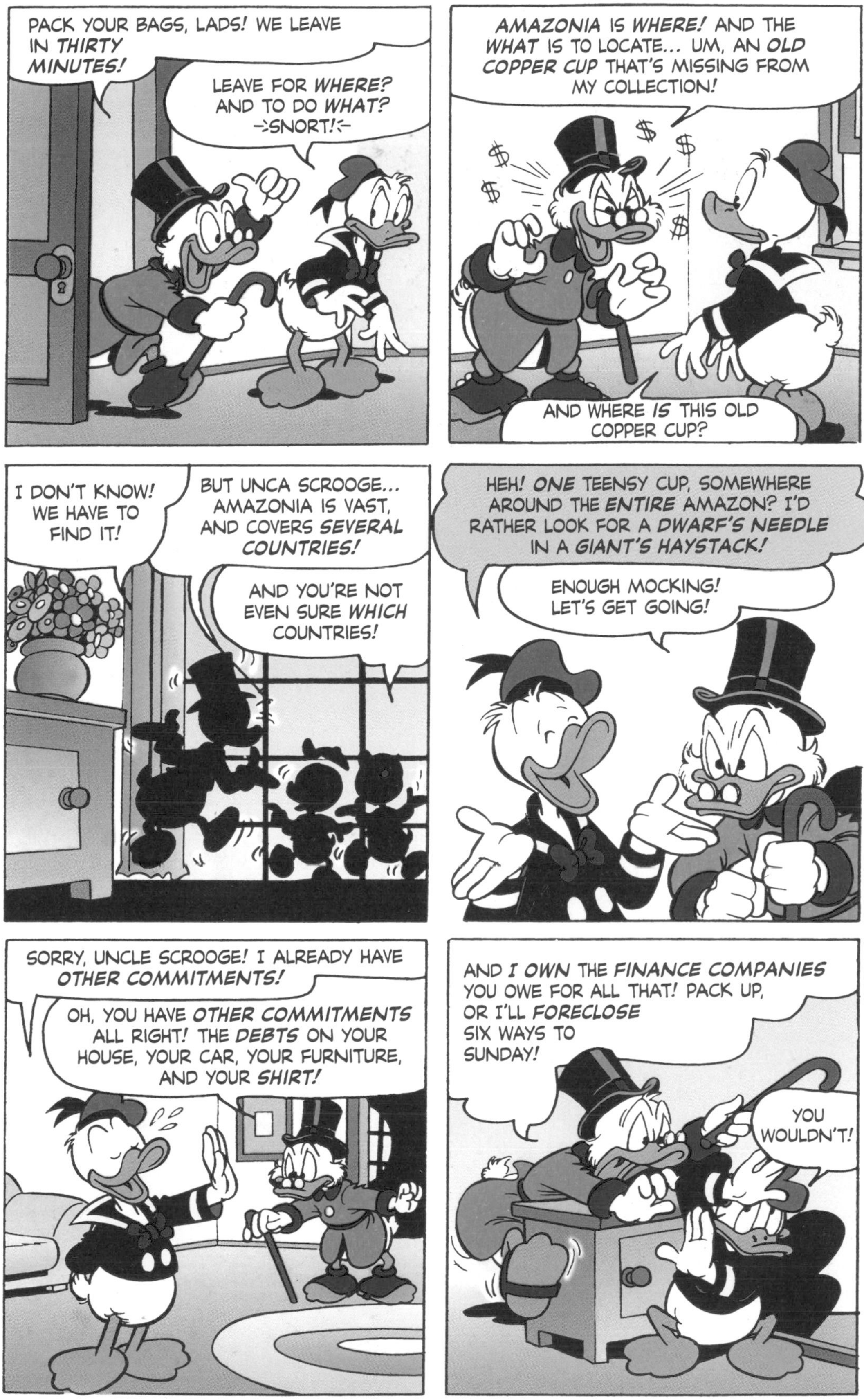

PACK YOUR BAGS, LADS! WE LEAVE IN THIRTY MINUTES!
LEAVE FOR WHERE? AND TO DO WHAT? -SNORT!-
AMAZONIA IS WHERE! AND THE WHAT IS TO LOCATE... UM, AN OLD COPPER CUP THAT'S MISSING FROM MY COLLECTION!
AND WHERE IS THIS OLD COPPER CUP?
I DON'T KNOW! WE HAVE TO FIND IT!
BUT UNCA SCROOGE... AMAZONIA IS VAST, AND COVERS SEVERAL COUNTRIES!
AND YOU'RE NOT EVEN SURE WHICH COUNTRIES!
HEH! ONE TEENSY CUP, SOMEWHERE AROUND THE ENTIRE AMAZON? I'D RATHER LOOK FOR A DWARF'S NEEDLE IN A GIANT'S HAYSTACK!
ENOUGH MOCKING! LET'S GET GOING!
SORRY, UNCLE SCROOGE! I ALREADY HAVE OTHER COMMITMENTS!
OH, YOU HAVE OTHER COMMITMENTS ALL RIGHT! THE DEBTS ON YOUR HOUSE, YOUR CAR, YOUR FURNITURE, AND YOUR SHIRT!
AND I OWN THE FINANCE COMPANIES YOU OWE FOR ALL THAT! PACK UP, OR I'LL FORECLOSE SIX WAYS TO SUNDAY!
YOU WOULDN'T!

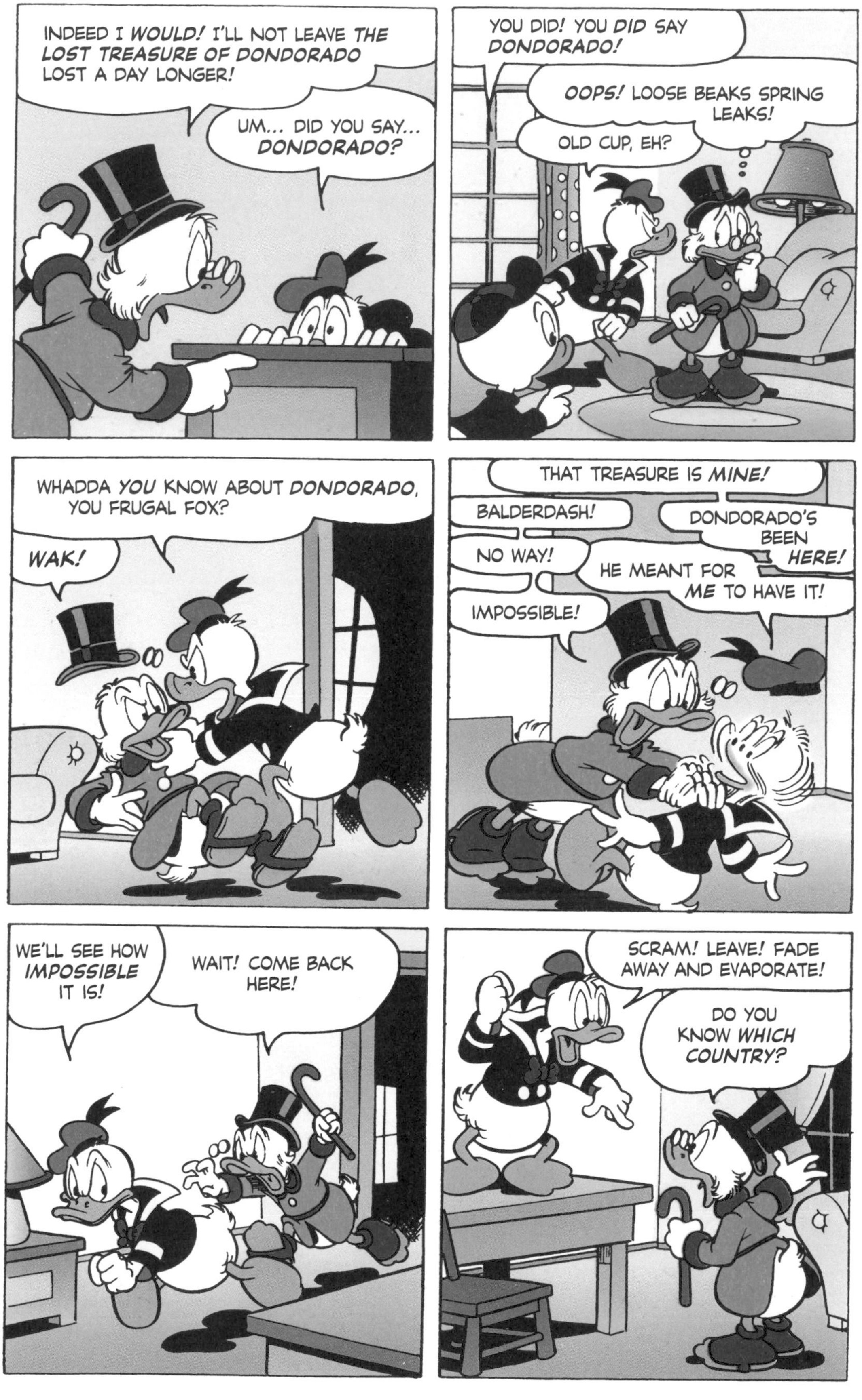
INDEED I WOULD! I'LL NOT LEAVE THE LOST TREASURE OF DONDORADO LOST A DAY LONGER!
UM... DID YOU SAY... DONDORADO?
YOU DID! YOU DID SAY DONDORADO!
OOPS! LOOSE BEAKS SPRING LEAKS!
OLD CUP, EH?
WHADDA YOU KNOW ABOUT DONDORADO, YOU FRUGAL FOX?
WAK!
THAT TREASURE IS MINE!
BALDERDASH!
DONDORADO'S BEEN HERE!
NO WAY!
HE MEANT FOR ME TO HAVE IT!
IMPOSSIBLE!
WE'LL SEE HOW IMPOSSIBLE IT IS!
WAIT! COME BACK HERE!
SCRAM! LEAVE! FADE AWAY AND EVAPORATE!
DO YOU KNOW WHICH COUNTRY?

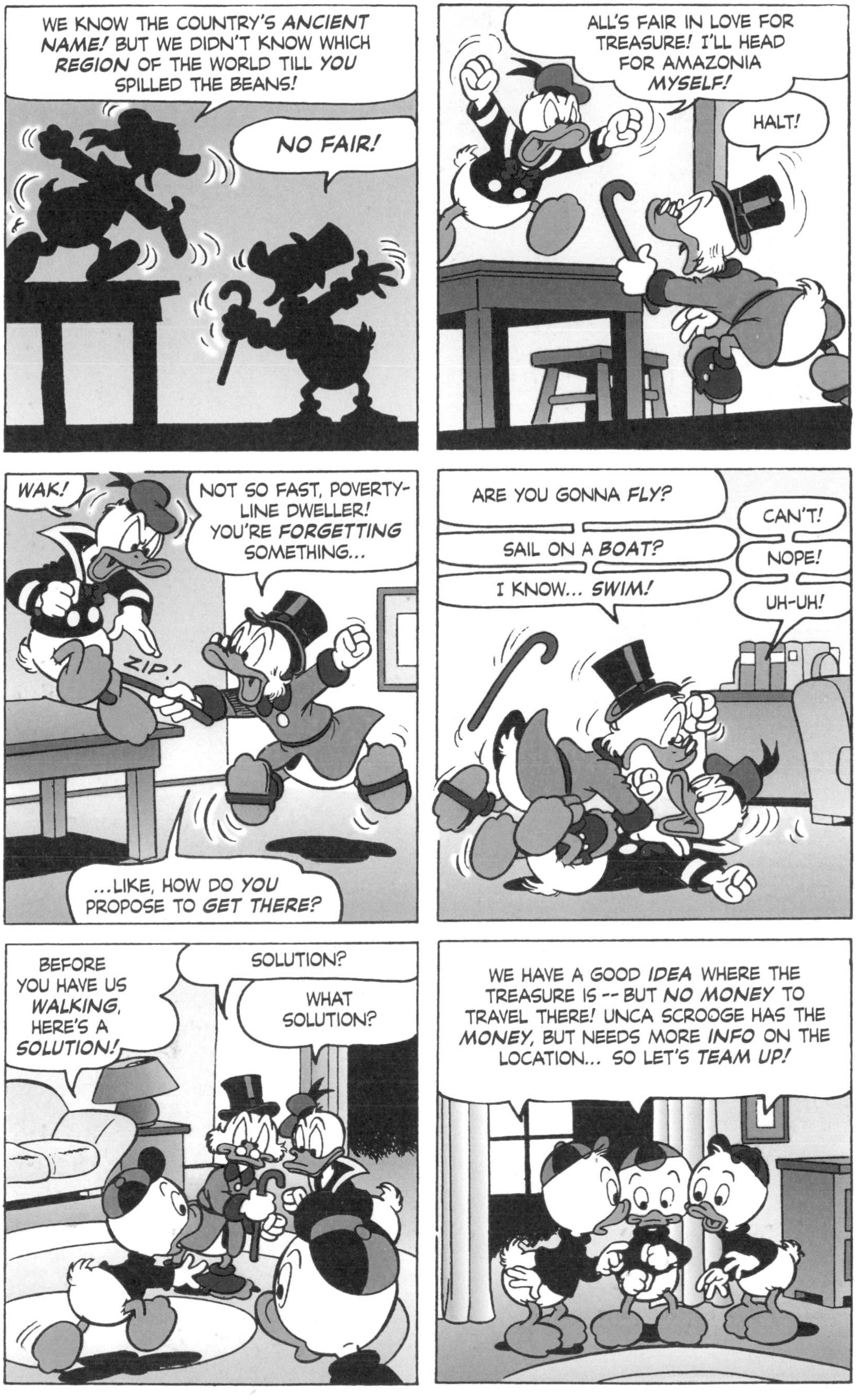
WE KNOW THE COUNTRY'S ANCIENT NAME! BUT WE DIDN'T KNOW WHICH REGION OF THE WORLD TILL YOU SPILLED THE BEANS!
NO FAIR!
ALL'S FAIR IN LOVE FOR TREASURE! I'LL HEAD FOR AMAZONIA MYSELF!
HALT!
WAK!
NOT SO FAST, POVERTY-LINE DWELLER! YOU'RE FORGETTING SOMETHING...
ZIP!
...LIKE, HOW DO YOU PROPOSE TO GET THERE?
ARE YOU GONNA FLY?
CAN'T!
SAIL ON A BOAT?
NOPE!
I KNOW... SWIM!
UH-UH!
BEFORE YOU HAVE US WALKING, HERE'S A SOLUTION!
SOLUTION?
WHAT SOLUTION?
WE HAVE A GOOD IDEA WHERE THE TREASURE IS -- BUT NO MONEY TO TRAVEL THERE! UNCA SCROOGE HAS THE MONEY, BUT NEEDS MORE INFO ON THE LOCATION... SO LET'S TEAM UP!

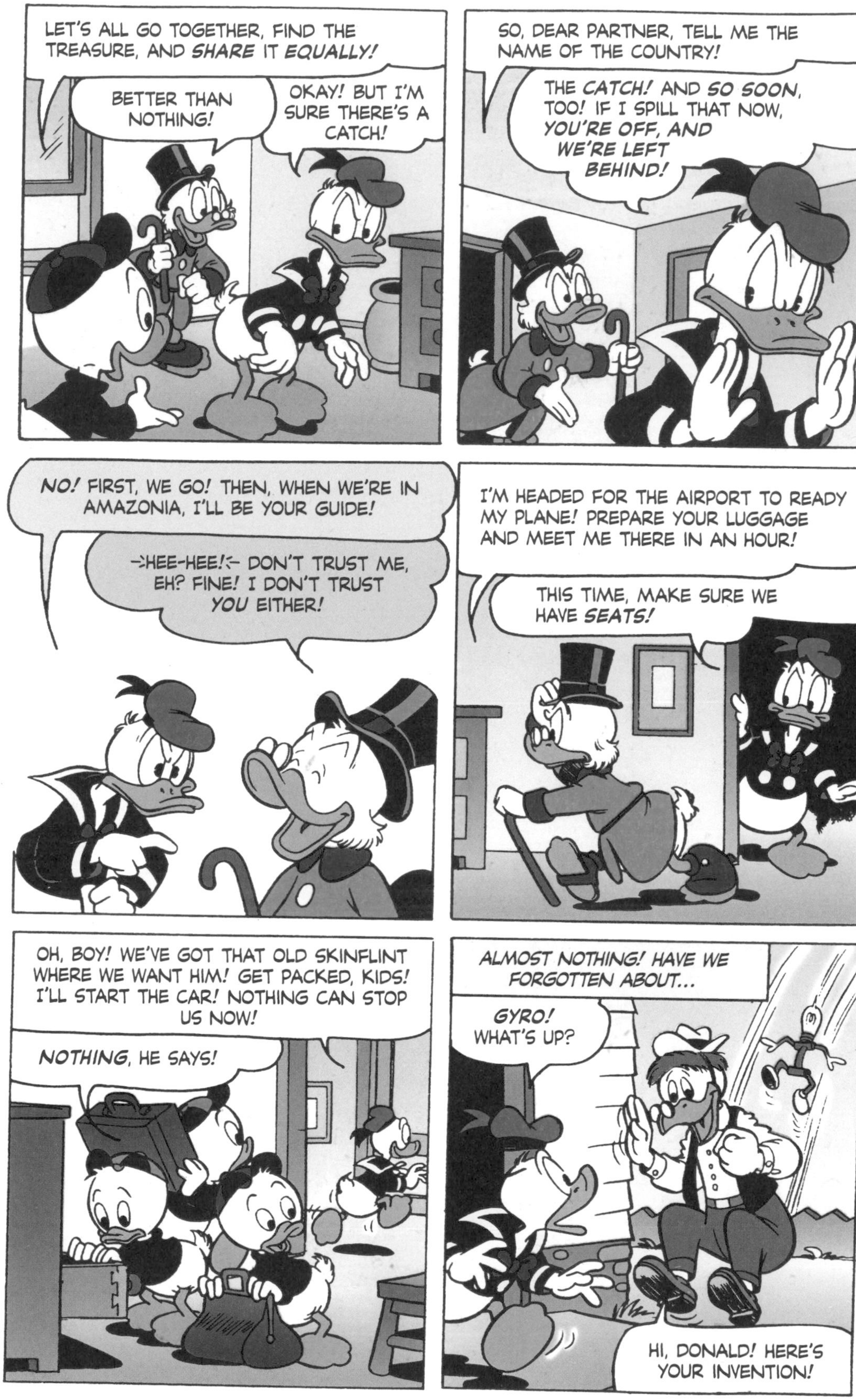
LET'S ALL GO TOGETHER, FIND THE TREASURE, AND SHARE IT EQUALLY!
BETTER THAN NOTHING!
OKAY! BUT I'M SURE THERE'S A CATCH!
SO, DEAR PARTNER, TELL ME THE NAME OF THE COUNTRY!
THE CATCH! AND SO SOON, TOO! IF I SPILL THAT NOW, YOU'RE OFF, AND WE'RE LEFT BEHIND!
NO! FIRST, WE GO! THEN, WHEN WE'RE IN AMAZONIA, I'LL BE YOUR GUIDE!
-HEE-HEE!- DON'T TRUST ME, EH? FINE! I DON'T TRUST YOU EITHER!
I'M HEADED FOR THE AIRPORT TO READY MY PLANE! PREPARE YOUR LUGGAGE AND MEET ME THERE IN AN HOUR!
THIS TIME, MAKE SURE WE HAVE SEATS!
OH, BOY! WE'VE GOT THAT OLD SKINFLINT WHERE WE WANT HIM! GET PACKED, KIDS! I'LL START THE CAR! NOTHING CAN STOP US NOW!
NOTHING, HE SAYS!
ALMOST NOTHING! HAVE WE FORGOTTEN ABOUT...
GYRO! WHAT'S UP?
HI, DONALD! HERE'S YOUR INVENTION!

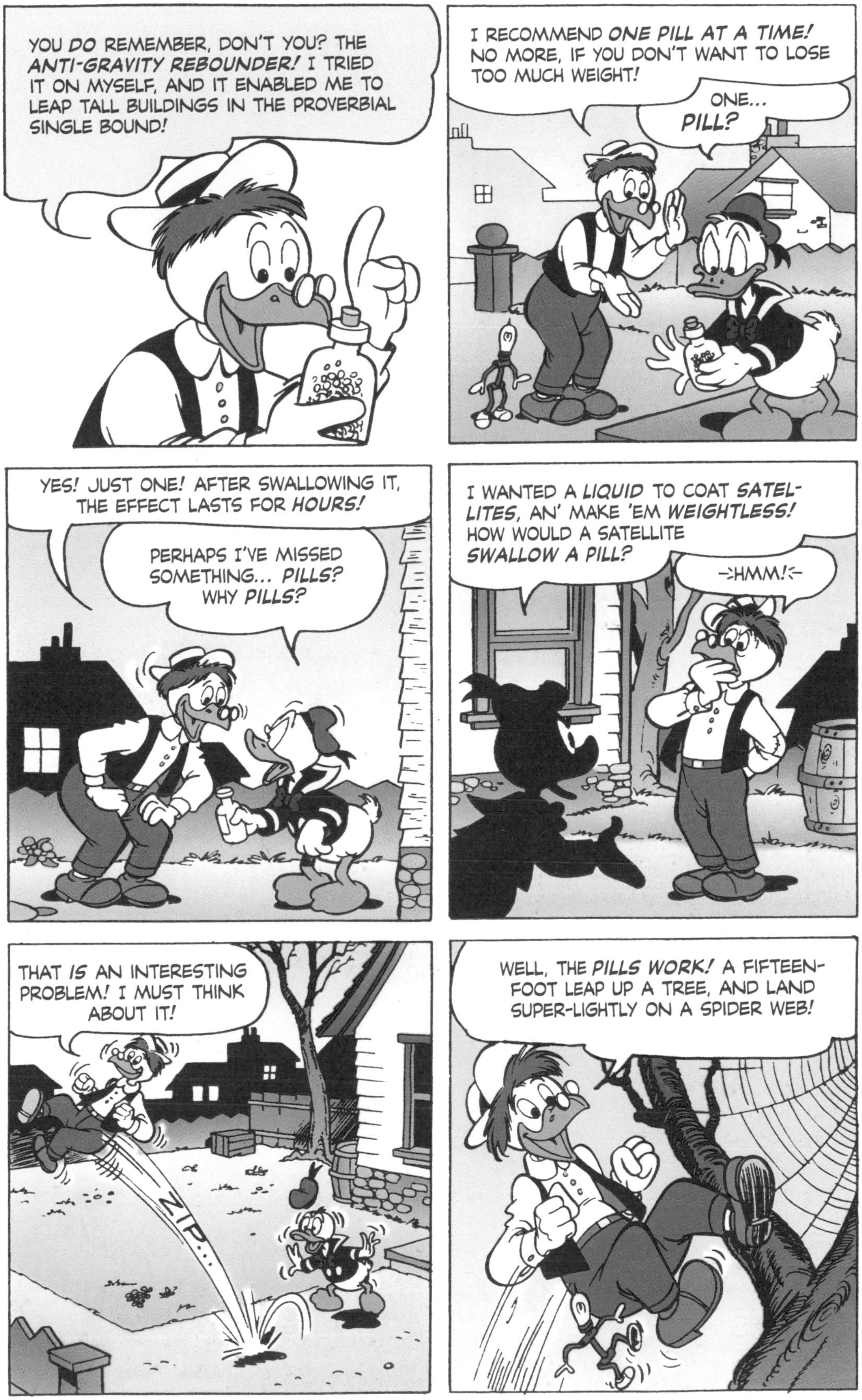
YOU DO REMEMBER, DON'T YOU? THE ANTI-GRAVITY REBOUNDER! I TRIED IT ON MYSELF, AND IT ENABLED ME TO LEAP TALL BUILDINGS IN THE PROVERBIAL SINGLE BOUND!
I RECOMMEND ONE PILL AT A TIME! NO MORE, IF YOU DON'T WANT TO LOSE TOO MUCH WEIGHT!
ONE... PILL?
YES! JUST ONE! AFTER SWALLOWING IT, THE EFFECT LASTS FOR HOURS!
PERHAPS I'VE MISSED SOMETHING... PILLS? WHY PILLS?
I WANTED A LIQUID TO COAT SATELLITES, AN' MAKE 'EM WEIGHTLESS! HOW WOULD A SATELLITE SWALLOW A PILL?
HMM!
THAT IS AN INTERESTING PROBLEM! I MUST THINK ABOUT IT!
ZIP...
WELL, THE PILLS WORK! A FIFTEEN-FOOT LEAP UP A TREE, AND LAND SUPER-LIGHTLY ON A SPIDER WEB!

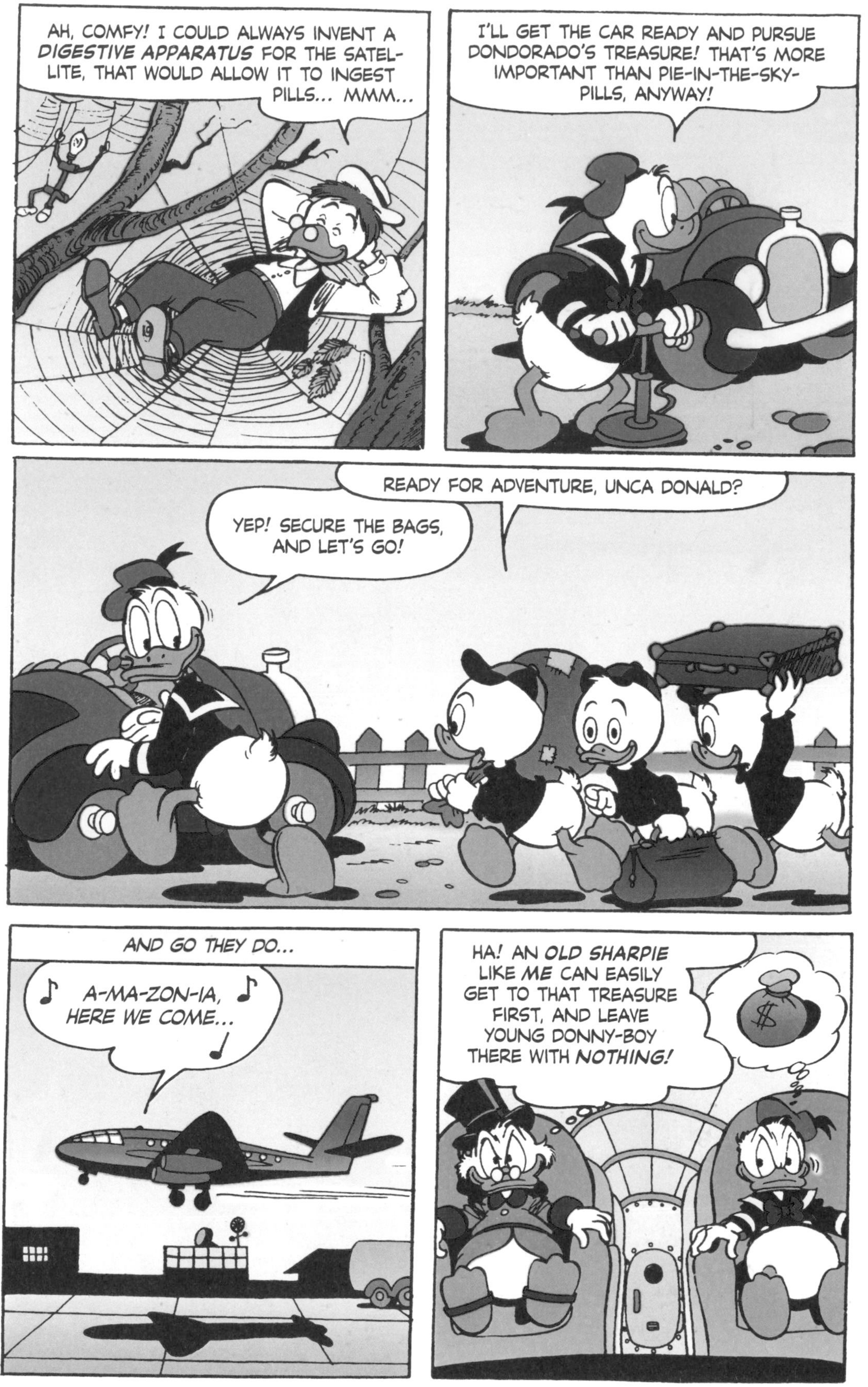
AH, COMFY! I COULD ALWAYS INVENT A DIGESTIVE APPARATUS FOR THE SATEL-LITE, THAT WOULD ALLOW IT TO INGEST PILLS... MMM...
I'LL GET THE CAR READY AND PURSUE DONDORADO'S TREASURE! THAT'S MORE IMPORTANT THAN PIE-IN-THE-SKY-PILLS, ANYWAY!
READY FOR ADVENTURE, UNCA DONALD?
YEP! SECURE THE BAGS, AND LET'S GO!
AND GO THEY DO...
♪ A-MA-ZON-IA, ♪ HERE WE COME... ♩
HA! AN OLD SHARPIE LIKE ME CAN EASILY GET TO THAT TREASURE FIRST, AND LEAVE YOUNG DONNY-BOY THERE WITH NOTHING!

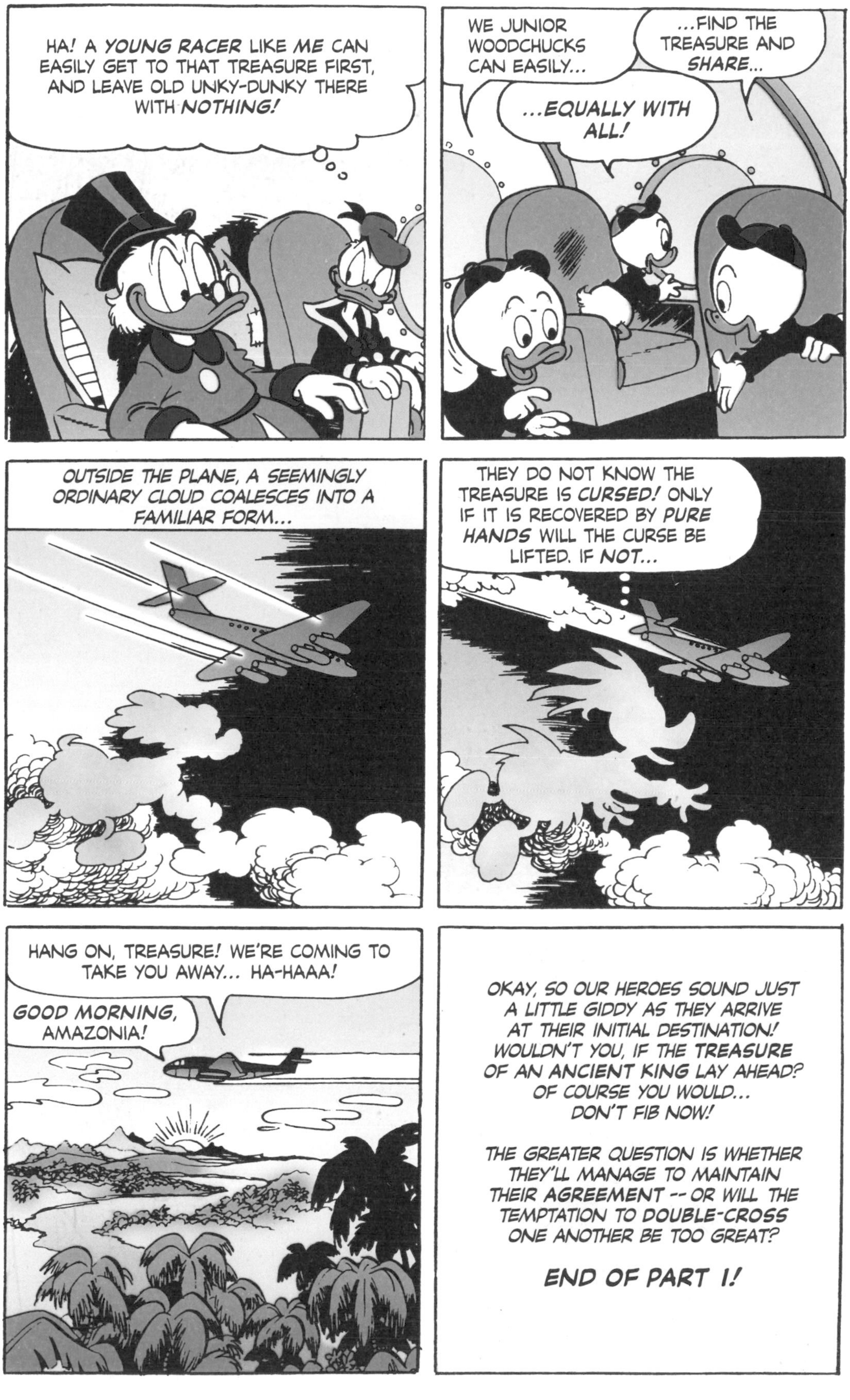
HA! A YOUNG RACER LIKE ME CAN EASILY GET TO THAT TREASURE FIRST, AND LEAVE OLD UNKY-DUNKY THERE WITH NOTHING!
WE JUNIOR WOODCHUCKS CAN EASILY...
...FIND THE TREASURE AND SHARE...
...EQUALLY WITH ALL!
OUTSIDE THE PLANE, A SEEMINGLY ORDINARY CLOUD COALESCES INTO A FAMILIAR FORM...
THEY DO NOT KNOW THE TREASURE IS CURSED! ONLY IF IT IS RECOVERED BY PURE HANDS WILL THE CURSE BE LIFTED. IF NOT...
HANG ON, TREASURE! WE'RE COMING TO TAKE YOU AWAY... HA-HAAA!
GOOD MORNING, AMAZONIA!
OKAY, SO OUR HEROES SOUND JUST A LITTLE GIDDY AS THEY ARRIVE AT THEIR INITIAL DESTINATION! WOULDN'T YOU, IF THE TREASURE OF AN ANCIENT KING LAY AHEAD? OF COURSE YOU WOULD... DON'T FIB NOW!
THE GREATER QUESTION IS WHETHER THEY'LL MANAGE TO MAINTAIN THEIR AGREEMENT -- OR WILL THE TEMPTATION TO DOUBLE-CROSS ONE ANOTHER BE TOO GREAT?
END OF PART 1!

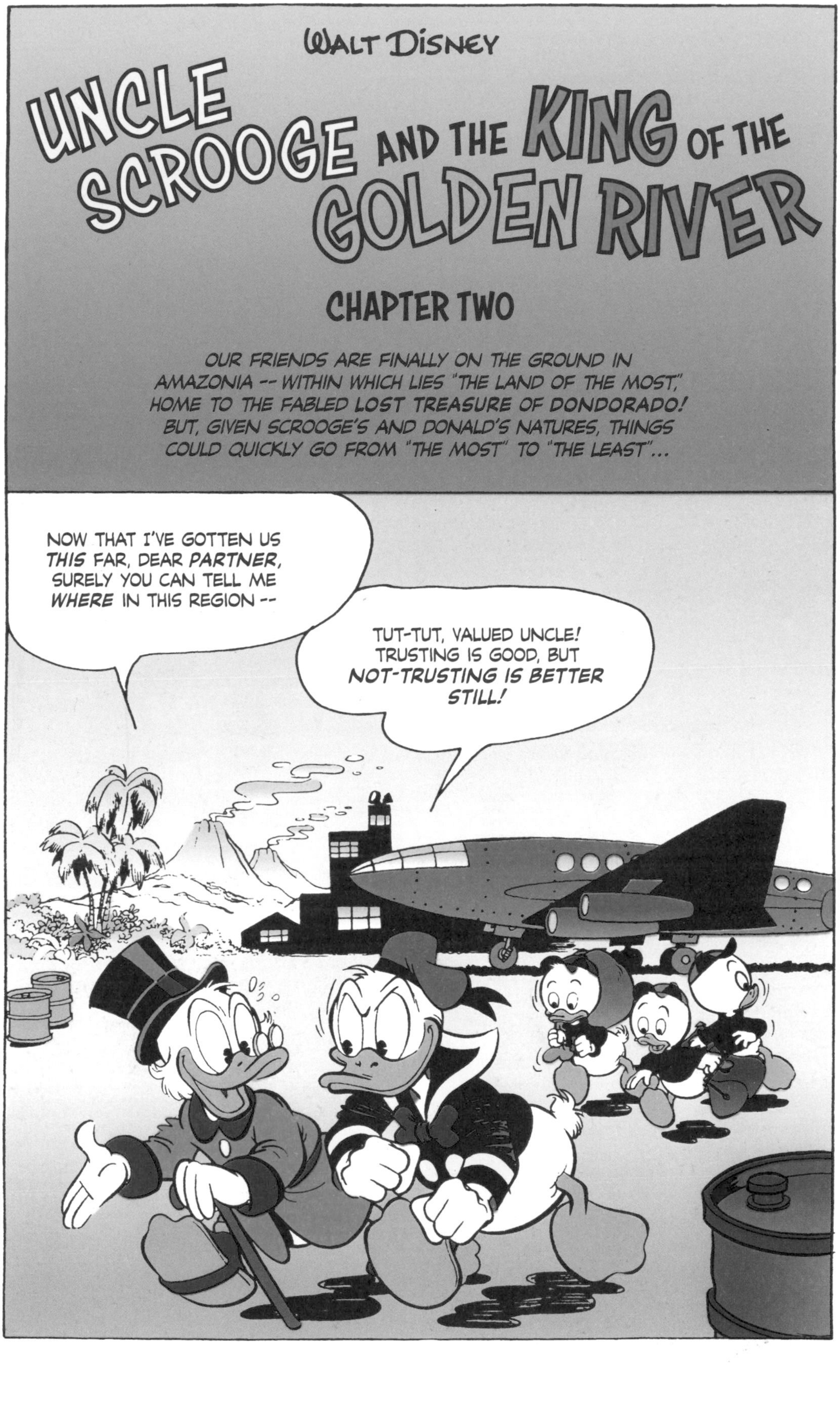
WALT DISNEY
UNCLE SCROOGE AND THE KING OF THE GOLDEN RIVER
CHAPTER TWO
OUR FRIENDS ARE FINALLY ON THE GROUND IN AMAZONIA -- WITHIN WHICH LIES "THE LAND OF THE MOST," HOME TO THE FABLED LOST TREASURE OF DONDORADO! BUT, GIVEN SCROOGE'S AND DONALD'S NATURES, THINGS COULD QUICKLY GO FROM "THE MOST" TO "THE LEAST"...
NOW THAT I'VE GOTTEN US THIS FAR, DEAR PARTNER, SURELY YOU CAN TELL ME WHERE IN THIS REGION --
TUT-TUT, VALUED UNCLE! TRUSTING IS GOOD, BUT NOT-TRUSTING IS BETTER STILL!

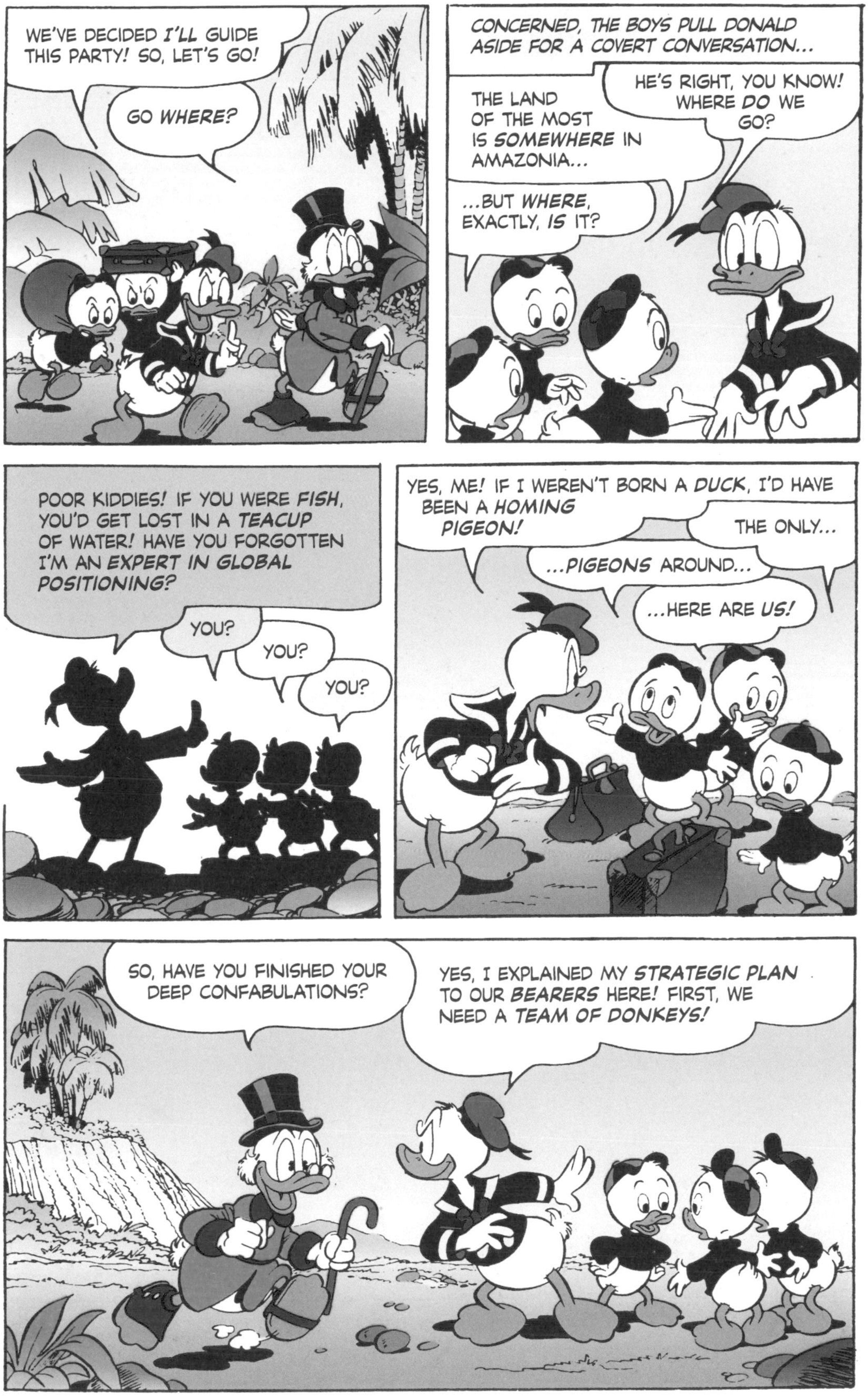

WE'VE DECIDED I'LL GUIDE THIS PARTY! SO, LET'S GO!
GO WHERE?
CONCERNED, THE BOYS PULL DONALD ASIDE FOR A COVERT CONVERSATION...
THE LAND OF THE MOST IS SOMEWHERE IN AMAZONIA...
HE'S RIGHT, YOU KNOW! WHERE DO WE GO?
...BUT WHERE, EXACTLY, IS IT?
POOR KIDDIES! IF YOU WERE FISH, YOU'D GET LOST IN A TEACUP OF WATER! HAVE YOU FORGOTTEN I'M AN EXPERT IN GLOBAL POSITIONING?
YOU?
YOU?
YOU?
YES, ME! IF I WEREN'T BORN A DUCK, I'D HAVE BEEN A HOMING PIGEON!
THE ONLY...
...PIGEONS AROUND...
...HERE ARE US!
SO, HAVE YOU FINISHED YOUR DEEP CONFABULATIONS?
YES, I EXPLAINED MY STRATEGIC PLAN TO OUR BEARERS HERE! FIRST, WE NEED A TEAM OF DONKEYS!

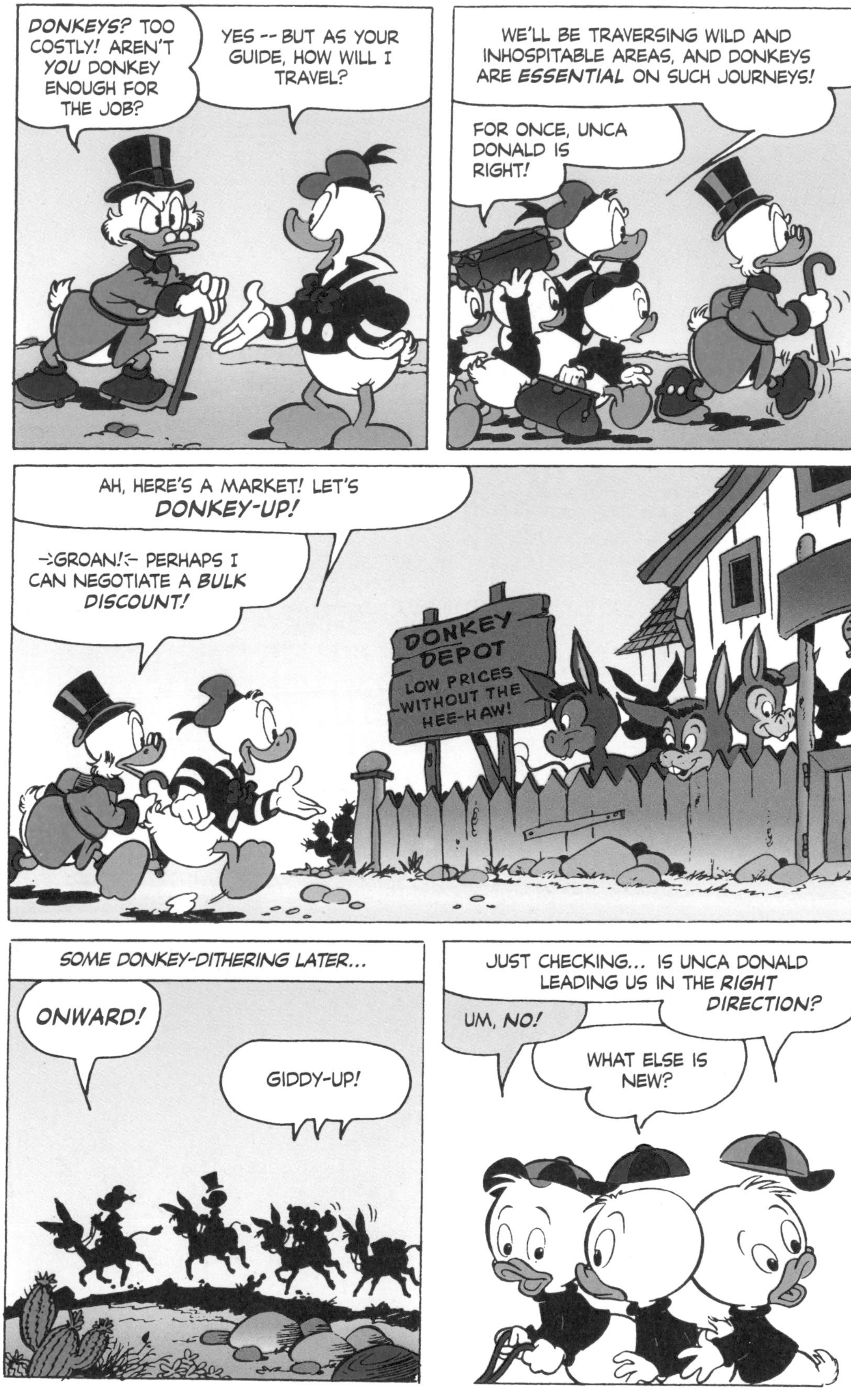
DONKEYS? TOO COSTLY! AREN'T YOU DONKEY ENOUGH FOR THE JOB?
YES -- BUT AS YOUR GUIDE, HOW WILL I TRAVEL?
WE'LL BE TRAVERSING WILD AND INHOSPITABLE AREAS, AND DONKEYS ARE ESSENTIAL ON SUCH JOURNEYS!
FOR ONCE, UNCA DONALD IS RIGHT!
AH, HERE'S A MARKET! LET'S DONKEY-UP!
-GROAN!- PERHAPS I CAN NEGOTIATE A BULK DISCOUNT!
DONKEY DEPOT
LOW PRICES WITHOUT THE HEE-HAW!
SOME DONKEY-DITHERING LATER...
ONWARD!
GIDDY-UP!
JUST CHECKING... IS UNCA DONALD LEADING US IN THE RIGHT DIRECTION?
UM, NO!
WHAT ELSE IS NEW?

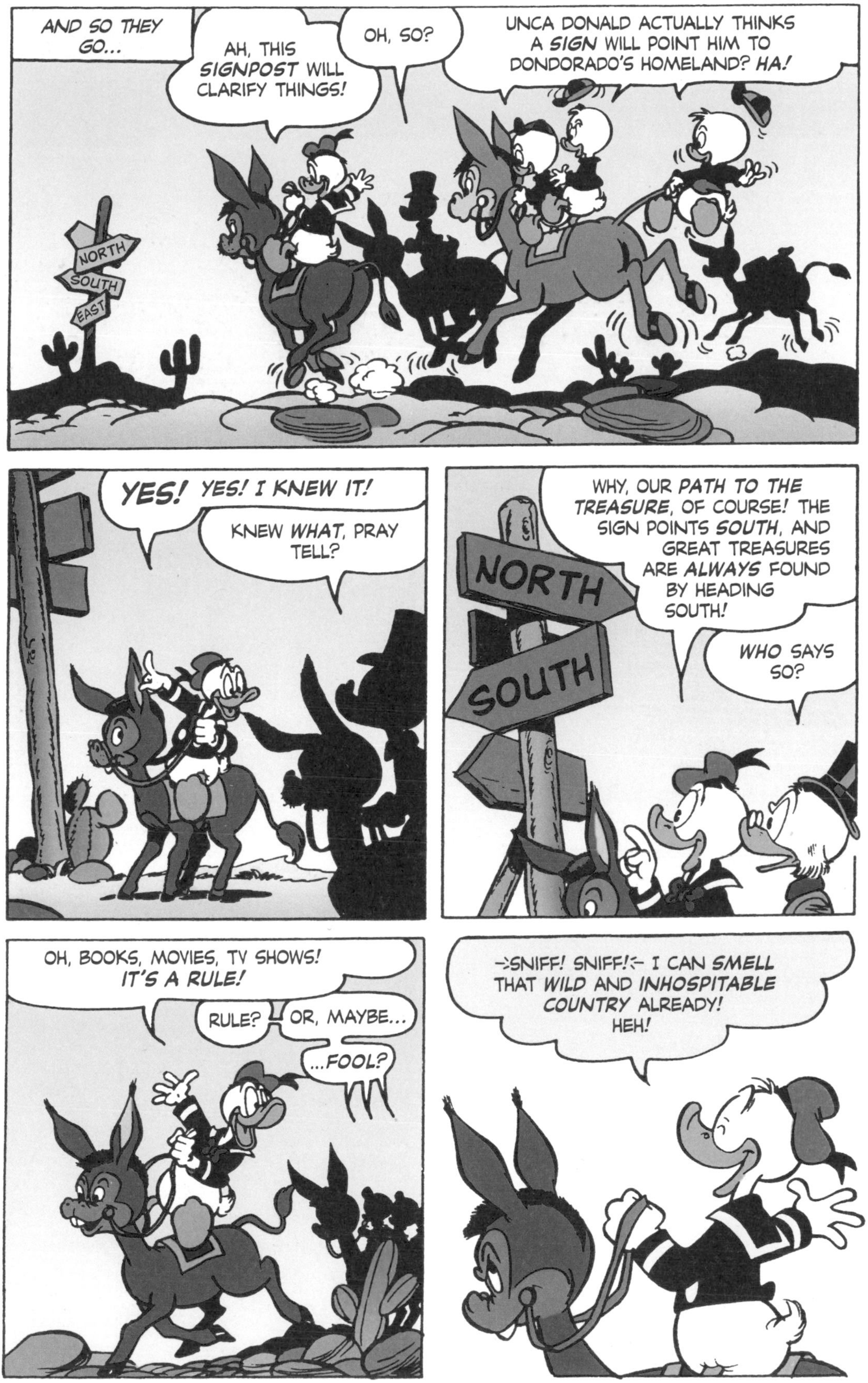
AND SO THEY GO...
AH, THIS SIGNPOST WILL CLARIFY THINGS!
OH, SO?
UNCA DONALD ACTUALLY THINKS A SIGN WILL POINT HIM TO DONDORADO'S HOMELAND? HA!
NORTH
SOUTH
EAST
YES! YES! I KNEW IT!
KNEW WHAT, PRAY TELL?
WHY, OUR PATH TO THE TREASURE, OF COURSE! THE SIGN POINTS SOUTH, AND GREAT TREASURES ARE ALWAYS FOUND BY HEADING SOUTH!
NORTH
SOUTH
WHO SAYS SO?
OH, BOOKS, MOVIES, TV SHOWS! IT'S A RULE!
RULE?
OR, MAYBE...
...FOOL?
-SNIFF! SNIFF!- I CAN SMELL THAT WILD AND INHOSPITABLE COUNTRY ALREADY! HEH!

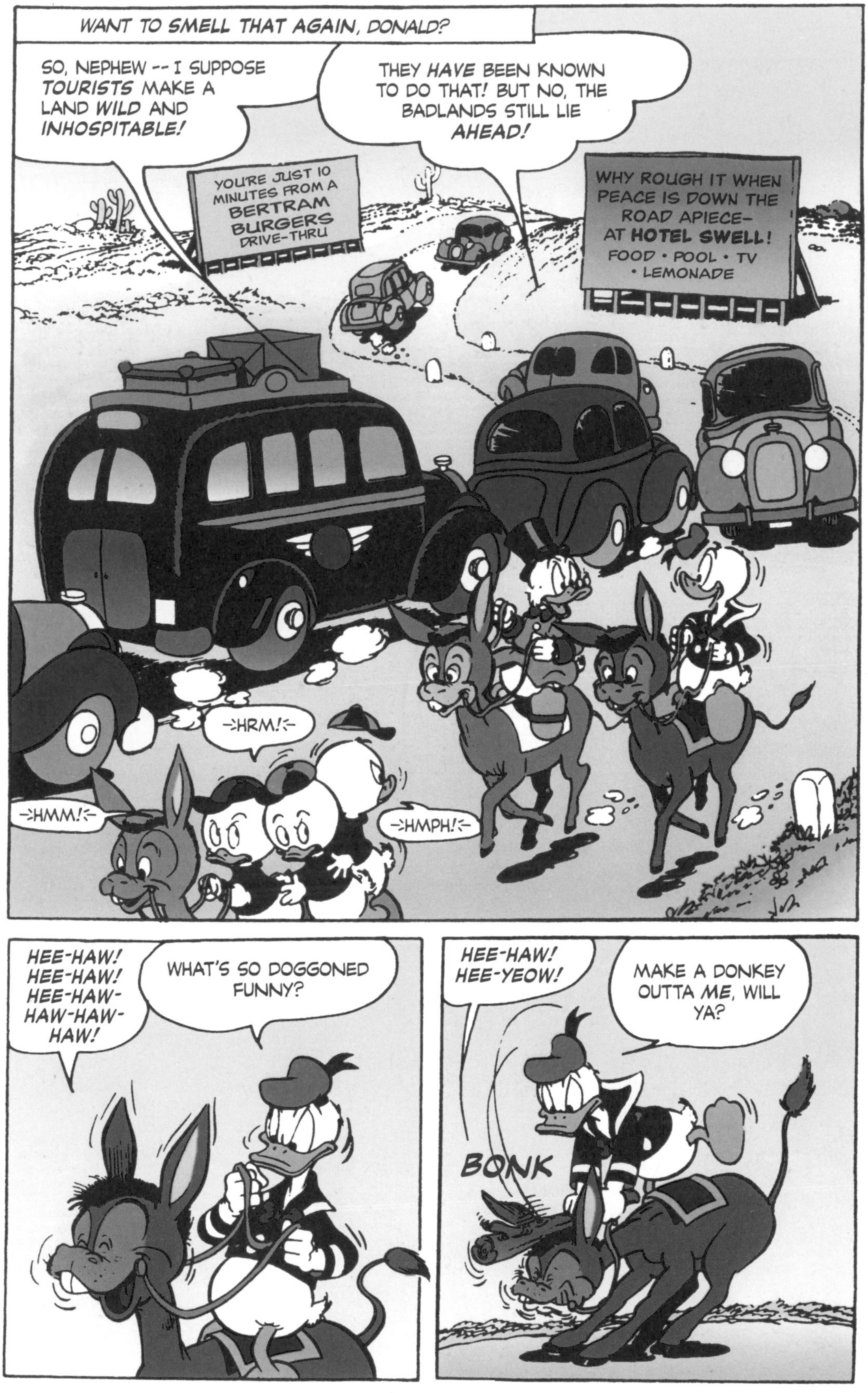
WANT TO SMELL THAT AGAIN, DONALD?
SO, NEPHEW -- I SUPPOSE TOURISTS MAKE A LAND WILD AND INHOSPITABLE!
THEY HAVE BEEN KNOWN TO DO THAT! BUT NO, THE BADLANDS STILL LIE AHEAD!
YOU'RE JUST 10 MINUTES FROM A BERTRAM BURGERS DRIVE-THRU
WHY ROUGH IT WHEN PEACE IS DOWN THE ROAD APIECE— AT HOTEL SWELL! FOOD • POOL • TV • LEMONADE
—HRM!—
—HMM!—
—HMPH!—
HEE-HAW! HEE-HAW! HEE-HAW-HAW-HAW-HAW!
WHAT'S SO DOGGONED FUNNY?
HEE-HAW! HEE-YEOW!
MAKE A DONKEY OUTTA ME, WILL YA?
BONK

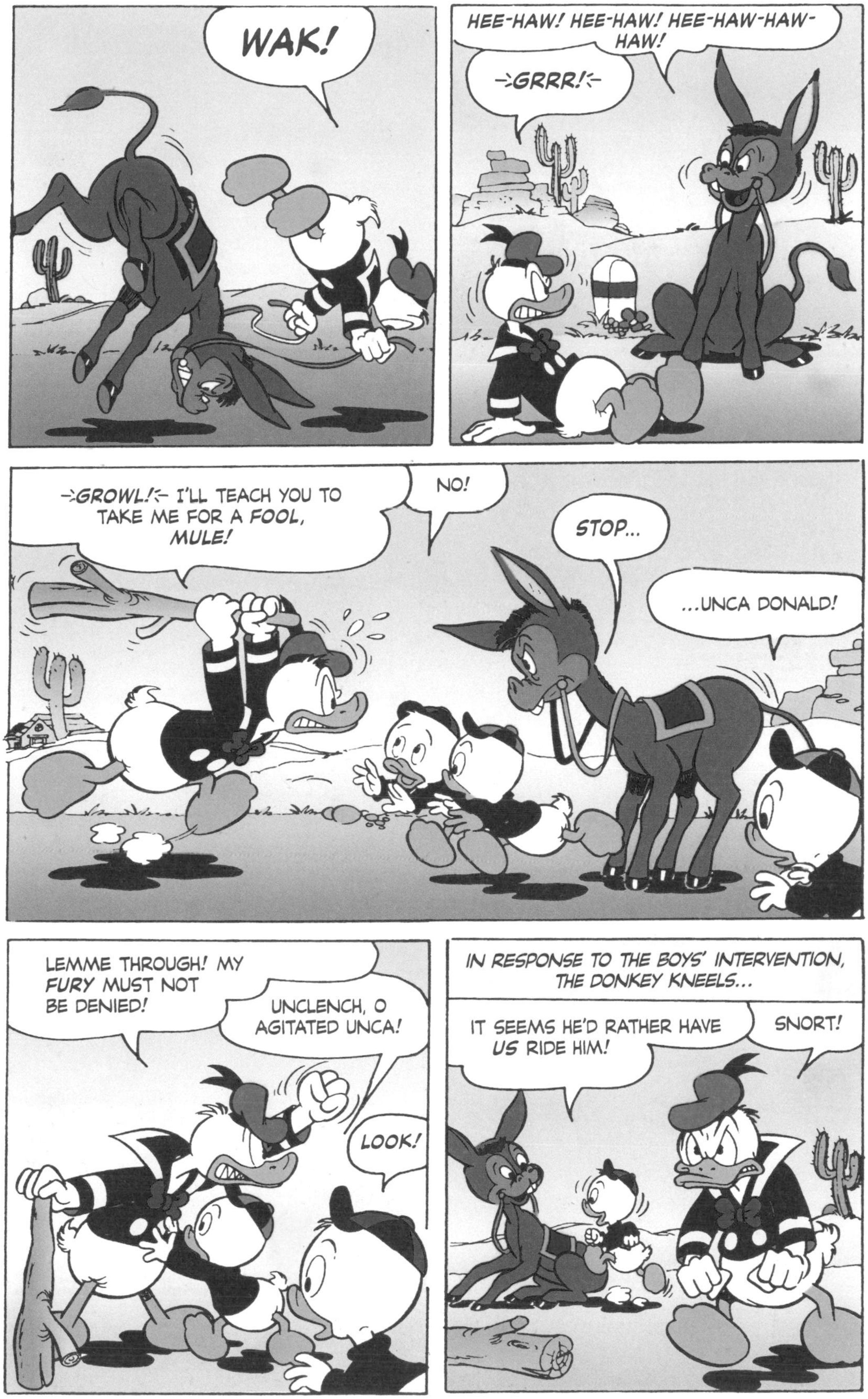

WAK!
HEE-HAW! HEE-HAW! HEE-HAW-HAW-HAW!
-GRRR!-
-GROWL!- I'LL TEACH YOU TO TAKE ME FOR A FOOL, MULE!
NO!
STOP...
...UNCA DONALD!
LEMME THROUGH! MY FURY MUST NOT BE DENIED!
UNCLENCH, O AGITATED UNCA!
LOOK!
IN RESPONSE TO THE BOYS' INTERVENTION, THE DONKEY KNEELS...
IT SEEMS HE'D RATHER HAVE US RIDE HIM!
SNORT!

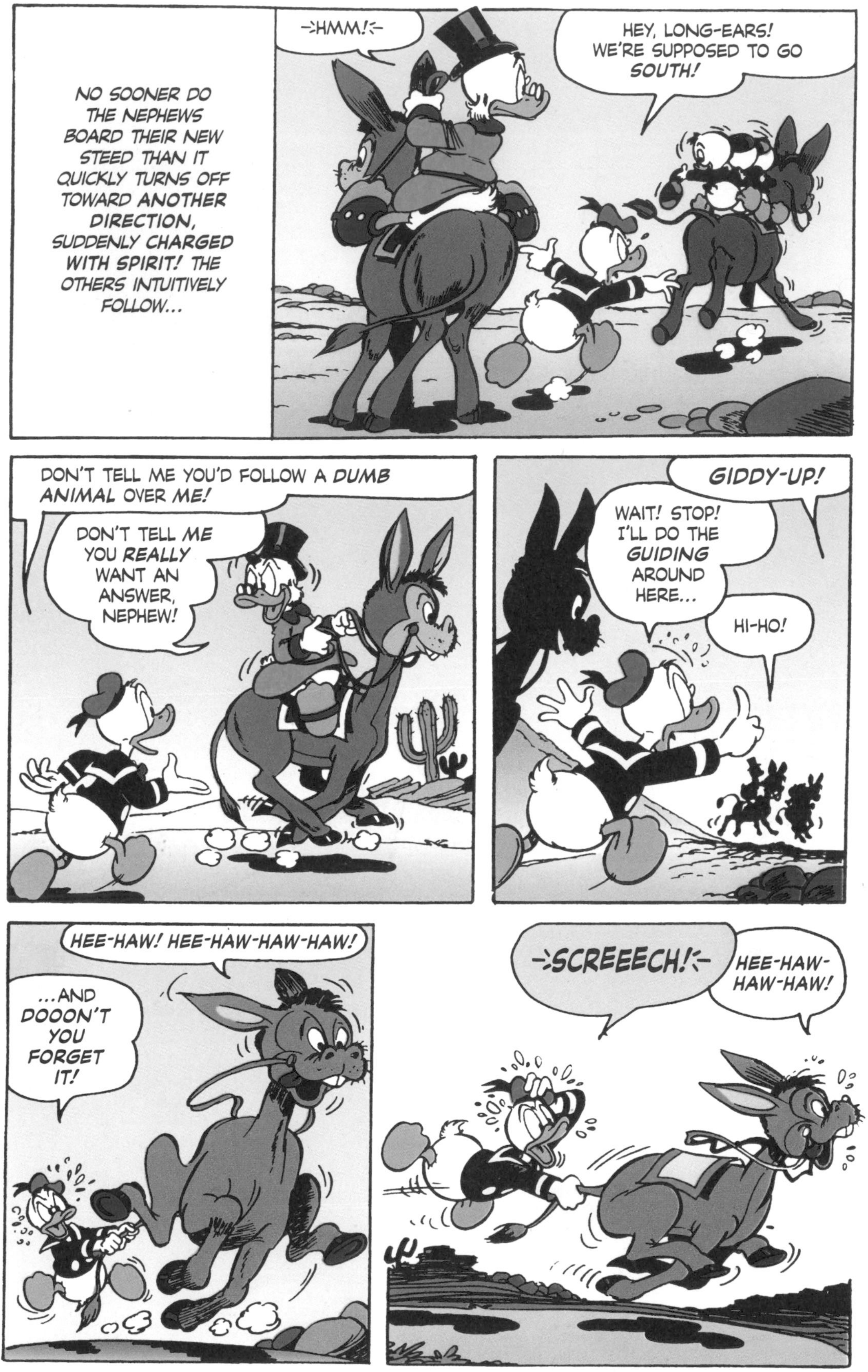
NO SOONER DO THE NEPHEWS BOARD THEIR NEW STEED THAN IT QUICKLY TURNS OFF TOWARD ANOTHER DIRECTION, SUDDENLY CHARGED WITH SPIRIT! THE OTHERS INTUITIVELY FOLLOW...
-HMM!-
HEY, LONG-EARS! WE'RE SUPPOSED TO GO SOUTH!
DON'T TELL ME YOU'D FOLLOW A DUMB ANIMAL OVER ME!
DON'T TELL ME YOU REALLY WANT AN ANSWER, NEPHEW!
GIDDY-UP!
WAIT! STOP! I'LL DO THE GUIDING AROUND HERE...
HI-HO!
HEE-HAW! HEE-HAW-HAW-HAW!
...AND DOOON'T YOU FORGET IT!
-SCREEECH!-
HEE-HAW-HAW-HAW!

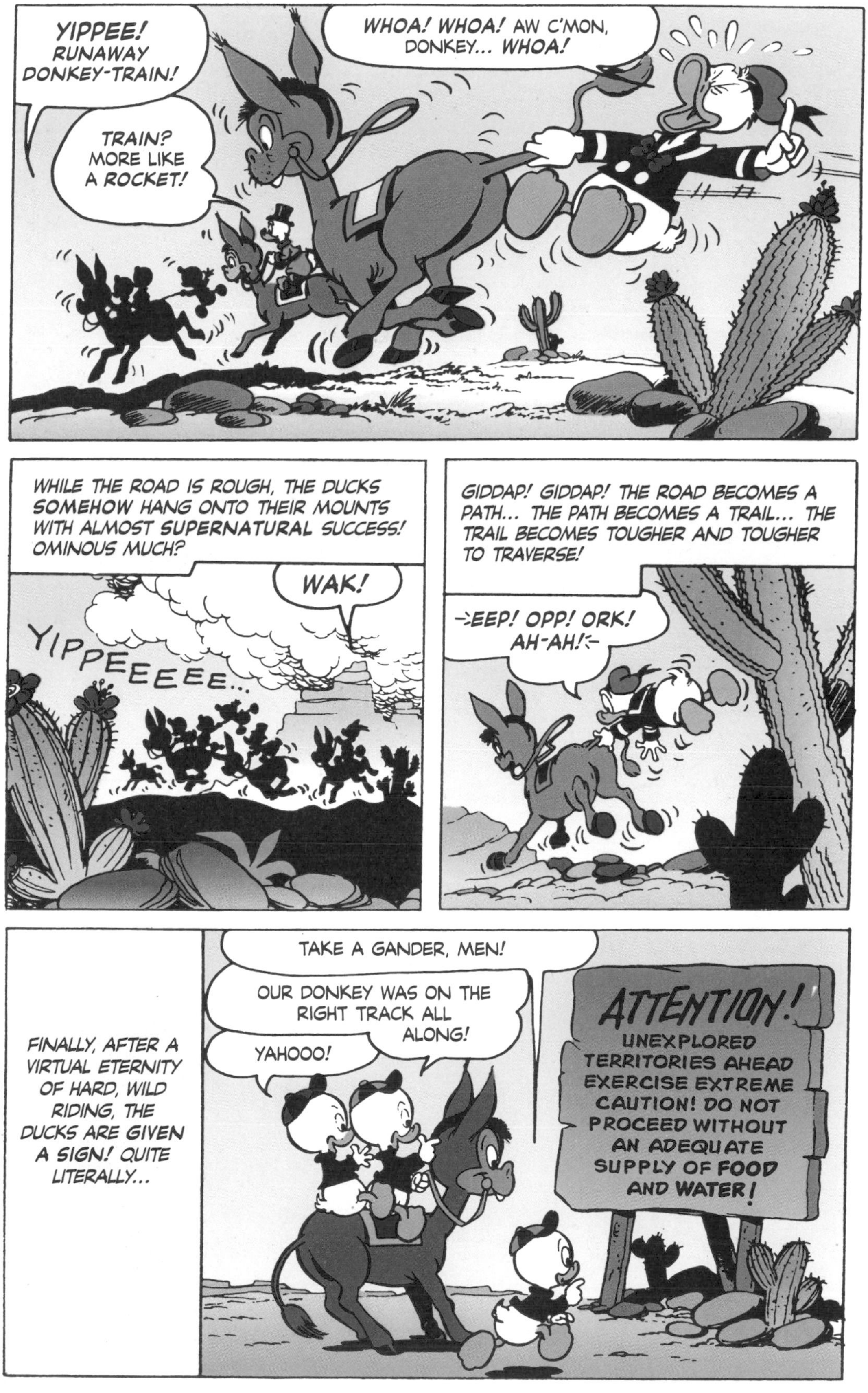
YIPPEE! RUNAWAY DONKEY-TRAIN!
WHOA! WHOA! AW C'MON, DONKEY... WHOA!
TRAIN? MORE LIKE A ROCKET!
WHILE THE ROAD IS ROUGH, THE DUCKS SOMEHOW HANG ONTO THEIR MOUNTS WITH ALMOST SUPERNATURAL SUCCESS! OMINOUS MUCH?
WAK!
YIPPEEEEEE...
GIDDAP! GIDDAP! THE ROAD BECOMES A PATH... THE PATH BECOMES A TRAIL... THE TRAIL BECOMES TOUGHER AND TOUGHER TO TRAVERSE!
EEP! OPP! ORK! AH-AH!
FINALLY, AFTER A VIRTUAL ETERNITY OF HARD, WILD RIDING, THE DUCKS ARE GIVEN A SIGN! QUITE LITERALLY...
TAKE A GANDER, MEN!
OUR DONKEY WAS ON THE RIGHT TRACK ALL ALONG!
YAHOOO!
ATTENTION! UNEXPLORED TERRITORIES AHEAD EXERCISE EXTREME CAUTION! DO NOT PROCEED WITHOUT AN ADEQUATE SUPPLY OF FOOD AND WATER!

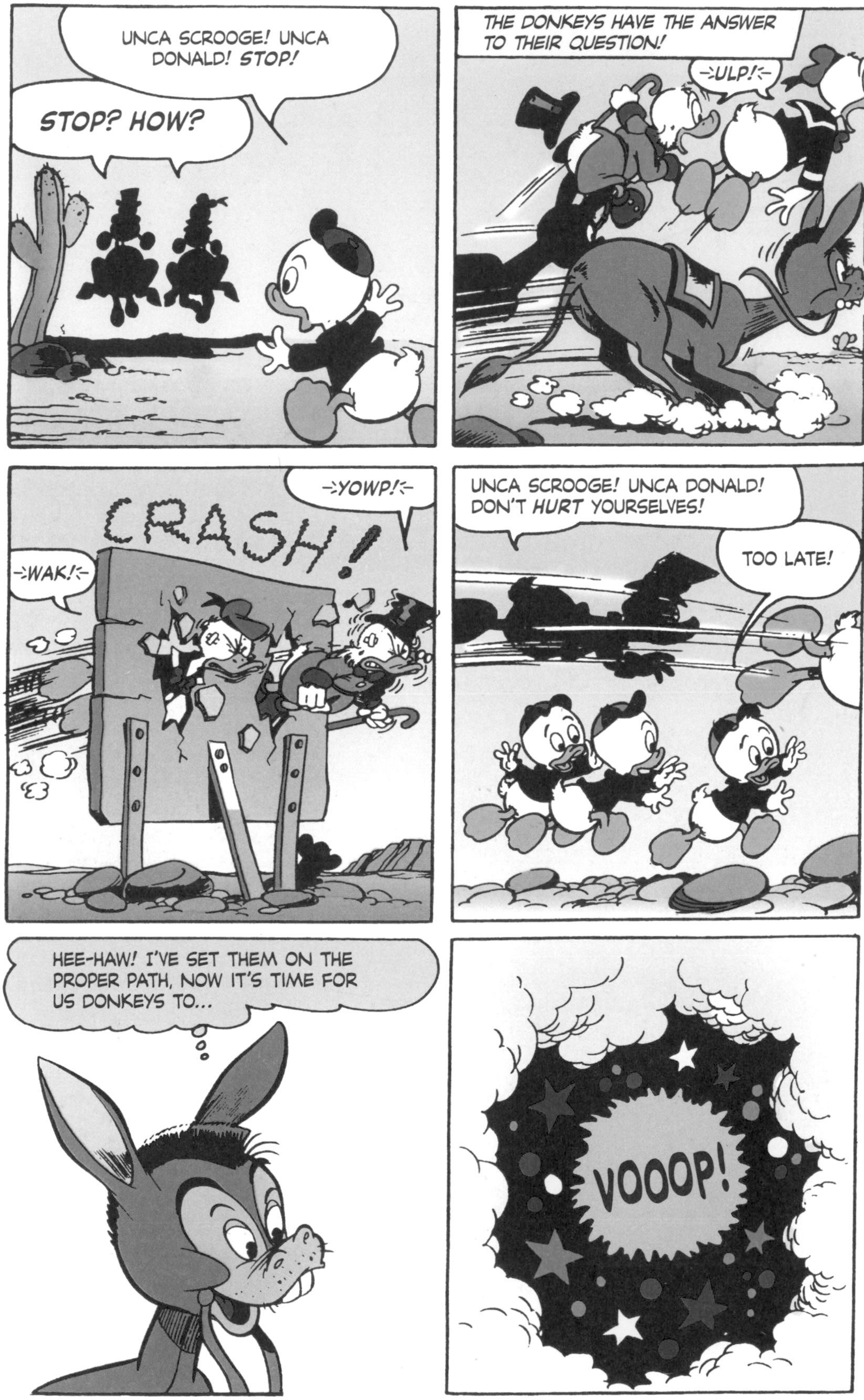
UNCA SCROOGE! UNCA DONALD! STOP!
STOP? HOW?
THE DONKEYS HAVE THE ANSWER TO THEIR QUESTION!
-ULP!-
-YOWP!-
CRASH!
-WAK!-
UNCA SCROOGE! UNCA DONALD! DON'T HURT YOURSELVES!
TOO LATE!
HEE-HAW! I'VE SET THEM ON THE PROPER PATH, NOW IT'S TIME FOR US DONKEYS TO...
VOOOP!

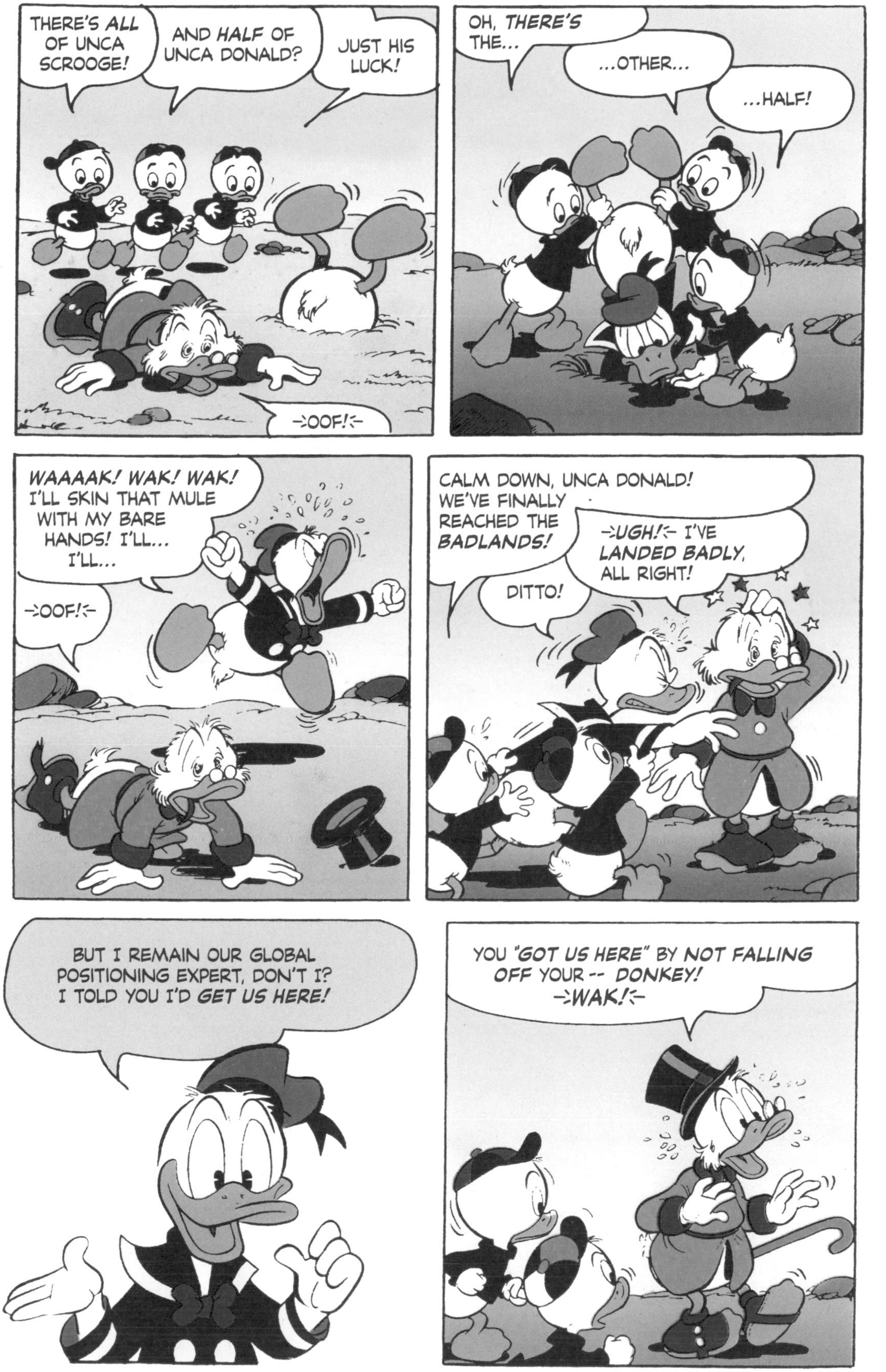
THERE'S ALL OF UNCA SCROOGE!
AND HALF OF UNCA DONALD?
JUST HIS LUCK!
-OOF!-
OH, THERE'S THE...
...OTHER...
...HALF!
WAAAAK! WAK! WAK! I'LL SKIN THAT MULE WITH MY BARE HANDS! I'LL... I'LL...
-OOF!-
CALM DOWN, UNCA DONALD! WE'VE FINALLY REACHED THE BADLANDS!
DITTO!
-UGH!- I'VE LANDED BADLY, ALL RIGHT!
BUT I REMAIN OUR GLOBAL POSITIONING EXPERT, DON'T I? I TOLD YOU I'D GET US HERE!
YOU "GOT US HERE" BY NOT FALLING OFF YOUR -- DONKEY!
-WAK!-

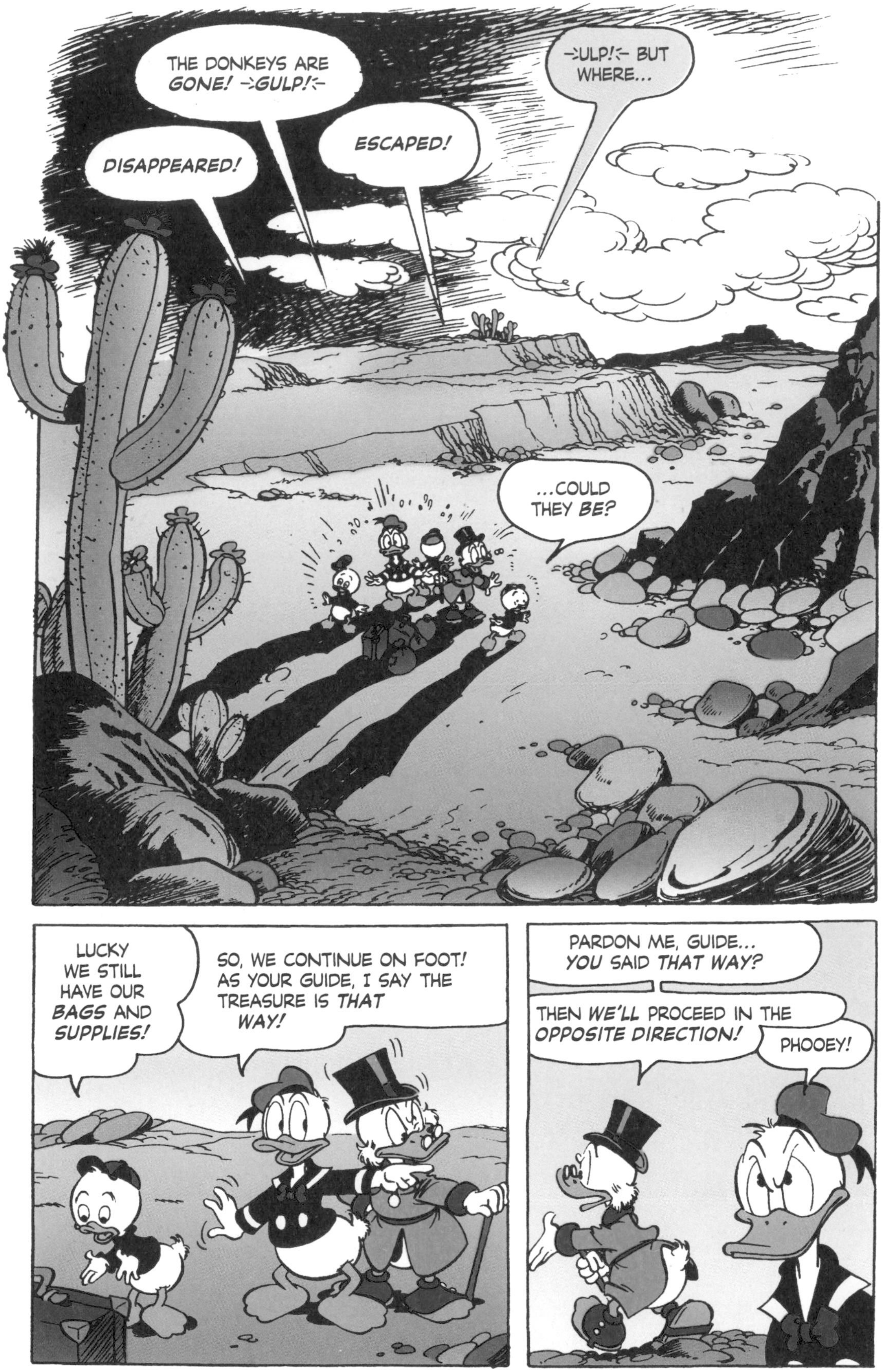
THE DONKEYS ARE GONE! ~GULP!~
DISAPPEARED!
ESCAPED!
~ULP!~ BUT WHERE...
...COULD THEY BE?
LUCKY WE STILL HAVE OUR BAGS AND SUPPLIES!
SO, WE CONTINUE ON FOOT! AS YOUR GUIDE, I SAY THE TREASURE IS THAT WAY!
PARDON ME, GUIDE... YOU SAID THAT WAY?
THEN WE'LL PROCEED IN THE OPPOSITE DIRECTION!
PHOOEY!

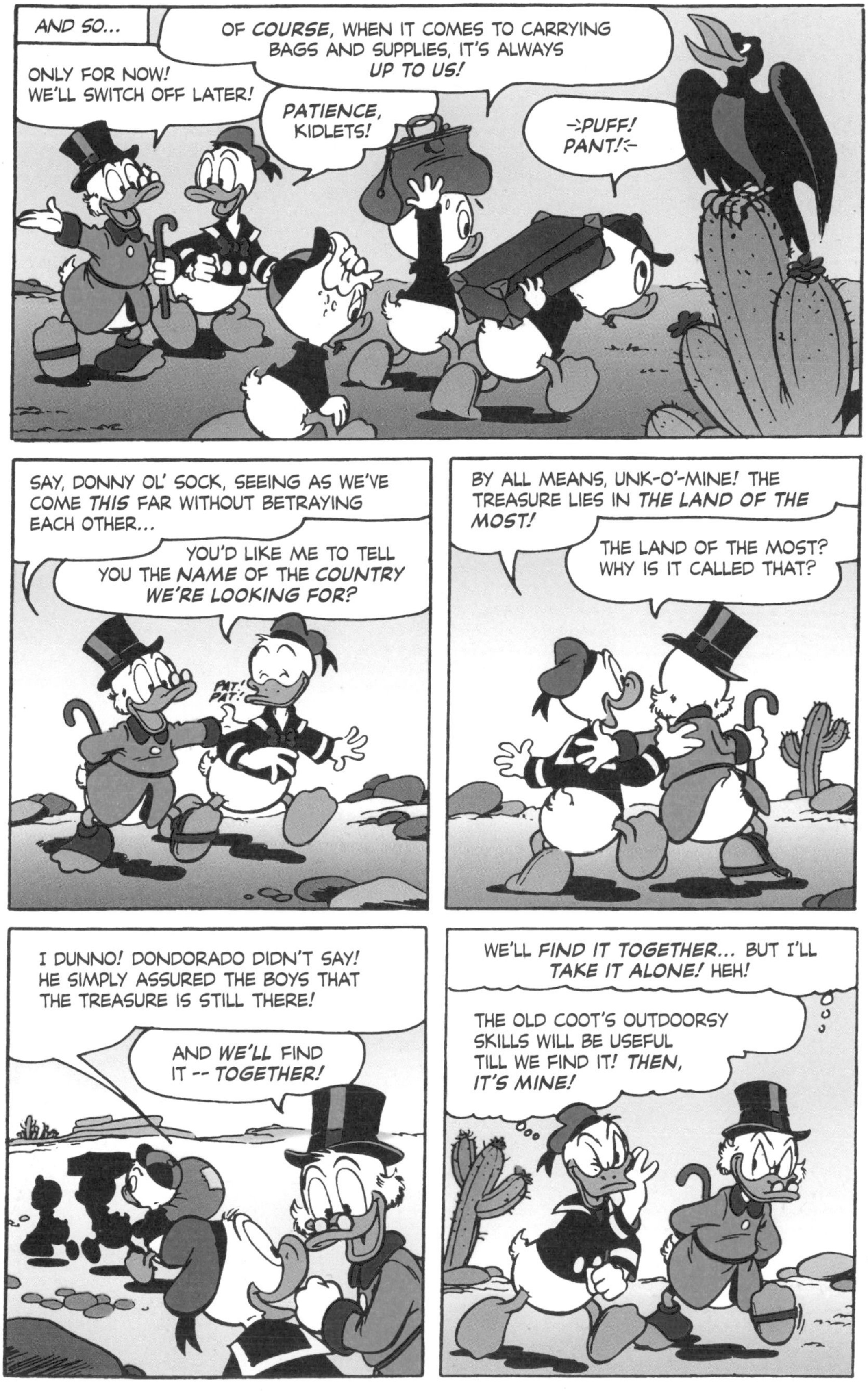
AND SO...
ONLY FOR NOW! WE'LL SWITCH OFF LATER!
OF COURSE, WHEN IT COMES TO CARRYING BAGS AND SUPPLIES, IT'S ALWAYS UP TO US!
PATIENCE, KIDLETS!
PUFF! PANT!
SAY, DONNY OL' SOCK, SEEING AS WE'VE COME THIS FAR WITHOUT BETRAYING EACH OTHER...
YOU'D LIKE ME TO TELL YOU THE NAME OF THE COUNTRY WE'RE LOOKING FOR?
PAT! PAT!
BY ALL MEANS, UNK-O'-MINE! THE TREASURE LIES IN THE LAND OF THE MOST!
THE LAND OF THE MOST? WHY IS IT CALLED THAT?
I DUNNO! DONDORADO DIDN'T SAY! HE SIMPLY ASSURED THE BOYS THAT THE TREASURE IS STILL THERE!
AND WE'LL FIND IT -- TOGETHER!
WE'LL FIND IT TOGETHER... BUT I'LL TAKE IT ALONE! HEH!
THE OLD COOT'S OUTDOORSY SKILLS WILL BE USEFUL TILL WE FIND IT! THEN, IT'S MINE!

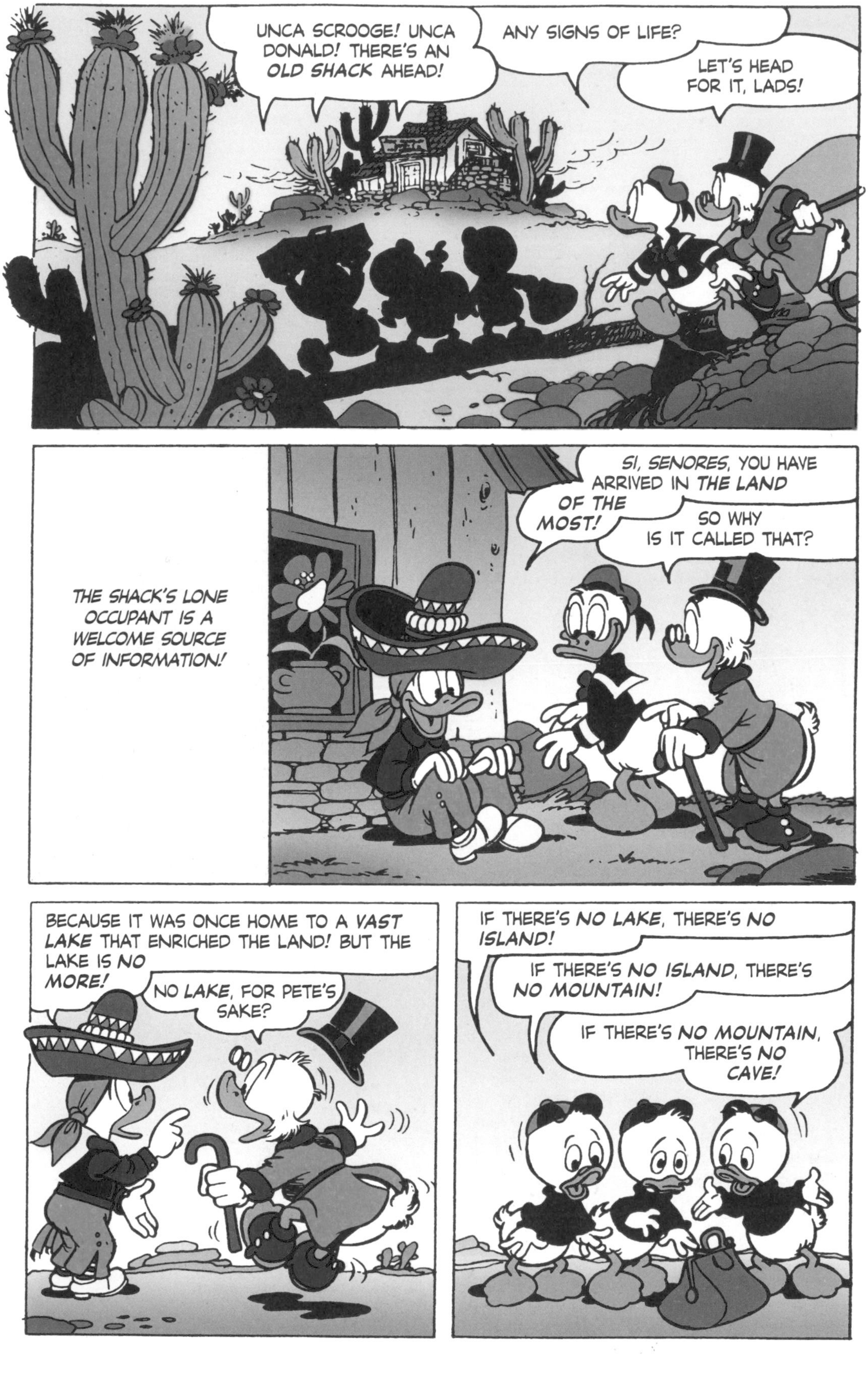
UNCA SCROOGE! UNCA DONALD! THERE'S AN OLD SHACK AHEAD!
ANY SIGNS OF LIFE?
LET'S HEAD FOR IT, LADS!
THE SHACK'S LONE OCCUPANT IS A WELCOME SOURCE OF INFORMATION!
SI, SENORES, YOU HAVE ARRIVED IN THE LAND OF THE MOST!
SO WHY IS IT CALLED THAT?
BECAUSE IT WAS ONCE HOME TO A VAST LAKE THAT ENRICHED THE LAND! BUT THE LAKE IS NO MORE!
NO LAKE, FOR PETE'S SAKE?
IF THERE'S NO LAKE, THERE'S NO ISLAND!
IF THERE'S NO ISLAND, THERE'S NO MOUNTAIN!
IF THERE'S NO MOUNTAIN, THERE'S NO CAVE!

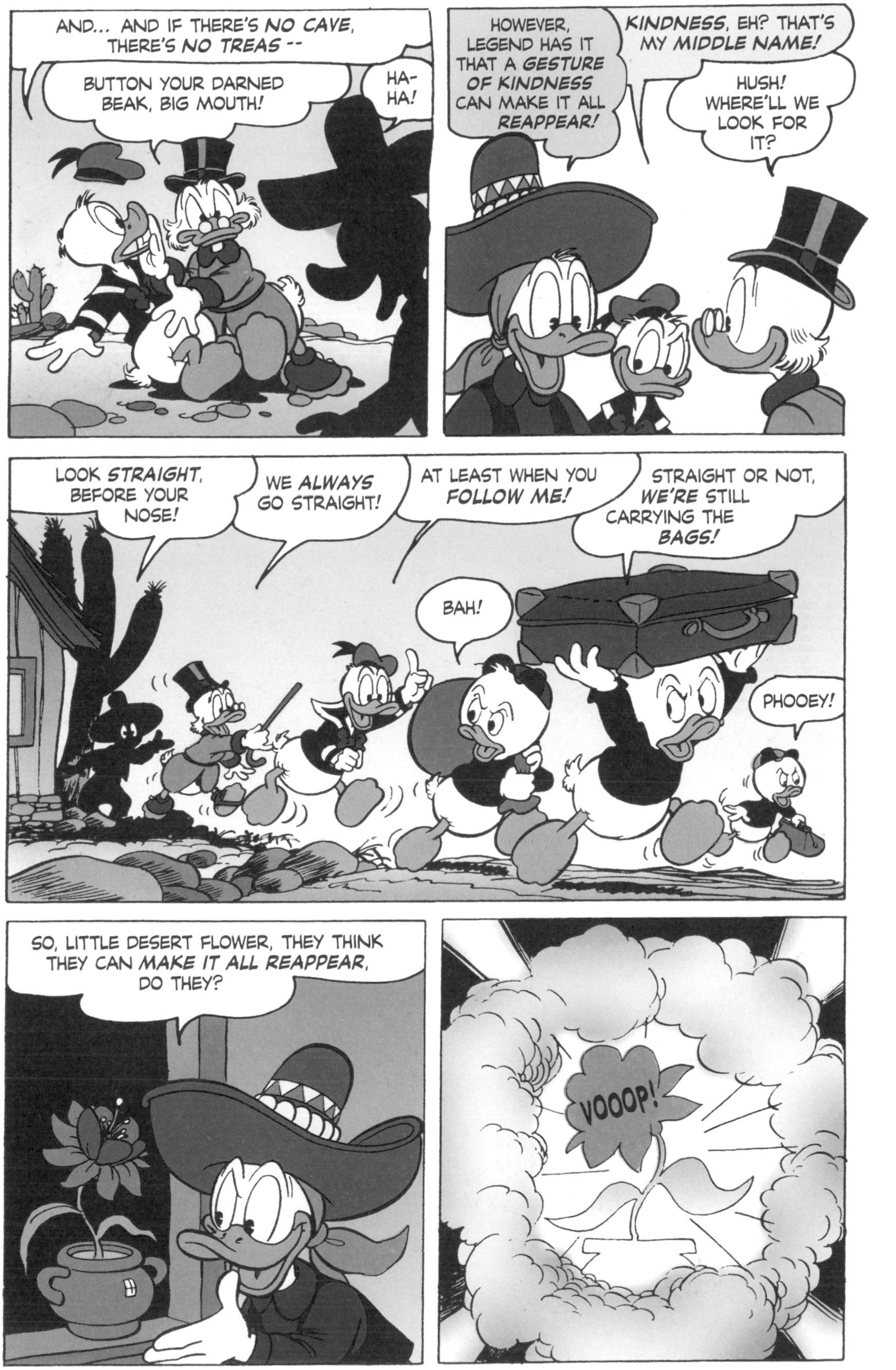
AND... AND IF THERE'S NO CAVE, THERE'S NO TREAS --
BUTTON YOUR DARNED BEAK, BIG MOUTH!
HA-HA!
HOWEVER, LEGEND HAS IT THAT A GESTURE OF KINDNESS CAN MAKE IT ALL REAPPEAR!
KINDNESS, EH? THAT'S MY MIDDLE NAME!
HUSH! WHERE'LL WE LOOK FOR IT?
LOOK STRAIGHT, BEFORE YOUR NOSE!
WE ALWAYS GO STRAIGHT!
AT LEAST WHEN YOU FOLLOW ME!
STRAIGHT OR NOT, WE'RE STILL CARRYING THE BAGS!
BAH!
PHOOEY!
SO, LITTLE DESERT FLOWER, THEY THINK THEY CAN MAKE IT ALL REAPPEAR, DO THEY?
VOOOP!

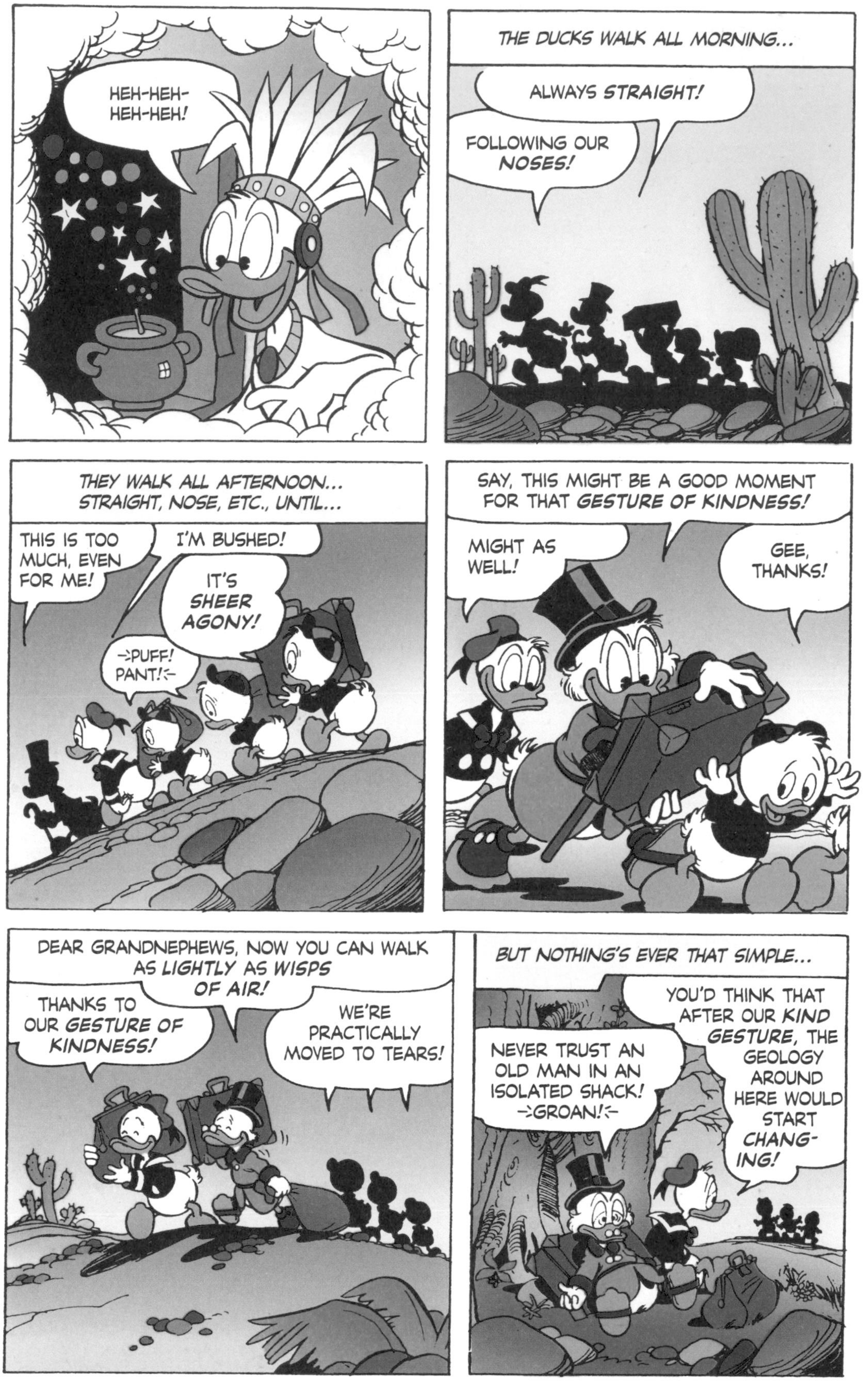
HEH-HEH-
HEH-HEH!
THE DUCKS WALK ALL MORNING...
FOLLOWING OUR NOSES!
ALWAYS STRAIGHT!
THEY WALK ALL AFTERNOON... STRAIGHT, NOSE, ETC., UNTIL...
THIS IS TOO MUCH, EVEN FOR ME!
I'M BUSHED!
IT'S SHEER AGONY!
-PUFF! PANT!-
SAY, THIS MIGHT BE A GOOD MOMENT FOR THAT GESTURE OF KINDNESS!
MIGHT AS WELL!
GEE, THANKS!
DEAR GRANDNEPHEWS, NOW YOU CAN WALK AS LIGHTLY AS WISPS OF AIR!
THANKS TO OUR GESTURE OF KINDNESS!
WE'RE PRACTICALLY MOVED TO TEARS!
BUT NOTHING'S EVER THAT SIMPLE...
YOU'D THINK THAT AFTER OUR KIND GESTURE, THE GEOLOGY AROUND HERE WOULD START CHANGING!
NEVER TRUST AN OLD MAN IN AN ISOLATED SHACK! -GROAN!-

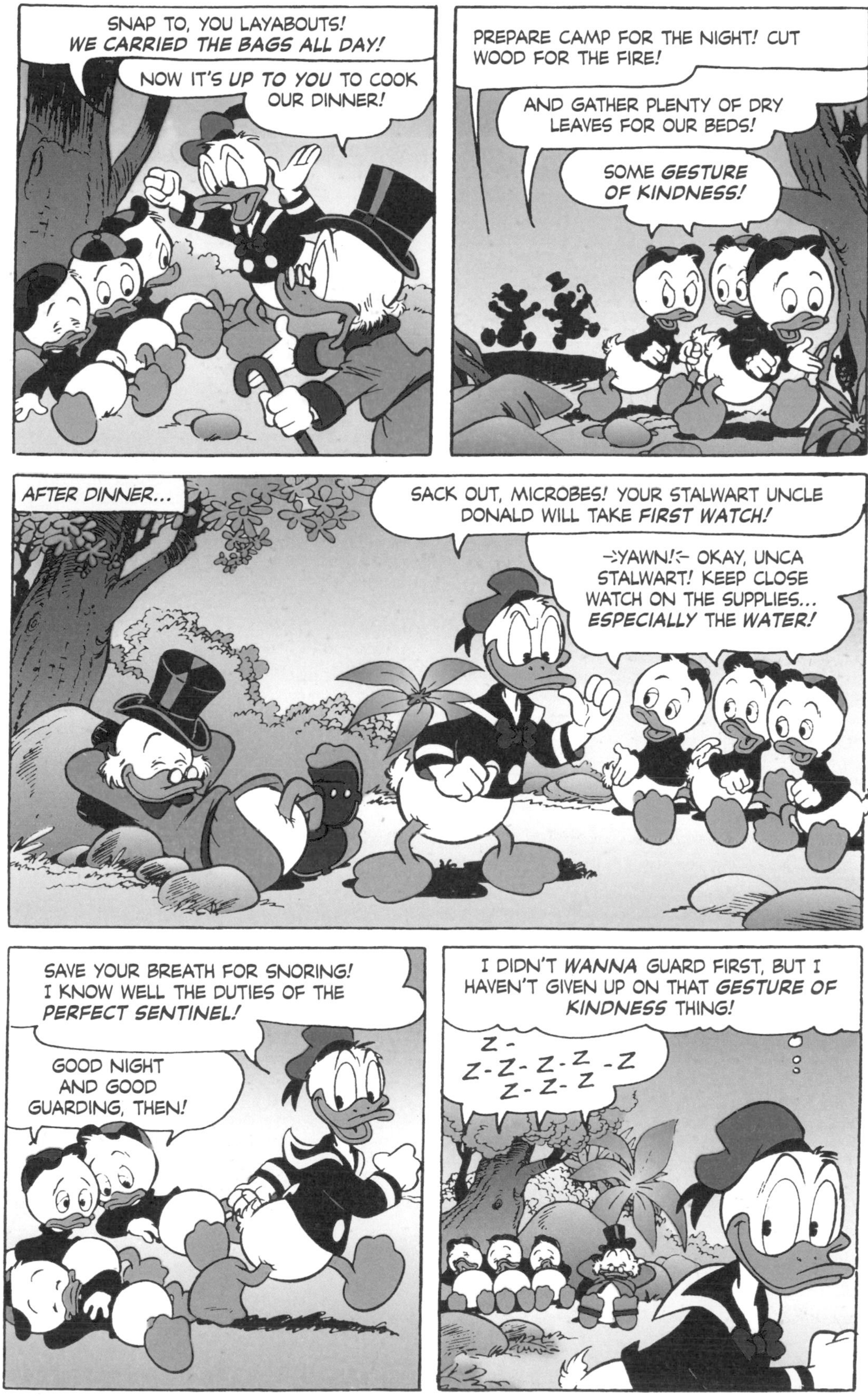
SNAP TO, YOU LAYABOUTS! WE CARRIED THE BAGS ALL DAY!
NOW IT'S UP TO YOU TO COOK OUR DINNER!
PREPARE CAMP FOR THE NIGHT! CUT WOOD FOR THE FIRE!
AND GATHER PLENTY OF DRY LEAVES FOR OUR BEDS!
SOME GESTURE OF KINDNESS!
AFTER DINNER...
SACK OUT, MICROBES! YOUR STALWART UNCLE DONALD WILL TAKE FIRST WATCH!
–YAWN!– OKAY, UNCA STALWART! KEEP CLOSE WATCH ON THE SUPPLIES... ESPECIALLY THE WATER!
SAVE YOUR BREATH FOR SNORING! I KNOW WELL THE DUTIES OF THE PERFECT SENTINEL!
GOOD NIGHT AND GOOD GUARDING, THEN!
I DIDN'T WANNA GUARD FIRST, BUT I HAVEN'T GIVEN UP ON THAT GESTURE OF KINDNESS THING!
Z-Z-Z-Z-Z-Z-Z-Z-Z-Z

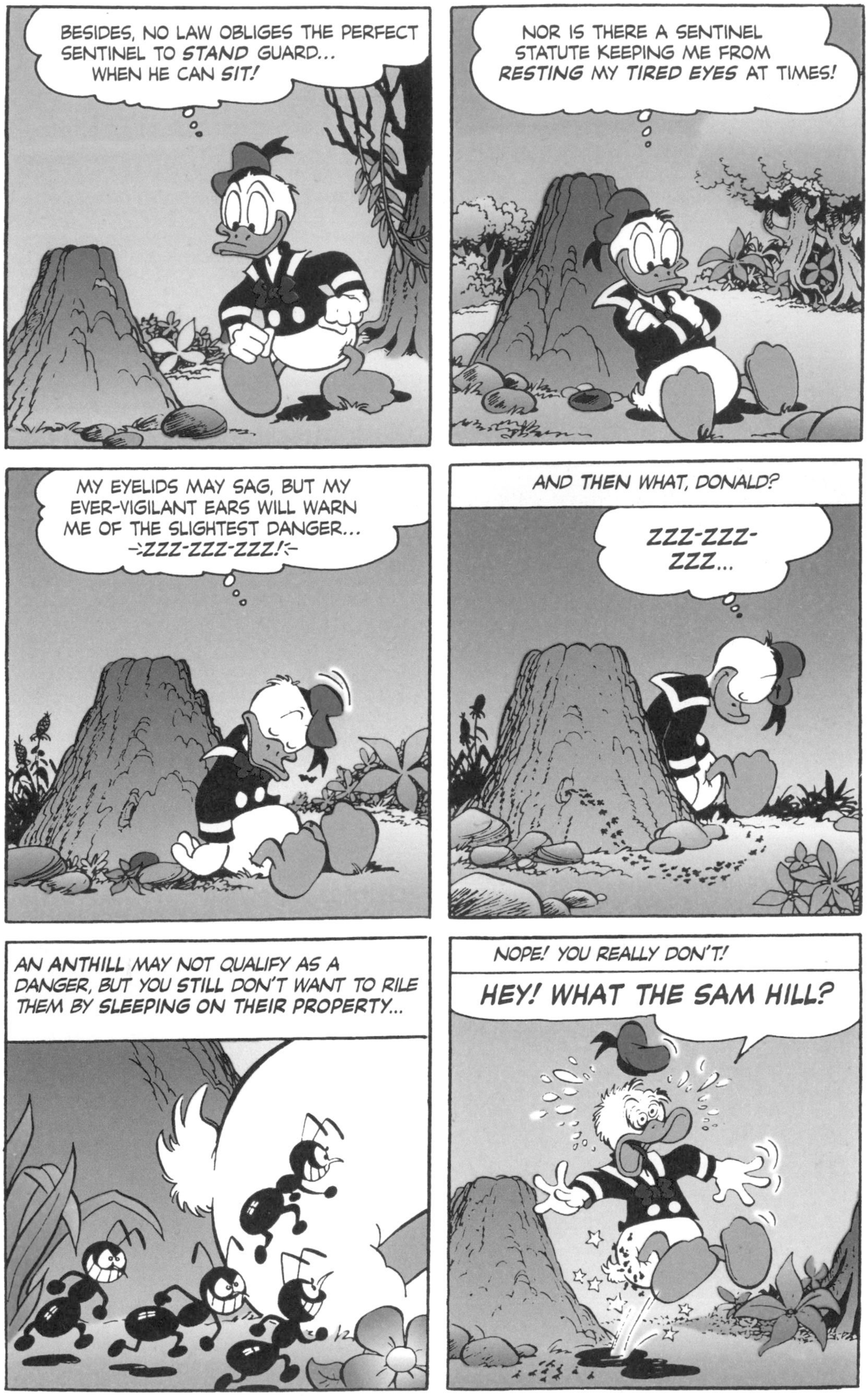

BESIDES, NO LAW OBLIGES THE PERFECT SENTINEL TO STAND GUARD... WHEN HE CAN SIT!
NOR IS THERE A SENTINEL STATUTE KEEPING ME FROM RESTING MY TIRED EYES AT TIMES!
MY EYELIDS MAY SAG, BUT MY EVER-VIGILANT EARS WILL WARN ME OF THE SLIGHTEST DANGER... ZZZ-ZZZ-ZZZ!
AND THEN WHAT, DONALD?
ZZZ-ZZZ-ZZZ...
AN ANTHILL MAY NOT QUALIFY AS A DANGER, BUT YOU STILL DON'T WANT TO RILE THEM BY SLEEPING ON THEIR PROPERTY...
NOPE! YOU REALLY DON'T!
HEY! WHAT THE SAM HILL?

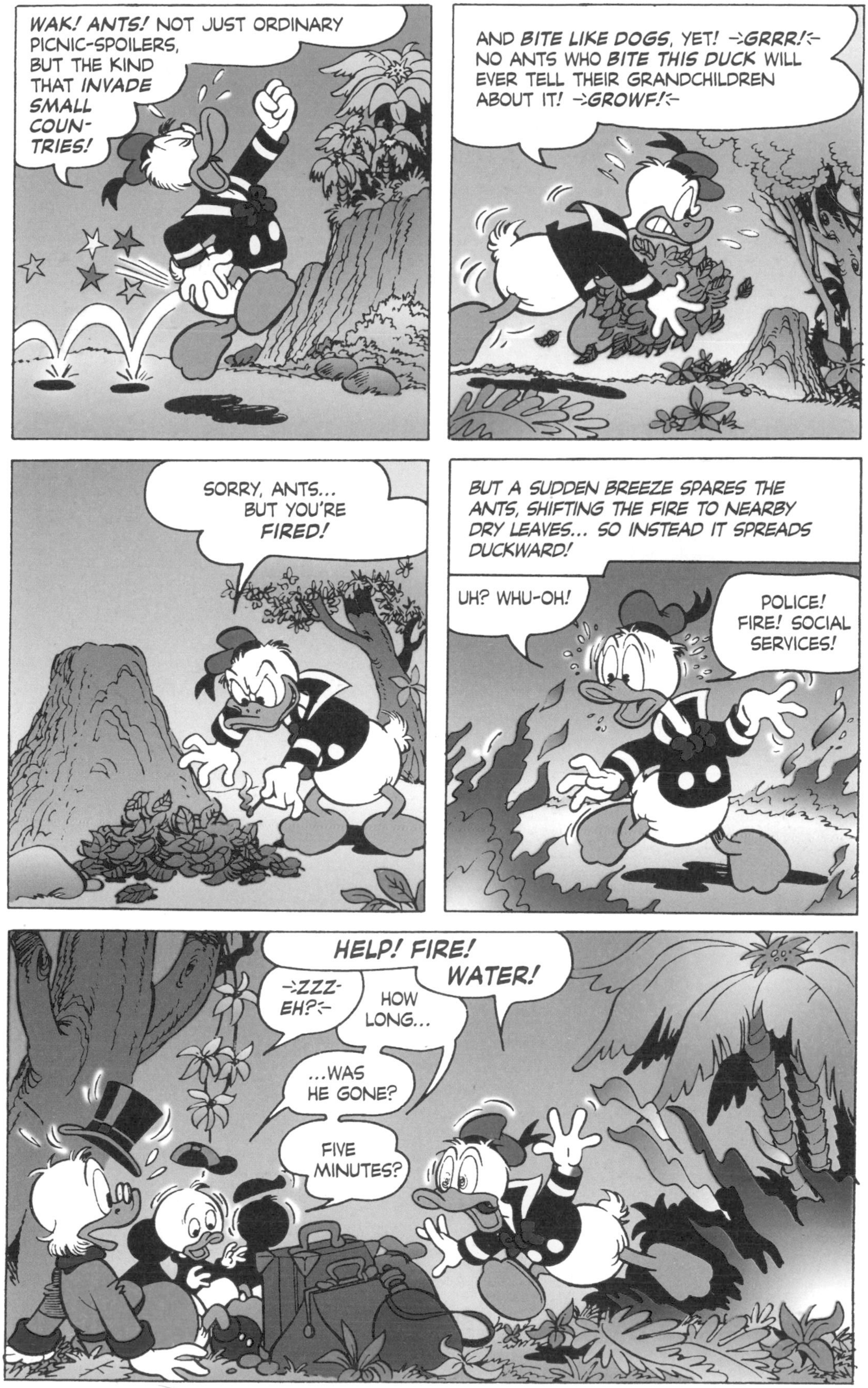
WAK! ANTS! NOT JUST ORDINARY PICNIC-SPOILERS, BUT THE KIND THAT INVADE SMALL COUN-TRIES!
AND BITE LIKE DOGS, YET! –GRRR!– NO ANTS WHO BITE THIS DUCK WILL EVER TELL THEIR GRANDCHILDREN ABOUT IT! –GROWF!–
SORRY, ANTS... BUT YOU'RE FIRED!
BUT A SUDDEN BREEZE SPARES THE ANTS, SHIFTING THE FIRE TO NEARBY DRY LEAVES... SO INSTEAD IT SPREADS DUCKWARD!
UH? WHU-OH!
POLICE! FIRE! SOCIAL SERVICES!
HELP! FIRE! WATER!
–ZZZ-EH?–
HOW LONG...
...WAS HE GONE?
FIVE MINUTES?

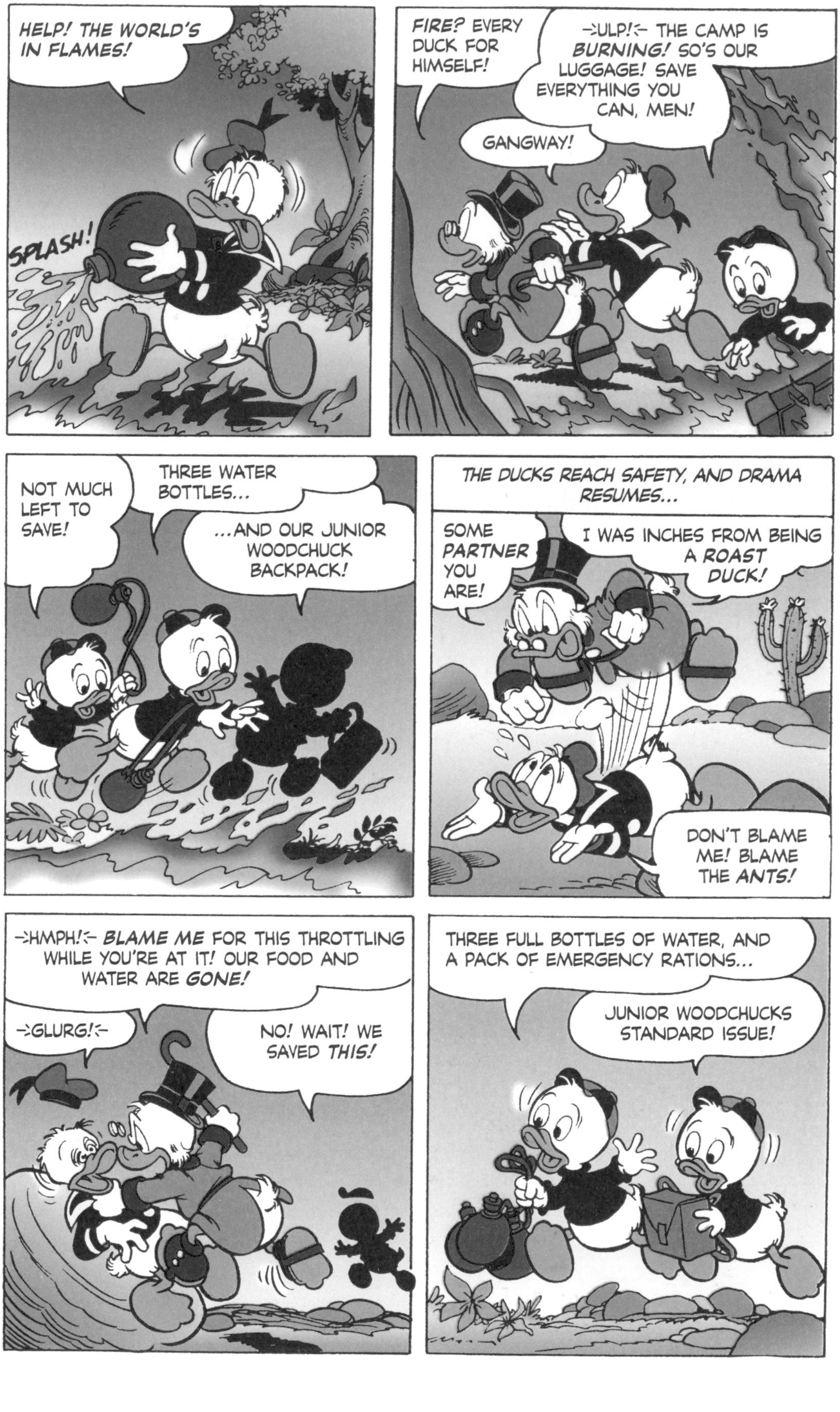
HELP! THE WORLD'S IN FLAMES!
SPLASH!
FIRE? EVERY DUCK FOR HIMSELF!
ULP! THE CAMP IS BURNING! SO'S OUR LUGGAGE! SAVE EVERYTHING YOU CAN, MEN!
GANGWAY!
NOT MUCH LEFT TO SAVE!
THREE WATER BOTTLES...
...AND OUR JUNIOR WOODCHUCK BACKPACK!
THE DUCKS REACH SAFETY, AND DRAMA RESUMES...
SOME PARTNER YOU ARE!
I WAS INCHES FROM BEING A ROAST DUCK!
DON'T BLAME ME! BLAME THE ANTS!
HMPH! BLAME ME FOR THIS THROTTLING WHILE YOU'RE AT IT! OUR FOOD AND WATER ARE GONE!
GLURG!
NO! WAIT! WE SAVED THIS!
THREE FULL BOTTLES OF WATER, AND A PACK OF EMERGENCY RATIONS...
JUNIOR WOODCHUCKS STANDARD ISSUE!

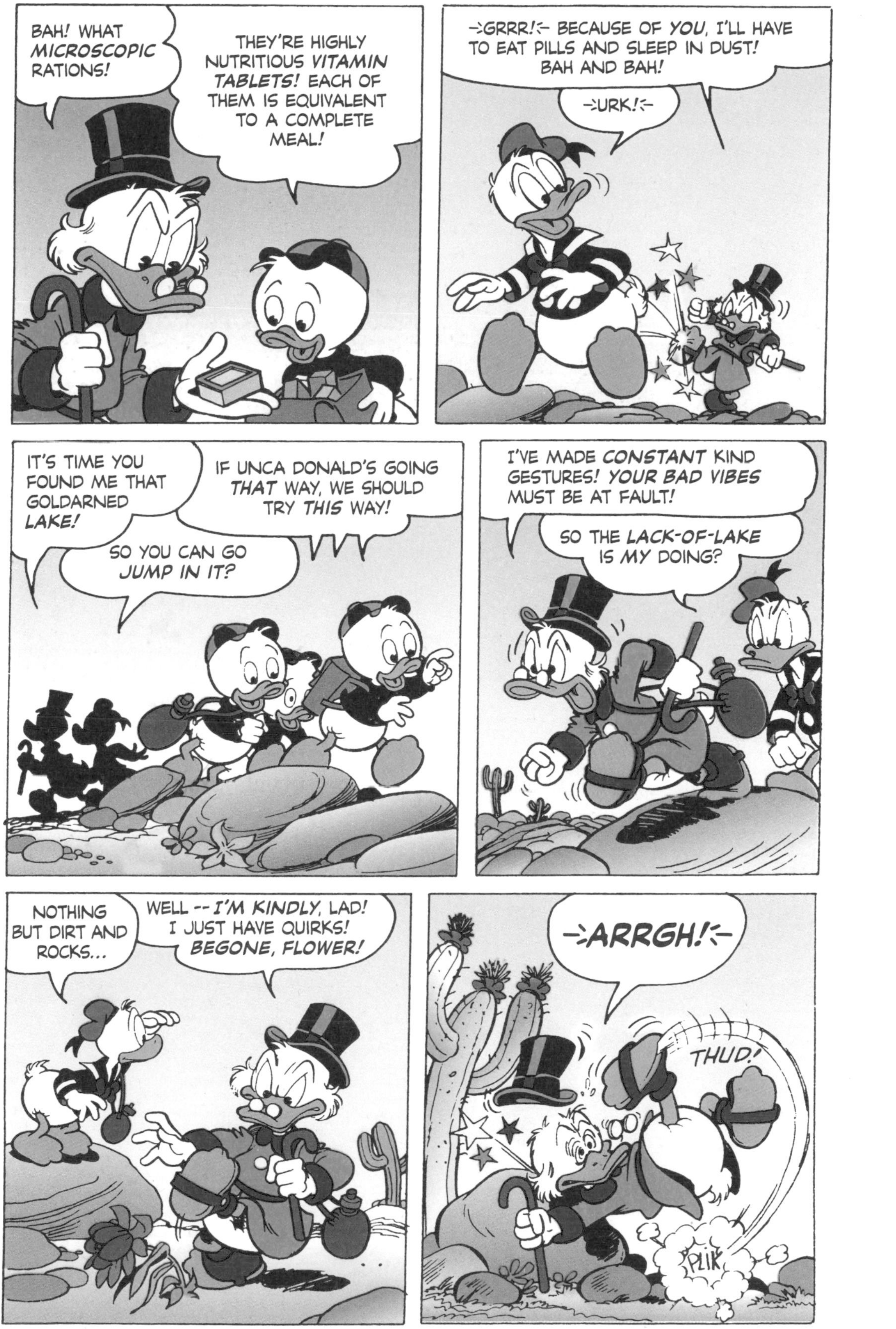

BAH! WHAT MICROSCOPIC RATIONS!
THEY'RE HIGHLY NUTRITIOUS VITAMIN TABLETS! EACH OF THEM IS EQUIVALENT TO A COMPLETE MEAL!
-GRRR!- BECAUSE OF YOU, I'LL HAVE TO EAT PILLS AND SLEEP IN DUST! BAH AND BAH!
-URK!-
IT'S TIME YOU FOUND ME THAT GOLDARNED LAKE!
SO YOU CAN GO JUMP IN IT?
IF UNCA DONALD'S GOING THAT WAY, WE SHOULD TRY THIS WAY!
I'VE MADE CONSTANT KIND GESTURES! YOUR BAD VIBES MUST BE AT FAULT!
SO THE LACK-OF-LAKE IS MY DOING?
NOTHING BUT DIRT AND ROCKS...
WELL -- I'M KINDLY, LAD! I JUST HAVE QUIRKS! BEGONE, FLOWER!
-ARRGH!-
THUD!
PLIK

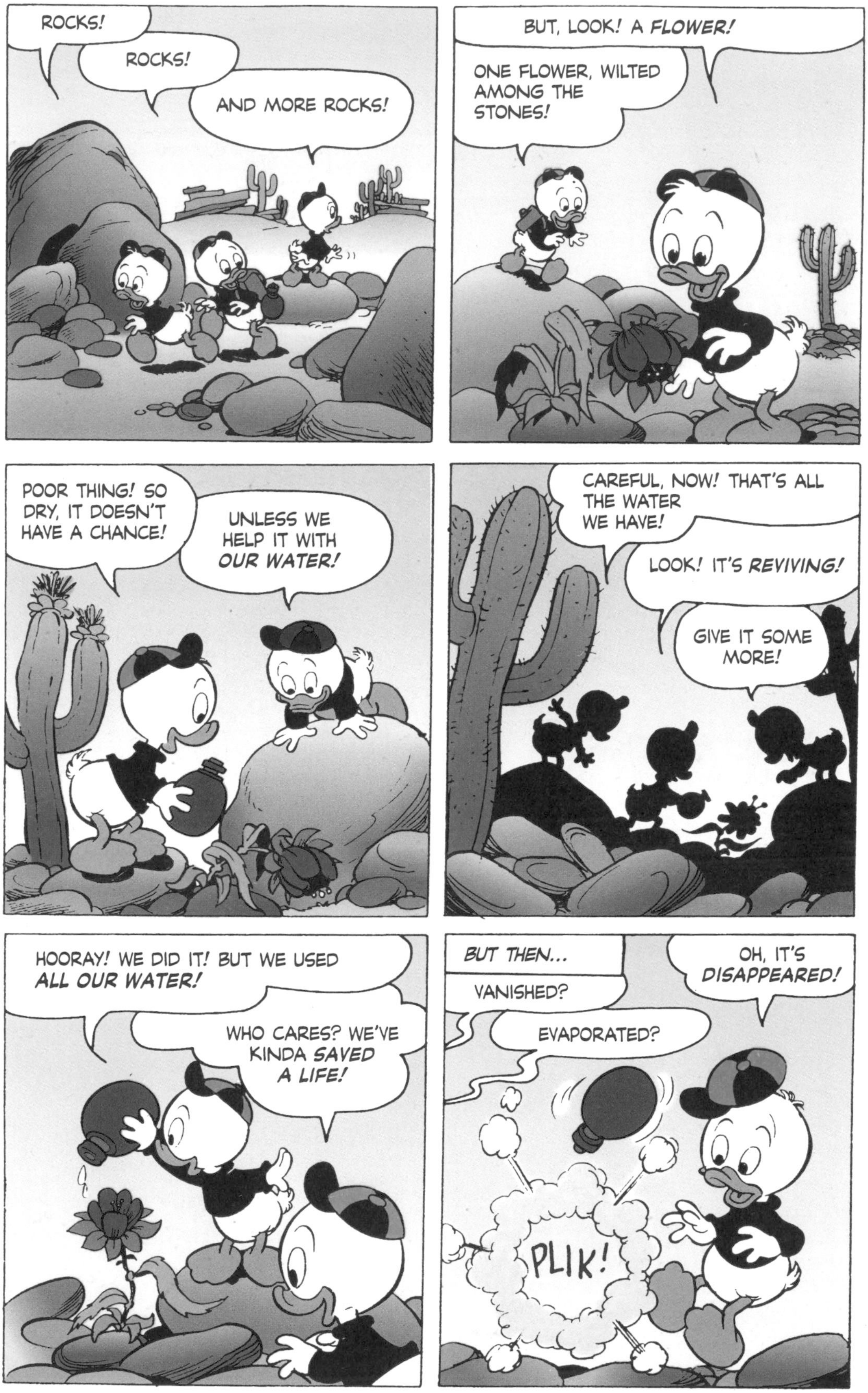
ROCKS!
ROCKS!
AND MORE ROCKS!
BUT, LOOK! A FLOWER!
ONE FLOWER, WILTED AMONG THE STONES!
POOR THING! SO DRY, IT DOESN'T HAVE A CHANCE!
UNLESS WE HELP IT WITH OUR WATER!
CAREFUL, NOW! THAT'S ALL THE WATER WE HAVE!
LOOK! IT'S REVIVING!
GIVE IT SOME MORE!
HOORAY! WE DID IT! BUT WE USED ALL OUR WATER!
WHO CARES? WE'VE KINDA SAVED A LIFE!
BUT THEN...
VANISHED?
OH, IT'S DISAPPEARED!
EVAPORATED?
PLIK!

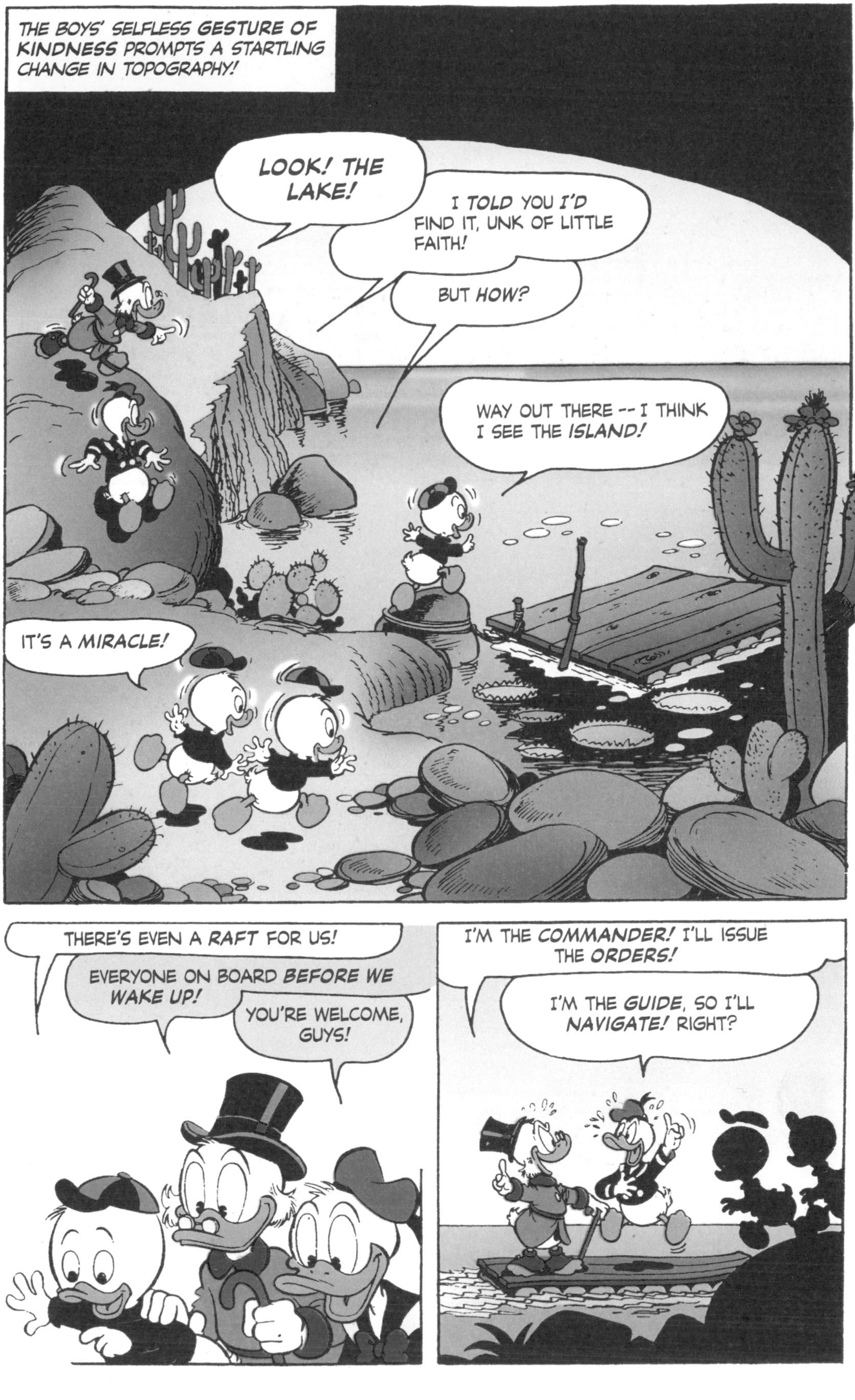

THE BOYS' SELFLESS GESTURE OF KINDNESS PROMPTS A STARTLING CHANGE IN TOPOGRAPHY!
LOOK! THE LAKE!
I TOLD YOU I'D FIND IT, UNK OF LITTLE FAITH!
BUT HOW?
WAY OUT THERE -- I THINK I SEE THE ISLAND!
IT'S A MIRACLE!
THERE'S EVEN A RAFT FOR US!
EVERYONE ON BOARD BEFORE WE WAKE UP!
YOU'RE WELCOME, GUYS!
I'M THE COMMANDER! I'LL ISSUE THE ORDERS!
I'M THE GUIDE, SO I'LL NAVIGATE! RIGHT?

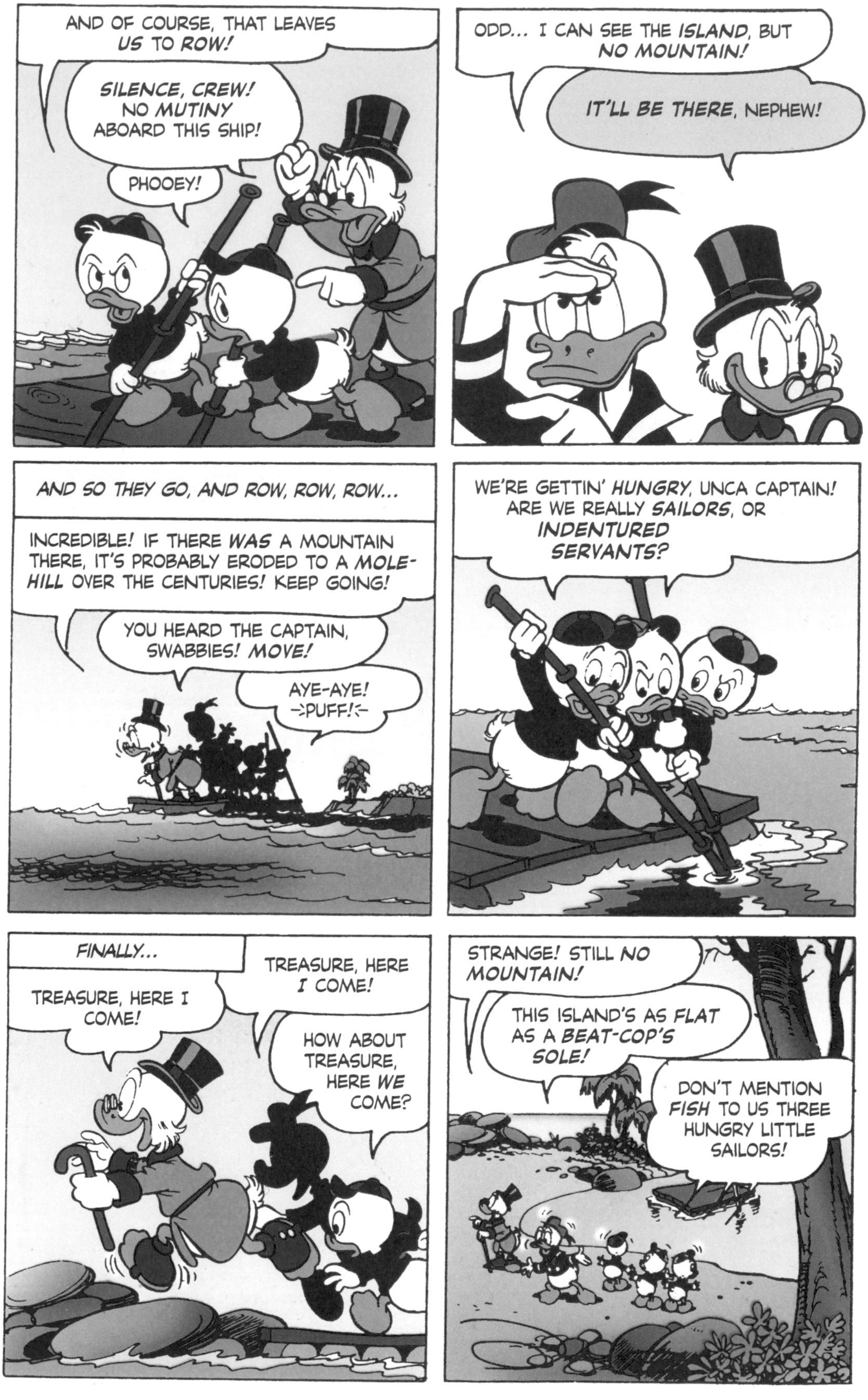
AND OF COURSE, THAT LEAVES US TO ROW!
SILENCE, CREW! NO MUTINY ABOARD THIS SHIP!
PHOOEY!
ODD... I CAN SEE THE ISLAND, BUT NO MOUNTAIN!
IT'LL BE THERE, NEPHEW!
AND SO THEY GO, AND ROW, ROW, ROW...
INCREDIBLE! IF THERE WAS A MOUNTAIN THERE, IT'S PROBABLY ERODED TO A MOLE-HILL OVER THE CENTURIES! KEEP GOING!
YOU HEARD THE CAPTAIN, SWABBIES! MOVE!
AYE-AYE! PUFF!
WE'RE GETTIN' HUNGRY, UNCA CAPTAIN! ARE WE REALLY SAILORS, OR INDENTURED SERVANTS?
FINALLY...
TREASURE, HERE I COME!
TREASURE, HERE I COME!
HOW ABOUT TREASURE, HERE WE COME?
STRANGE! STILL NO MOUNTAIN!
THIS ISLAND'S AS FLAT AS A BEAT-COP'S SOLE!
DON'T MENTION FISH TO US THREE HUNGRY LITTLE SAILORS!

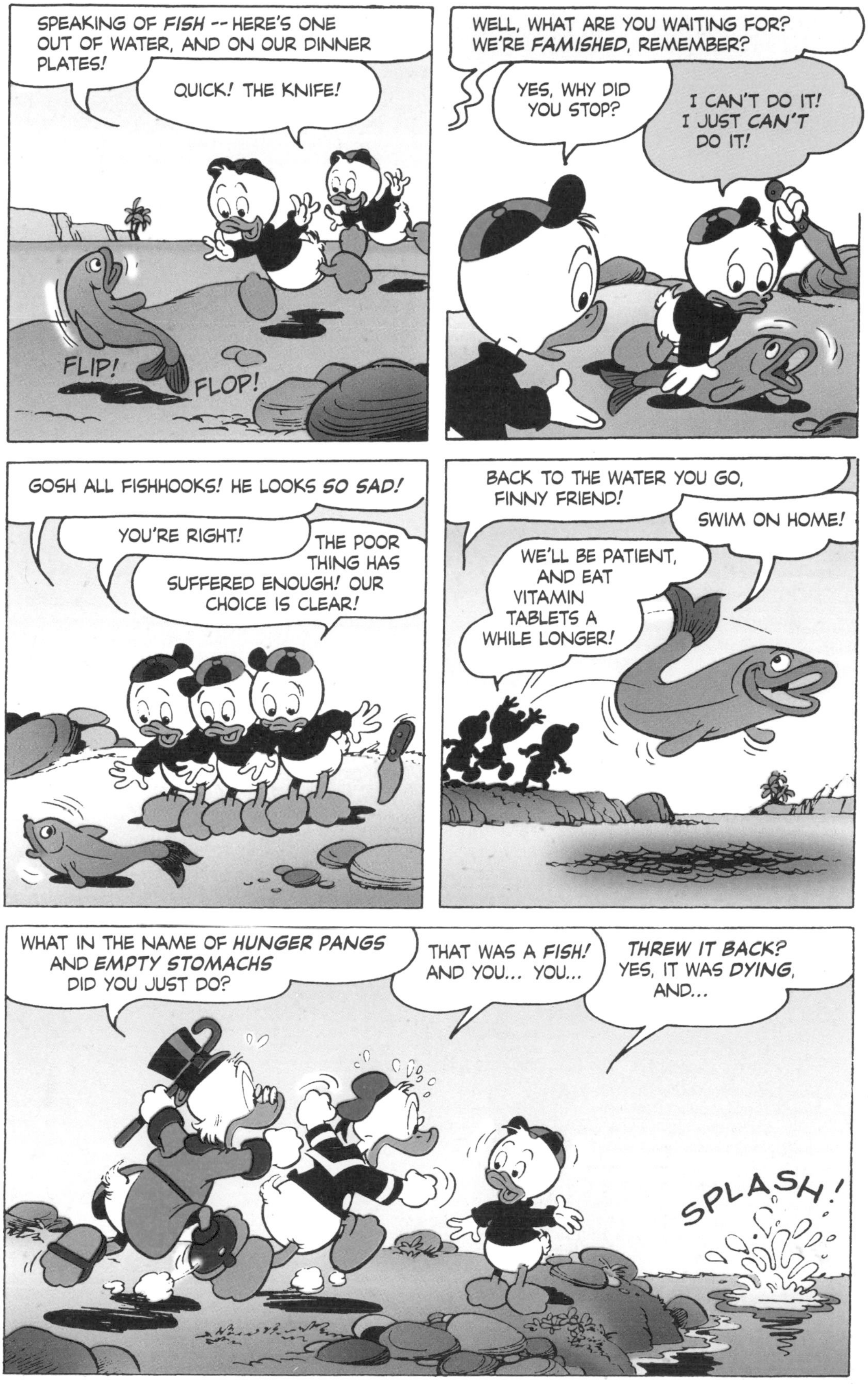
SPEAKING OF FISH -- HERE'S ONE OUT OF WATER, AND ON OUR DINNER PLATES!
QUICK! THE KNIFE!
FLIP!
FLOP!
WELL, WHAT ARE YOU WAITING FOR? WE'RE FAMISHED, REMEMBER?
YES, WHY DID YOU STOP?
I CAN'T DO IT! I JUST CAN'T DO IT!
GOSH ALL FISHHOOKS! HE LOOKS SO SAD!
YOU'RE RIGHT!
THE POOR THING HAS SUFFERED ENOUGH! OUR CHOICE IS CLEAR!
BACK TO THE WATER YOU GO, FINNY FRIEND!
SWIM ON HOME!
WE'LL BE PATIENT, AND EAT VITAMIN TABLETS A WHILE LONGER!
WHAT IN THE NAME OF HUNGER PANGS AND EMPTY STOMACHS DID YOU JUST DO?
THAT WAS A FISH! AND YOU... YOU...
THREW IT BACK? YES, IT WAS DYING, AND...
SPLASH!

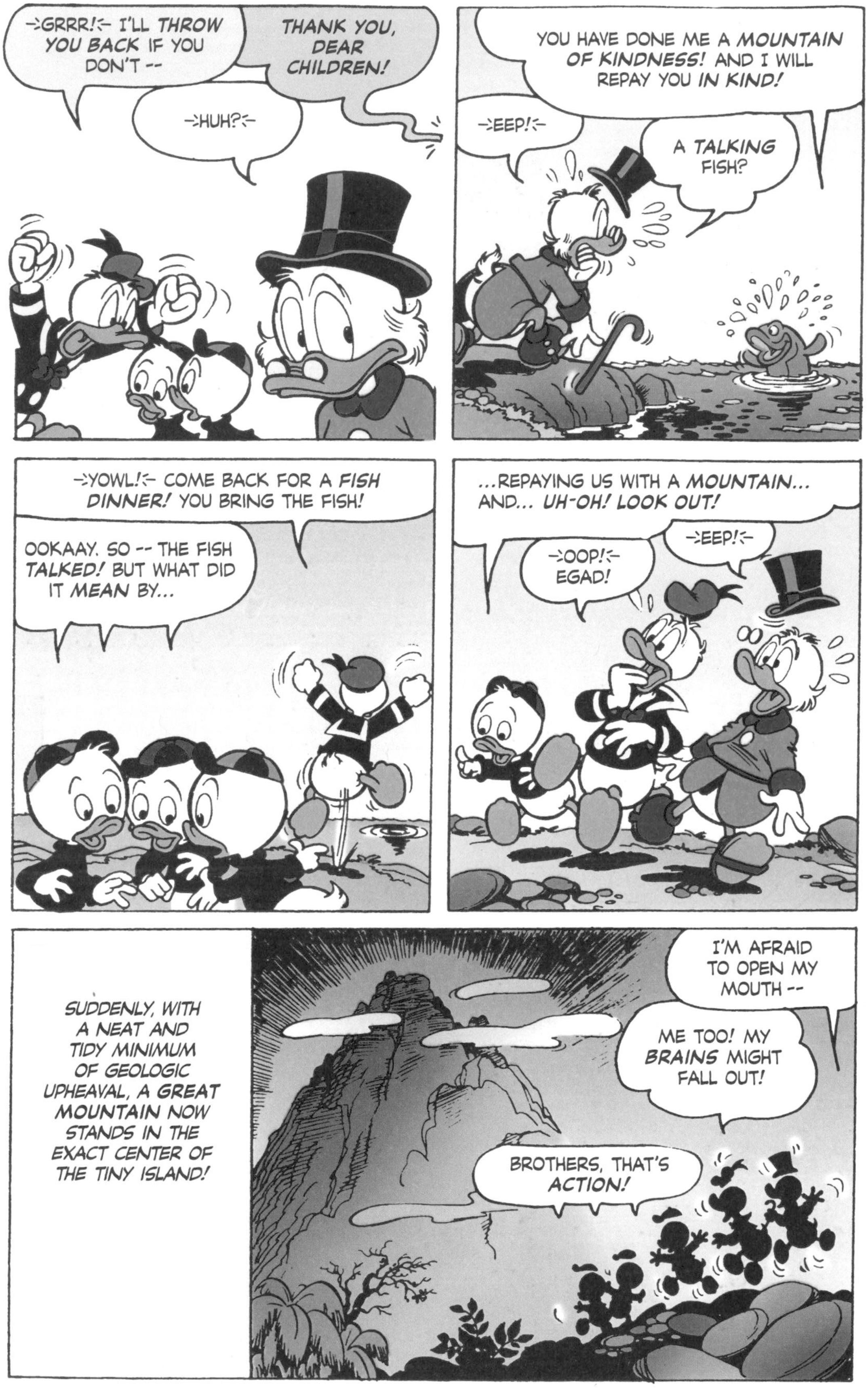

⇒GRRR!⇐ I'LL THROW YOU BACK IF YOU DON'T --
⇒HUH?⇐
THANK YOU, DEAR CHILDREN!
YOU HAVE DONE ME A MOUNTAIN OF KINDNESS! AND I WILL REPAY YOU IN KIND!
⇒EEP!⇐
A TALKING FISH?
⇒YOWL!⇐ COME BACK FOR A FISH DINNER! YOU BRING THE FISH!
OOKAAY. SO -- THE FISH TALKED! BUT WHAT DID IT MEAN BY...
...REPAYING US WITH A MOUNTAIN... AND... UH-OH! LOOK OUT!
⇒OOP!⇐ EGAD!
⇒EEP!⇐
SUDDENLY, WITH A NEAT AND TIDY MINIMUM OF GEOLOGIC UPHEAVAL, A GREAT MOUNTAIN NOW STANDS IN THE EXACT CENTER OF THE TINY ISLAND!
I'M AFRAID TO OPEN MY MOUTH --
ME TOO! MY BRAINS MIGHT FALL OUT!
BROTHERS, THAT'S ACTION!

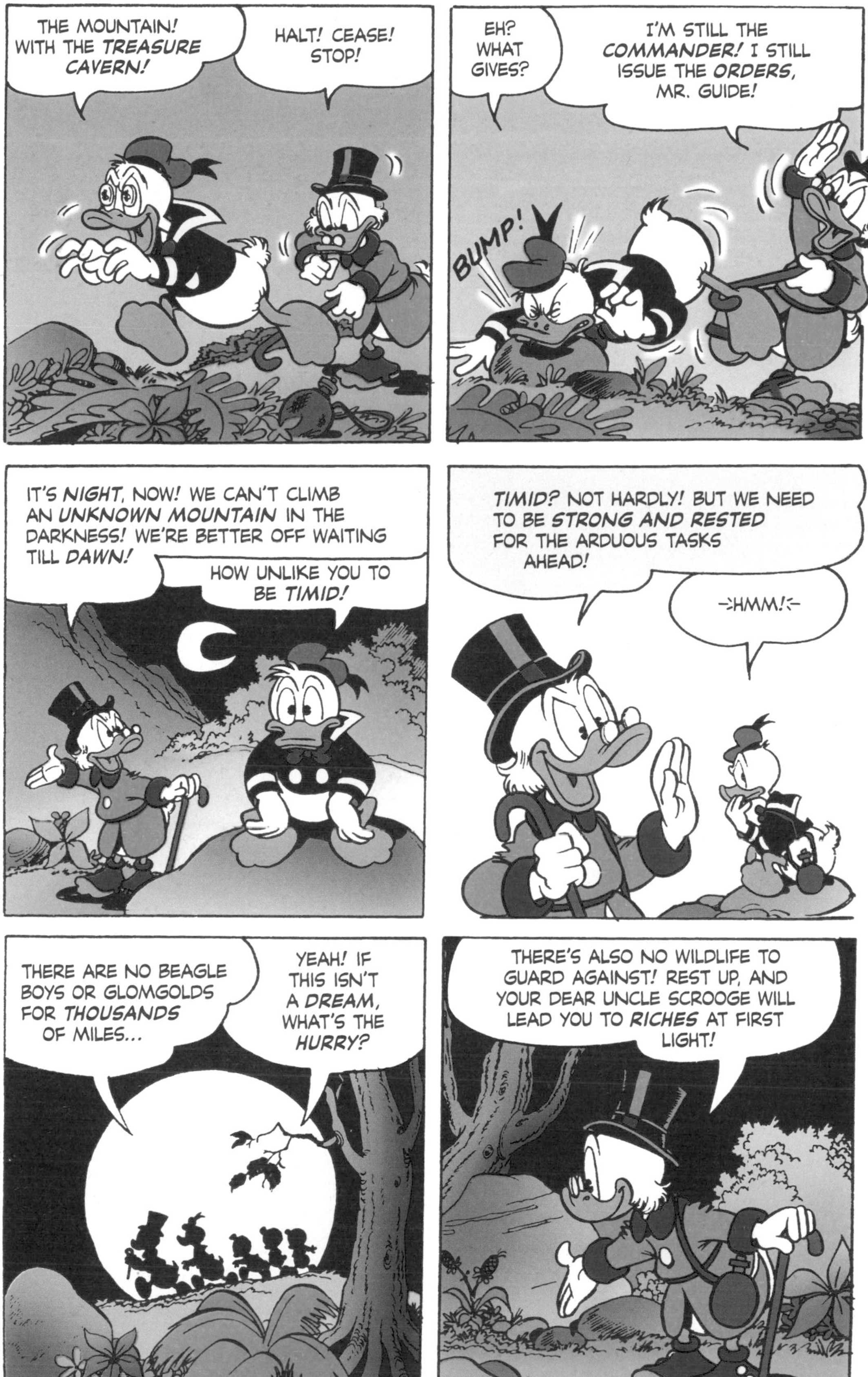
THE MOUNTAIN! WITH THE TREASURE CAVERN!
HALT! CEASE! STOP!
EH? WHAT GIVES?
I'M STILL THE COMMANDER! I STILL ISSUE THE ORDERS, MR. GUIDE!
BUMP!
IT'S NIGHT, NOW! WE CAN'T CLIMB AN UNKNOWN MOUNTAIN IN THE DARKNESS! WE'RE BETTER OFF WAITING TILL DAWN!
HOW UNLIKE YOU TO BE TIMID!
TIMID? NOT HARDLY! BUT WE NEED TO BE STRONG AND RESTED FOR THE ARDUOUS TASKS AHEAD!
HMM!
THERE ARE NO BEAGLE BOYS OR GLOMGOLDS FOR THOUSANDS OF MILES...
YEAH! IF THIS ISN'T A DREAM, WHAT'S THE HURRY?
THERE'S ALSO NO WILDLIFE TO GUARD AGAINST! REST UP, AND YOUR DEAR UNCLE SCROOGE WILL LEAD YOU TO RICHES AT FIRST LIGHT!

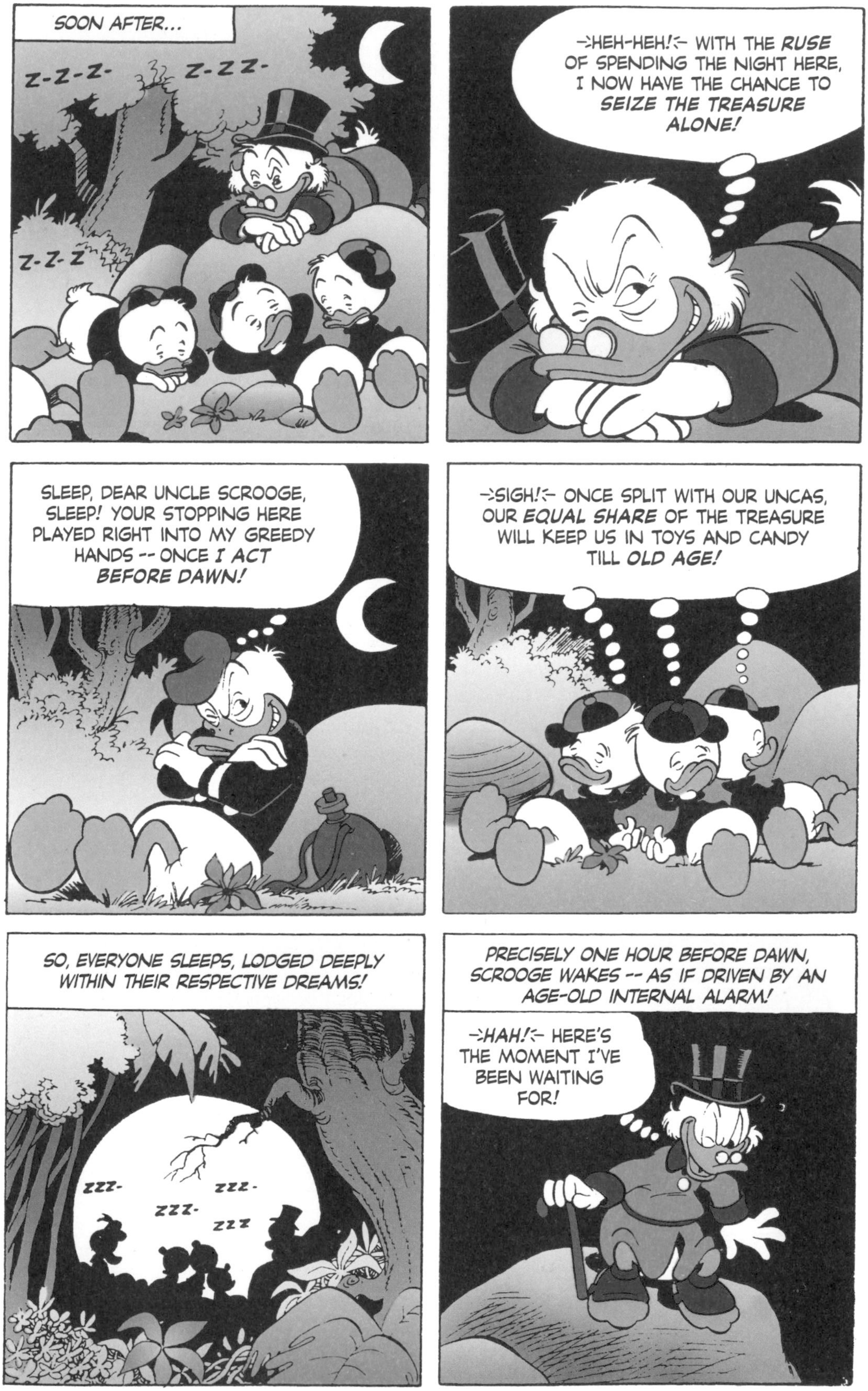
SOON AFTER...
Z-Z-Z-
Z-Z Z-
Z-Z-Z
-HEH-HEH!- WITH THE RUSE OF SPENDING THE NIGHT HERE, I NOW HAVE THE CHANCE TO SEIZE THE TREASURE ALONE!
SLEEP, DEAR UNCLE SCROOGE, SLEEP! YOUR STOPPING HERE PLAYED RIGHT INTO MY GREEDY HANDS -- ONCE I ACT BEFORE DAWN!
-SIGH!- ONCE SPLIT WITH OUR UNCAS, OUR EQUAL SHARE OF THE TREASURE WILL KEEP US IN TOYS AND CANDY TILL OLD AGE!
SO, EVERYONE SLEEPS, LODGED DEEPLY WITHIN THEIR RESPECTIVE DREAMS!
ZZZ-
ZZZ-
ZZZ-
ZZZ
PRECISELY ONE HOUR BEFORE DAWN, SCROOGE WAKES -- AS IF DRIVEN BY AN AGE-OLD INTERNAL ALARM!
-HAH!- HERE'S THE MOMENT I'VE BEEN WAITING FOR!

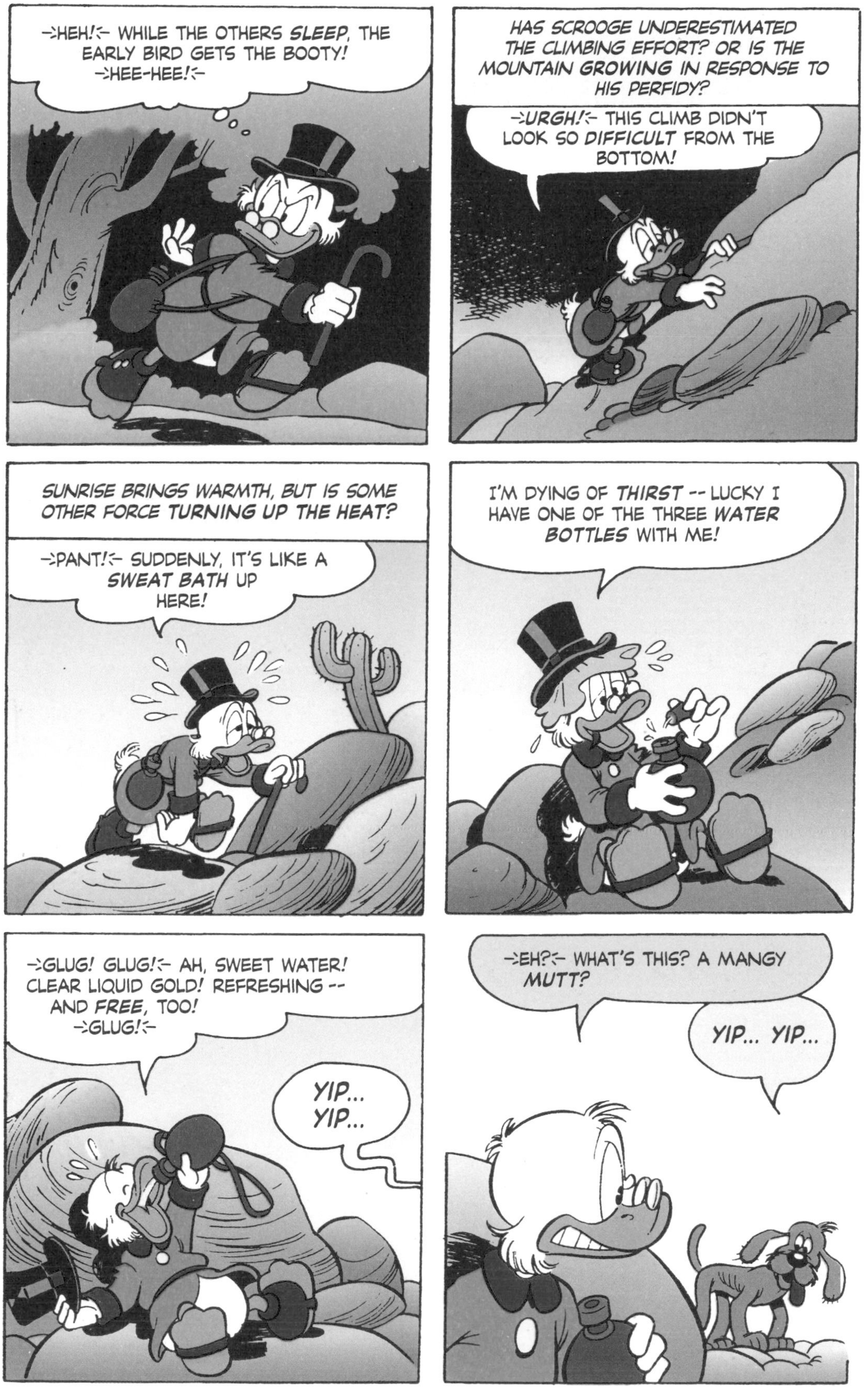
–HEH!– WHILE THE OTHERS SLEEP, THE EARLY BIRD GETS THE BOOTY! –HEE-HEE!–
HAS SCROOGE UNDERESTIMATED THE CLIMBING EFFORT? OR IS THE MOUNTAIN GROWING IN RESPONSE TO HIS PERFIDY?
–URGH!– THIS CLIMB DIDN'T LOOK SO DIFFICULT FROM THE BOTTOM!
SUNRISE BRINGS WARMTH, BUT IS SOME OTHER FORCE TURNING UP THE HEAT?
–PANT!– SUDDENLY, IT'S LIKE A SWEAT BATH UP HERE!
I'M DYING OF THIRST -- LUCKY I HAVE ONE OF THE THREE WATER BOTTLES WITH ME!
–GLUG! GLUG!– AH, SWEET WATER! CLEAR LIQUID GOLD! REFRESHING -- AND FREE, TOO! –GLUG!–
YIP... YIP...
–EH?– WHAT'S THIS? A MANGY MUTT?
YIP... YIP...

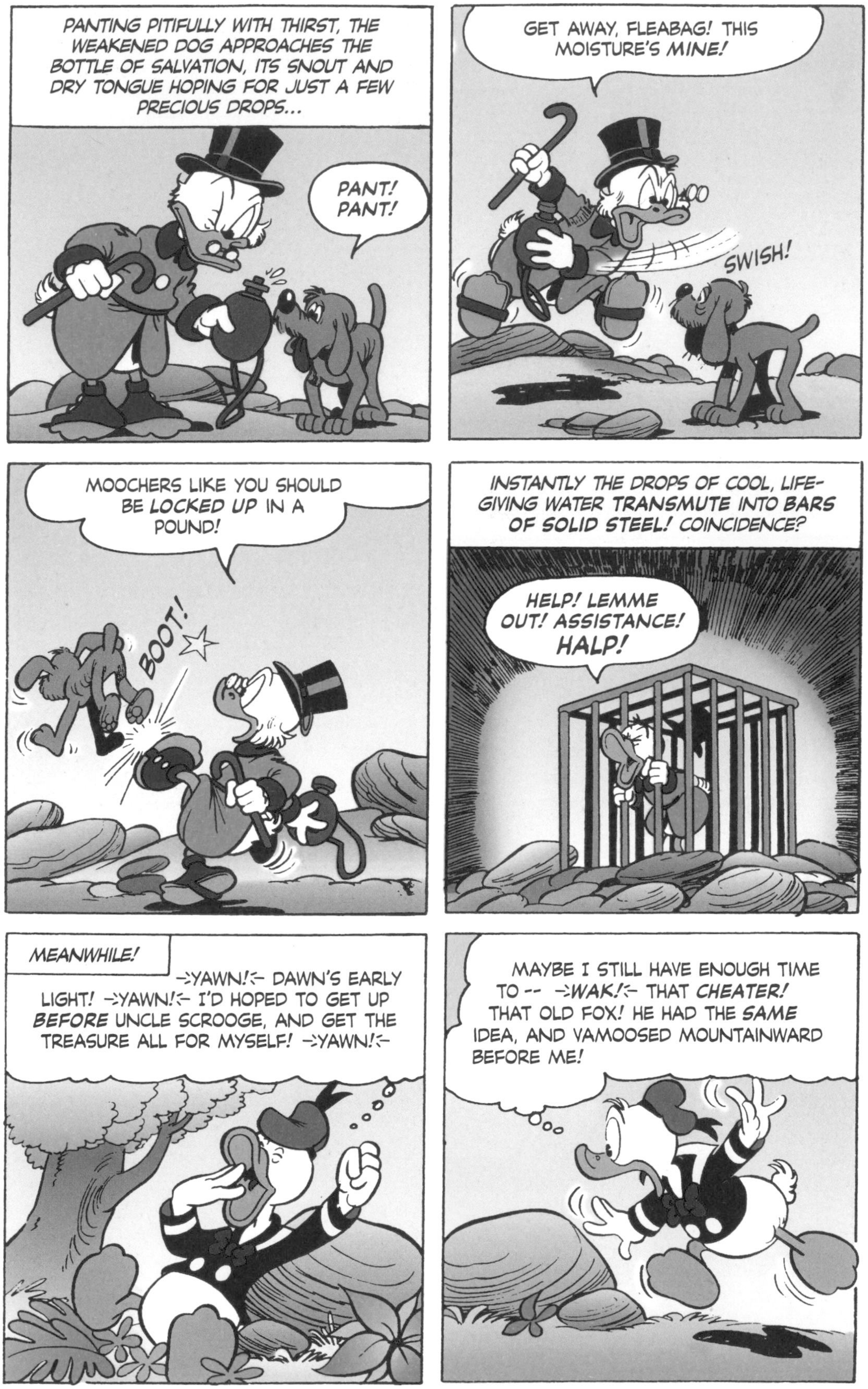

PANTING PITIFULLY WITH THIRST, THE WEAKENED DOG APPROACHES THE BOTTLE OF SALVATION, ITS SNOUT AND DRY TONGUE HOPING FOR JUST A FEW PRECIOUS DROPS...
PANT! PANT!
GET AWAY, FLEABAG! THIS MOISTURE'S MINE!
SWISH!
MOOCHERS LIKE YOU SHOULD BE LOCKED UP IN A POUND!
BOOT!
INSTANTLY THE DROPS OF COOL, LIFE-GIVING WATER TRANSMUTE INTO BARS OF SOLID STEEL! COINCIDENCE?
HELP! LEMME OUT! ASSISTANCE! HALP!
MEANWHILE!
-YAWN!- DAWN'S EARLY LIGHT! -YAWN!- I'D HOPED TO GET UP BEFORE UNCLE SCROOGE, AND GET THE TREASURE ALL FOR MYSELF! -YAWN!-
MAYBE I STILL HAVE ENOUGH TIME TO -- -WAK!- THAT CHEATER! THAT OLD FOX! HE HAD THE SAME IDEA, AND VAMOOSED MOUNTAINWARD BEFORE ME!

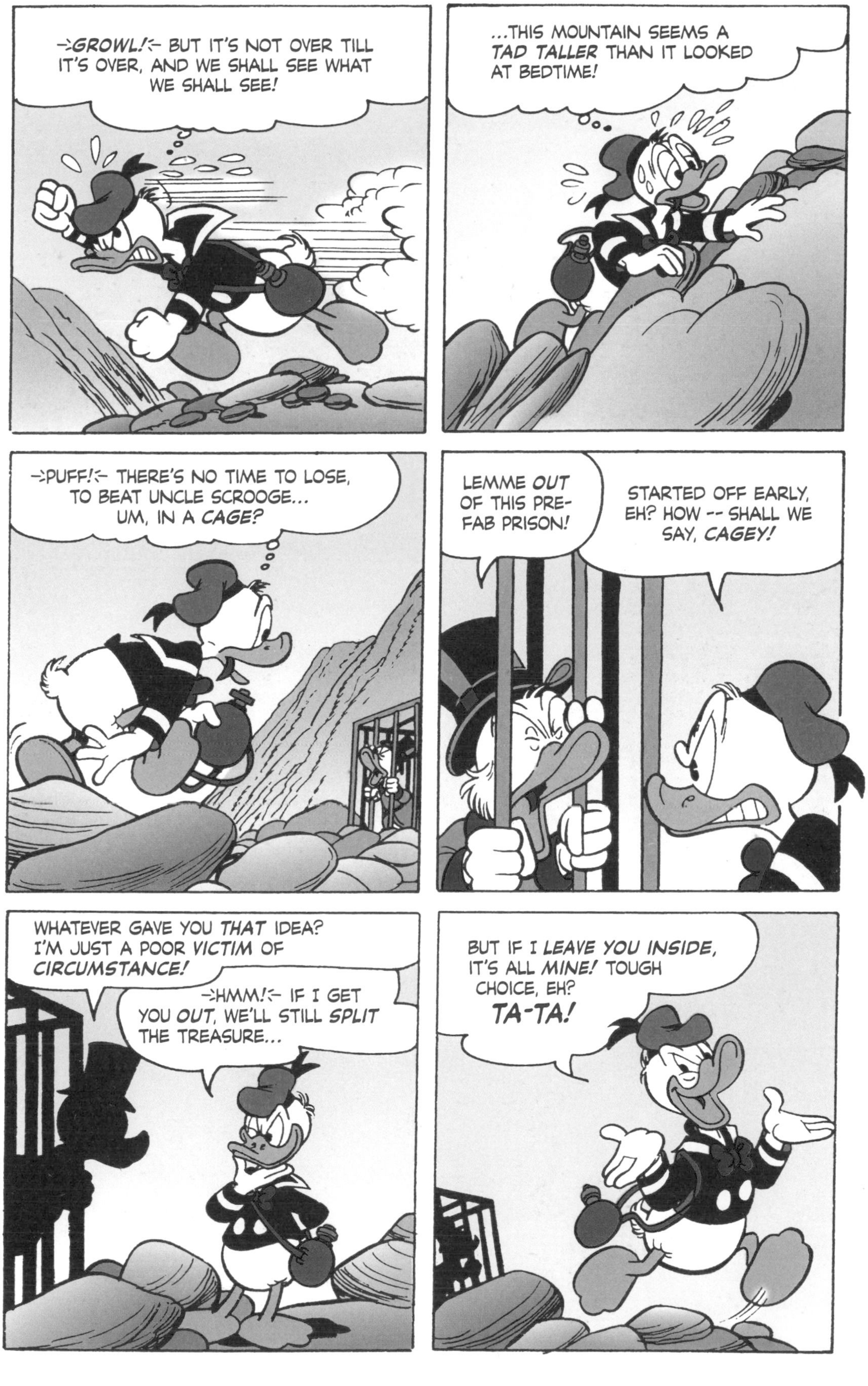
-GROWL!- BUT IT'S NOT OVER TILL IT'S OVER, AND WE SHALL SEE WHAT WE SHALL SEE!
...THIS MOUNTAIN SEEMS A TAD TALLER THAN IT LOOKED AT BEDTIME!
-PUFF!- THERE'S NO TIME TO LOSE, TO BEAT UNCLE SCROOGE... UM, IN A CAGE?
LEMME OUT OF THIS PRE-FAB PRISON!
STARTED OFF EARLY, EH? HOW -- SHALL WE SAY, CAGEY!
WHATEVER GAVE YOU THAT IDEA? I'M JUST A POOR VICTIM OF CIRCUMSTANCE!
-HMM!- IF I GET YOU OUT, WE'LL STILL SPLIT THE TREASURE...
BUT IF I LEAVE YOU INSIDE, IT'S ALL MINE! TOUGH CHOICE, EH? TA-TA!

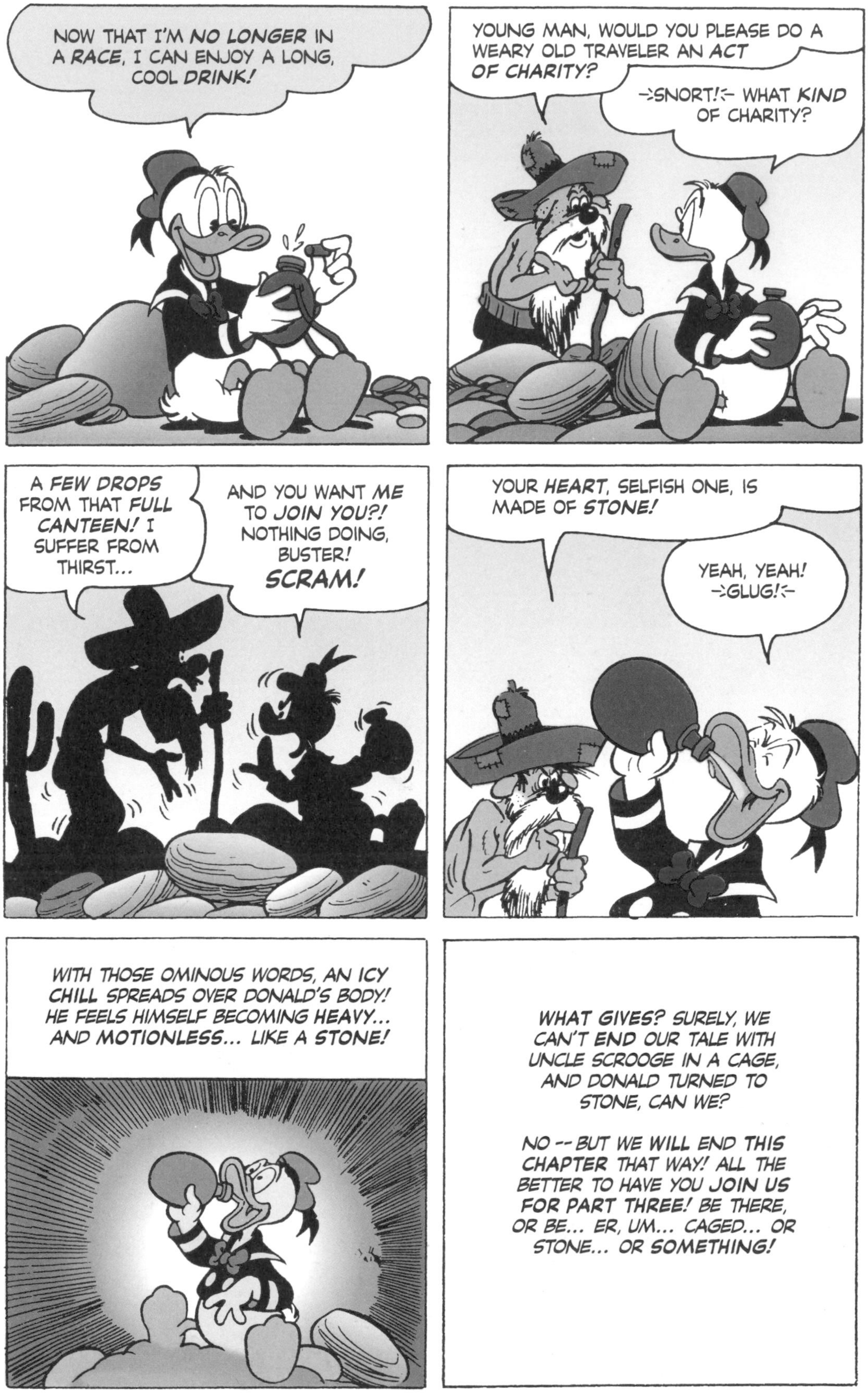
NOW THAT I'M NO LONGER IN A RACE, I CAN ENJOY A LONG, COOL DRINK!
YOUNG MAN, WOULD YOU PLEASE DO A WEARY OLD TRAVELER AN ACT OF CHARITY?
-SNORT!- WHAT KIND OF CHARITY?
A FEW DROPS FROM THAT FULL CANTEEN! I SUFFER FROM THIRST...
AND YOU WANT ME TO JOIN YOU?! NOTHING DOING, BUSTER! SCRAM!
YOUR HEART, SELFISH ONE, IS MADE OF STONE!
YEAH, YEAH! -GLUG!-
WITH THOSE OMINOUS WORDS, AN ICY CHILL SPREADS OVER DONALD'S BODY! HE FEELS HIMSELF BECOMING HEAVY... AND MOTIONLESS... LIKE A STONE!
WHAT GIVES? SURELY, WE CAN'T END OUR TALE WITH UNCLE SCROOGE IN A CAGE, AND DONALD TURNED TO STONE, CAN WE?
NO -- BUT WE WILL END THIS CHAPTER THAT WAY! ALL THE BETTER TO HAVE YOU JOIN US FOR PART THREE! BE THERE, OR BE... ER, UM... CAGED... OR STONE... OR SOMETHING!

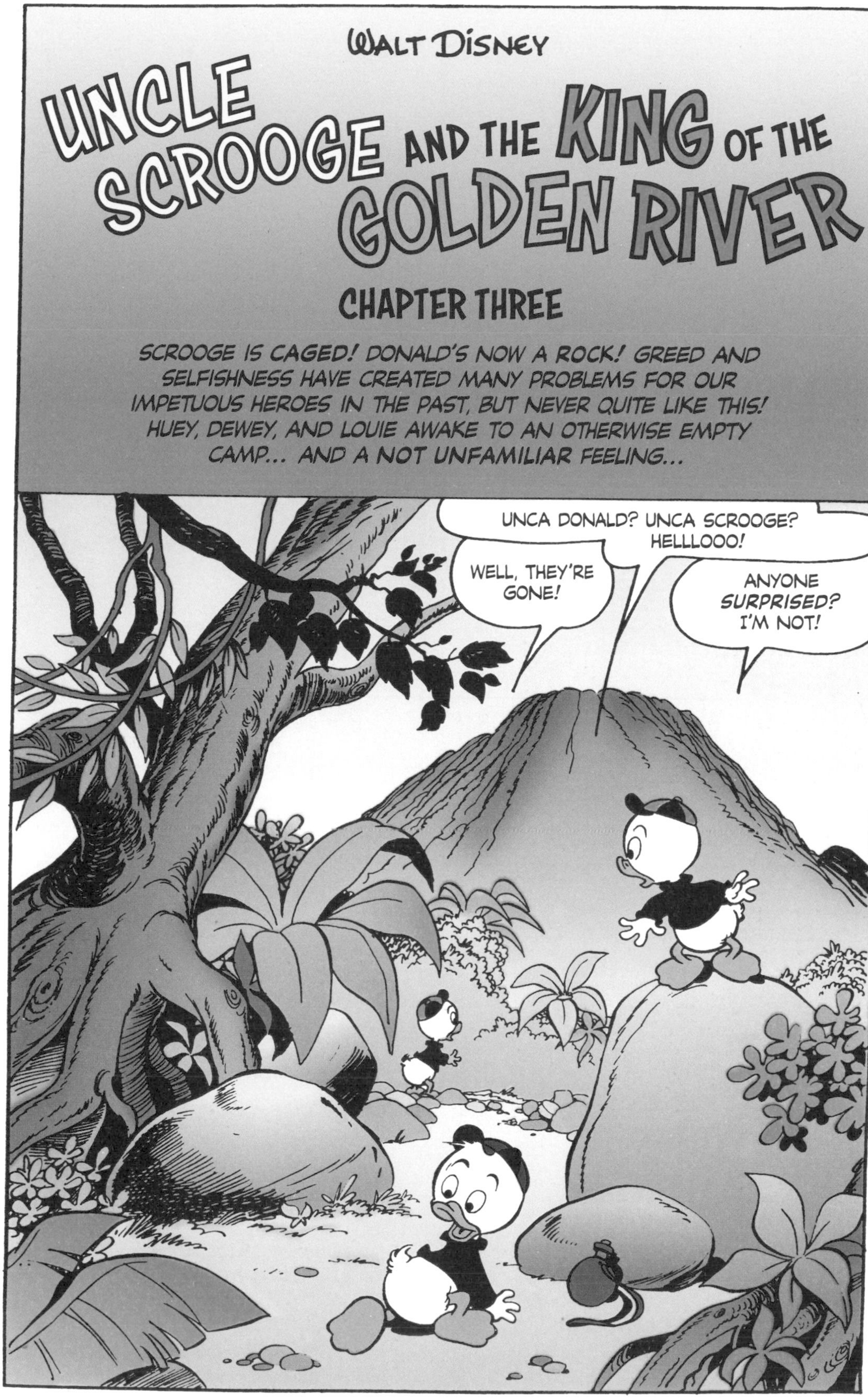
WALT DISNEY
UNCLE SCROOGE AND THE KING OF THE GOLDEN RIVER
CHAPTER THREE
SCROOGE IS CAGED! DONALD'S NOW A ROCK! GREED AND SELFISHNESS HAVE CREATED MANY PROBLEMS FOR OUR IMPETUOUS HEROES IN THE PAST, BUT NEVER QUITE LIKE THIS! HUEY, DEWEY, AND LOUIE AWAKE TO AN OTHERWISE EMPTY CAMP... AND A NOT UNFAMILIAR FEELING...
UNCA DONALD? UNCA SCROOGE? HELLLOOO!
WELL, THEY'RE GONE!
ANYONE SURPRISED? I'M NOT!

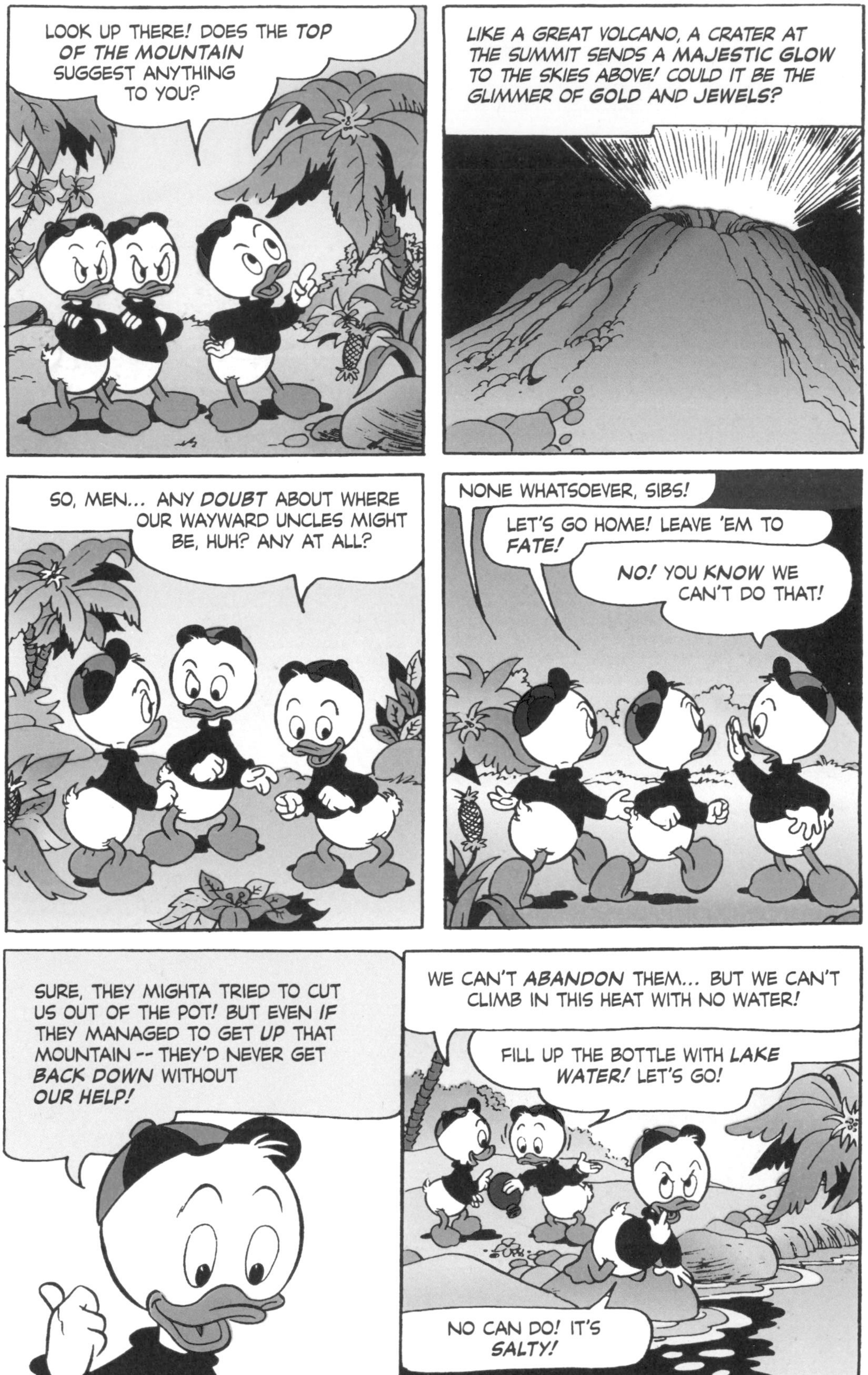
LOOK UP THERE! DOES THE TOP OF THE MOUNTAIN SUGGEST ANYTHING TO YOU?
LIKE A GREAT VOLCANO, A CRATER AT THE SUMMIT SENDS A MAJESTIC GLOW TO THE SKIES ABOVE! COULD IT BE THE GLIMMER OF GOLD AND JEWELS?
SO, MEN... ANY DOUBT ABOUT WHERE OUR WAYWARD UNCLES MIGHT BE, HUH? ANY AT ALL?
NONE WHATSOEVER, SIBS!
LET'S GO HOME! LEAVE 'EM TO FATE!
NO! YOU KNOW WE CAN'T DO THAT!
SURE, THEY MIGHTA TRIED TO CUT US OUT OF THE POT! BUT EVEN IF THEY MANAGED TO GET UP THAT MOUNTAIN -- THEY'D NEVER GET BACK DOWN WITHOUT OUR HELP!
WE CAN'T ABANDON THEM... BUT WE CAN'T CLIMB IN THIS HEAT WITH NO WATER!
FILL UP THE BOTTLE WITH LAKE WATER! LET'S GO!
NO CAN DO! IT'S SALTY!

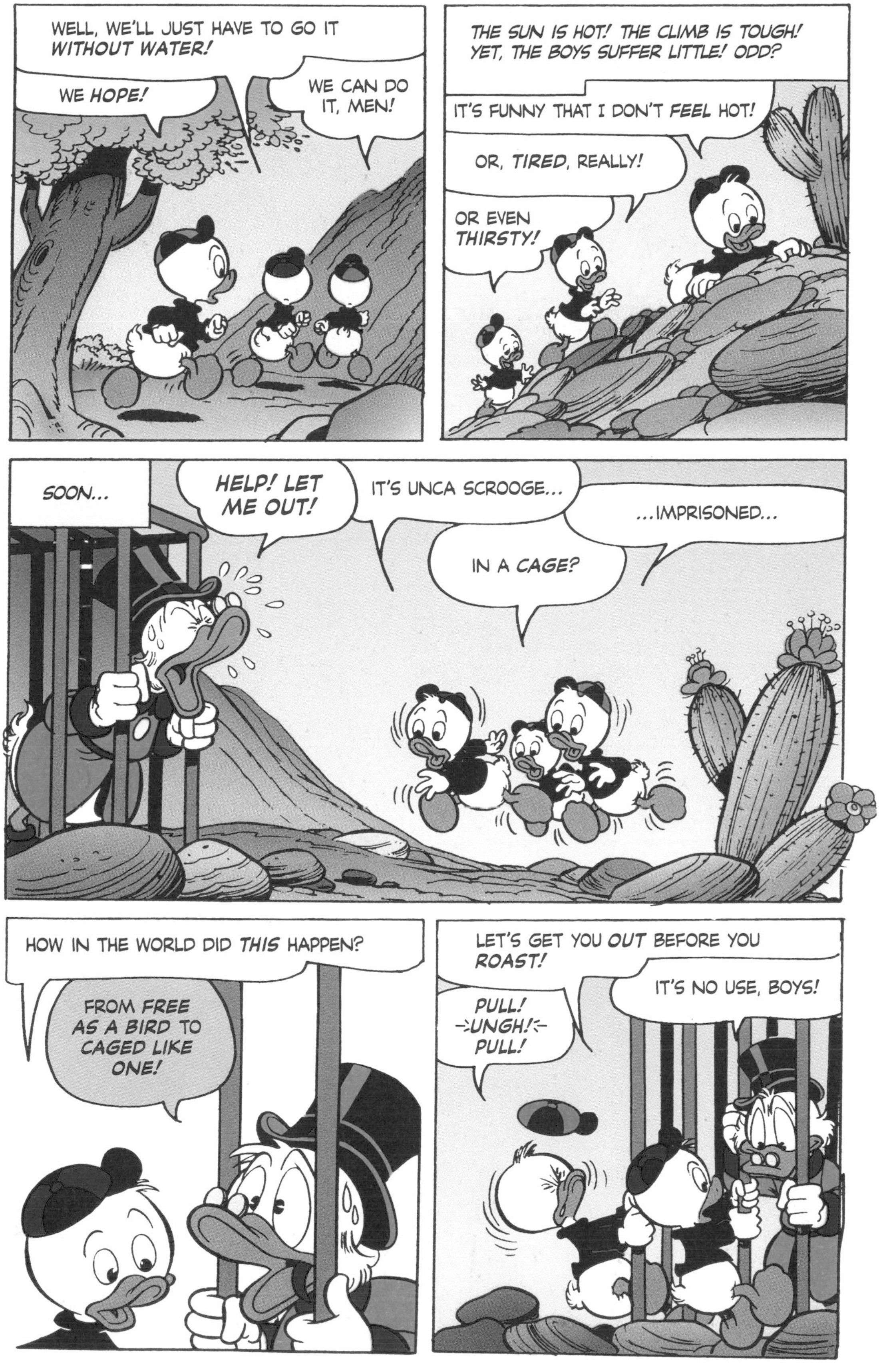
WELL, WE'LL JUST HAVE TO GO IT *WITHOUT WATER!*
WE *HOPE!*
WE CAN DO IT, MEN!
THE SUN IS HOT! THE CLIMB IS TOUGH! YET, THE BOYS SUFFER LITTLE! ODD?
IT'S FUNNY THAT I DON'T *FEEL* HOT!
OR, *TIRED*, REALLY!
OR EVEN *THIRSTY!*
SOON...
HELP! LET ME OUT!
IT'S UNCA SCROOGE...
...IMPRISONED...
IN A *CAGE?*
HOW IN THE WORLD DID *THIS* HAPPEN?
FROM FREE AS A BIRD TO CAGED LIKE ONE!
LET'S GET YOU *OUT* BEFORE YOU *ROAST!*
PULL! UNGH! PULL!
IT'S NO USE, BOYS!

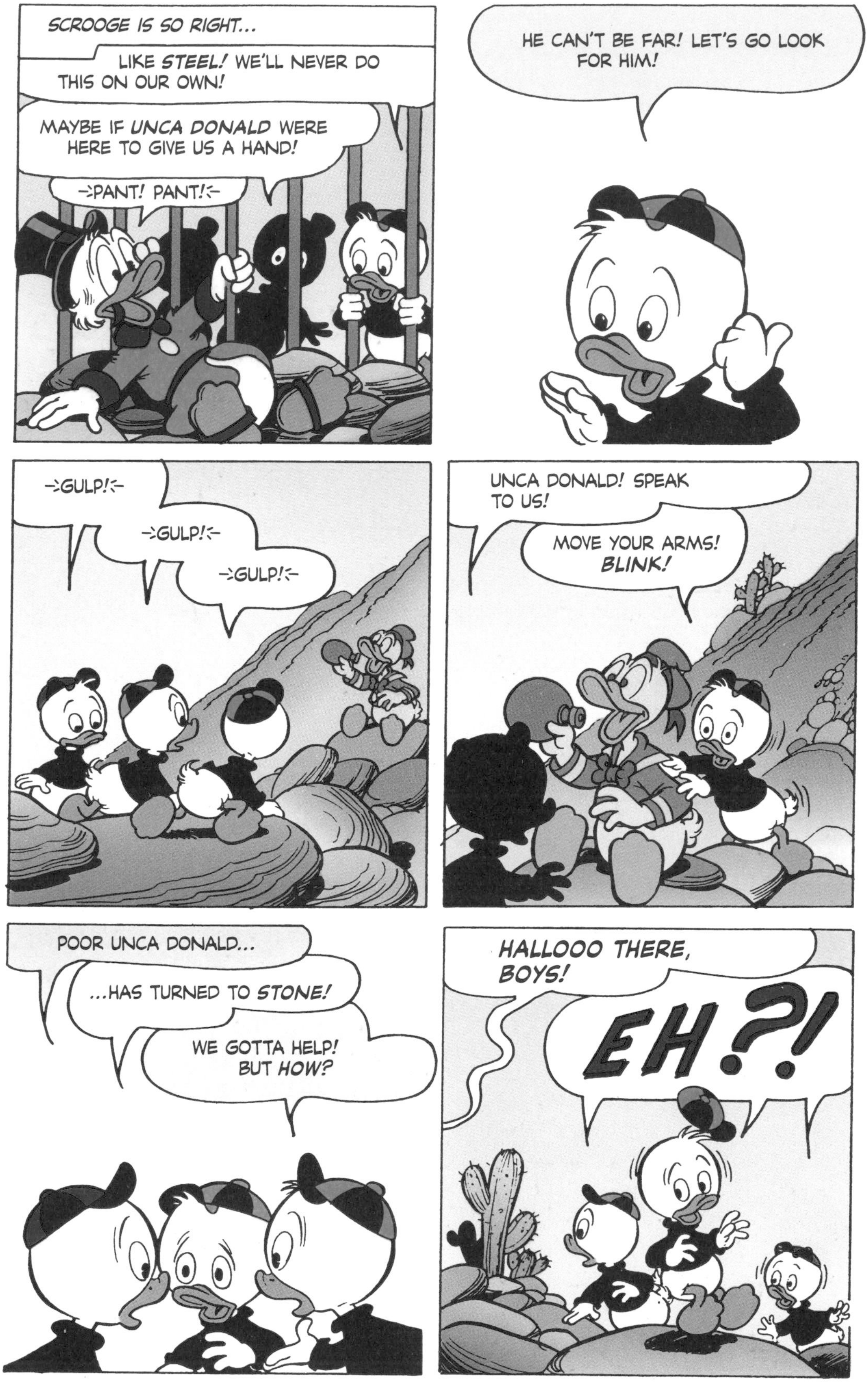

SCROOGE IS SO RIGHT...
LIKE STEEL! WE'LL NEVER DO THIS ON OUR OWN!
MAYBE IF UNCA DONALD WERE HERE TO GIVE US A HAND!
PANT! PANT!
HE CAN'T BE FAR! LET'S GO LOOK FOR HIM!
GULP!
GULP!
GULP!
UNCA DONALD! SPEAK TO US!
MOVE YOUR ARMS! BLINK!
POOR UNCA DONALD...
...HAS TURNED TO STONE!
WE GOTTA HELP! BUT HOW?
HALLOOO THERE, BOYS!
EH?!

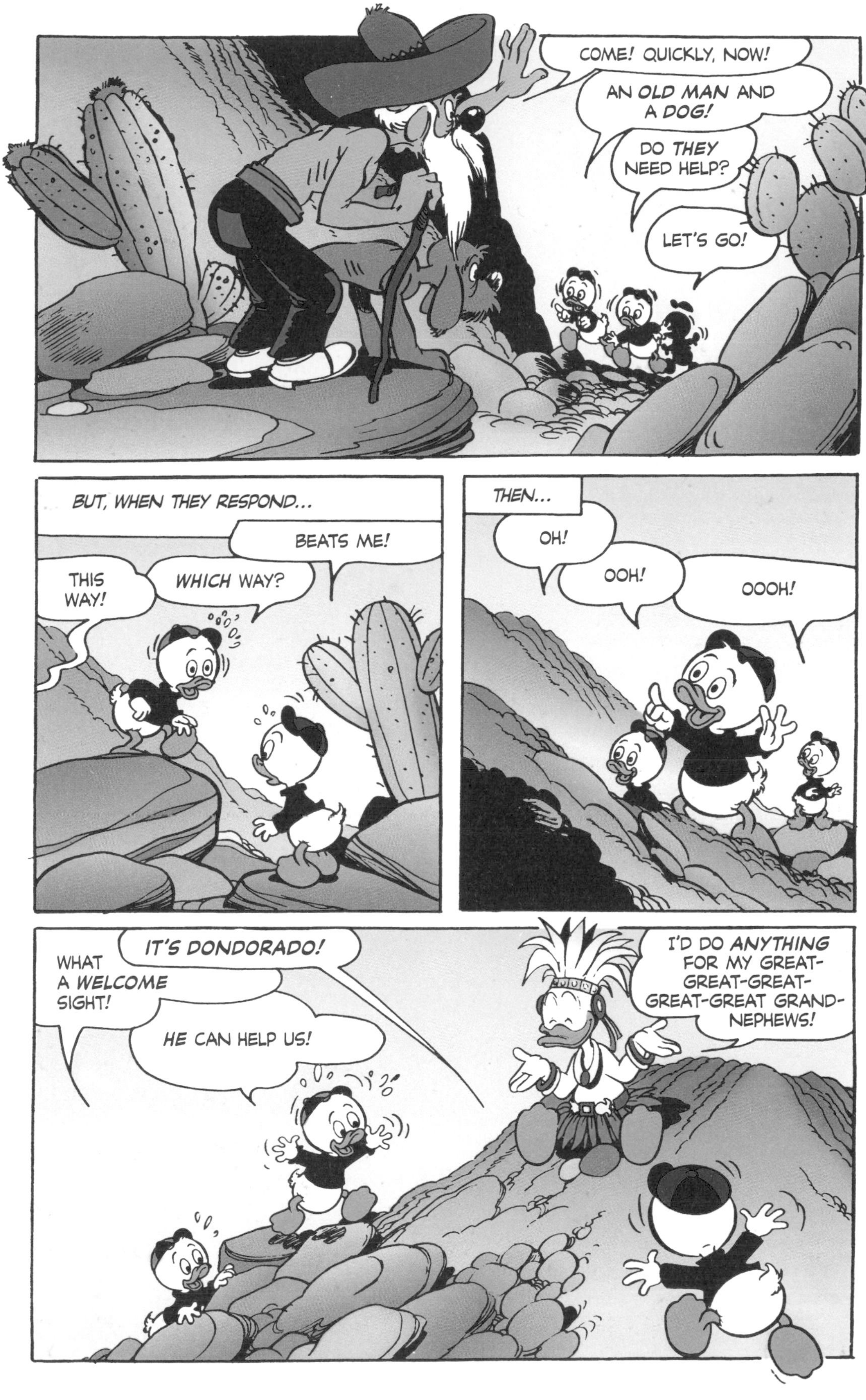
COME! QUICKLY, NOW!
AN OLD MAN AND A DOG!
DO THEY NEED HELP?
LET'S GO!
BUT, WHEN THEY RESPOND...
THIS WAY!
WHICH WAY?
BEATS ME!
THEN...
OH!
OOH!
OOOH!
WHAT A WELCOME SIGHT!
IT'S DONDORADO!
HE CAN HELP US!
I'D DO ANYTHING FOR MY GREAT-GREAT-GREAT-GREAT-GREAT GRAND-NEPHEWS!

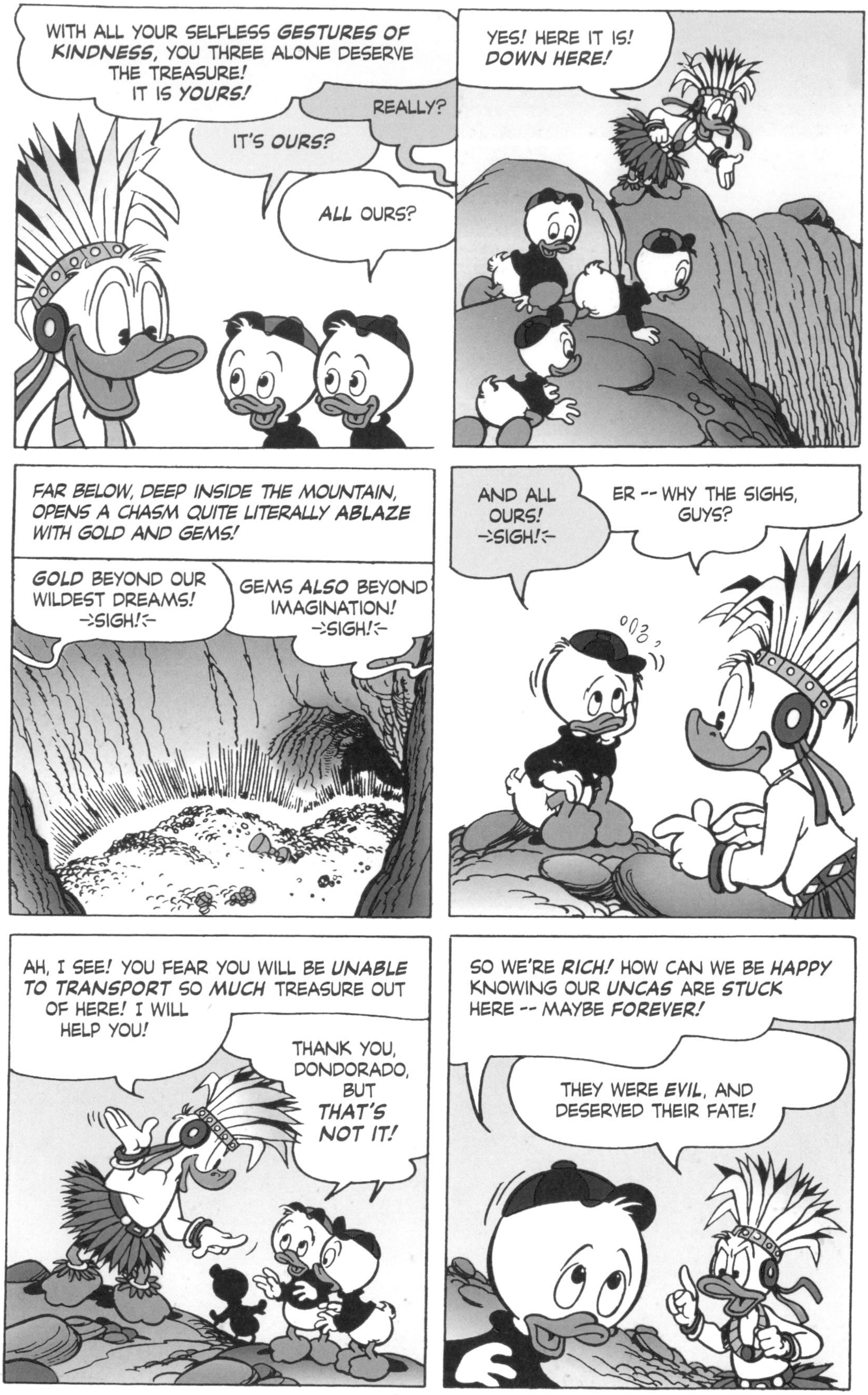

WITH ALL YOUR SELFLESS GESTURES OF KINDNESS, YOU THREE ALONE DESERVE THE TREASURE! IT IS YOURS!
REALLY?
IT'S OURS?
ALL OURS?
YES! HERE IT IS! DOWN HERE!
FAR BELOW, DEEP INSIDE THE MOUNTAIN, OPENS A CHASM QUITE LITERALLY ABLAZE WITH GOLD AND GEMS!
GOLD BEYOND OUR WILDEST DREAMS! -SIGH!-
GEMS ALSO BEYOND IMAGINATION! -SIGH!-
AND ALL OURS! -SIGH!-
ER -- WHY THE SIGHS, GUYS?
AH, I SEE! YOU FEAR YOU WILL BE UNABLE TO TRANSPORT SO MUCH TREASURE OUT OF HERE! I WILL HELP YOU!
THANK YOU, DONDORADO, BUT THAT'S NOT IT!
SO WE'RE RICH! HOW CAN WE BE HAPPY KNOWING OUR UNCAS ARE STUCK HERE -- MAYBE FOREVER!
THEY WERE EVIL, AND DESERVED THEIR FATE!

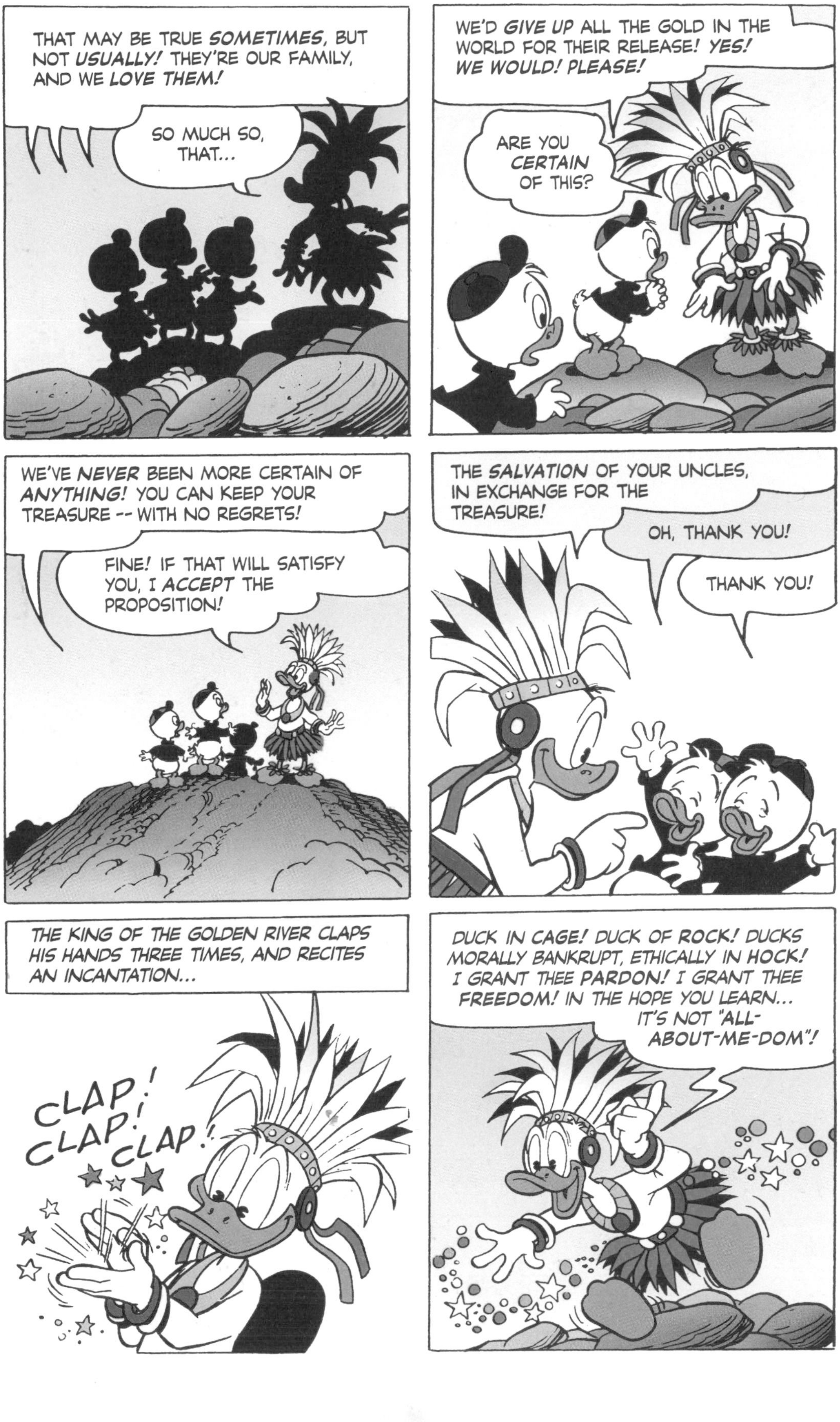

THAT MAY BE TRUE SOMETIMES, BUT NOT USUALLY! THEY'RE OUR FAMILY, AND WE LOVE THEM!
SO MUCH SO, THAT...
WE'D GIVE UP ALL THE GOLD IN THE WORLD FOR THEIR RELEASE! YES! WE WOULD! PLEASE!
ARE YOU CERTAIN OF THIS?
WE'VE NEVER BEEN MORE CERTAIN OF ANYTHING! YOU CAN KEEP YOUR TREASURE -- WITH NO REGRETS!
FINE! IF THAT WILL SATISFY YOU, I ACCEPT THE PROPOSITION!
THE SALVATION OF YOUR UNCLES, IN EXCHANGE FOR THE TREASURE!
OH, THANK YOU!
THANK YOU!
THE KING OF THE GOLDEN RIVER CLAPS HIS HANDS THREE TIMES, AND RECITES AN INCANTATION...
CLAP! CLAP! CLAP!
DUCK IN CAGE! DUCK OF ROCK! DUCKS MORALLY BANKRUPT, ETHICALLY IN HOCK! I GRANT THEE PARDON! I GRANT THEE FREEDOM! IN THE HOPE YOU LEARN... IT'S NOT "ALL-ABOUT-ME-DOM"!

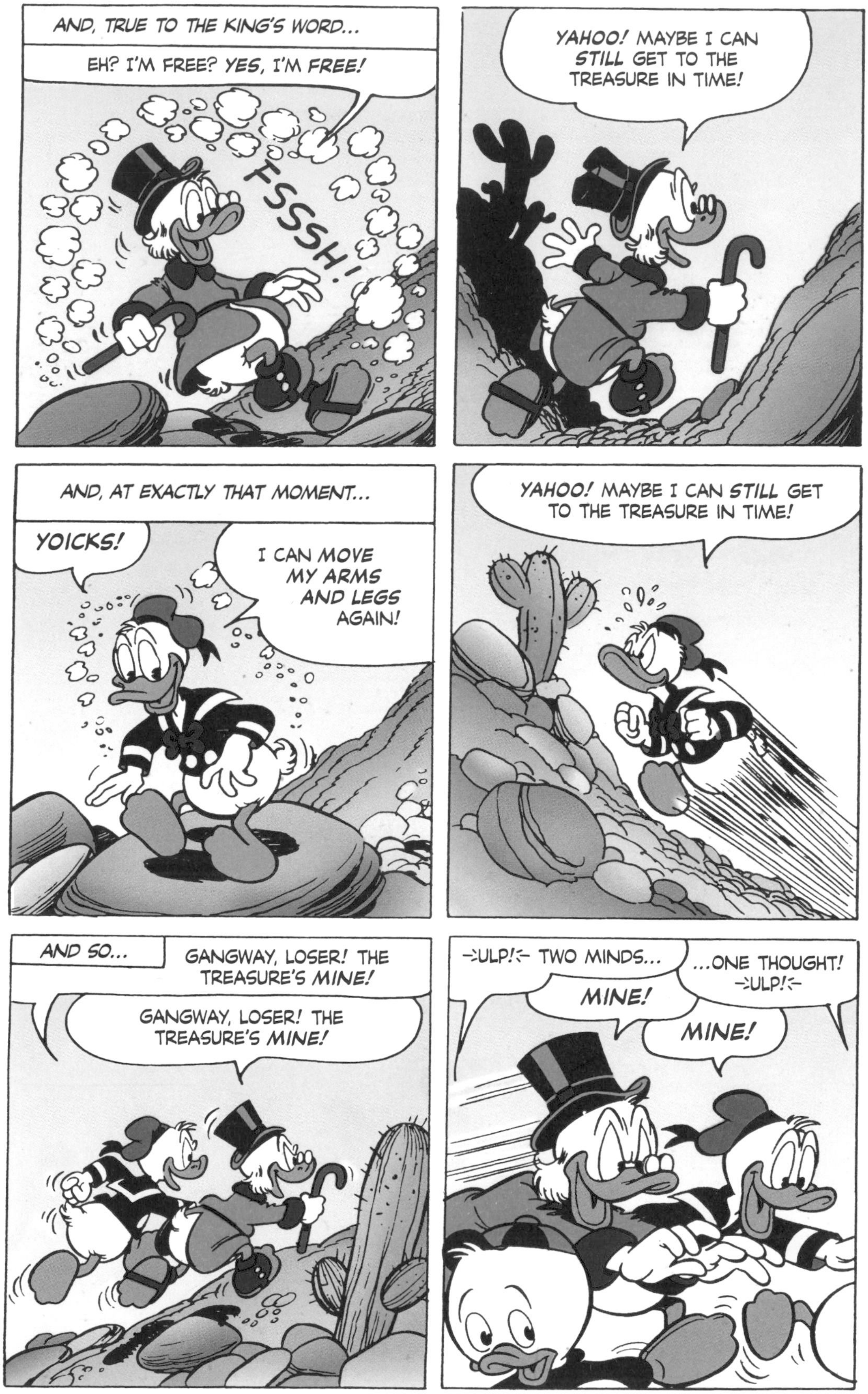
AND, TRUE TO THE KING'S WORD...
EH? I'M FREE? YES, I'M FREE!
FSSSH!
YAHOO! MAYBE I CAN STILL GET TO THE TREASURE IN TIME!
AND, AT EXACTLY THAT MOMENT...
YOICKS!
I CAN MOVE MY ARMS AND LEGS AGAIN!
YAHOO! MAYBE I CAN STILL GET TO THE TREASURE IN TIME!
AND SO...
GANGWAY, LOSER! THE TREASURE'S MINE!
GANGWAY, LOSER! THE TREASURE'S MINE!
-ULP!- TWO MINDS...
MINE!
...ONE THOUGHT! -ULP!-
MINE!

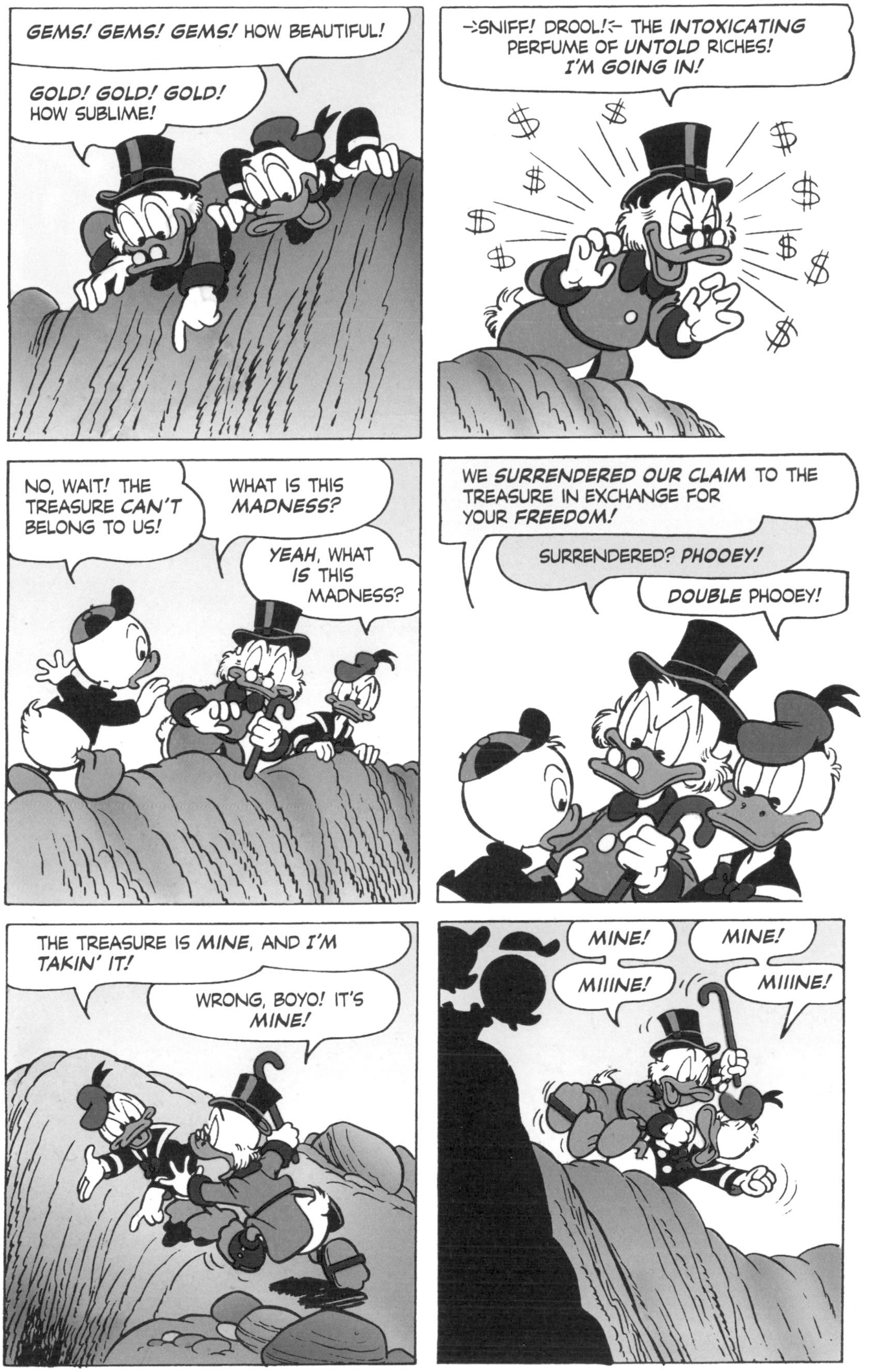
GEMS! GEMS! GEMS! HOW BEAUTIFUL!
GOLD! GOLD! GOLD! HOW SUBLIME!
SNIFF! DROOL! THE INTOXICATING PERFUME OF UNTOLD RICHES! I'M GOING IN!
NO, WAIT! THE TREASURE CAN'T BELONG TO US!
WHAT IS THIS MADNESS?
YEAH, WHAT IS THIS MADNESS?
WE SURRENDERED OUR CLAIM TO THE TREASURE IN EXCHANGE FOR YOUR FREEDOM!
SURRENDERED? PHOOEY!
DOUBLE PHOOEY!
THE TREASURE IS MINE, AND I'M TAKIN' IT!
WRONG, BOYO! IT'S MINE!
MINE!
MINE!
MIIINE!
MIIINE!

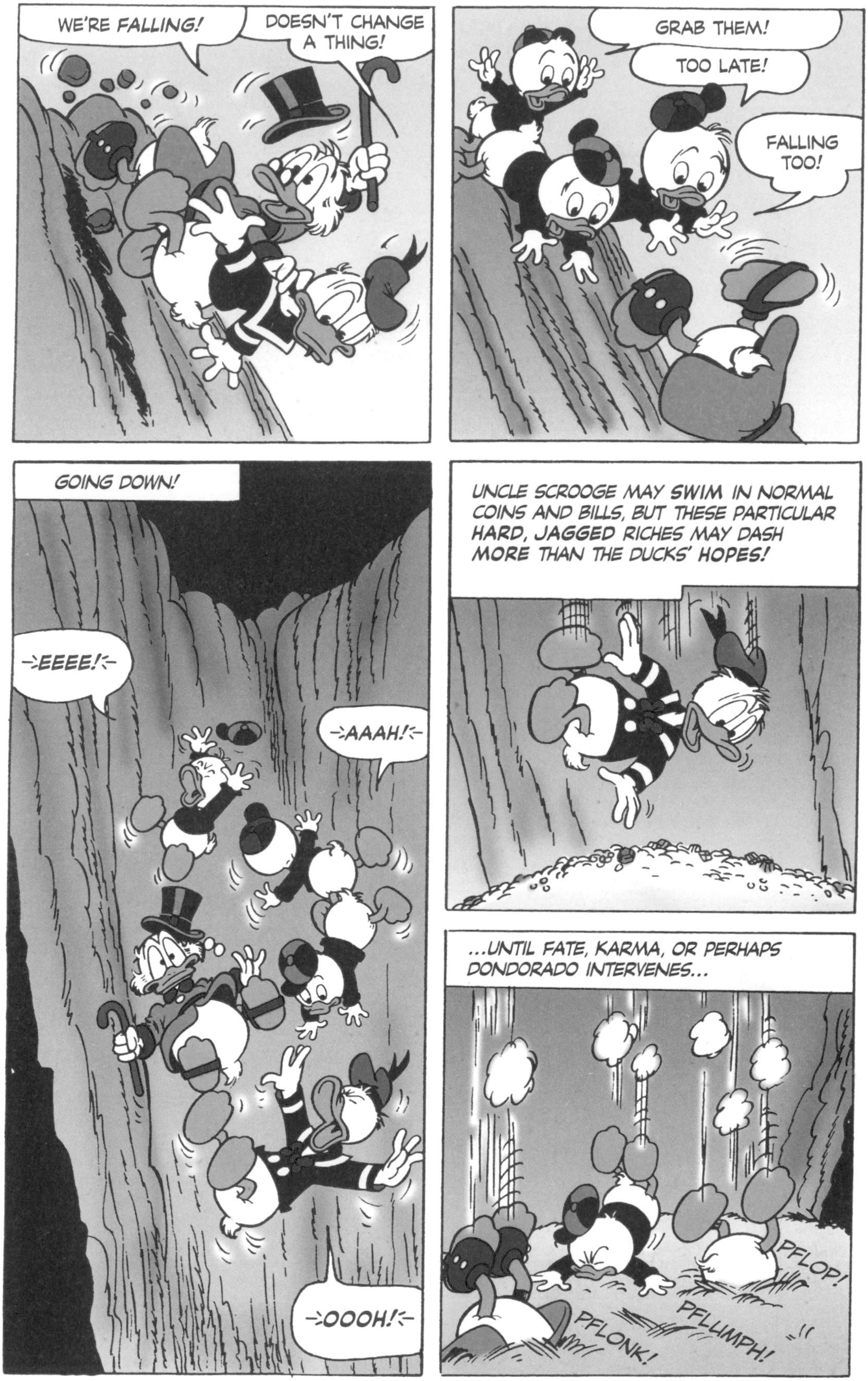
WE'RE FALLING!
DOESN'T CHANGE A THING!
GRAB THEM!
TOO LATE!
FALLING TOO!
GOING DOWN!
-EEEE!-
-AAAH!-
-OOOH!-
UNCLE SCROOGE MAY SWIM IN NORMAL COINS AND BILLS, BUT THESE PARTICULAR HARD, JAGGED RICHES MAY DASH MORE THAN THE DUCKS' HOPES!
...UNTIL FATE, KARMA, OR PERHAPS DONDORADO INTERVENES...
PFLOP!
PFLUMPH!
PFLONK!

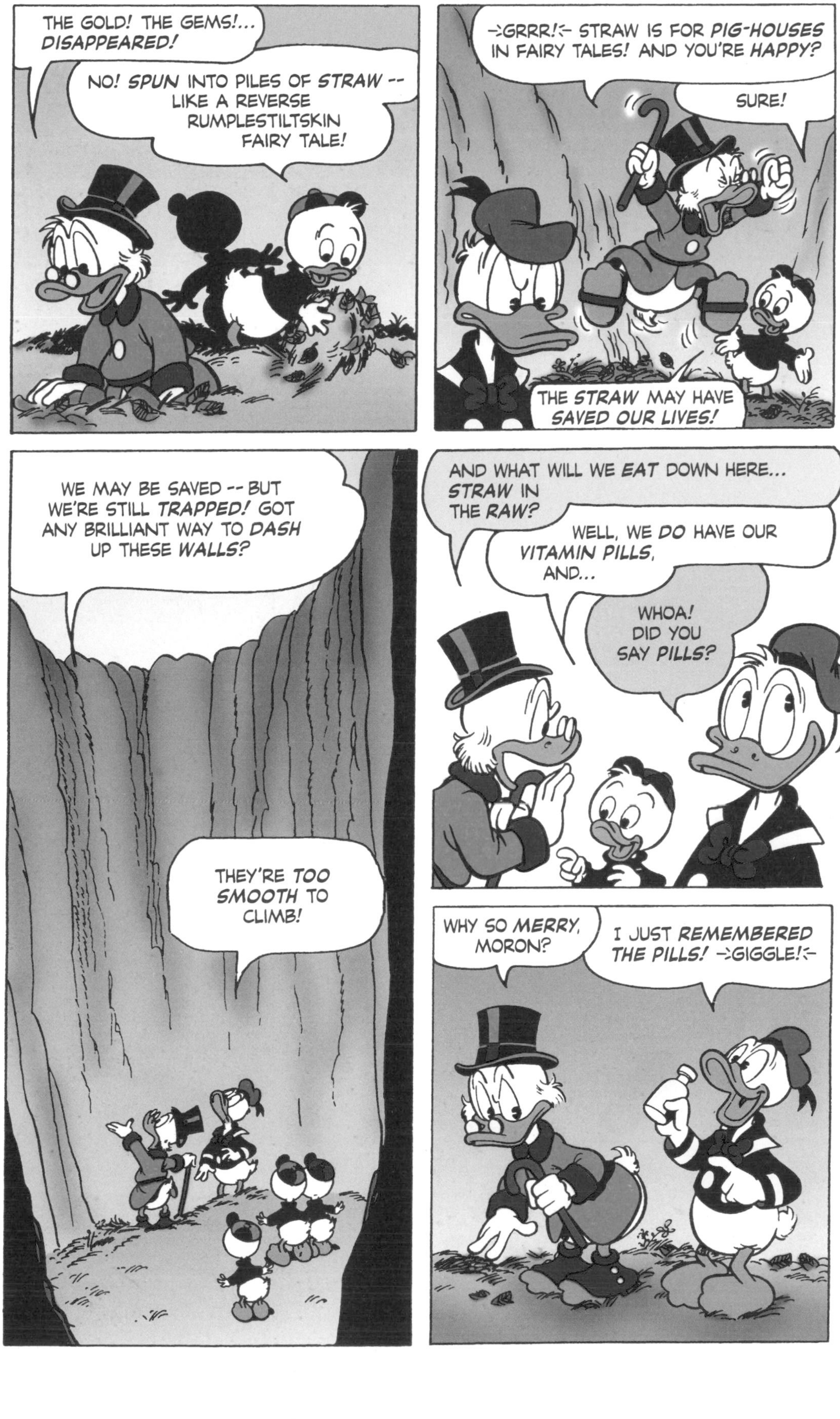
THE GOLD! THE GEMS!... DISAPPEARED!
NO! SPUN INTO PILES OF STRAW -- LIKE A REVERSE RUMPLESTILTSKIN FAIRY TALE!
-GRRR!- STRAW IS FOR PIG-HOUSES IN FAIRY TALES! AND YOU'RE HAPPY?
SURE!
THE STRAW MAY HAVE SAVED OUR LIVES!
WE MAY BE SAVED -- BUT WE'RE STILL TRAPPED! GOT ANY BRILLIANT WAY TO DASH UP THESE WALLS?
THEY'RE TOO SMOOTH TO CLIMB!
AND WHAT WILL WE EAT DOWN HERE... STRAW IN THE RAW?
WELL, WE DO HAVE OUR VITAMIN PILLS, AND...
WHOA! DID YOU SAY PILLS?
WHY SO MERRY, MORON?
I JUST REMEMBERED THE PILLS! -GIGGLE!-

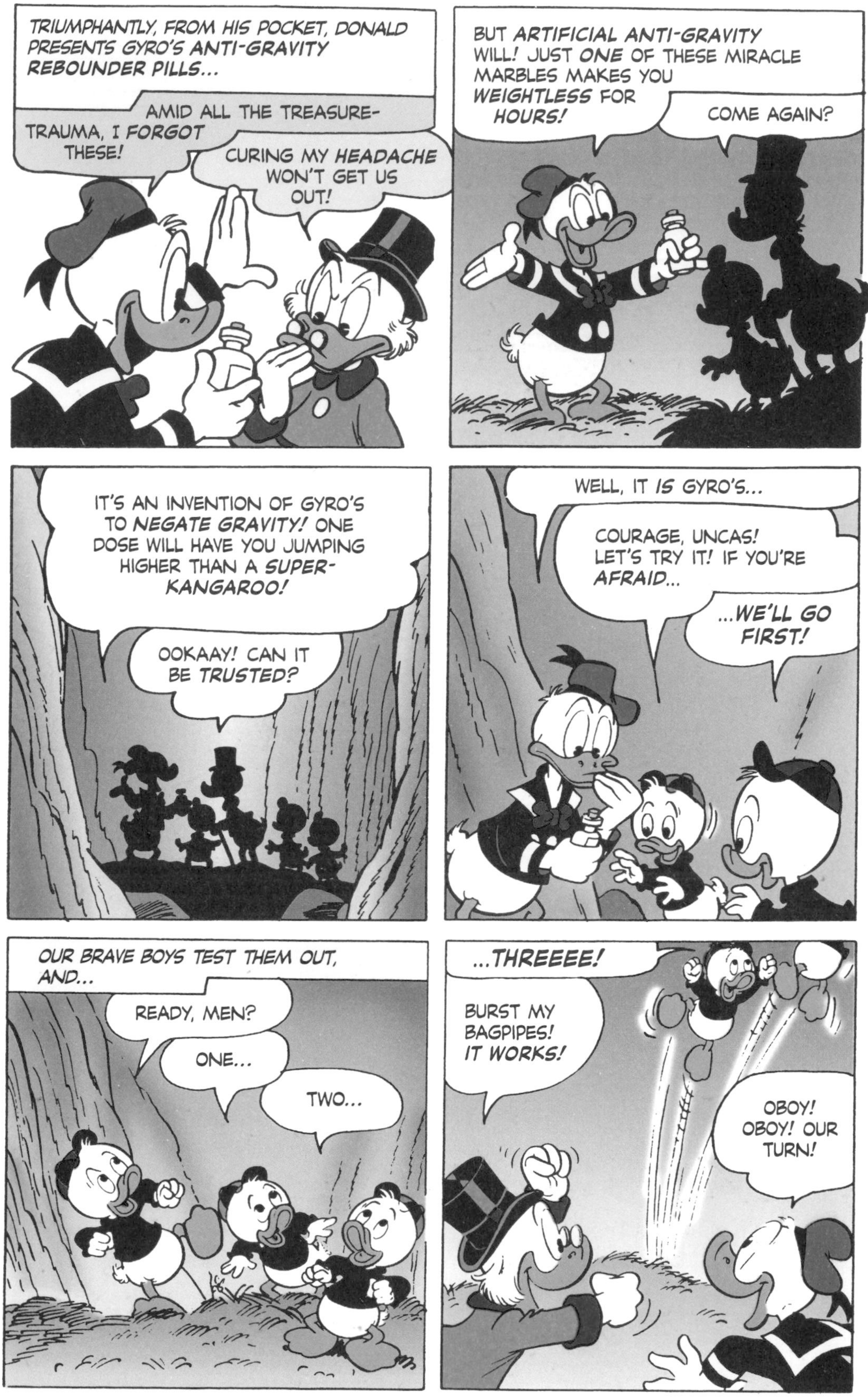
TRIUMPHANTLY, FROM HIS POCKET, DONALD PRESENTS GYRO'S ANTI-GRAVITY REBOUNDER PILLS...
AMID ALL THE TREASURE-TRAUMA, I FORGOT THESE!
CURING MY HEADACHE WON'T GET US OUT!
BUT ARTIFICIAL ANTI-GRAVITY WILL! JUST ONE OF THESE MIRACLE MARBLES MAKES YOU WEIGHTLESS FOR HOURS!
COME AGAIN?
IT'S AN INVENTION OF GYRO'S TO NEGATE GRAVITY! ONE DOSE WILL HAVE YOU JUMPING HIGHER THAN A SUPER-KANGAROO!
OOKAAY! CAN IT BE TRUSTED?
WELL, IT IS GYRO'S...
COURAGE, UNCAS! LET'S TRY IT! IF YOU'RE AFRAID...
...WE'LL GO FIRST!
OUR BRAVE BOYS TEST THEM OUT, AND...
READY, MEN?
ONE...
TWO...
...THREEEE!
BURST MY BAGPIPES! IT WORKS!
OBOY! OBOY! OUR TURN!

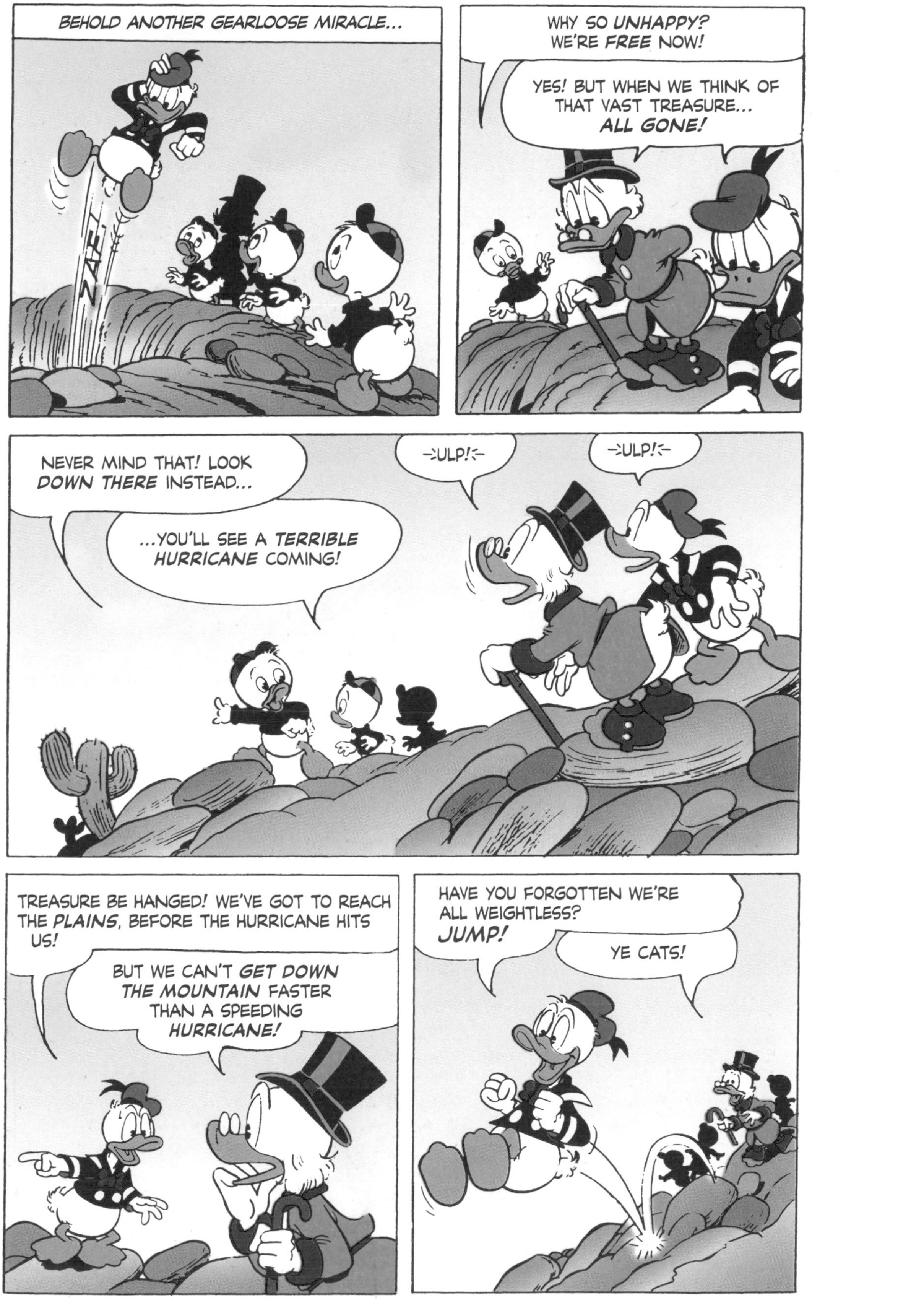
BEHOLD ANOTHER GEARLOOSE MIRACLE...
ZAP!
WHY SO UNHAPPY? WE'RE FREE NOW!
YES! BUT WHEN WE THINK OF THAT VAST TREASURE... ALL GONE!
NEVER MIND THAT! LOOK DOWN THERE INSTEAD...
...YOU'LL SEE A TERRIBLE HURRICANE COMING!
-ULP!-
-ULP!-
TREASURE BE HANGED! WE'VE GOT TO REACH THE PLAINS, BEFORE THE HURRICANE HITS US!
BUT WE CAN'T GET DOWN THE MOUNTAIN FASTER THAN A SPEEDING HURRICANE!
HAVE YOU FORGOTTEN WE'RE ALL WEIGHTLESS? JUMP!
YE CATS!

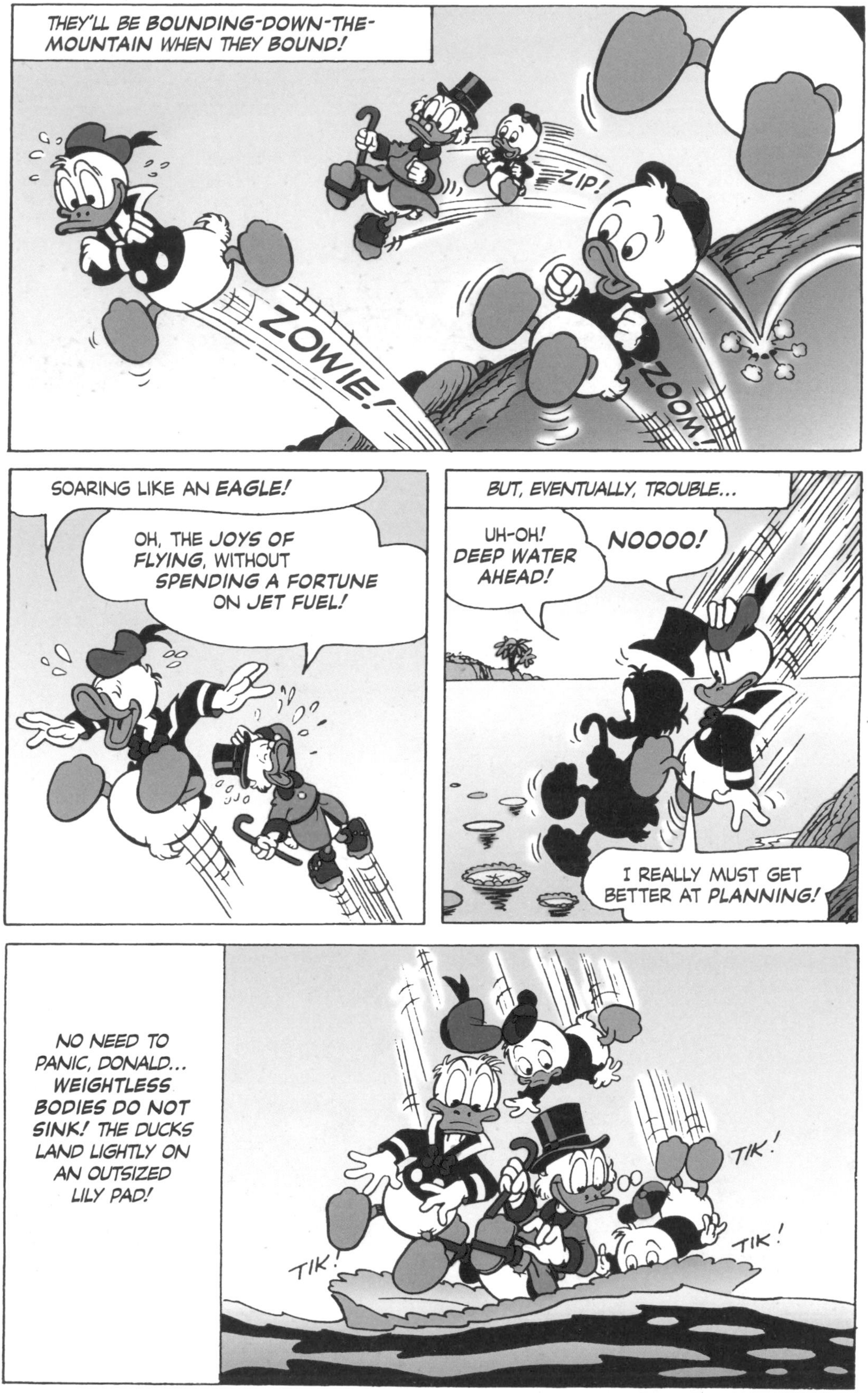
THEY'LL BE BOUNDING-DOWN-THE-MOUNTAIN WHEN THEY BOUND!
ZIP!
ZOWIE!
ZOOM!
SOARING LIKE AN EAGLE!
OH, THE JOYS OF FLYING, WITHOUT SPENDING A FORTUNE ON JET FUEL!
BUT, EVENTUALLY, TROUBLE...
UH-OH! DEEP WATER AHEAD!
NOOOO!
I REALLY MUST GET BETTER AT PLANNING!
NO NEED TO PANIC, DONALD... WEIGHTLESS BODIES DO NOT SINK! THE DUCKS LAND LIGHTLY ON AN OUTSIZED LILY PAD!
TIK!
TIK!
TIK!

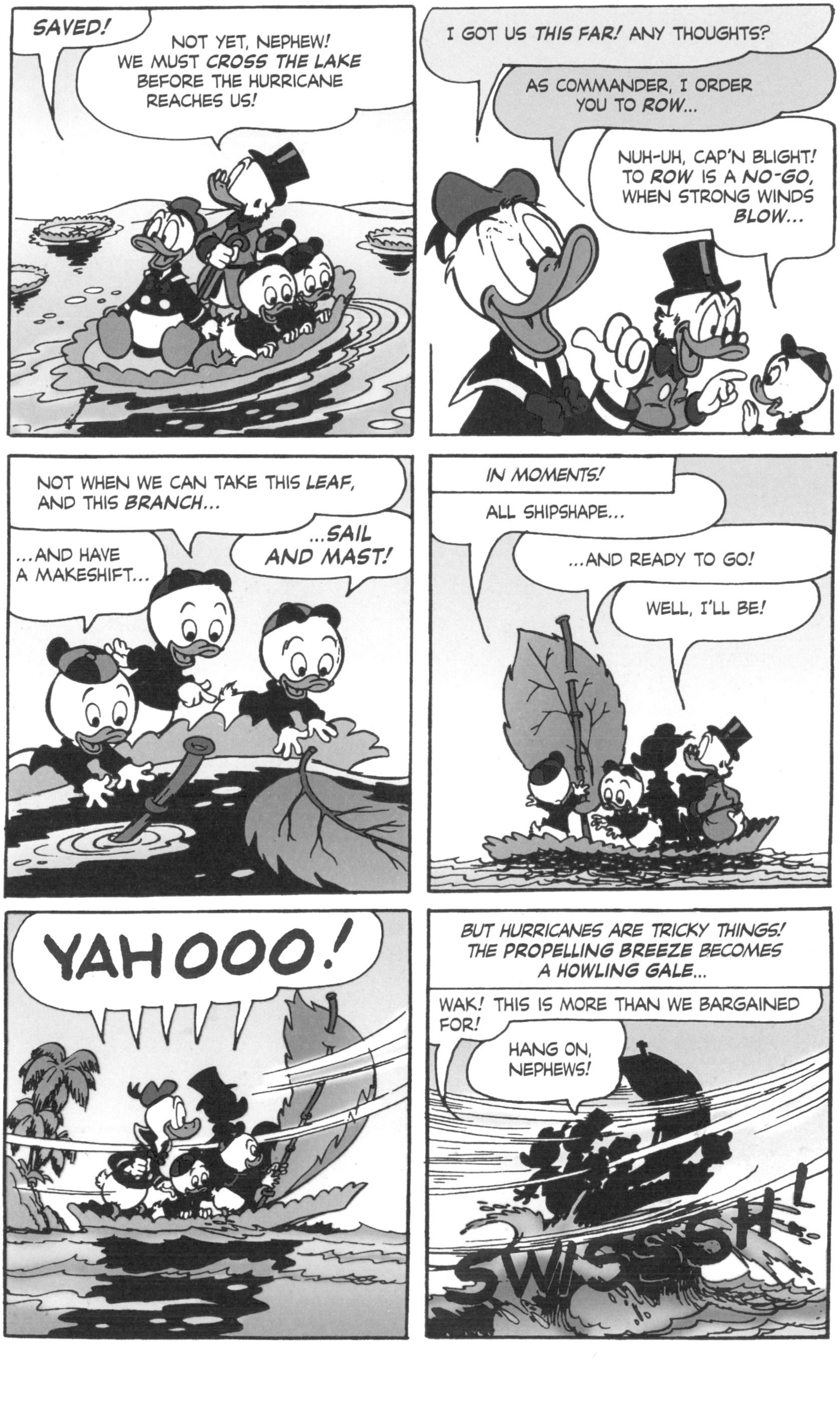
SAVED!
NOT YET, NEPHEW! WE MUST CROSS THE LAKE BEFORE THE HURRICANE REACHES US!
I GOT US THIS FAR! ANY THOUGHTS?
AS COMMANDER, I ORDER YOU TO ROW...
NUH-UH, CAP'N BLIGHT! TO ROW IS A NO-GO, WHEN STRONG WINDS BLOW...
NOT WHEN WE CAN TAKE THIS LEAF, AND THIS BRANCH...
...AND HAVE A MAKESHIFT...
...SAIL AND MAST!
IN MOMENTS!
ALL SHIPSHAPE...
...AND READY TO GO!
WELL, I'LL BE!
YAHOOO!
BUT HURRICANES ARE TRICKY THINGS! THE PROPELLING BREEZE BECOMES A HOWLING GALE...
WAK! THIS IS MORE THAN WE BARGAINED FOR!
HANG ON, NEPHEWS!
SWISSSH!

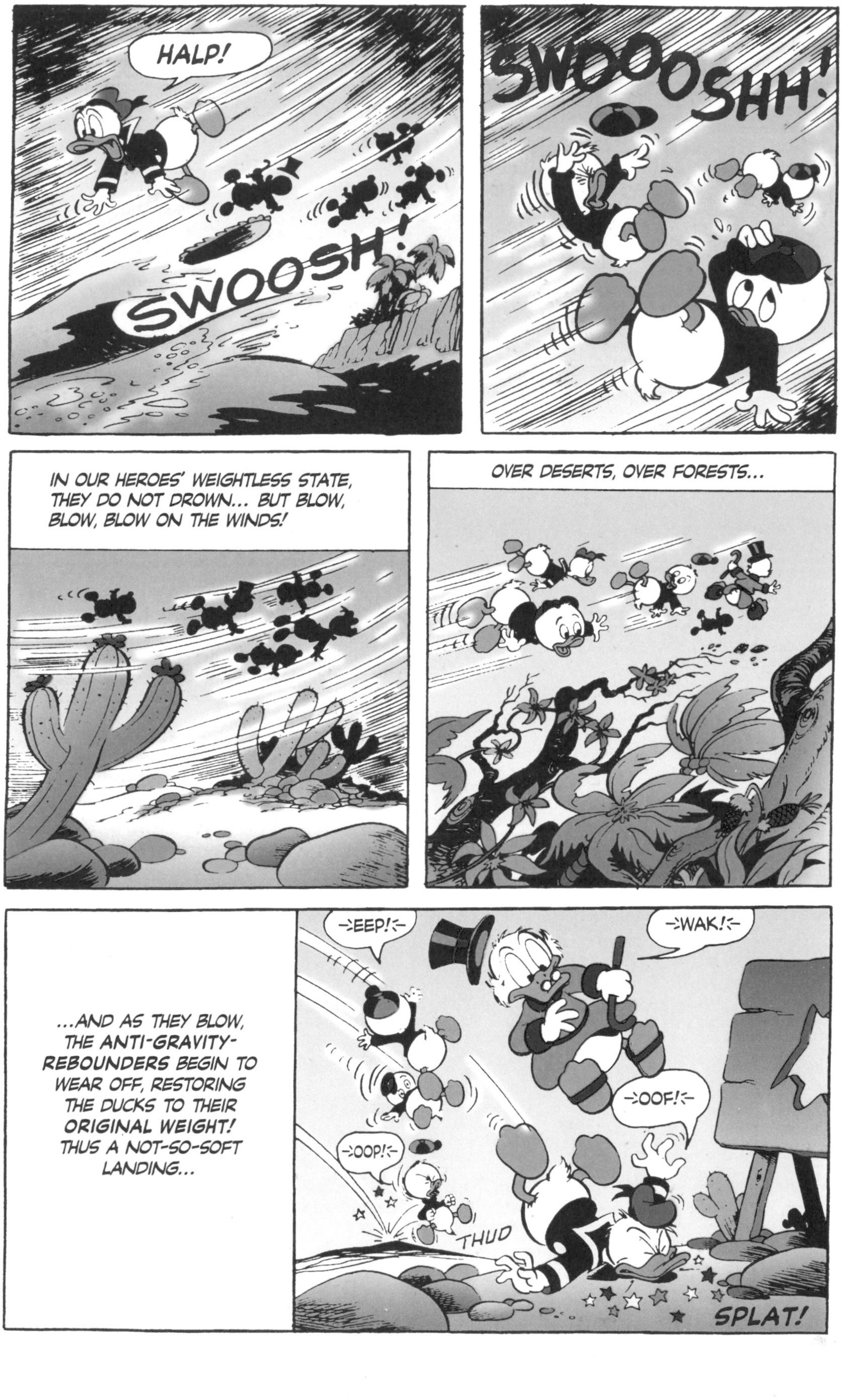
HALP!
SWOOSH!
SWOOOOSHH!
IN OUR HEROES' WEIGHTLESS STATE, THEY DO NOT DROWN... BUT BLOW, BLOW, BLOW ON THE WINDS!
OVER DESERTS, OVER FORESTS...
...AND AS THEY BLOW, THE ANTI-GRAVITY-REBOUNDERS BEGIN TO WEAR OFF, RESTORING THE DUCKS TO THEIR ORIGINAL WEIGHT! THUS A NOT-SO-SOFT LANDING...
EEP!
WAK!
OOF!
OOP!
THUD
SPLAT!

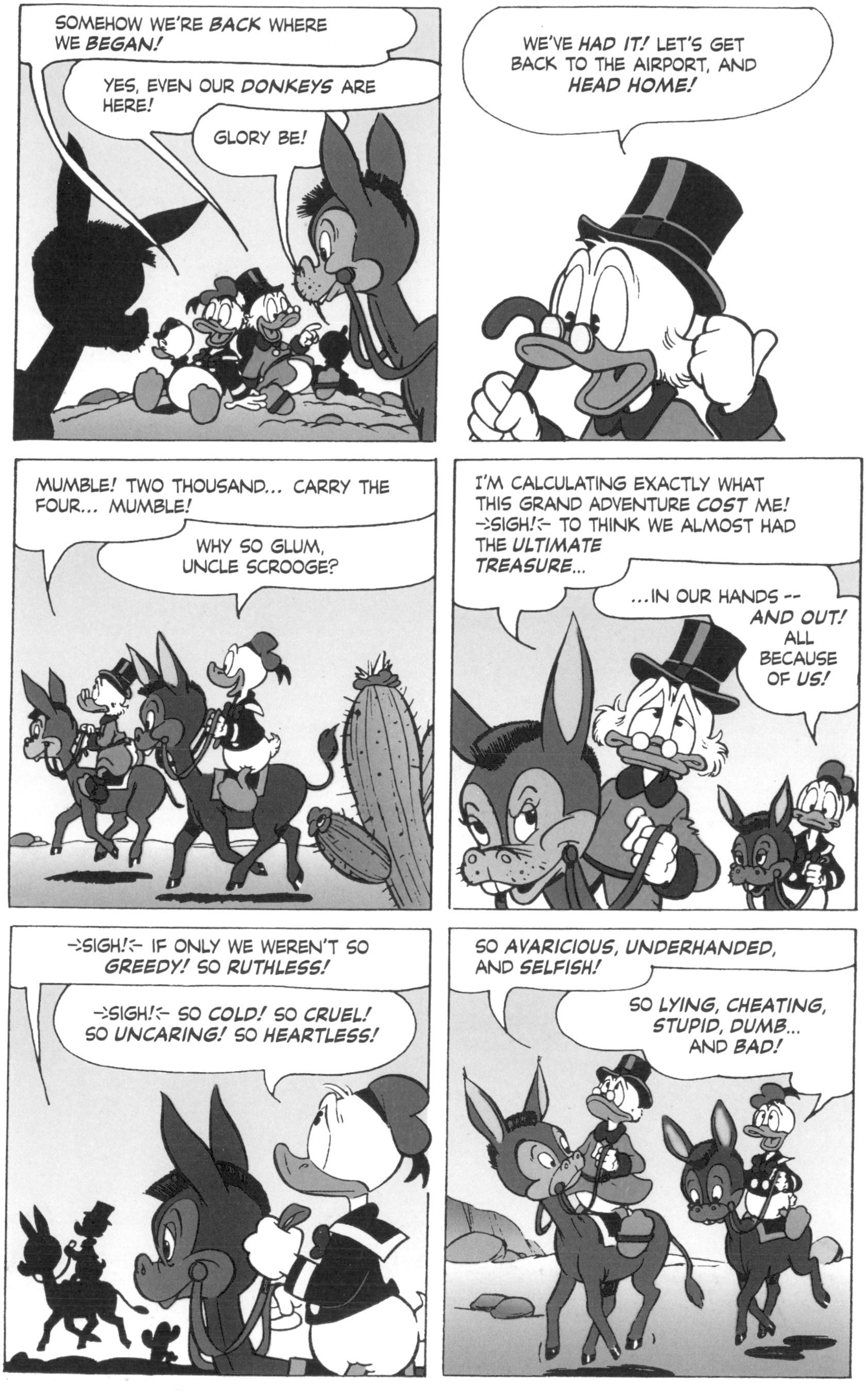
SOMEHOW WE'RE BACK WHERE WE BEGAN!
YES, EVEN OUR DONKEYS ARE HERE!
GLORY BE!
WE'VE HAD IT! LET'S GET BACK TO THE AIRPORT, AND HEAD HOME!
MUMBLE! TWO THOUSAND... CARRY THE FOUR... MUMBLE!
WHY SO GLUM, UNCLE SCROOGE?
I'M CALCULATING EXACTLY WHAT THIS GRAND ADVENTURE COST ME! ⇢SIGH!⇠ TO THINK WE ALMOST HAD THE ULTIMATE TREASURE...
...IN OUR HANDS -- AND OUT! ALL BECAUSE OF US!
⇢SIGH!⇠ IF ONLY WE WEREN'T SO GREEDY! SO RUTHLESS!
⇢SIGH!⇠ SO COLD! SO CRUEL! SO UNCARING! SO HEARTLESS!
SO AVARICIOUS, UNDERHANDED, AND SELFISH!
SO LYING, CHEATING, STUPID, DUMB... AND BAD!

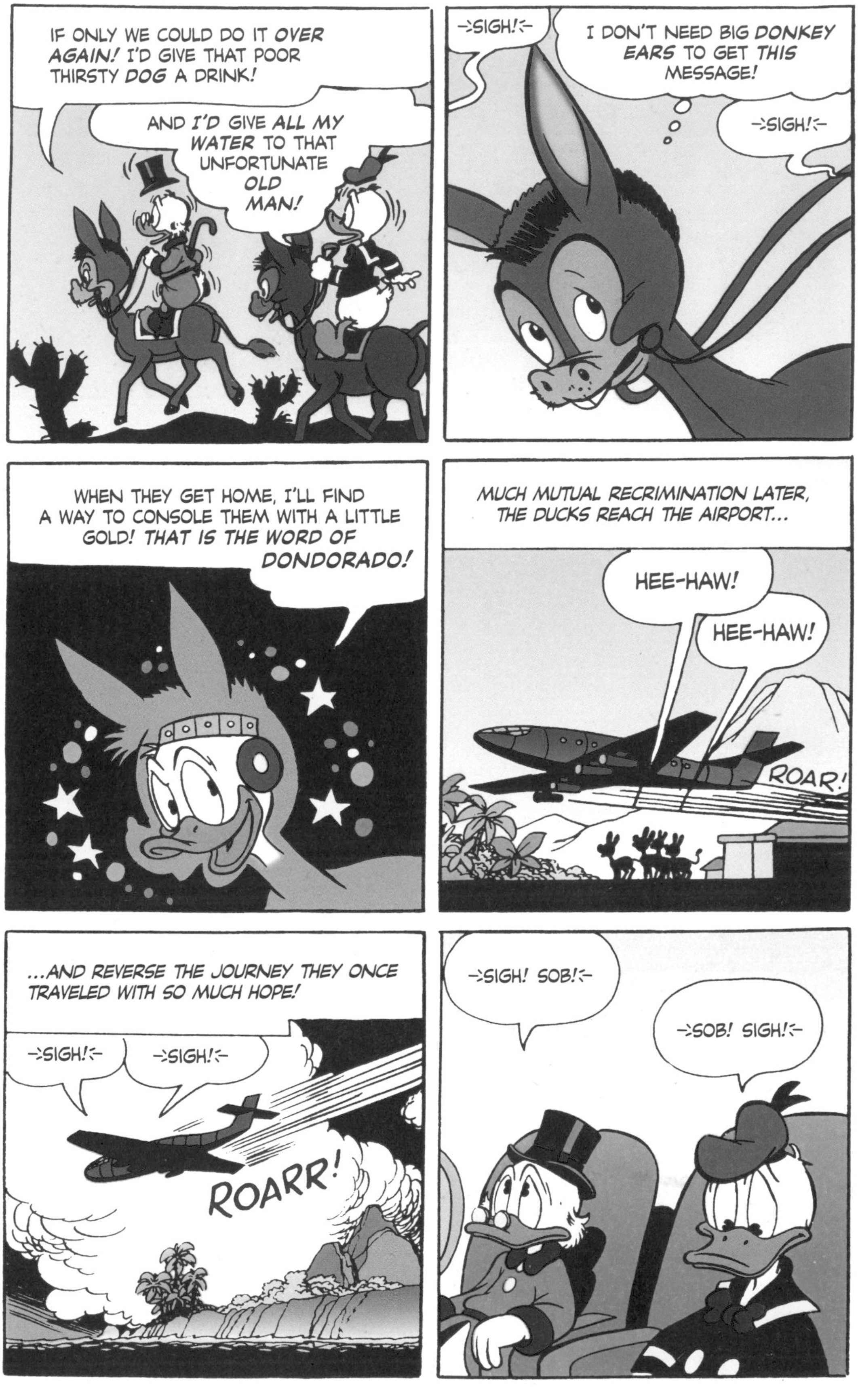
IF ONLY WE COULD DO IT OVER AGAIN! I'D GIVE THAT POOR THIRSTY DOG A DRINK!
AND I'D GIVE ALL MY WATER TO THAT UNFORTUNATE OLD MAN!
-SIGH!-
I DON'T NEED BIG DONKEY EARS TO GET THIS MESSAGE!
-SIGH!-
WHEN THEY GET HOME, I'LL FIND A WAY TO CONSOLE THEM WITH A LITTLE GOLD! THAT IS THE WORD OF DONDORADO!
MUCH MUTUAL RECRIMINATION LATER, THE DUCKS REACH THE AIRPORT...
HEE-HAW!
HEE-HAW!
ROAR!
...AND REVERSE THE JOURNEY THEY ONCE TRAVELED WITH SO MUCH HOPE!
-SIGH!-
-SIGH!-
ROARR!
-SIGH! SOB!-
-SOB! SIGH!-

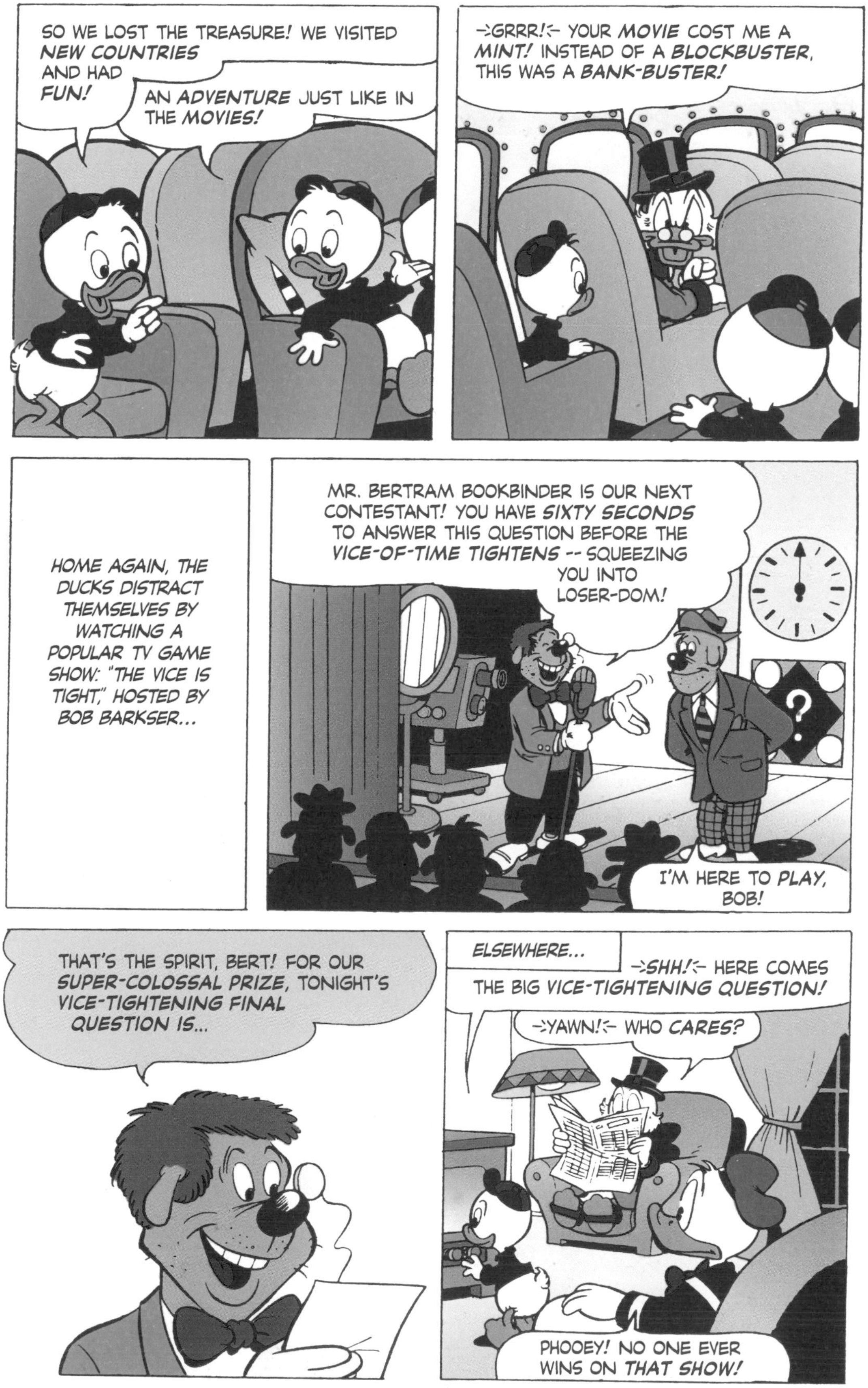
SO WE LOST THE TREASURE! WE VISITED NEW COUNTRIES AND HAD FUN!
AN ADVENTURE JUST LIKE IN THE MOVIES!
–GRRR!– YOUR MOVIE COST ME A MINT! INSTEAD OF A BLOCKBUSTER, THIS WAS A BANK-BUSTER!
HOME AGAIN, THE DUCKS DISTRACT THEMSELVES BY WATCHING A POPULAR TV GAME SHOW: "THE VICE IS TIGHT," HOSTED BY BOB BARKSER...
MR. BERTRAM BOOKBINDER IS OUR NEXT CONTESTANT! YOU HAVE SIXTY SECONDS TO ANSWER THIS QUESTION BEFORE THE VICE-OF-TIME TIGHTENS -- SQUEEZING YOU INTO LOSER-DOM!
I'M HERE TO PLAY, BOB!
THAT'S THE SPIRIT, BERT! FOR OUR SUPER-COLOSSAL PRIZE, TONIGHT'S VICE-TIGHTENING FINAL QUESTION IS...
ELSEWHERE...
–SHH!– HERE COMES THE BIG VICE-TIGHTENING QUESTION!
–YAWN!– WHO CARES?
PHOOEY! NO ONE EVER WINS ON THAT SHOW!

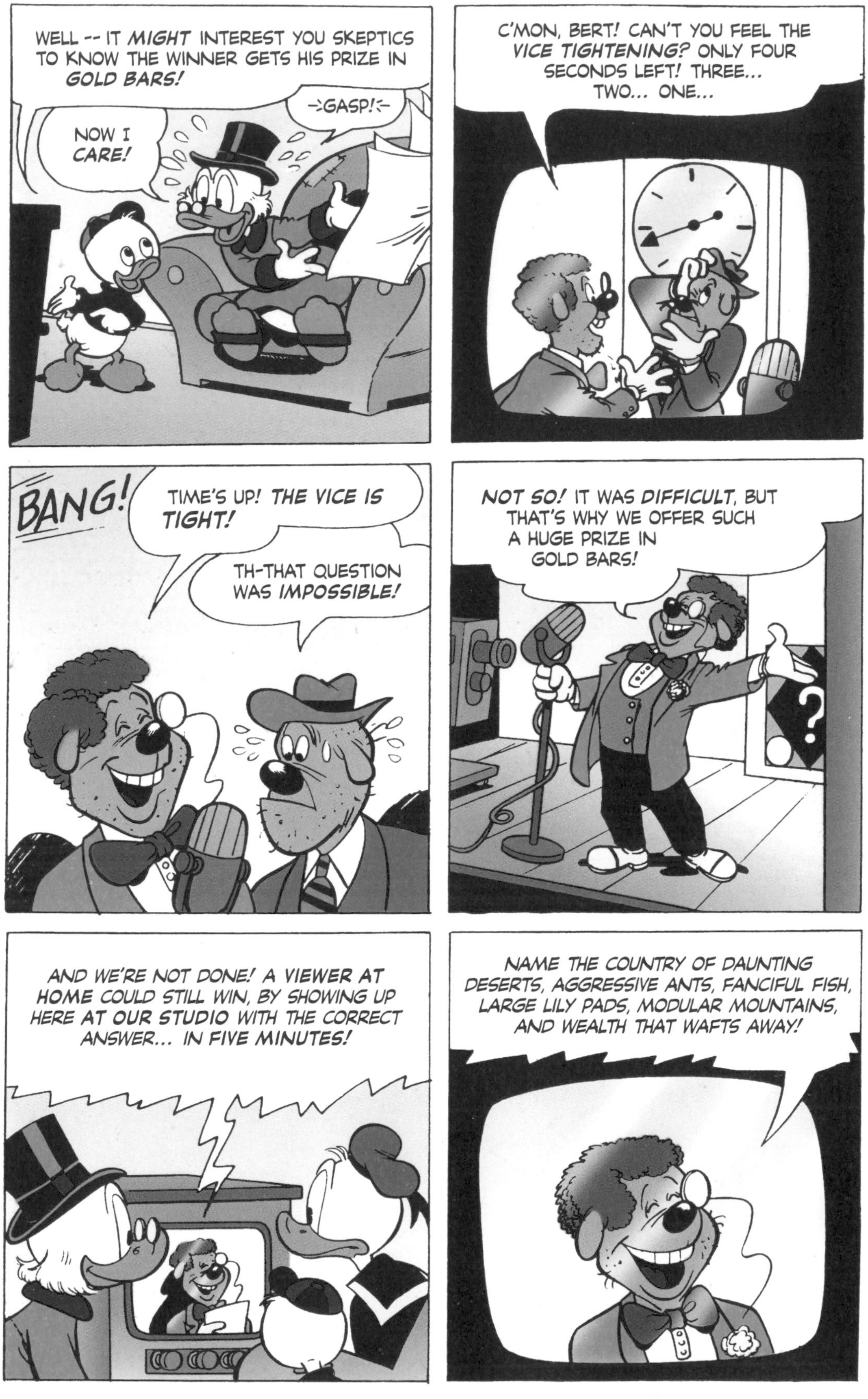
WELL -- IT MIGHT INTEREST YOU SKEPTICS TO KNOW THE WINNER GETS HIS PRIZE IN GOLD BARS!
NOW I CARE!
-GASP!-
C'MON, BERT! CAN'T YOU FEEL THE VICE TIGHTENING? ONLY FOUR SECONDS LEFT! THREE... TWO... ONE...
BANG!
TIME'S UP! THE VICE IS TIGHT!
TH-THAT QUESTION WAS IMPOSSIBLE!
NOT SO! IT WAS DIFFICULT, BUT THAT'S WHY WE OFFER SUCH A HUGE PRIZE IN GOLD BARS!
AND WE'RE NOT DONE! A VIEWER AT HOME COULD STILL WIN, BY SHOWING UP HERE AT OUR STUDIO WITH THE CORRECT ANSWER... IN FIVE MINUTES!
NAME THE COUNTRY OF DAUNTING DESERTS, AGGRESSIVE ANTS, FANCIFUL FISH, LARGE LILY PADS, MODULAR MOUNTAINS, AND WEALTH THAT WAFTS AWAY!

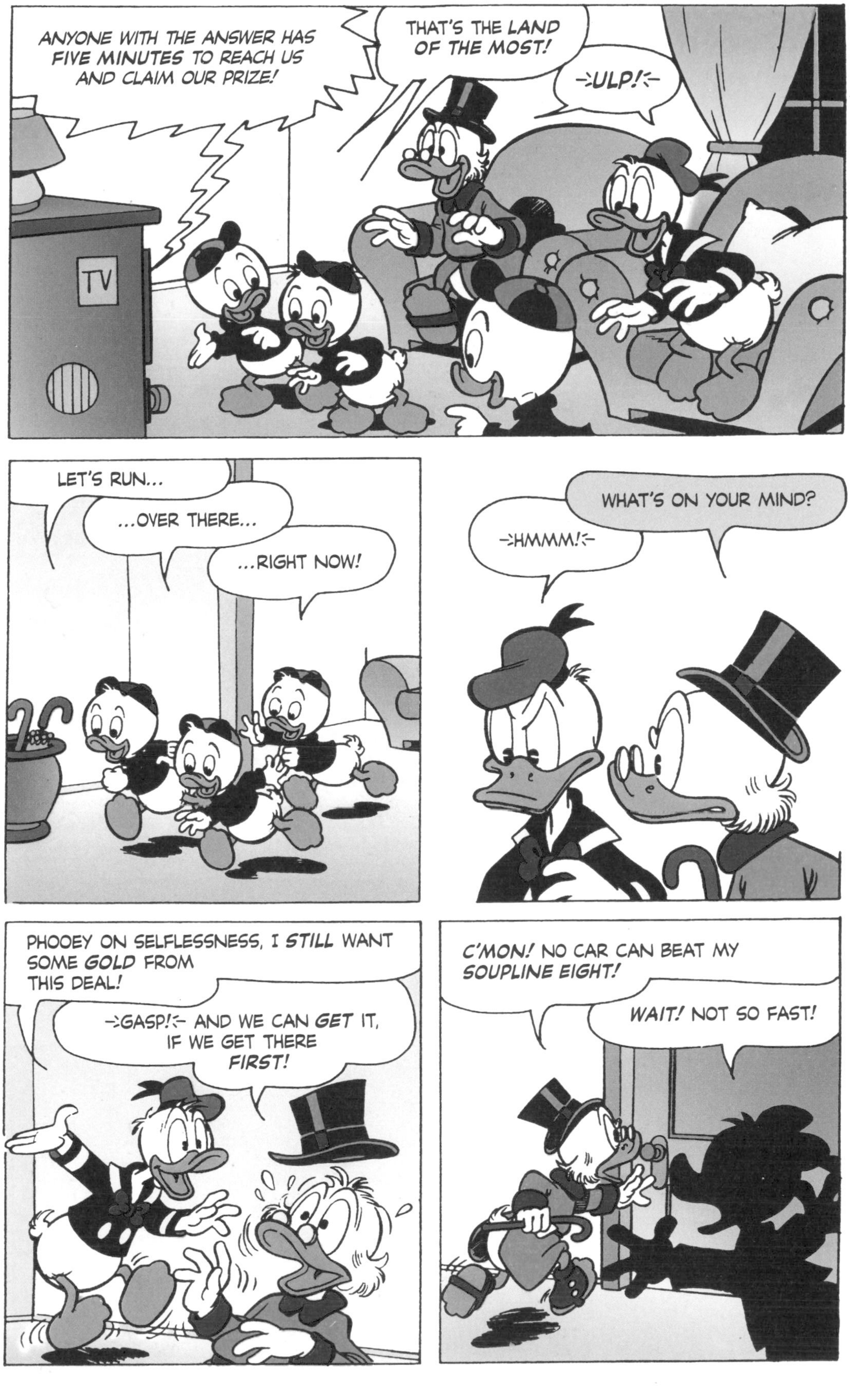
ANYONE WITH THE ANSWER HAS FIVE MINUTES TO REACH US AND CLAIM OUR PRIZE!
THAT'S THE LAND OF THE MOST!
-ULP!-
LET'S RUN...
...OVER THERE...
...RIGHT NOW!
WHAT'S ON YOUR MIND?
-HMMM!-
PHOOEY ON SELFLESSNESS, I STILL WANT SOME GOLD FROM THIS DEAL!
-GASP!- AND WE CAN GET IT, IF WE GET THERE FIRST!
C'MON! NO CAR CAN BEAT MY SOUPLINE EIGHT!
WAIT! NOT SO FAST!

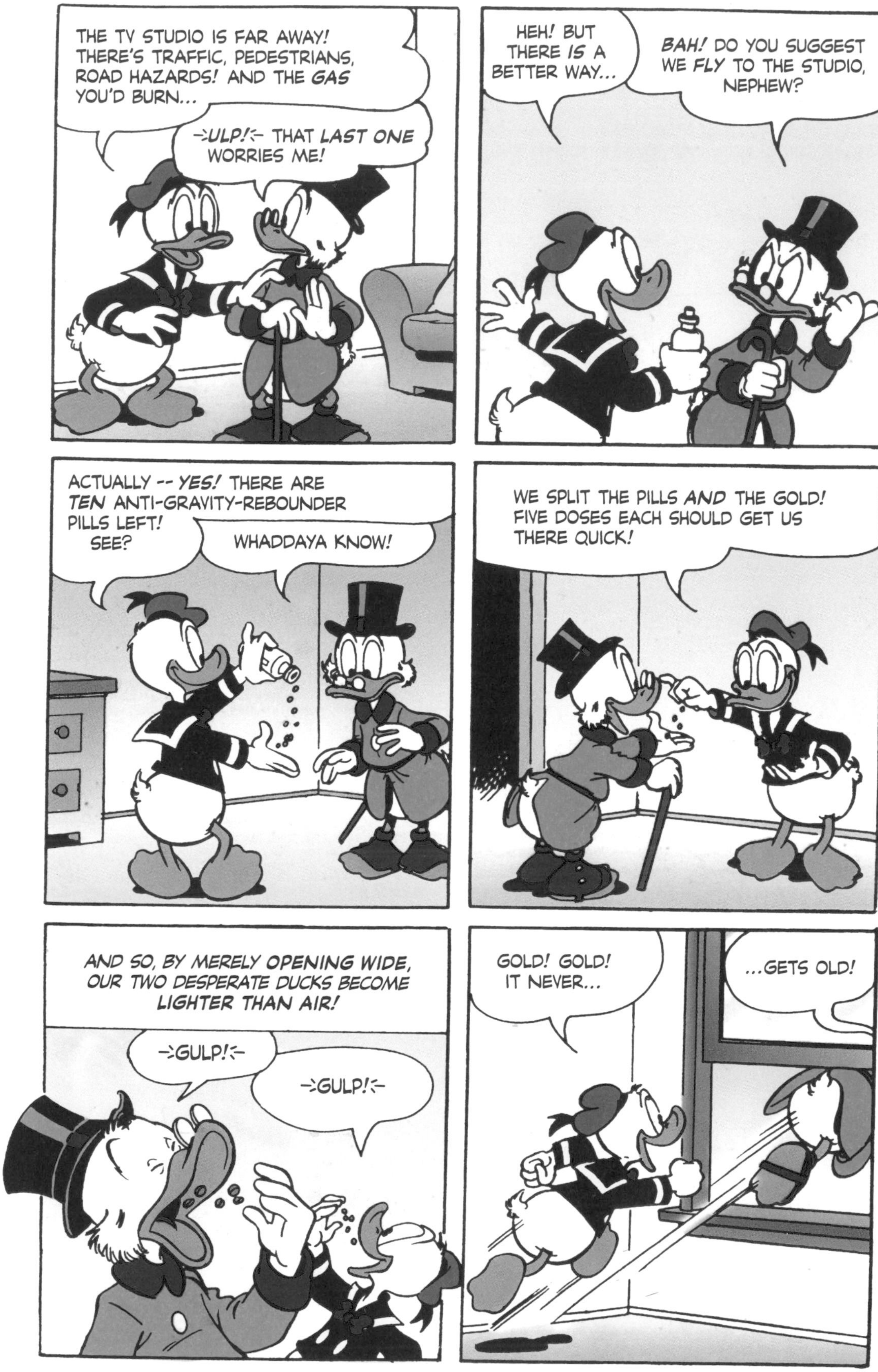

THE TV STUDIO IS FAR AWAY! THERE'S TRAFFIC, PEDESTRIANS, ROAD HAZARDS! AND THE GAS YOU'D BURN...
-ULP!- THAT LAST ONE WORRIES ME!
HEH! BUT THERE IS A BETTER WAY...
BAH! DO YOU SUGGEST WE FLY TO THE STUDIO, NEPHEW?
ACTUALLY -- YES! THERE ARE TEN ANTI-GRAVITY-REBOUNDER PILLS LEFT! SEE?
WHADDAYA KNOW!
WE SPLIT THE PILLS AND THE GOLD! FIVE DOSES EACH SHOULD GET US THERE QUICK!
AND SO, BY MERELY OPENING WIDE, OUR TWO DESPERATE DUCKS BECOME LIGHTER THAN AIR!
-GULP!-
-GULP!-
GOLD! GOLD! IT NEVER...
...GETS OLD!

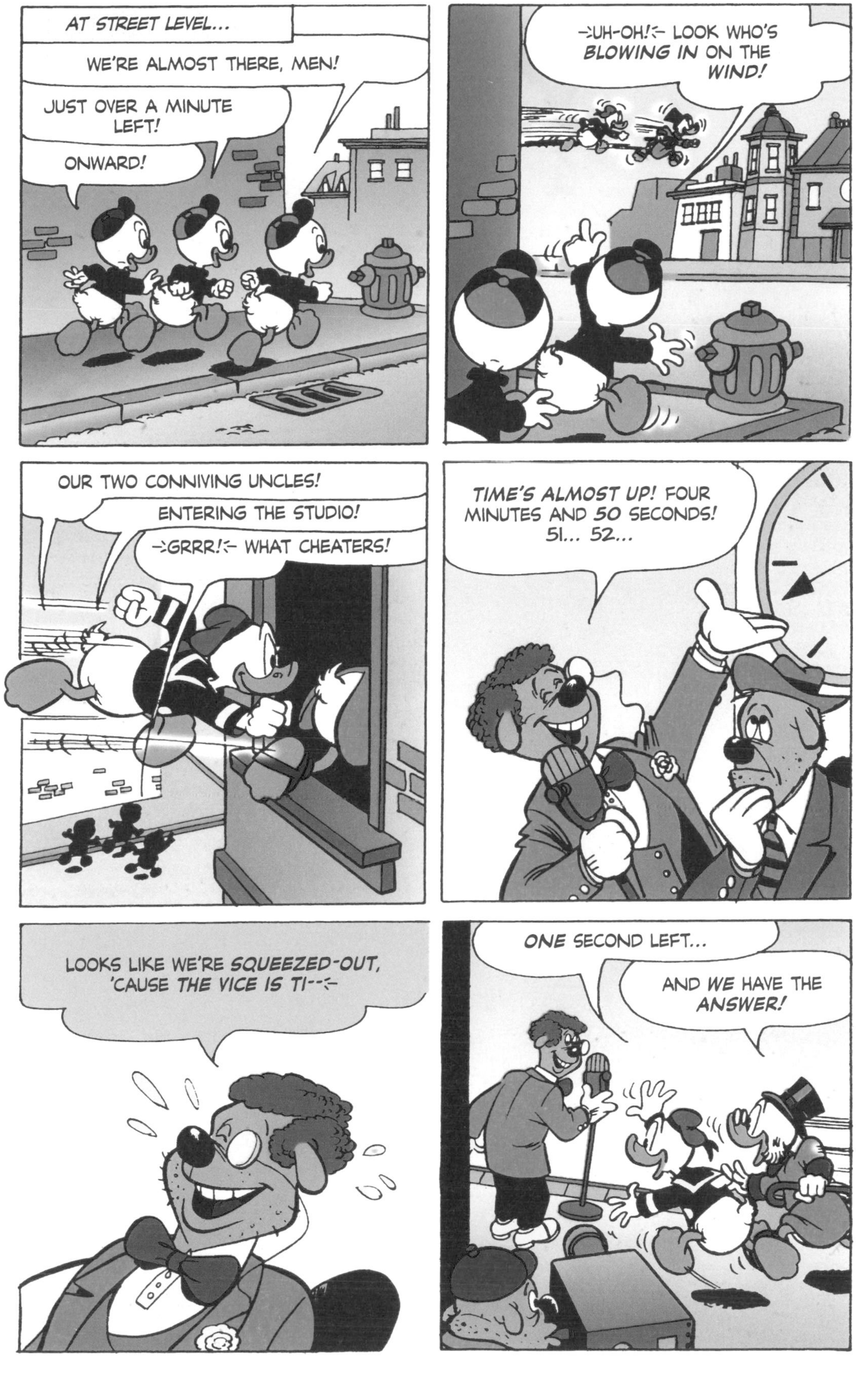
AT STREET LEVEL...
WE'RE ALMOST THERE, MEN!
JUST OVER A MINUTE LEFT!
ONWARD!
-UH-OH!- LOOK WHO'S *BLOWING IN* ON THE *WIND!*
OUR TWO CONNIVING UNCLES!
ENTERING THE STUDIO!
-GRRR!- WHAT CHEATERS!
TIME'S ALMOST UP! FOUR MINUTES AND *50* SECONDS! 51... 52...
LOOKS LIKE WE'RE *SQUEEZED-OUT,* 'CAUSE *THE VICE IS TI--*
ONE SECOND LEFT...
AND *WE* HAVE THE *ANSWER!*

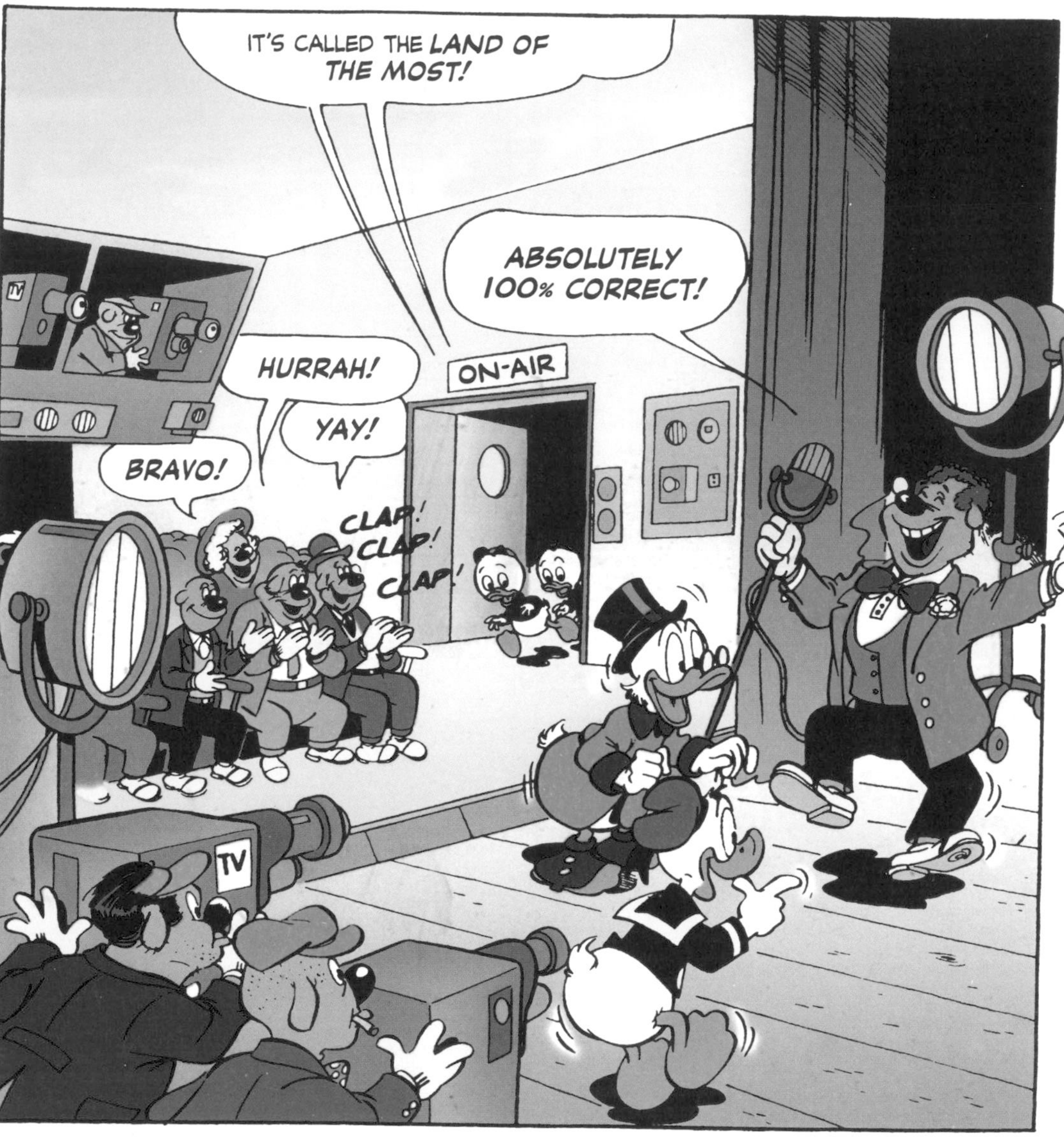
IT'S CALLED THE LAND OF THE MOST!
ABSOLUTELY 100% CORRECT!
HURRAH!
ON-AIR
YAY!
BRAVO!
CLAP! CLAP! CLAP!
TV
TV

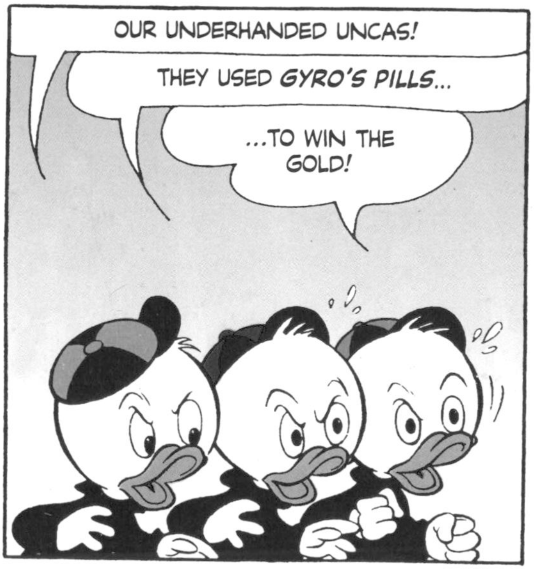
OUR UNDERHANDED UNCAS!
THEY USED GYRO'S PILLS...
...TO WIN THE GOLD!

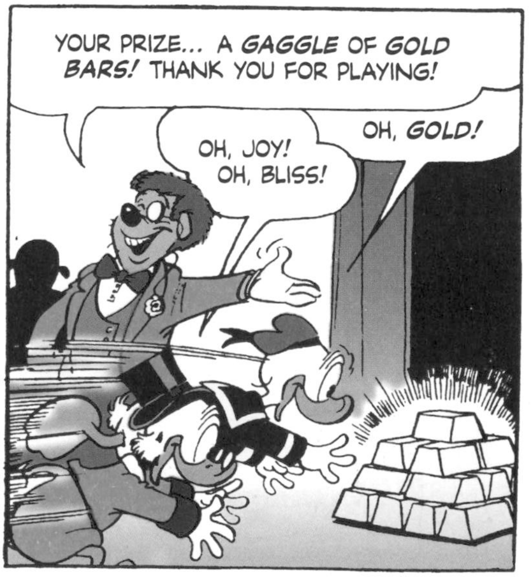
YOUR PRIZE... A GAGGLE OF GOLD BARS! THANK YOU FOR PLAYING!
OH, JOY! OH, BLISS!
OH, GOLD!

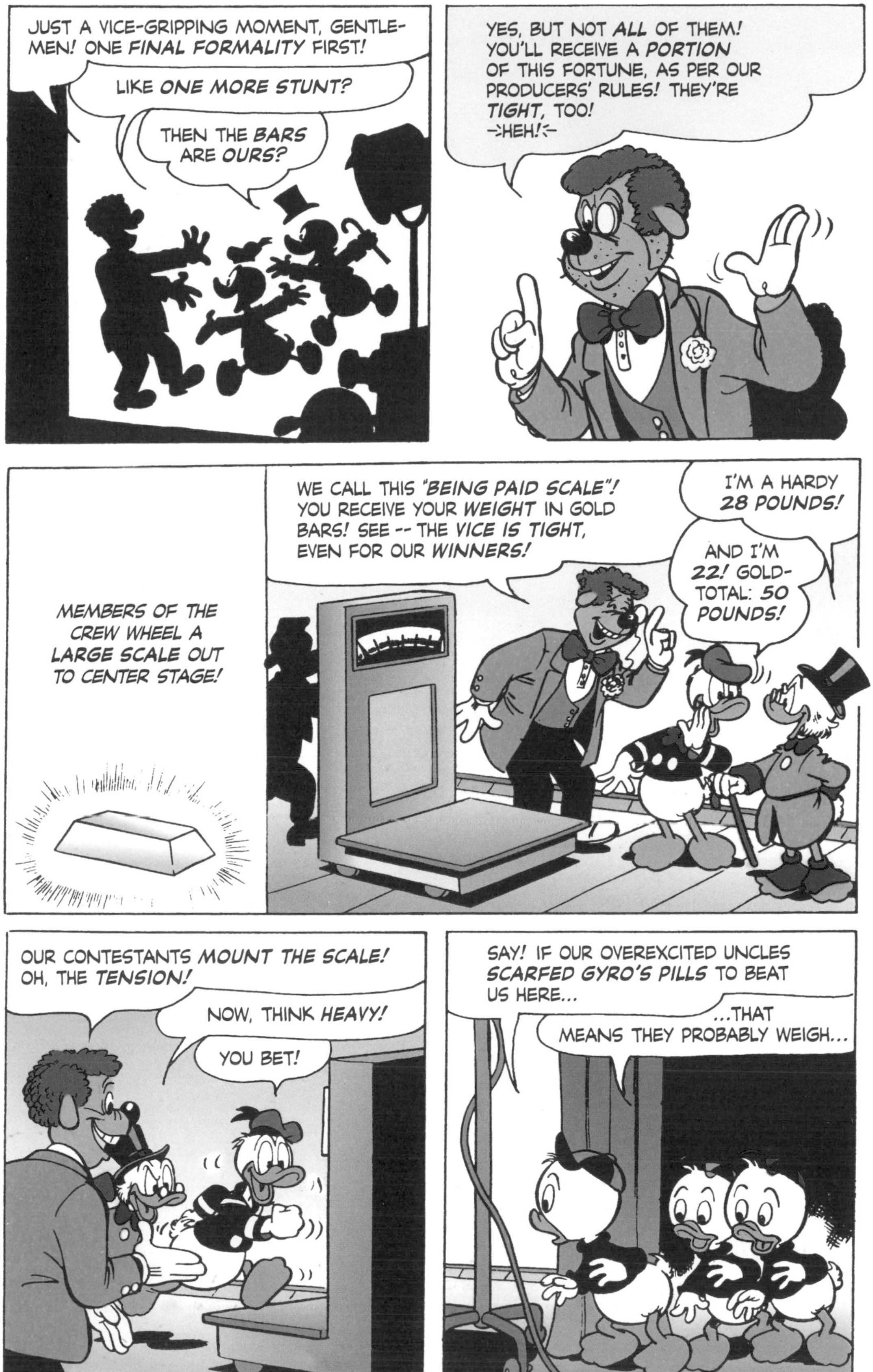
JUST A VICE-GRIPPING MOMENT, GENTLEMEN! ONE FINAL FORMALITY FIRST!
LIKE ONE MORE STUNT?
THEN THE BARS ARE OURS?
YES, BUT NOT ALL OF THEM! YOU'LL RECEIVE A PORTION OF THIS FORTUNE, AS PER OUR PRODUCERS' RULES! THEY'RE TIGHT, TOO! -HEH!-
MEMBERS OF THE CREW WHEEL A LARGE SCALE OUT TO CENTER STAGE!
WE CALL THIS "BEING PAID SCALE"! YOU RECEIVE YOUR WEIGHT IN GOLD BARS! SEE -- THE VICE IS TIGHT, EVEN FOR OUR WINNERS!
I'M A HARDY 28 POUNDS!
AND I'M 22! GOLD-TOTAL: 50 POUNDS!
OUR CONTESTANTS MOUNT THE SCALE! OH, THE TENSION!
NOW, THINK HEAVY!
YOU BET!
SAY! IF OUR OVEREXCITED UNCLES SCARFED GYRO'S PILLS TO BEAT US HERE...
...THAT MEANS THEY PROBABLY WEIGH...

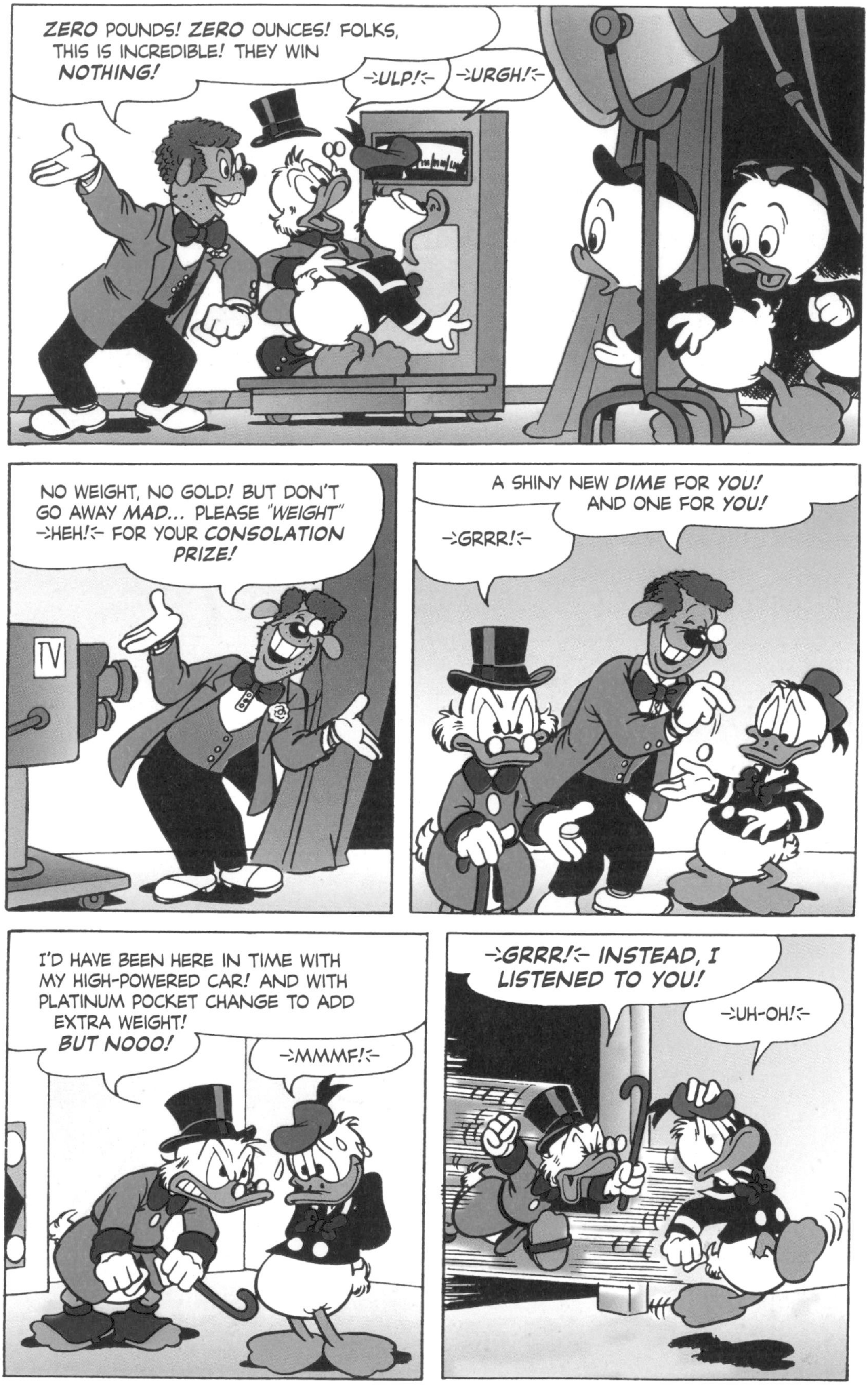
ZERO POUNDS! ZERO OUNCES! FOLKS, THIS IS INCREDIBLE! THEY WIN NOTHING!
ULP!
URGH!
NO WEIGHT, NO GOLD! BUT DON'T GO AWAY MAD... PLEASE "WEIGHT" HEH! FOR YOUR CONSOLATION PRIZE!
TV
A SHINY NEW DIME FOR YOU! AND ONE FOR YOU!
GRRR!
I'D HAVE BEEN HERE IN TIME WITH MY HIGH-POWERED CAR! AND WITH PLATINUM POCKET CHANGE TO ADD EXTRA WEIGHT! BUT NOOO!
MMMF!
GRRR! INSTEAD, I LISTENED TO YOU!
UH-OH!

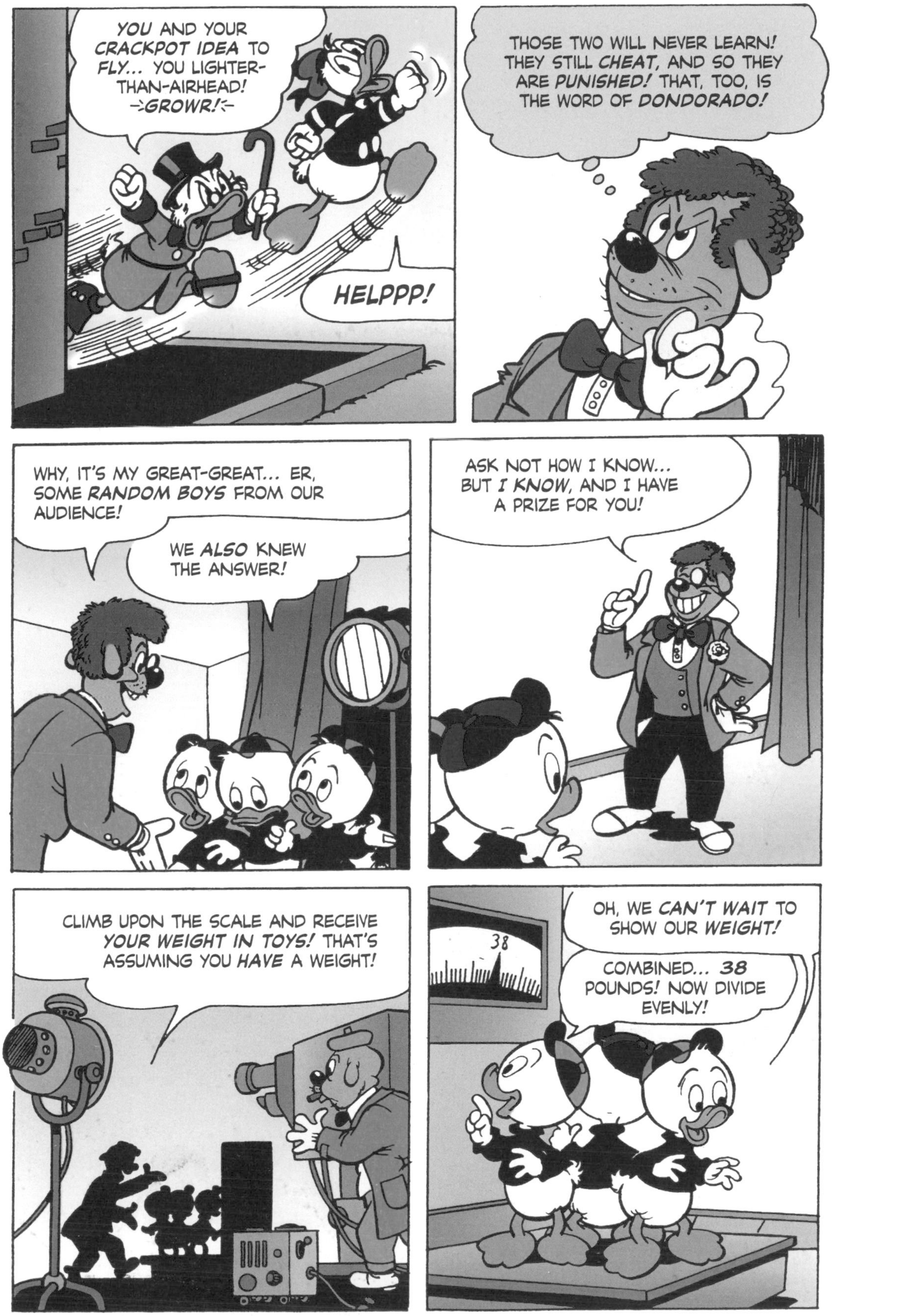

YOU AND YOUR CRACKPOT IDEA TO FLY... YOU LIGHTER-THAN-AIRHEAD! -GROWR!-
HELPPP!
THOSE TWO WILL NEVER LEARN! THEY STILL CHEAT, AND SO THEY ARE PUNISHED! THAT, TOO, IS THE WORD OF DONDORADO!
WHY, IT'S MY GREAT-GREAT... ER, SOME RANDOM BOYS FROM OUR AUDIENCE!
WE ALSO KNEW THE ANSWER!
ASK NOT HOW I KNOW... BUT I KNOW, AND I HAVE A PRIZE FOR YOU!
CLIMB UPON THE SCALE AND RECEIVE YOUR WEIGHT IN TOYS! THAT'S ASSUMING YOU HAVE A WEIGHT!
38
OH, WE CAN'T WAIT TO SHOW OUR WEIGHT!
COMBINED... 38 POUNDS! NOW DIVIDE EVENLY!

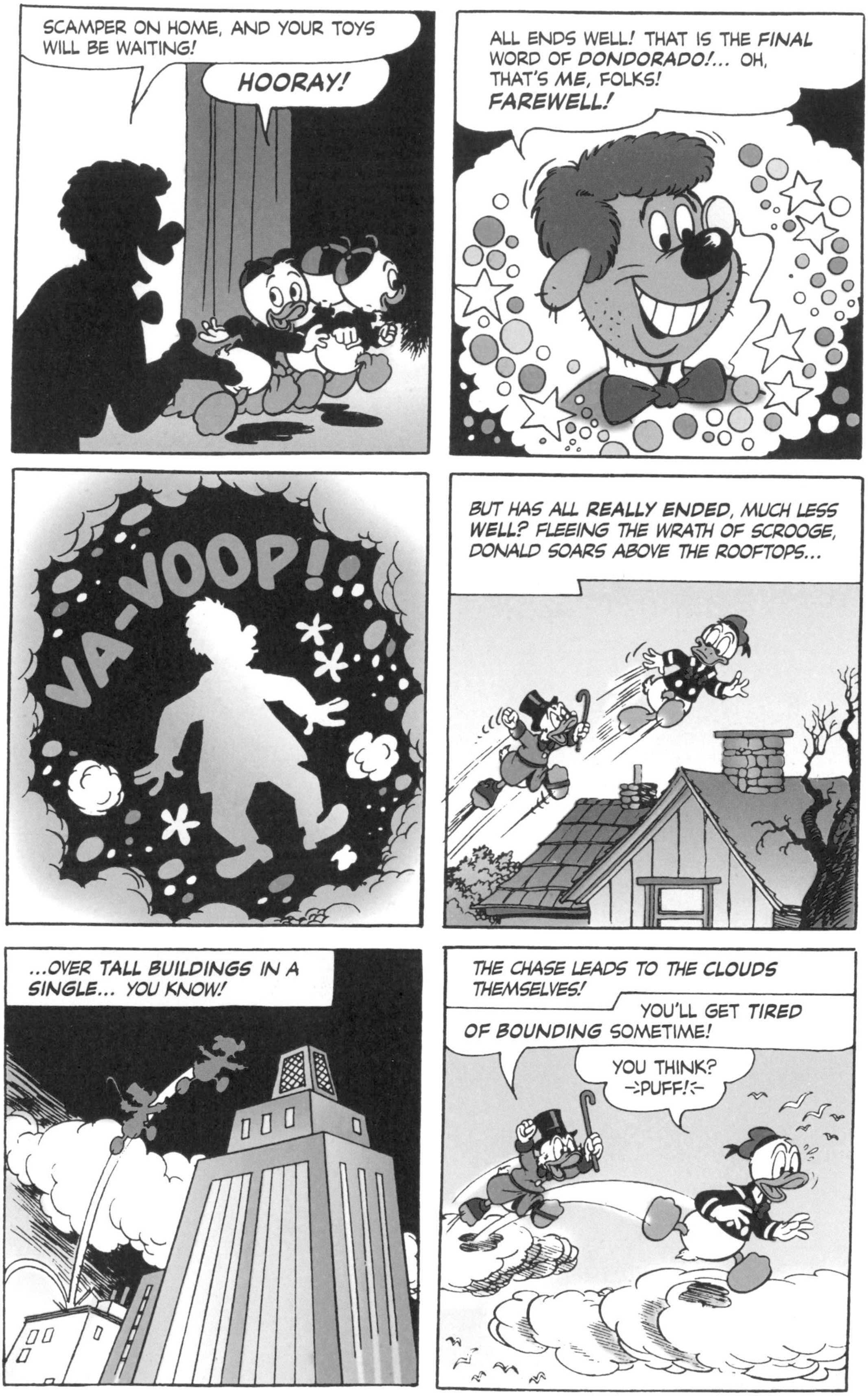
SCAMPER ON HOME, AND YOUR TOYS WILL BE WAITING!
HOORAY!
ALL ENDS WELL! THAT IS THE FINAL WORD OF DONDORADO!... OH, THAT'S ME, FOLKS! FAREWELL!
VA-VOOP!
BUT HAS ALL REALLY ENDED, MUCH LESS WELL? FLEEING THE WRATH OF SCROOGE, DONALD SOARS ABOVE THE ROOFTOPS...
...OVER TALL BUILDINGS IN A SINGLE... YOU KNOW!
THE CHASE LEADS TO THE CLOUDS THEMSELVES!
YOU'LL GET TIRED OF BOUNDING SOMETIME!
YOU THINK? -PUFF!-

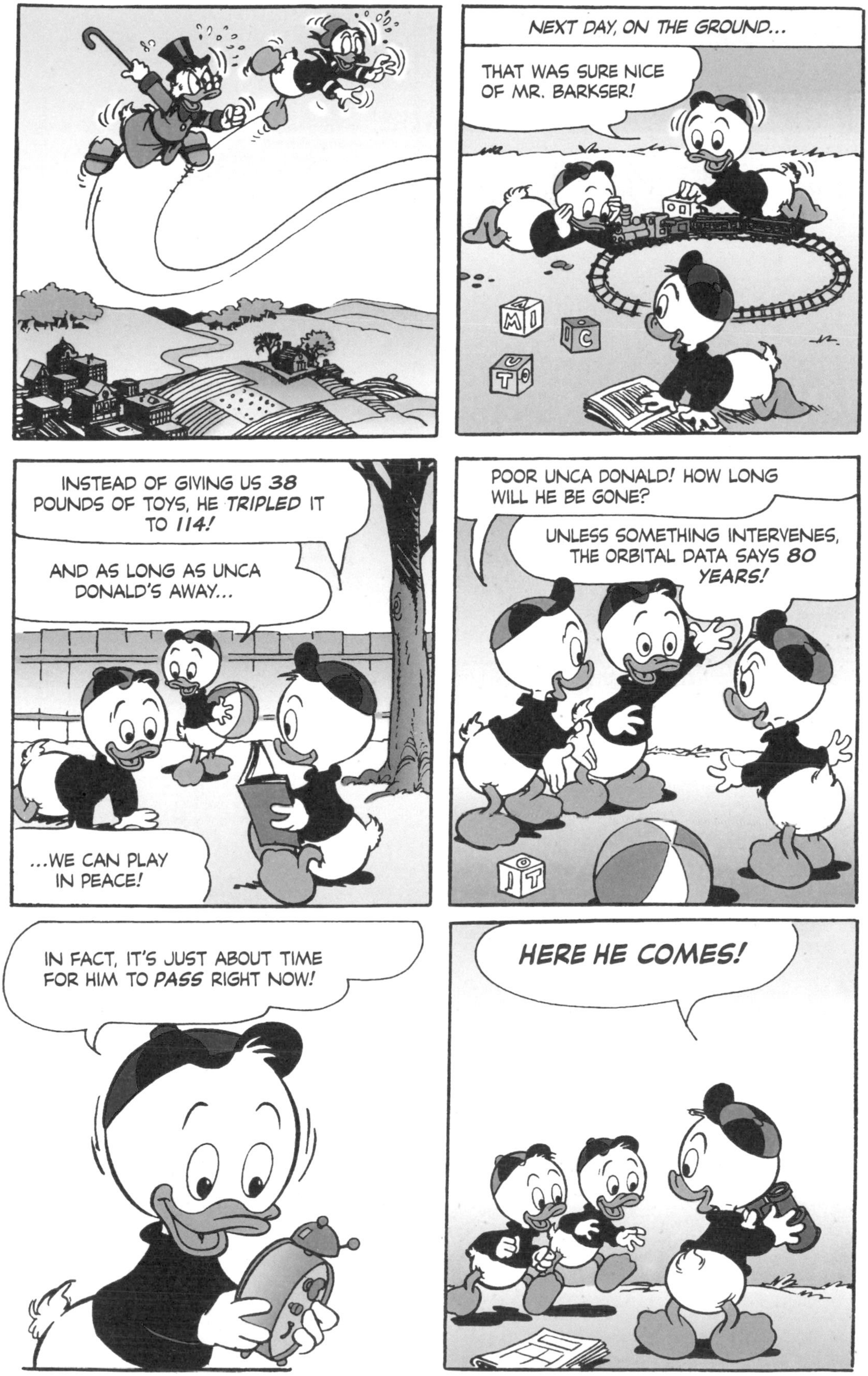
NEXT DAY, ON THE GROUND...
THAT WAS SURE NICE OF MR. BARKSER!
INSTEAD OF GIVING US 38 POUNDS OF TOYS, HE TRIPLED IT TO 114!
AND AS LONG AS UNCA DONALD'S AWAY...
...WE CAN PLAY IN PEACE!
POOR UNCA DONALD! HOW LONG WILL HE BE GONE?
UNLESS SOMETHING INTERVENES, THE ORBITAL DATA SAYS 80 YEARS!
IN FACT, IT'S JUST ABOUT TIME FOR HIM TO PASS RIGHT NOW!
HERE HE COMES!

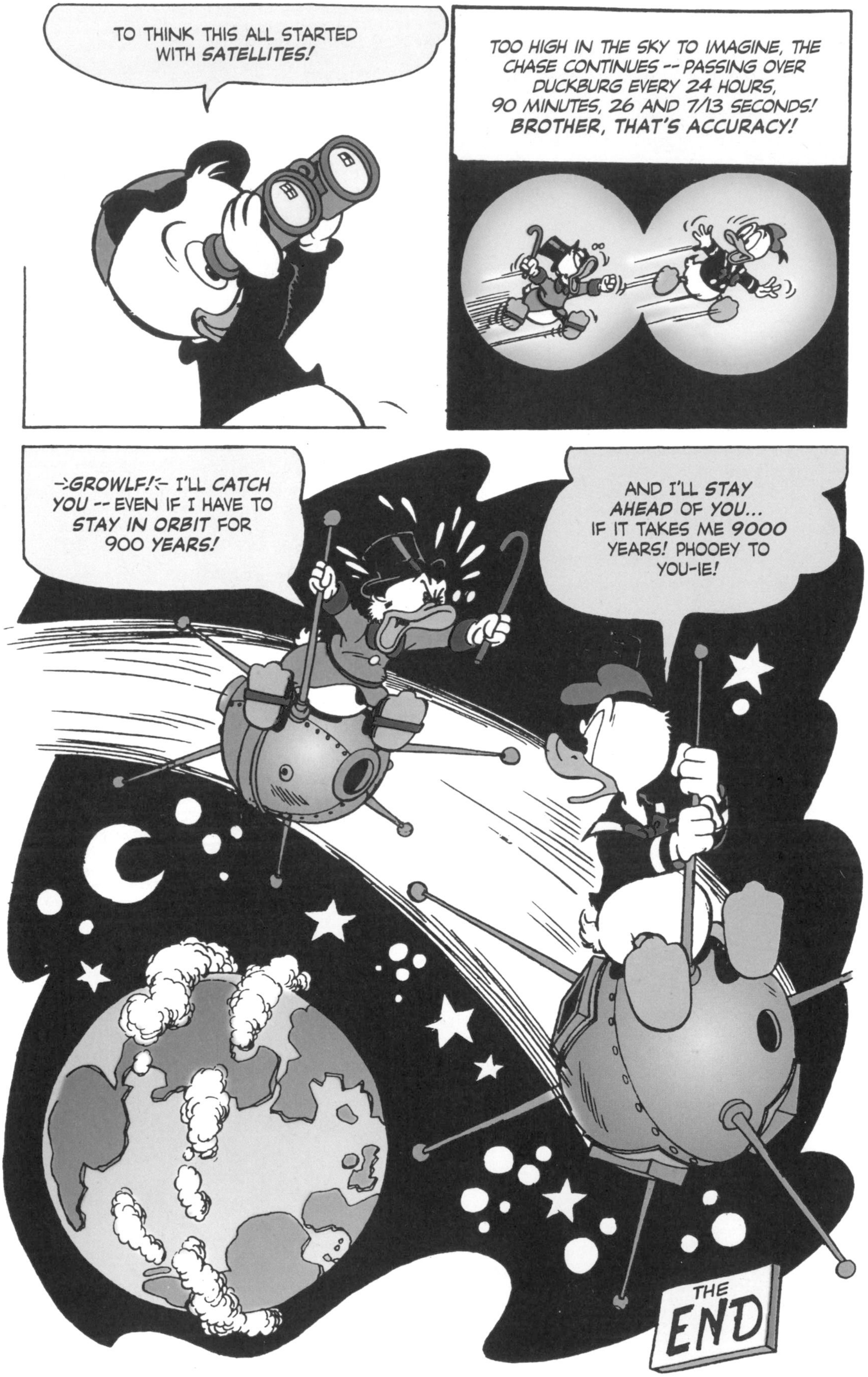
TO THINK THIS ALL STARTED WITH SATELLITES!
TOO HIGH IN THE SKY TO IMAGINE, THE CHASE CONTINUES -- PASSING OVER DUCKBURG EVERY 24 HOURS, 90 MINUTES, 26 AND 7/13 SECONDS! BROTHER, THAT'S ACCURACY!
-GROWLF!- I'LL CATCH YOU -- EVEN IF I HAVE TO STAY IN ORBIT FOR 900 YEARS!
AND I'LL STAY AHEAD OF YOU... IF IT TAKES ME 9000 YEARS! PHOOEY TO YOU-IE!
THE END

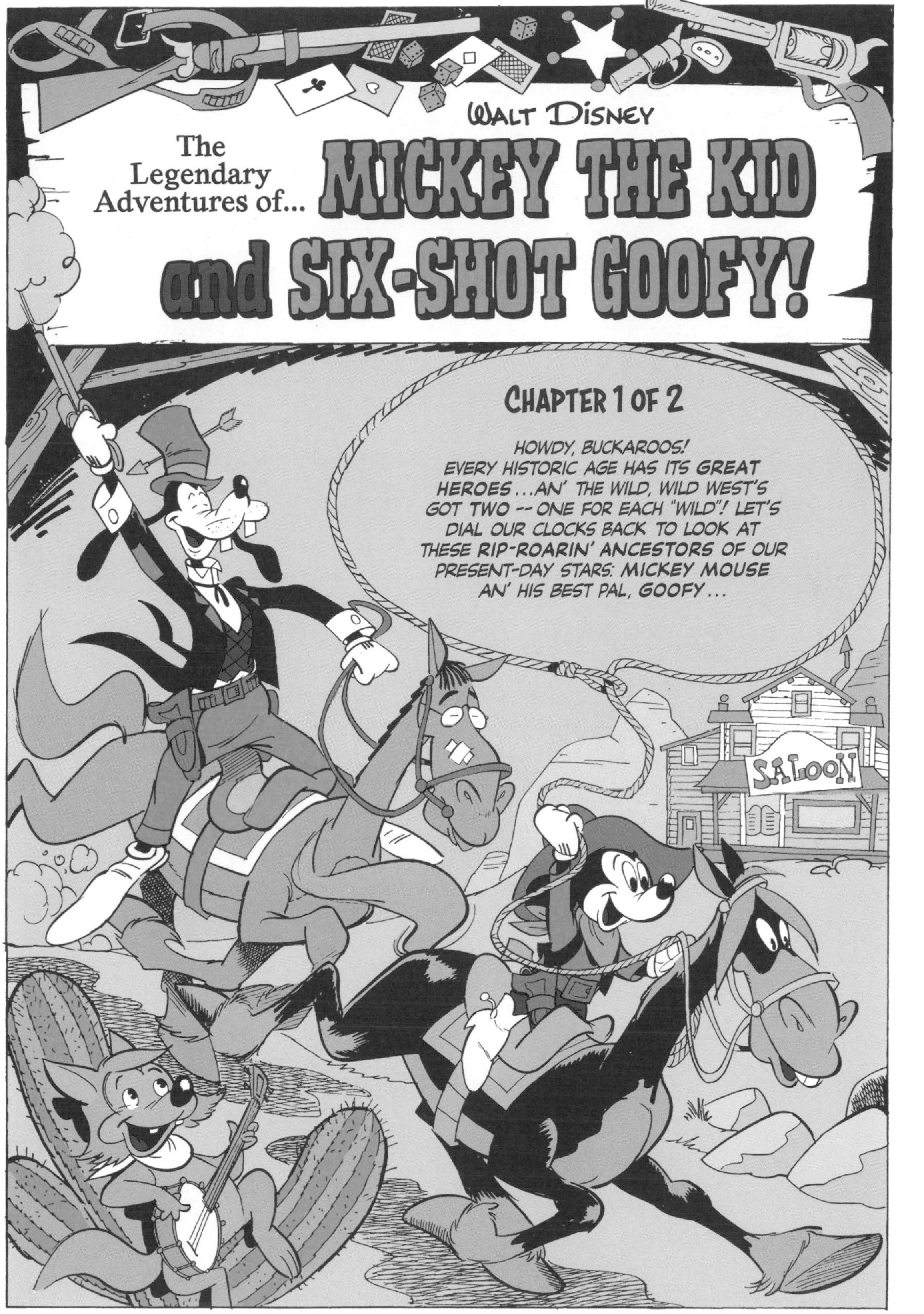
WALT DISNEY
The Legendary Adventures of...
MICKEY THE KID and SIX-SHOT GOOFY!
CHAPTER 1 OF 2
HOWDY, BUCKAROOS! EVERY HISTORIC AGE HAS ITS GREAT HEROES ...AN' THE WILD, WILD WEST'S GOT TWO -- ONE FOR EACH "WILD"! LET'S DIAL OUR CLOCKS BACK TO LOOK AT THESE RIP-ROARIN' ANCESTORS OF OUR PRESENT-DAY STARS: MICKEY MOUSE AN' HIS BEST PAL, GOOFY ...
SALOON

STORY BY GUIDO MARTINA • ART BY GIOVAN BATTISTA CARPI
DIALOGUE AND TRANSLATION BY JONATHAN H. GRAY

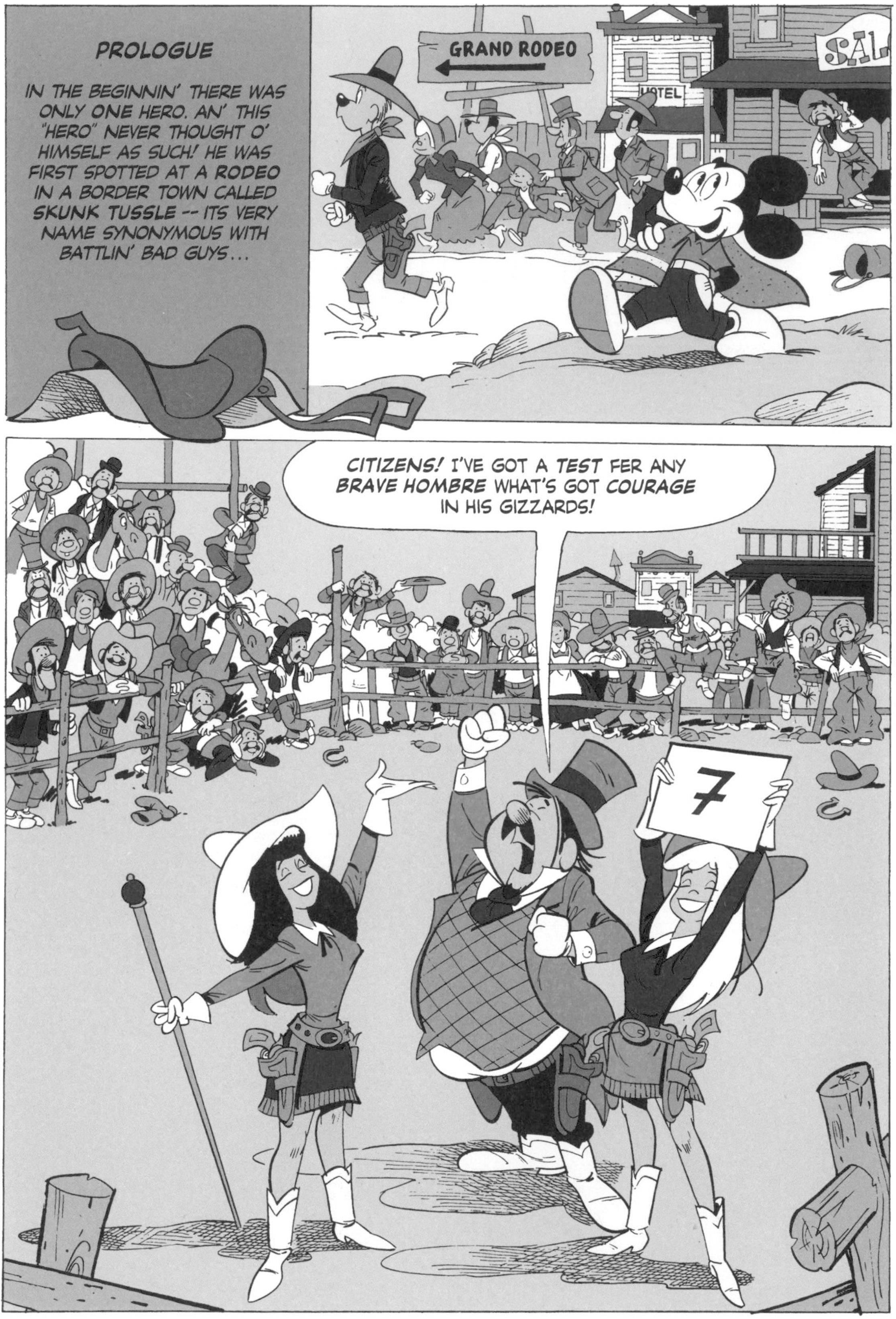
PROLOGUE
IN THE BEGINNIN' THERE WAS ONLY ONE HERO. AN' THIS "HERO" NEVER THOUGHT O' HIMSELF AS SUCH! HE WAS FIRST SPOTTED AT A RODEO IN A BORDER TOWN CALLED SKUNK TUSSLE -- ITS VERY NAME SYNONYMOUS WITH BATTLIN' BAD GUYS...
GRAND RODEO
HOTEL
CITIZENS! I'VE GOT A TEST FER ANY BRAVE HOMBRE WHAT'S GOT COURAGE IN HIS GIZZARDS!
7

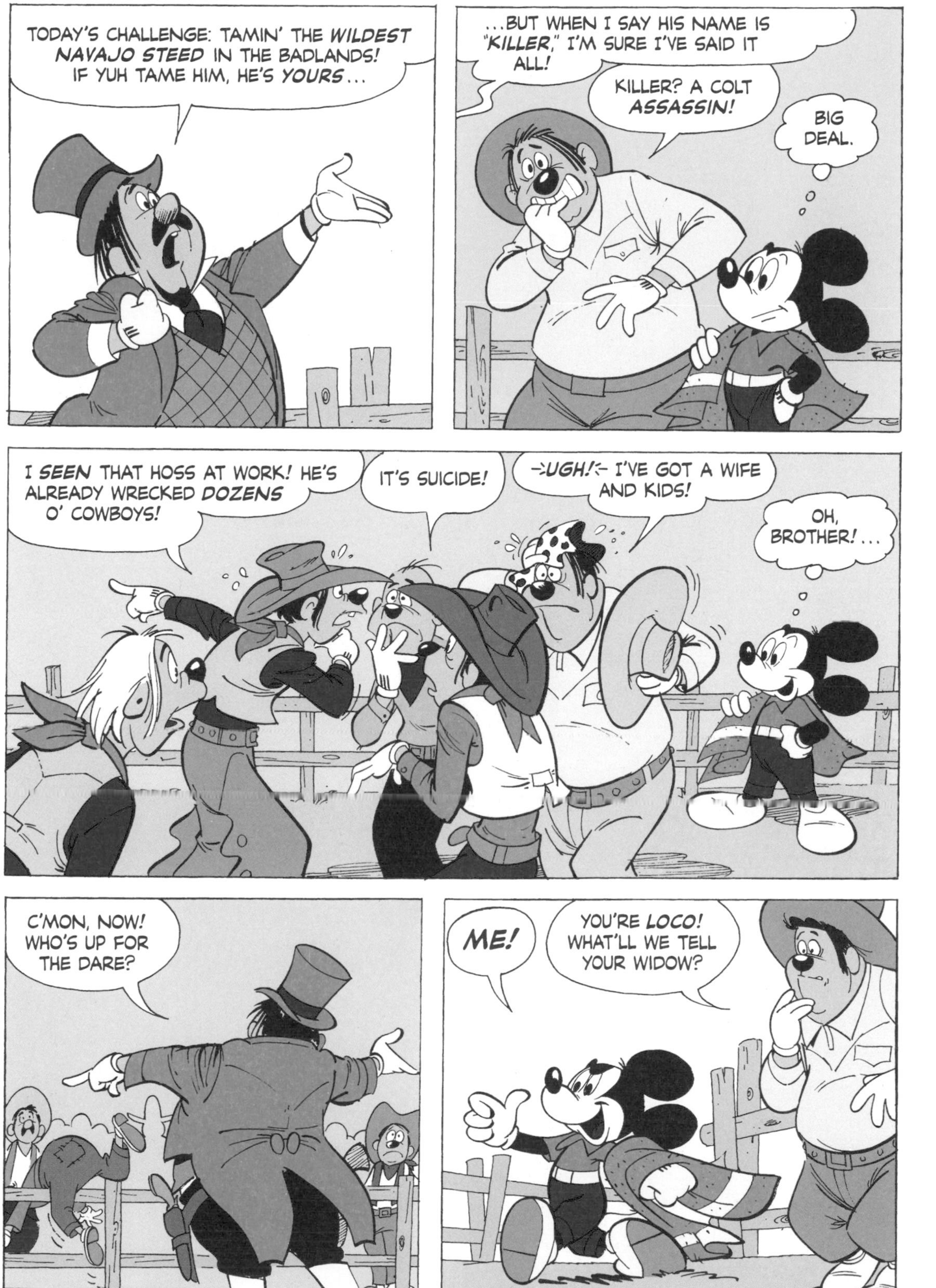
TODAY'S CHALLENGE: TAMIN' THE WILDEST NAVAJO STEED IN THE BADLANDS! IF YUH TAME HIM, HE'S YOURS...
...BUT WHEN I SAY HIS NAME IS "KILLER," I'M SURE I'VE SAID IT ALL!
KILLER? A COLT ASSASSIN!
BIG DEAL.
I SEEN THAT HOSS AT WORK! HE'S ALREADY WRECKED DOZENS O' COWBOYS!
IT'S SUICIDE!
UGH! I'VE GOT A WIFE AND KIDS!
OH, BROTHER!...
C'MON, NOW! WHO'S UP FOR THE DARE?
ME!
YOU'RE LOCO! WHAT'LL WE TELL YOUR WIDOW?

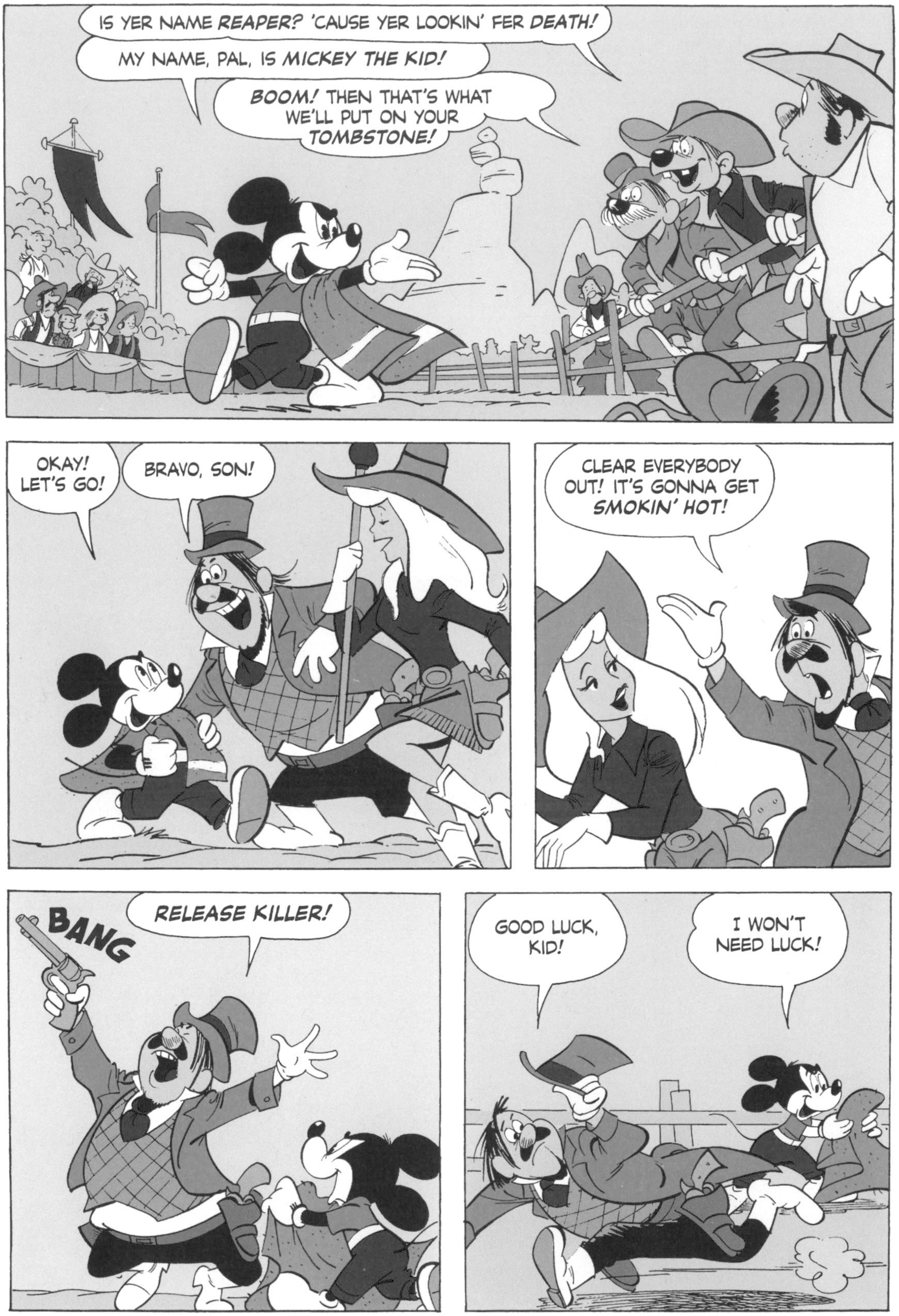
IS YER NAME REAPER? 'CAUSE YER LOOKIN' FER DEATH!
MY NAME, PAL, IS MICKEY THE KID!
BOOM! THEN THAT'S WHAT WE'LL PUT ON YOUR TOMBSTONE!
OKAY! LET'S GO!
BRAVO, SON!
CLEAR EVERYBODY OUT! IT'S GONNA GET SMOKIN' HOT!
BANG
RELEASE KILLER!
GOOD LUCK, KID!
I WON'T NEED LUCK!

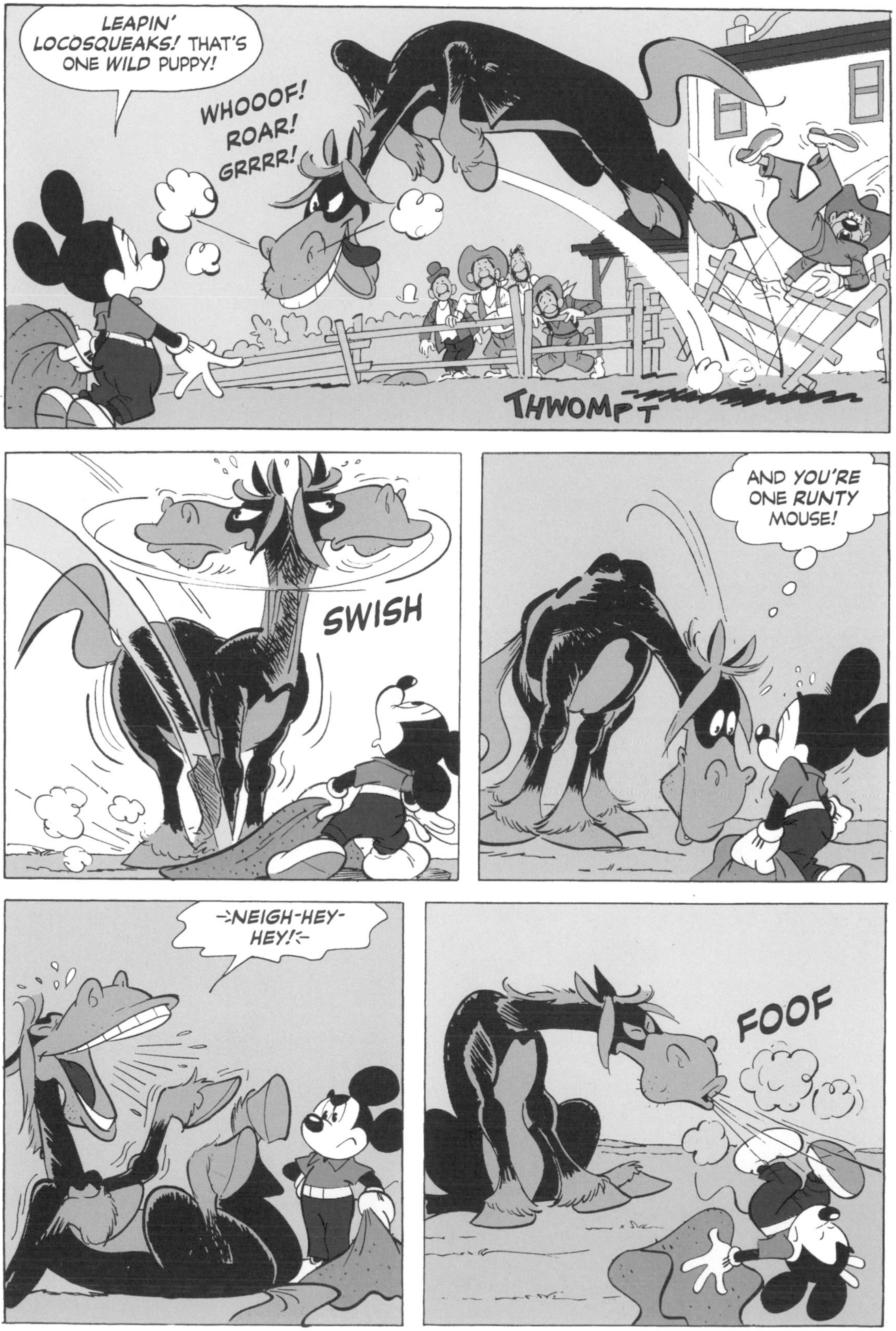
LEAPIN' LOCOSQUEAKS! THAT'S ONE WILD PUPPY!
WHOOOF! ROAR! GRRRR!
THWOMPT
SWISH
AND YOU'RE ONE RUNTY MOUSE!
-NEIGH-HEY-HEY!-
FOOF

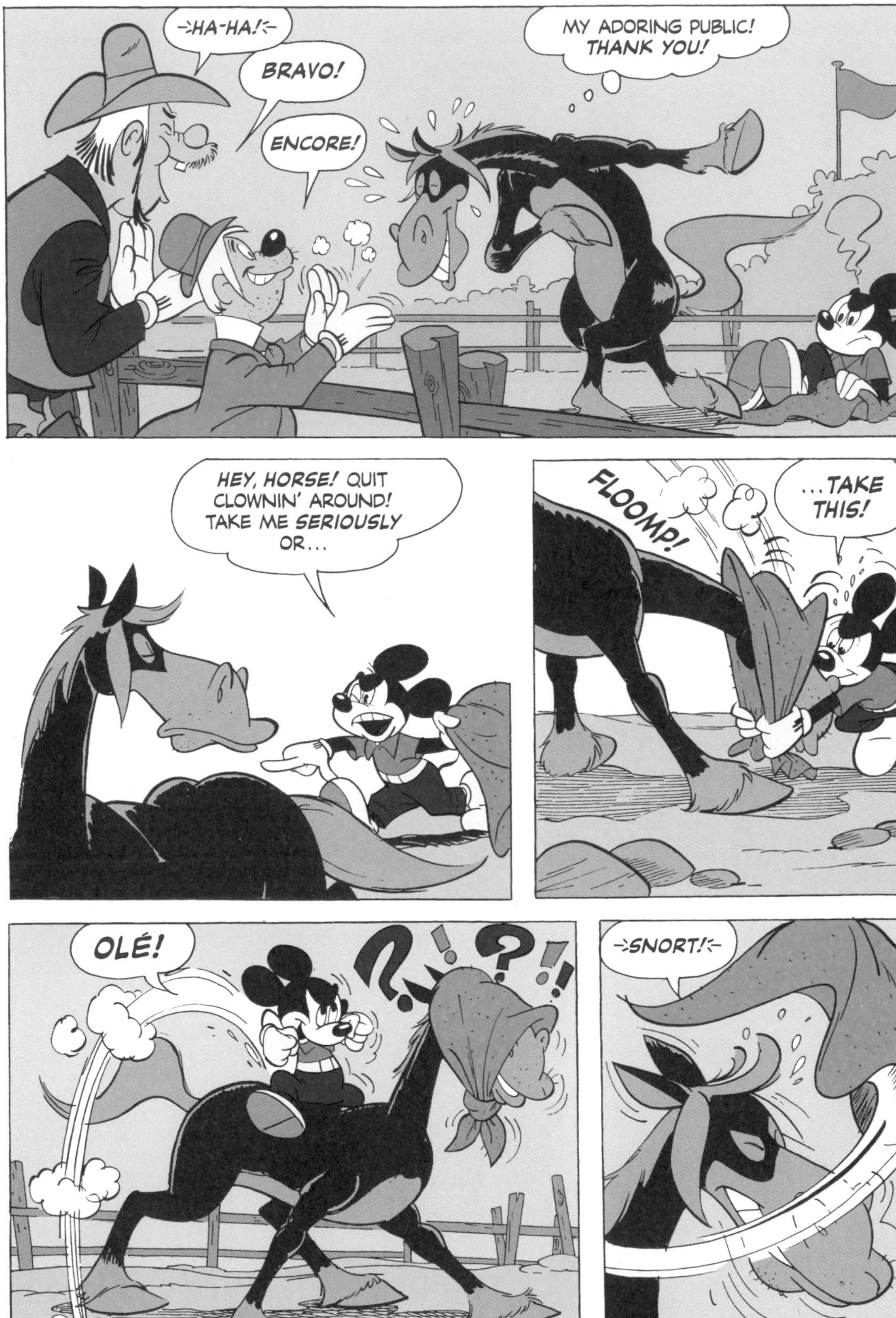

-HA-HA!-
BRAVO!
ENCORE!
MY ADORING PUBLIC! THANK YOU!
HEY, HORSE! QUIT CLOWNIN' AROUND! TAKE ME SERIOUSLY OR...
FLOOMP!
...TAKE THIS!
OLÉ!
-SNORT!-

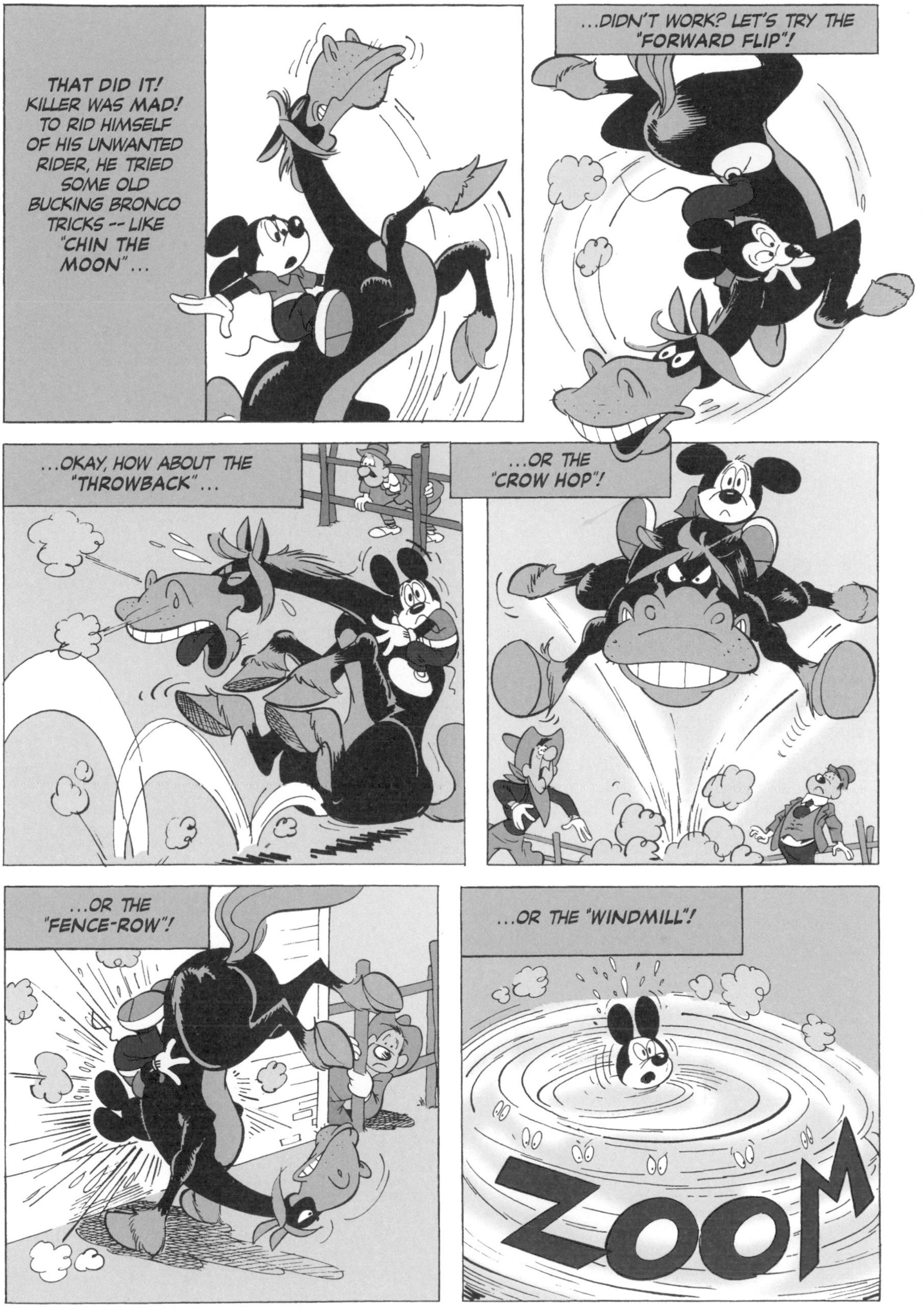
THAT DID IT! KILLER WAS MAD! TO RID HIMSELF OF HIS UNWANTED RIDER, HE TRIED SOME OLD BUCKING BRONCO TRICKS -- LIKE "CHIN THE MOON"...
...DIDN'T WORK? LET'S TRY THE "FORWARD FLIP"!
...OKAY, HOW ABOUT THE "THROWBACK"...
...OR THE "CROW HOP"!
...OR THE "FENCE-ROW"!
...OR THE "WINDMILL"!
ZOOM

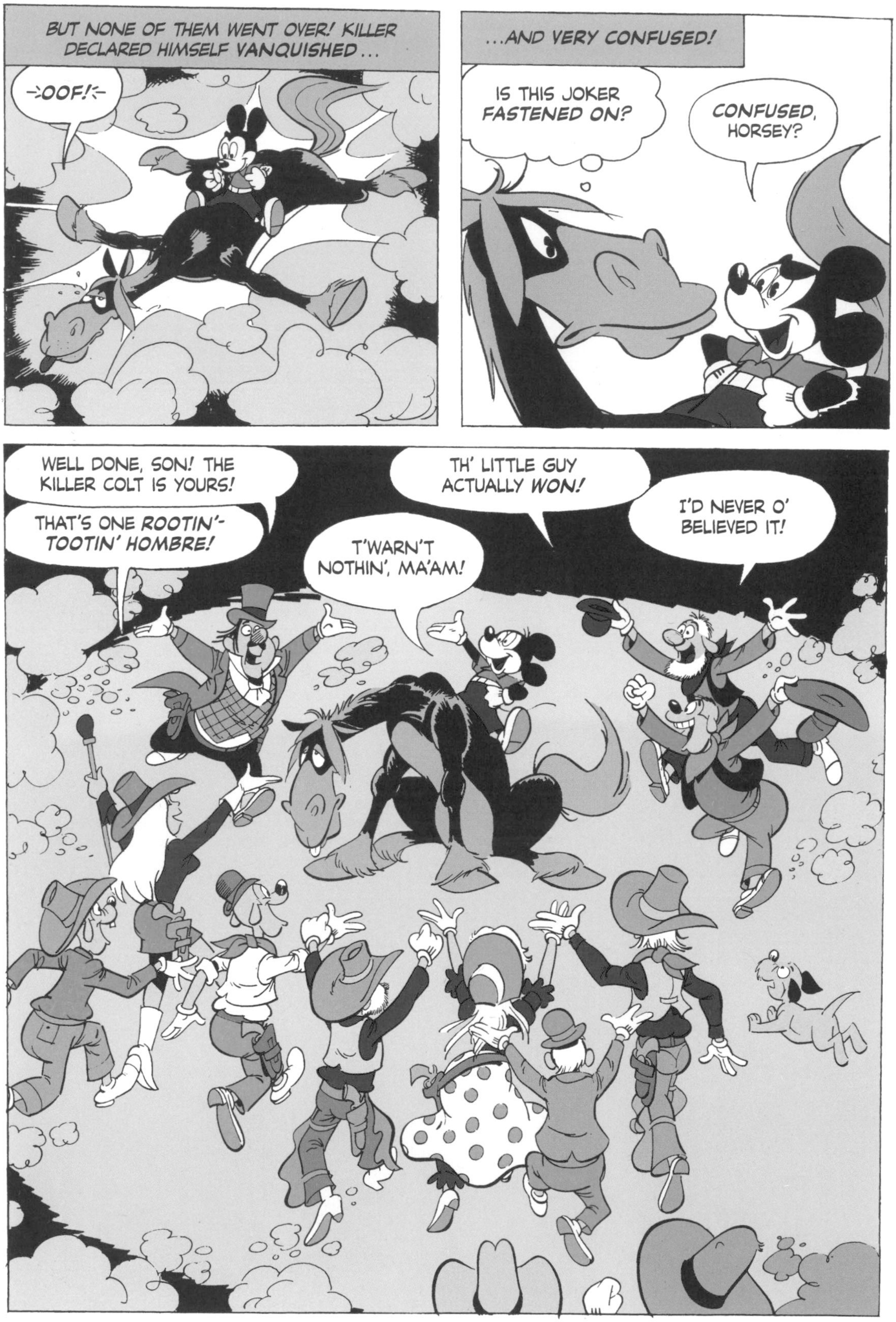
BUT NONE OF THEM WENT OVER! KILLER DECLARED HIMSELF VANQUISHED...
OOF!
...AND VERY CONFUSED!
IS THIS JOKER FASTENED ON?
CONFUSED, HORSEY?
WELL DONE, SON! THE KILLER COLT IS YOURS!
THAT'S ONE ROOTIN'-TOOTIN' HOMBRE!
T'WARN'T NOTHIN', MA'AM!
TH' LITTLE GUY ACTUALLY WON!
I'D NEVER O' BELIEVED IT!

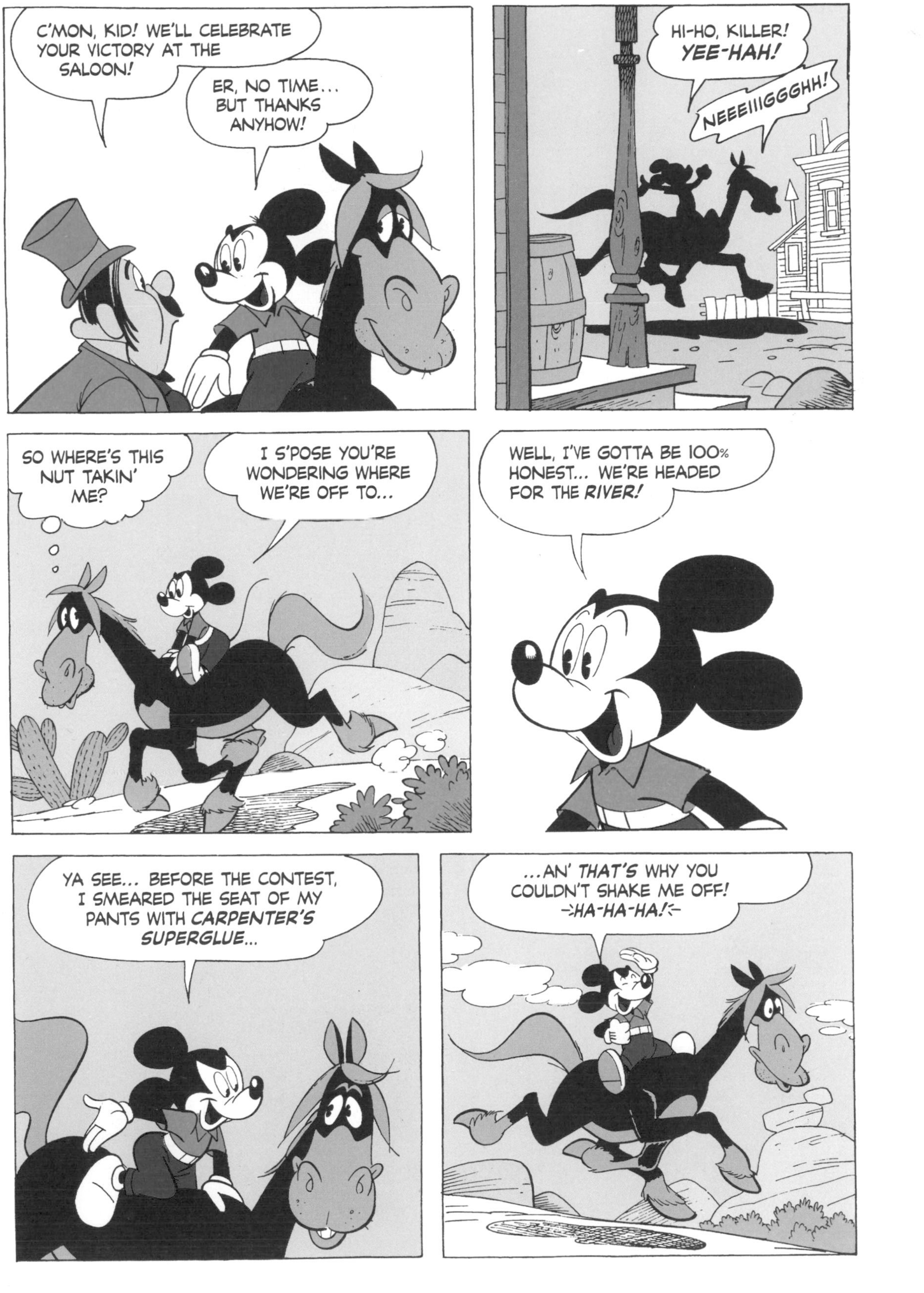
C'MON, KID! WE'LL CELEBRATE YOUR VICTORY AT THE SALOON!
ER, NO TIME... BUT THANKS ANYHOW!
HI-HO, KILLER! YEE-HAH!
NEEEIIIGGGHH!
SO WHERE'S THIS NUT TAKIN' ME?
I S'POSE YOU'RE WONDERING WHERE WE'RE OFF TO...
WELL, I'VE GOTTA BE 100% HONEST... WE'RE HEADED FOR THE RIVER!
YA SEE... BEFORE THE CONTEST, I SMEARED THE SEAT OF MY PANTS WITH CARPENTER'S SUPERGLUE...
...AN' THAT'S WHY YOU COULDN'T SHAKE ME OFF! HA-HA-HA!

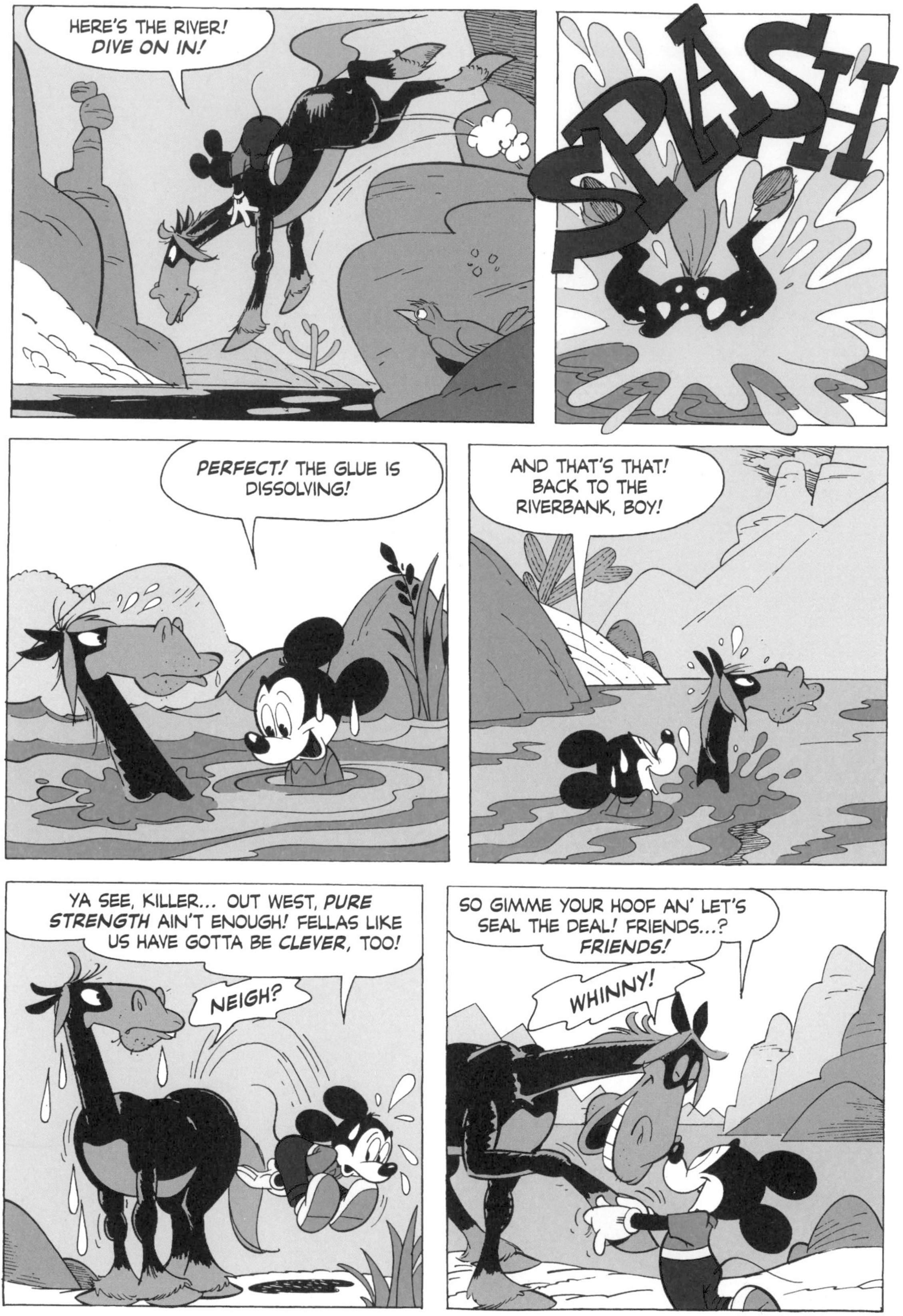
HERE'S THE RIVER! *DIVE ON IN!*
SPLASH
PERFECT! THE GLUE IS DISSOLVING!
AND THAT'S THAT! BACK TO THE RIVERBANK, BOY!
YA SEE, KILLER... OUT WEST, *PURE STRENGTH* AIN'T ENOUGH! FELLAS LIKE US HAVE GOTTA BE *CLEVER*, TOO!
NEIGH?
SO GIMME YOUR HOOF AN' LET'S SEAL THE DEAL! FRIENDS...? *FRIENDS!*
WHINNY!

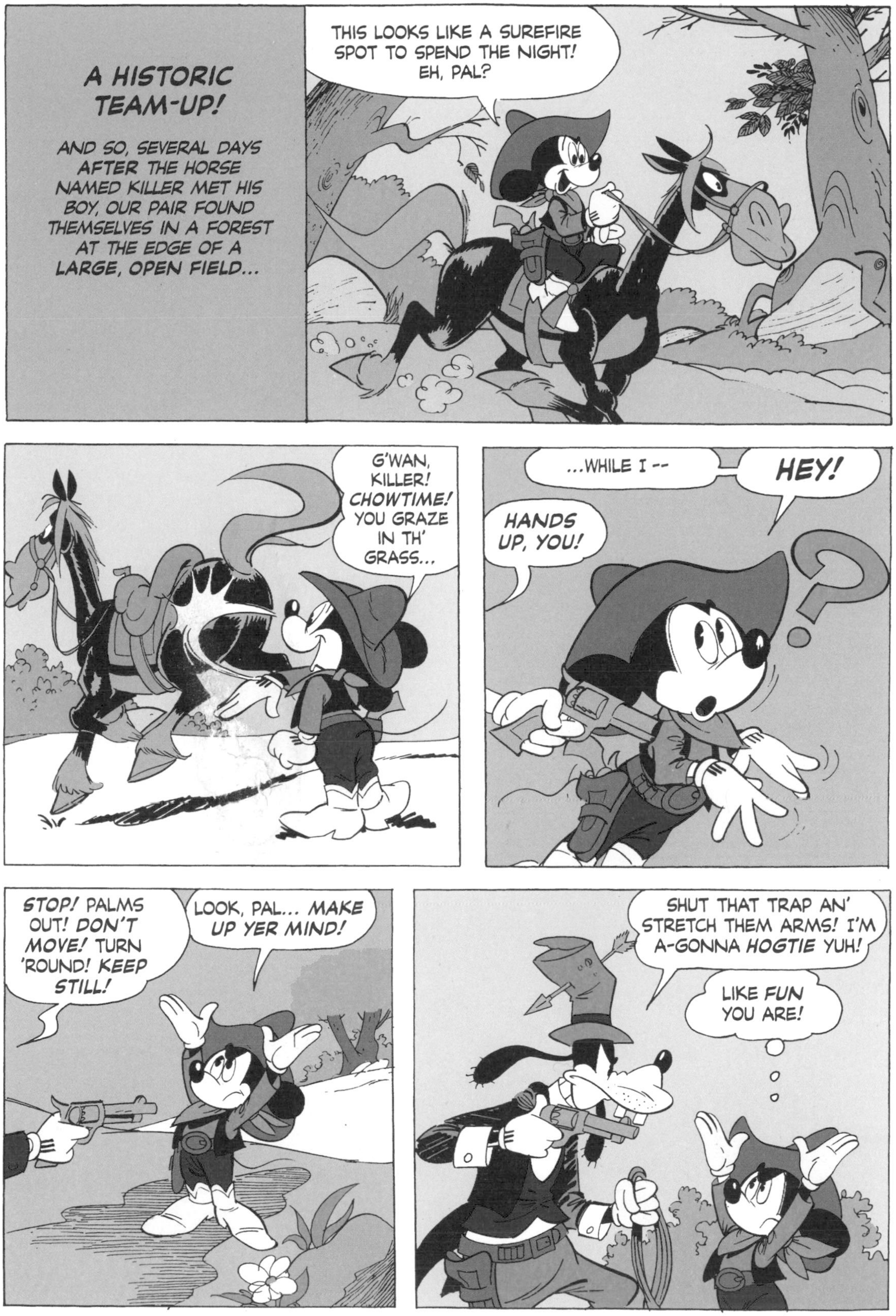
A HISTORIC TEAM-UP!
AND SO, SEVERAL DAYS AFTER THE HORSE NAMED KILLER MET HIS BOY, OUR PAIR FOUND THEMSELVES IN A FOREST AT THE EDGE OF A LARGE, OPEN FIELD...
THIS LOOKS LIKE A SUREFIRE SPOT TO SPEND THE NIGHT! EH, PAL?
G'WAN, KILLER! CHOWTIME! YOU GRAZE IN TH' GRASS...
...WHILE I --
HEY!
HANDS UP, YOU!
STOP! PALMS OUT! DON'T MOVE! TURN 'ROUND! KEEP STILL!
LOOK, PAL... MAKE UP YER MIND!
SHUT THAT TRAP AN' STRETCH THEM ARMS! I'M A-GONNA HOGTIE YUH!
LIKE FUN YOU ARE!

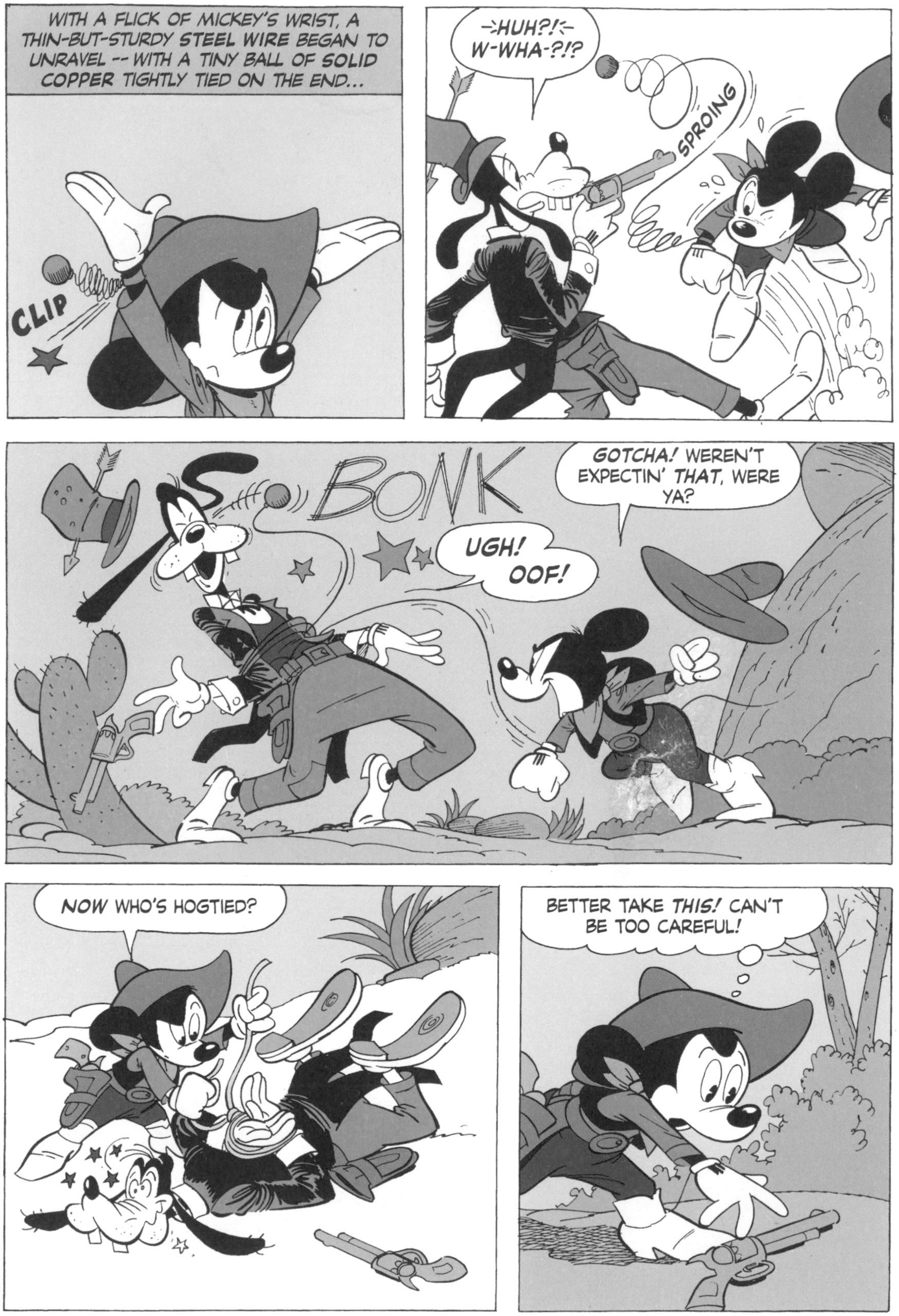
WITH A FLICK OF MICKEY'S WRIST, A THIN-BUT-STURDY STEEL WIRE BEGAN TO UNRAVEL -- WITH A TINY BALL OF SOLID COPPER TIGHTLY TIED ON THE END...
CLIP
-HUH?!- W-WHA-?!?
SPROING
BONK
GOTCHA! WEREN'T EXPECTIN' THAT, WERE YA?
UGH! OOF!
NOW WHO'S HOGTIED?
BETTER TAKE THIS! CAN'T BE TOO CAREFUL!

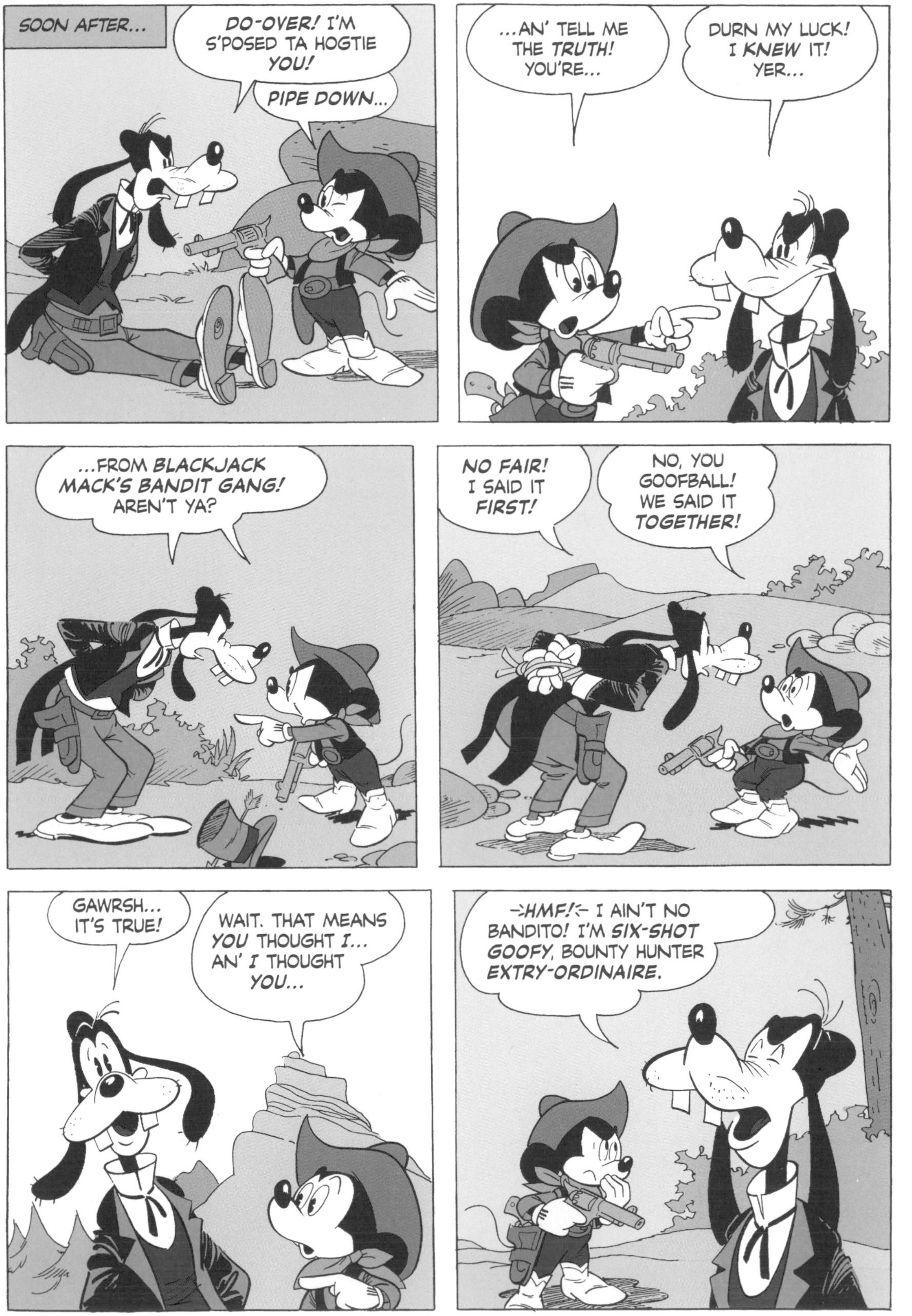
SOON AFTER...
DO-OVER! I'M S'POSED TA HOGTIE YOU!
PIPE DOWN...
...AN' TELL ME THE TRUTH! YOU'RE...
DURN MY LUCK! I KNEW IT! YER...
...FROM BLACKJACK MACK'S BANDIT GANG! AREN'T YA?
NO FAIR! I SAID IT FIRST!
NO, YOU GOOFBALL! WE SAID IT TOGETHER!
GAWRSH... IT'S TRUE!
WAIT. THAT MEANS YOU THOUGHT I... AN' I THOUGHT YOU...
-HMF!- I AIN'T NO BANDITO! I'M SIX-SHOT GOOFY, BOUNTY HUNTER EXTRY-ORDINAIRE.

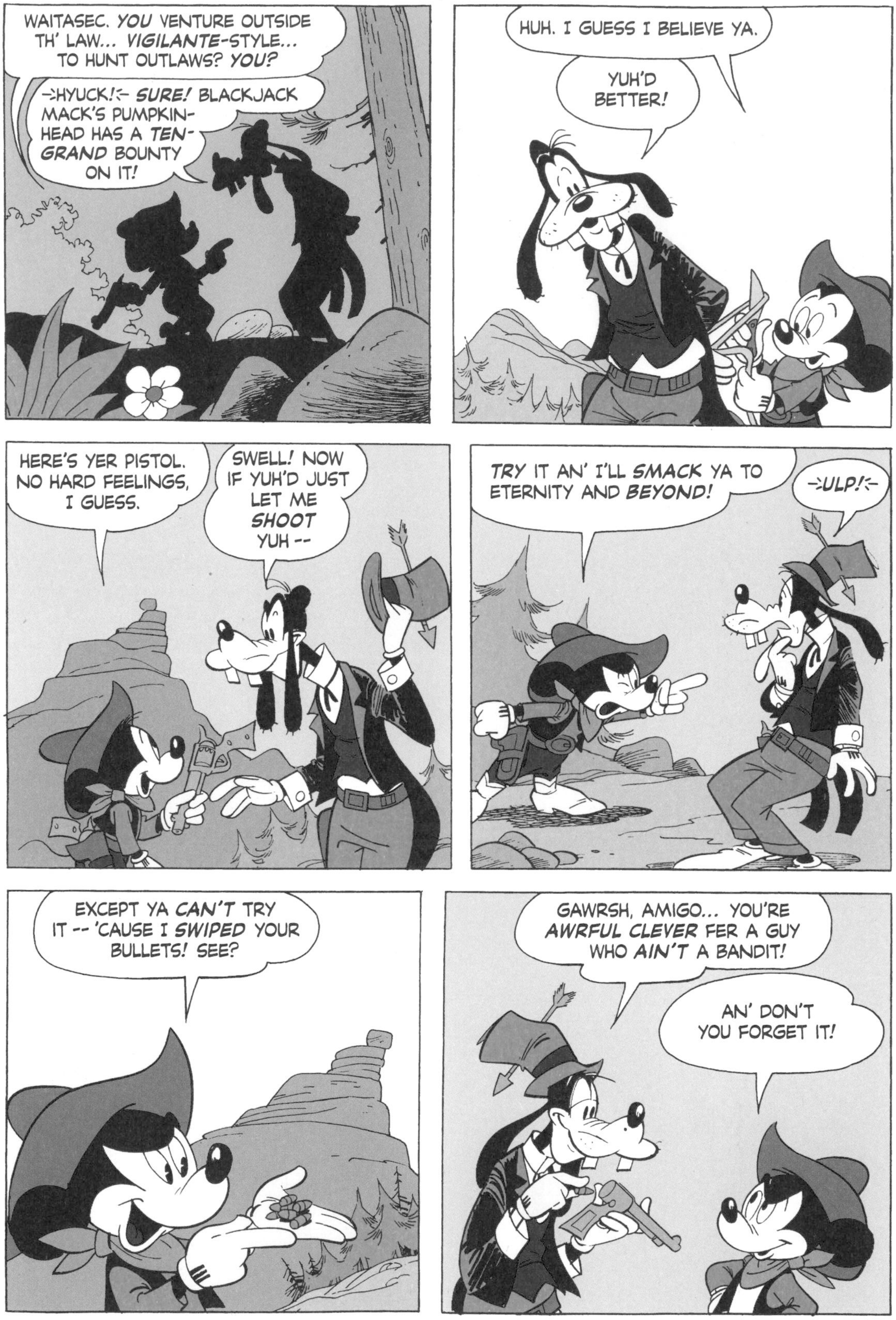
WAITASEC. *YOU* VENTURE OUTSIDE TH' LAW... *VIGILANTE*-STYLE... TO HUNT OUTLAWS? *YOU?*
-HYUCK!- *SURE!* BLACKJACK MACK'S PUMPKIN-HEAD HAS A *TEN-GRAND* BOUNTY ON IT!
HUH. I GUESS I BELIEVE YA.
YUH'D BETTER!
HERE'S YER PISTOL. NO HARD FEELINGS, I GUESS.
SWELL! NOW IF YUH'D JUST LET ME *SHOOT* YUH --
TRY IT AN' I'LL *SMACK* YA TO ETERNITY AND *BEYOND!*
-*ULP!*-
EXCEPT YA *CAN'T* TRY IT -- 'CAUSE I *SWIPED* YOUR BULLETS! SEE?
GAWRSH, AMIGO... YOU'RE *AWRFUL CLEVER* FER A GUY WHO *AIN'T* A BANDIT!
AN' DON'T YOU FORGET IT!

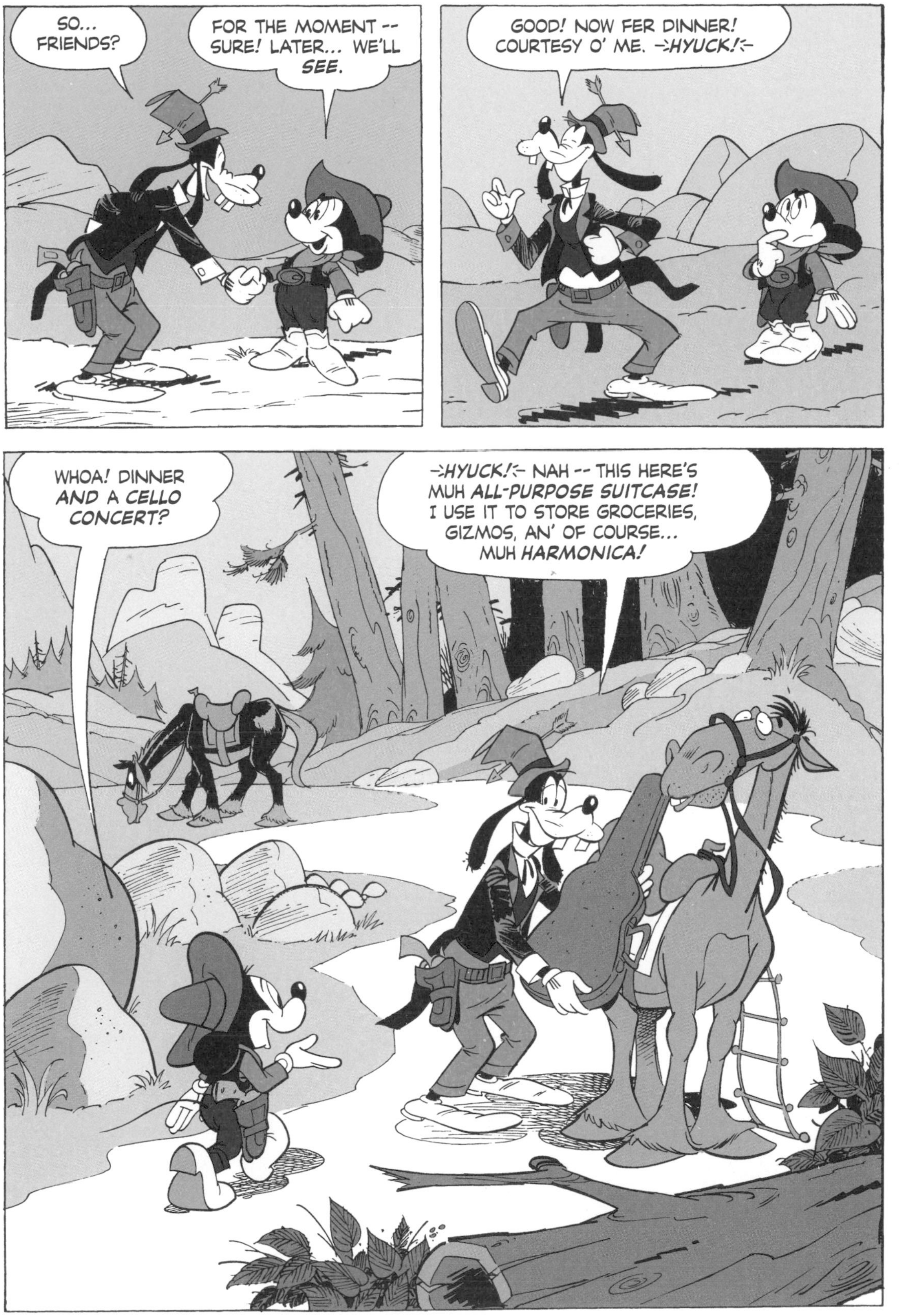
SO... FRIENDS?
FOR THE MOMENT -- SURE! LATER... WE'LL SEE.
GOOD! NOW FER DINNER! COURTESY O' ME. -HYUCK!-
WHOA! DINNER AND A CELLO CONCERT?
-HYUCK!- NAH -- THIS HERE'S MUH ALL-PURPOSE SUITCASE! I USE IT TO STORE GROCERIES, GIZMOS, AN' OF COURSE... MUH HARMONICA!

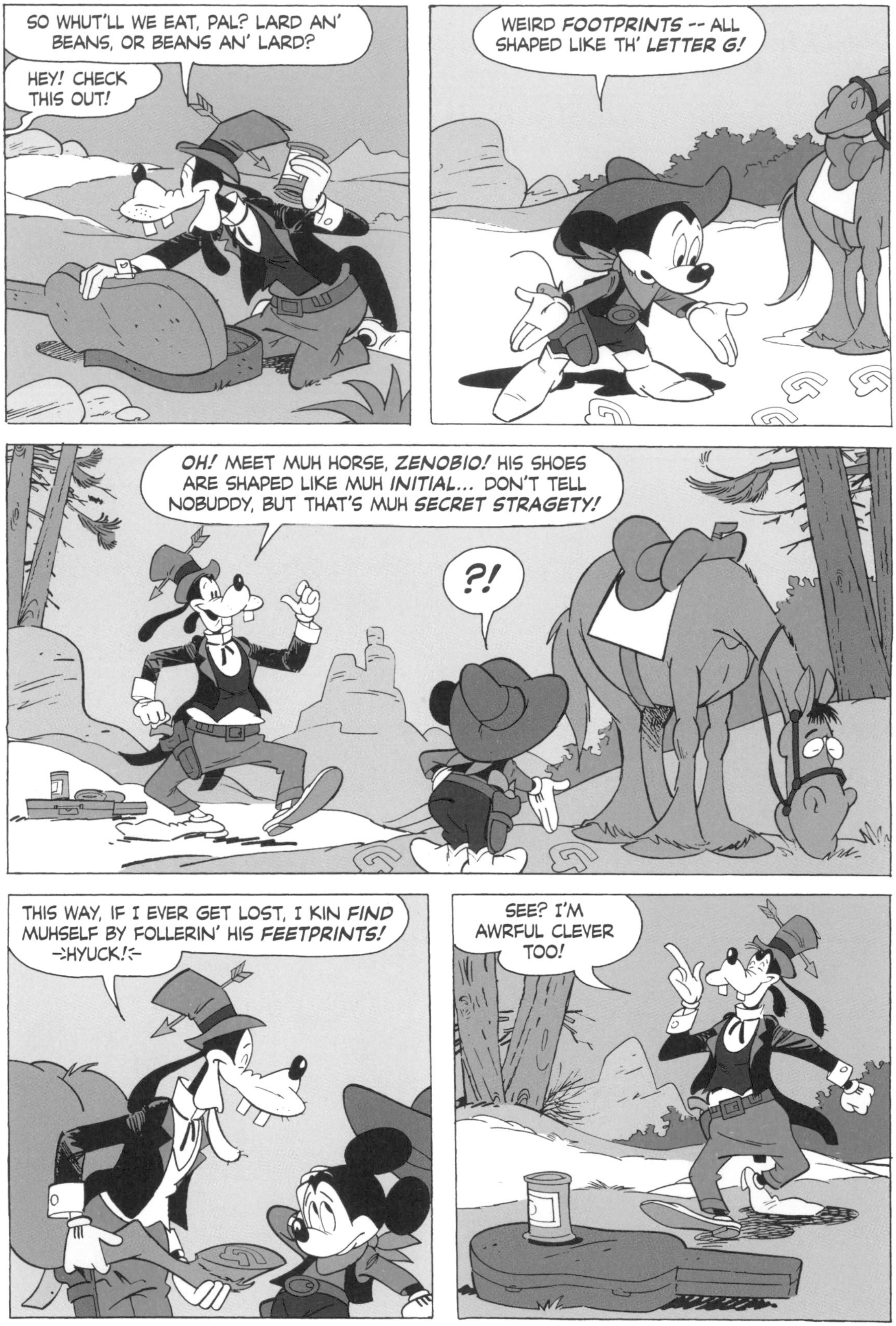
SO WHUT'LL WE EAT, PAL? LARD AN' BEANS, OR BEANS AN' LARD?
HEY! CHECK THIS OUT!
WEIRD FOOTPRINTS -- ALL SHAPED LIKE TH' LETTER G!
OH! MEET MUH HORSE, ZENOBIO! HIS SHOES ARE SHAPED LIKE MUH INITIAL... DON'T TELL NOBUDDY, BUT THAT'S MUH SECRET STRAGETY!
?!
THIS WAY, IF I EVER GET LOST, I KIN FIND MUHSELF BY FOLLERIN' HIS FEETPRINTS! -HYUCK!-
SEE? I'M AWRFUL CLEVER TOO!

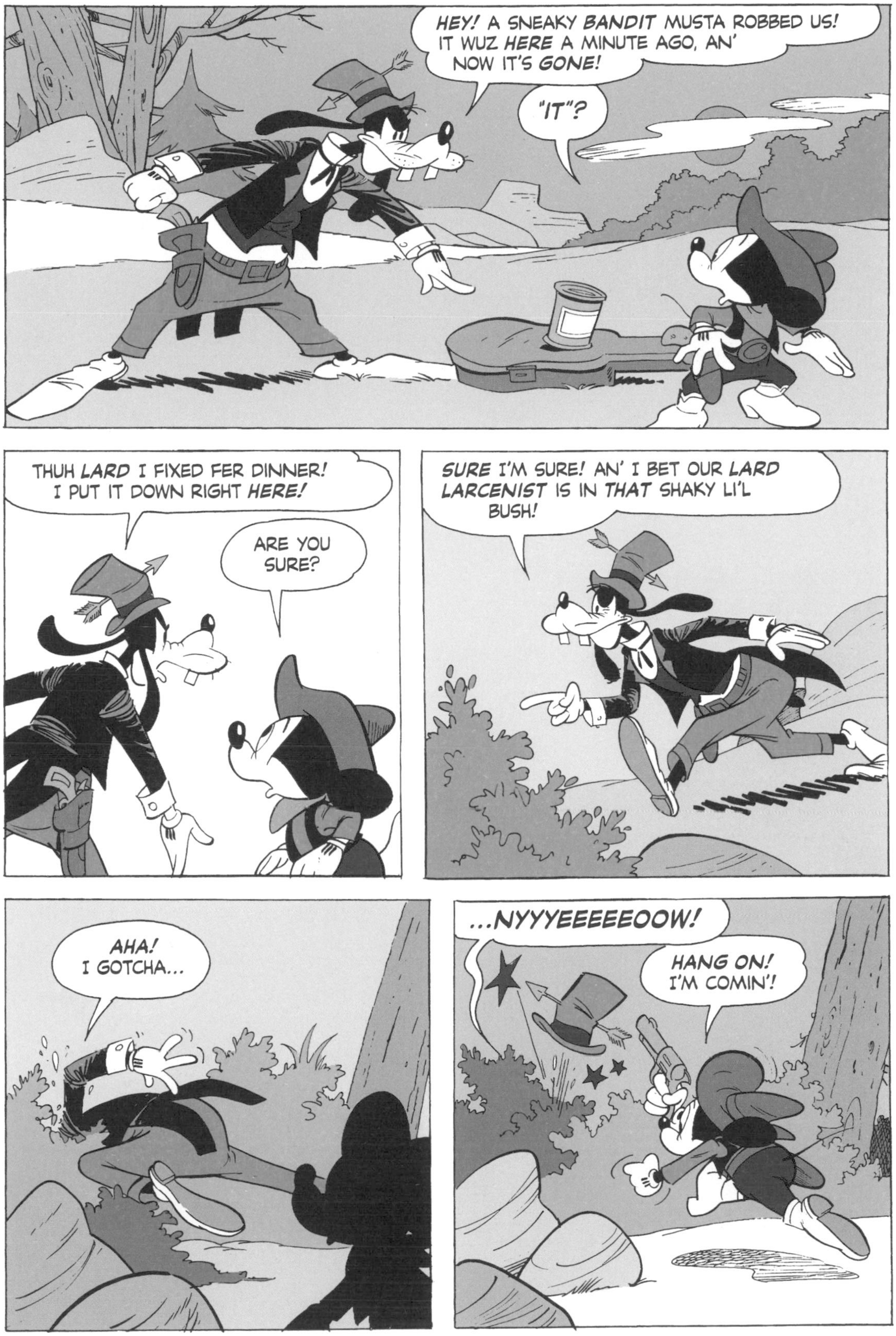
HEY! A SNEAKY BANDIT MUSTA ROBBED US! IT WUZ HERE A MINUTE AGO, AN' NOW IT'S GONE!
"IT"?
THUH LARD I FIXED FER DINNER! I PUT IT DOWN RIGHT HERE!
ARE YOU SURE?
SURE I'M SURE! AN' I BET OUR LARD LARCENIST IS IN THAT SHAKY LI'L BUSH!
AHA! I GOTCHA...
...NYYYEEEEEOOW!
HANG ON! I'M COMIN'!

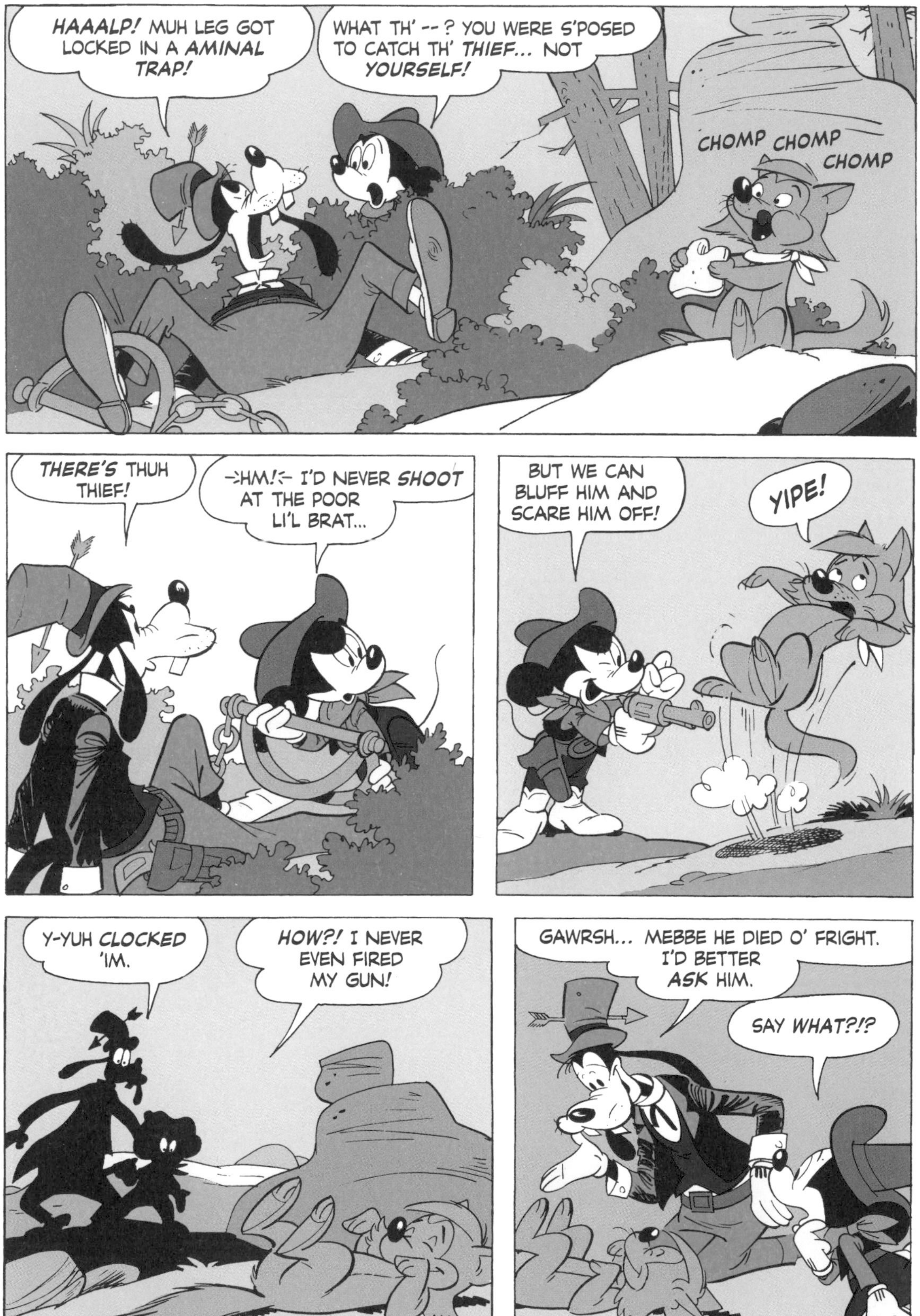
HAAALP! MUH LEG GOT LOCKED IN A AMINAL TRAP!
WHAT TH' --? YOU WERE S'POSED TO CATCH TH' THIEF... NOT YOURSELF!
CHOMP CHOMP CHOMP
THERE'S THUH THIEF!
-HM!- I'D NEVER SHOOT AT THE POOR LI'L BRAT...
BUT WE CAN BLUFF HIM AND SCARE HIM OFF!
YIPE!
Y-YUH CLOCKED 'IM.
HOW?! I NEVER EVEN FIRED MY GUN!
GAWRSH... MEBBE HE DIED O' FRIGHT. I'D BETTER ASK HIM.
SAY WHAT?!?

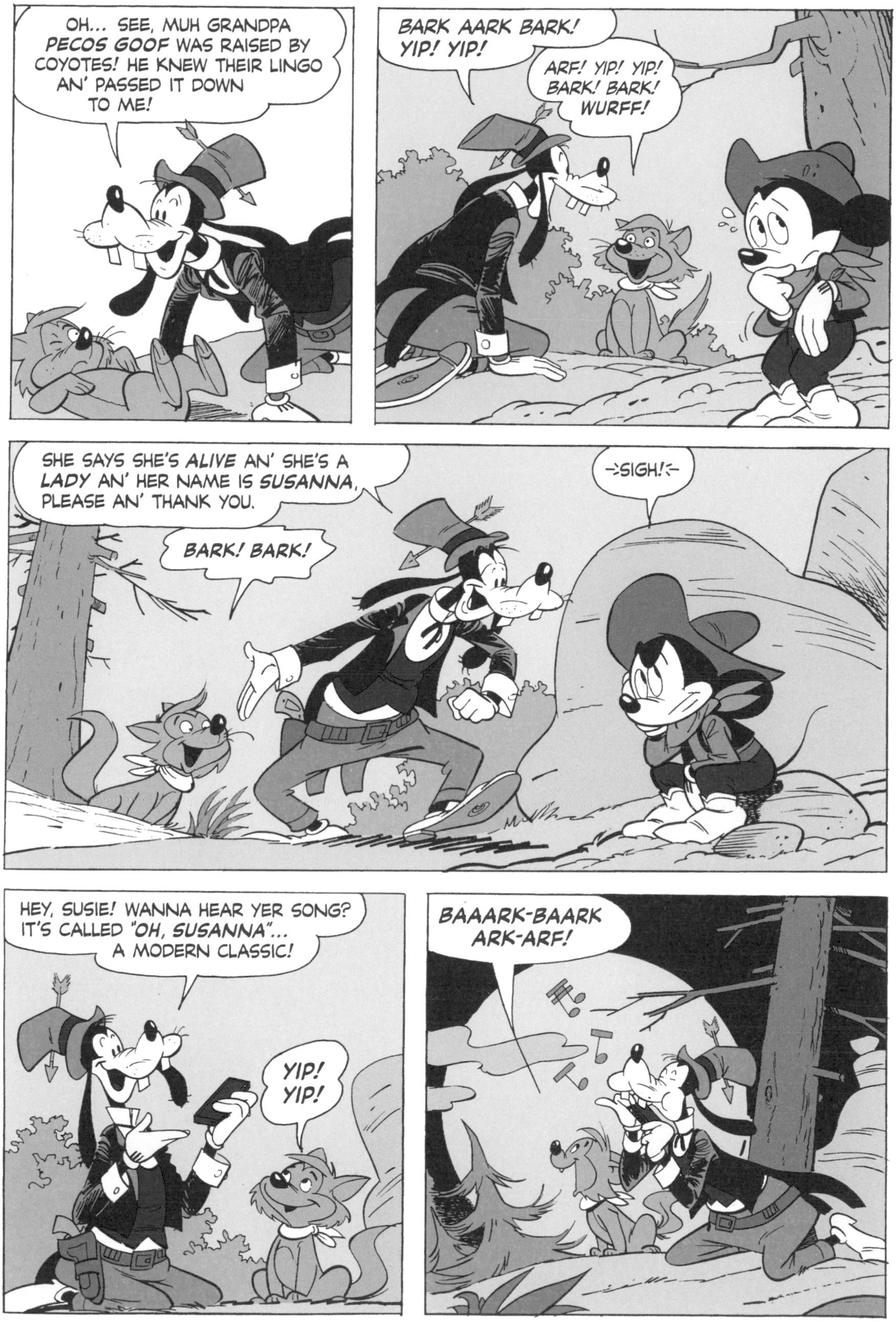
OH... SEE, MUH GRANDPA PECOS GOOF WAS RAISED BY COYOTES! HE KNEW THEIR LINGO AN' PASSED IT DOWN TO ME!
BARK AARK BARK! YIP! YIP!
ARF! YIP! YIP! BARK! BARK! WURFF!
SHE SAYS SHE'S ALIVE AN' SHE'S A LADY AN' HER NAME IS SUSANNA, PLEASE AN' THANK YOU.
BARK! BARK!
-SIGH!-
HEY, SUSIE! WANNA HEAR YER SONG? IT'S CALLED "OH, SUSANNA"... A MODERN CLASSIC!
YIP! YIP!
BAAARK-BAARK ARK-ARF!

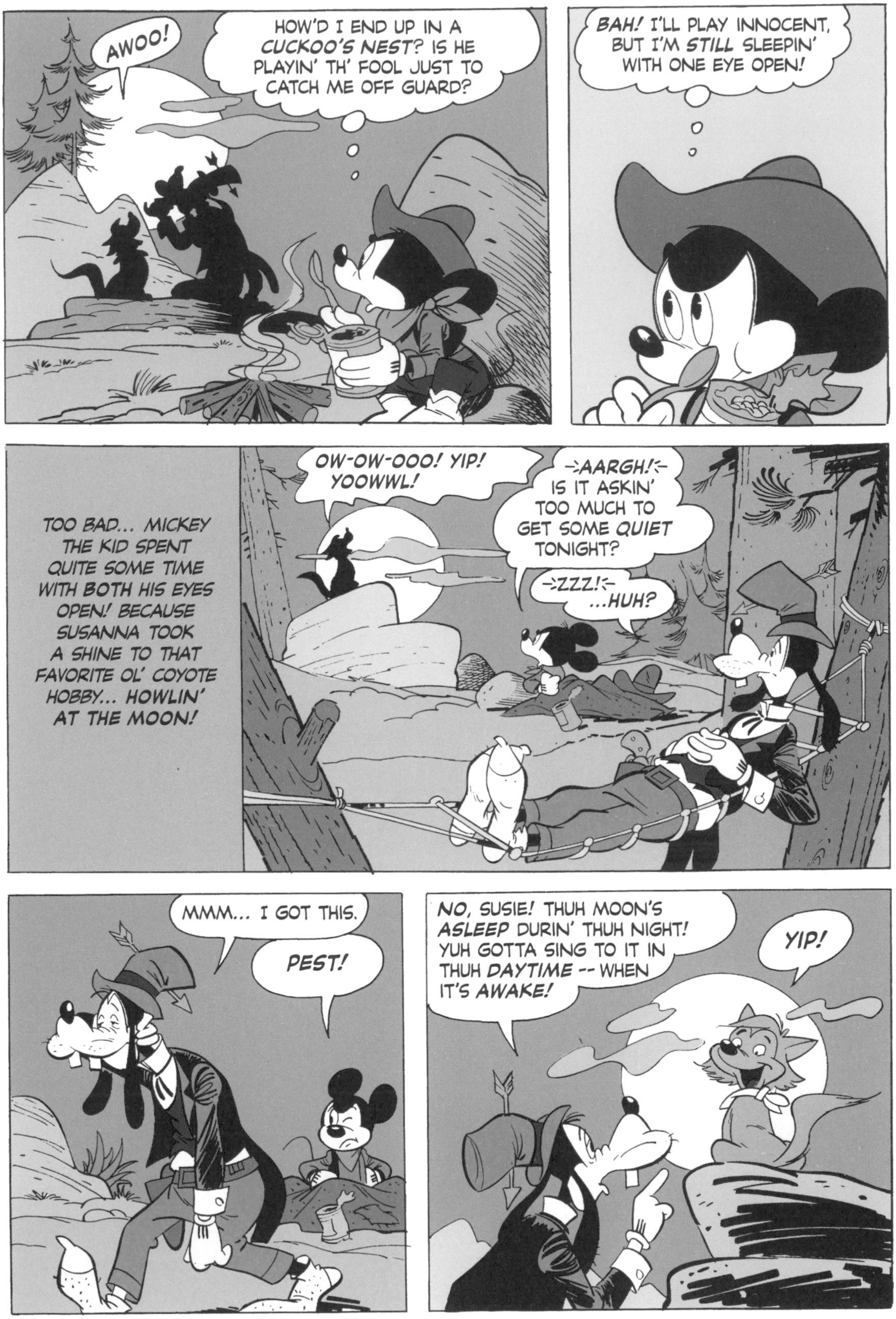
AWOO!
HOW'D I END UP IN A CUCKOO'S NEST? IS HE PLAYIN' TH' FOOL JUST TO CATCH ME OFF GUARD?
BAH! I'LL PLAY INNOCENT, BUT I'M STILL SLEEPIN' WITH ONE EYE OPEN!
TOO BAD... MICKEY THE KID SPENT QUITE SOME TIME WITH BOTH HIS EYES OPEN! BECAUSE SUSANNA TOOK A SHINE TO THAT FAVORITE OL' COYOTE HOBBY... HOWLIN' AT THE MOON!
OW-OW-OOO! YIP! YOOWWL!
AARGH! IS IT ASKIN' TOO MUCH TO GET SOME QUIET TONIGHT?
ZZZ! ...HUH?
MMM... I GOT THIS.
PEST!
NO, SUSIE! THUH MOON'S ASLEEP DURIN' THUH NIGHT! YUH GOTTA SING TO IT IN THUH DAYTIME -- WHEN IT'S AWAKE!
YIP!

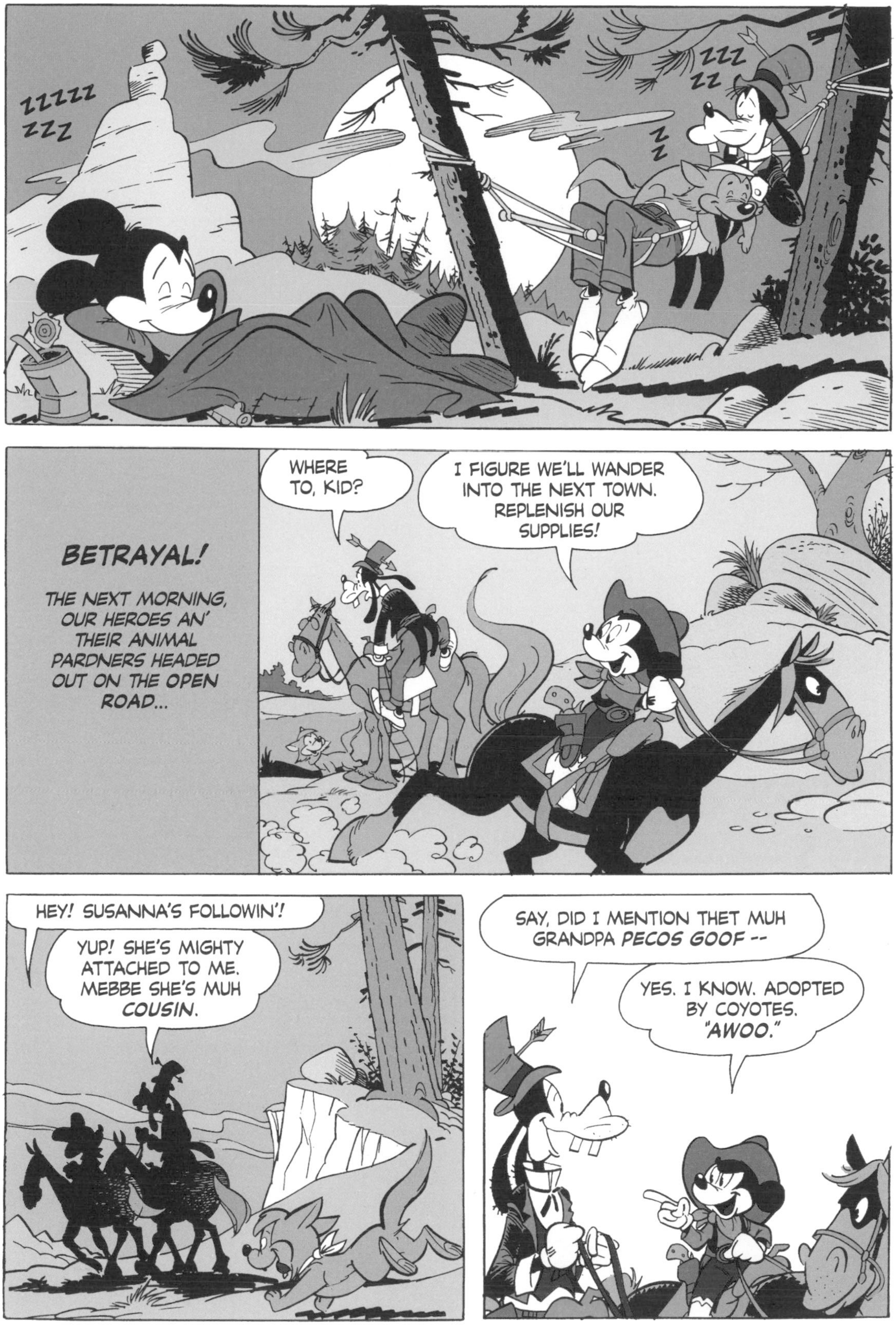
ZZZZZ
ZZZ
ZZZ
ZZ
ZZ
BETRAYAL!
THE NEXT MORNING, OUR HEROES AN' THEIR ANIMAL PARDNERS HEADED OUT ON THE OPEN ROAD...
WHERE TO, KID?
I FIGURE WE'LL WANDER INTO THE NEXT TOWN. REPLENISH OUR SUPPLIES!
HEY! SUSANNA'S FOLLOWIN'!
YUP! SHE'S MIGHTY ATTACHED TO ME. MEBBE SHE'S MUH *COUSIN*.
SAY, DID I MENTION THET MUH GRANDPA *PECOS GOOF* --
YES. I KNOW. ADOPTED BY COYOTES. *"AWOO."*

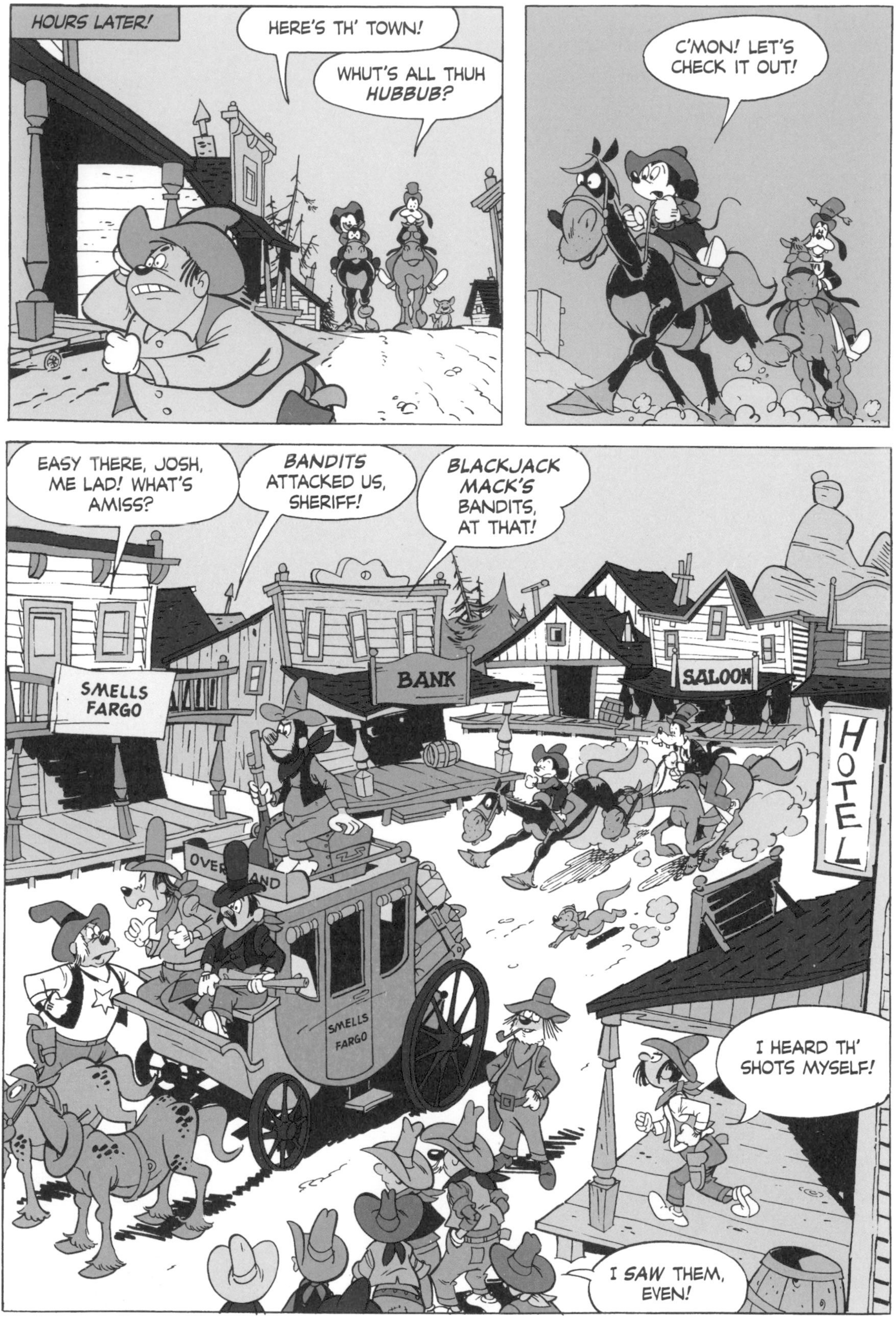
HOURS LATER!
HERE'S TH' TOWN!
WHUT'S ALL THUH *HUBBUB?*
C'MON! LET'S CHECK IT OUT!
EASY THERE, JOSH, ME LAD! WHAT'S AMISS?
BANDITS ATTACKED US, SHERIFF!
BLACKJACK MACK'S BANDITS, AT THAT!
SMELLS FARGO
BANK
SALOON
HOTEL
OVERLAND
SMELLS FARGO
I HEARD TH' SHOTS MYSELF!
I *SAW* THEM, EVEN!

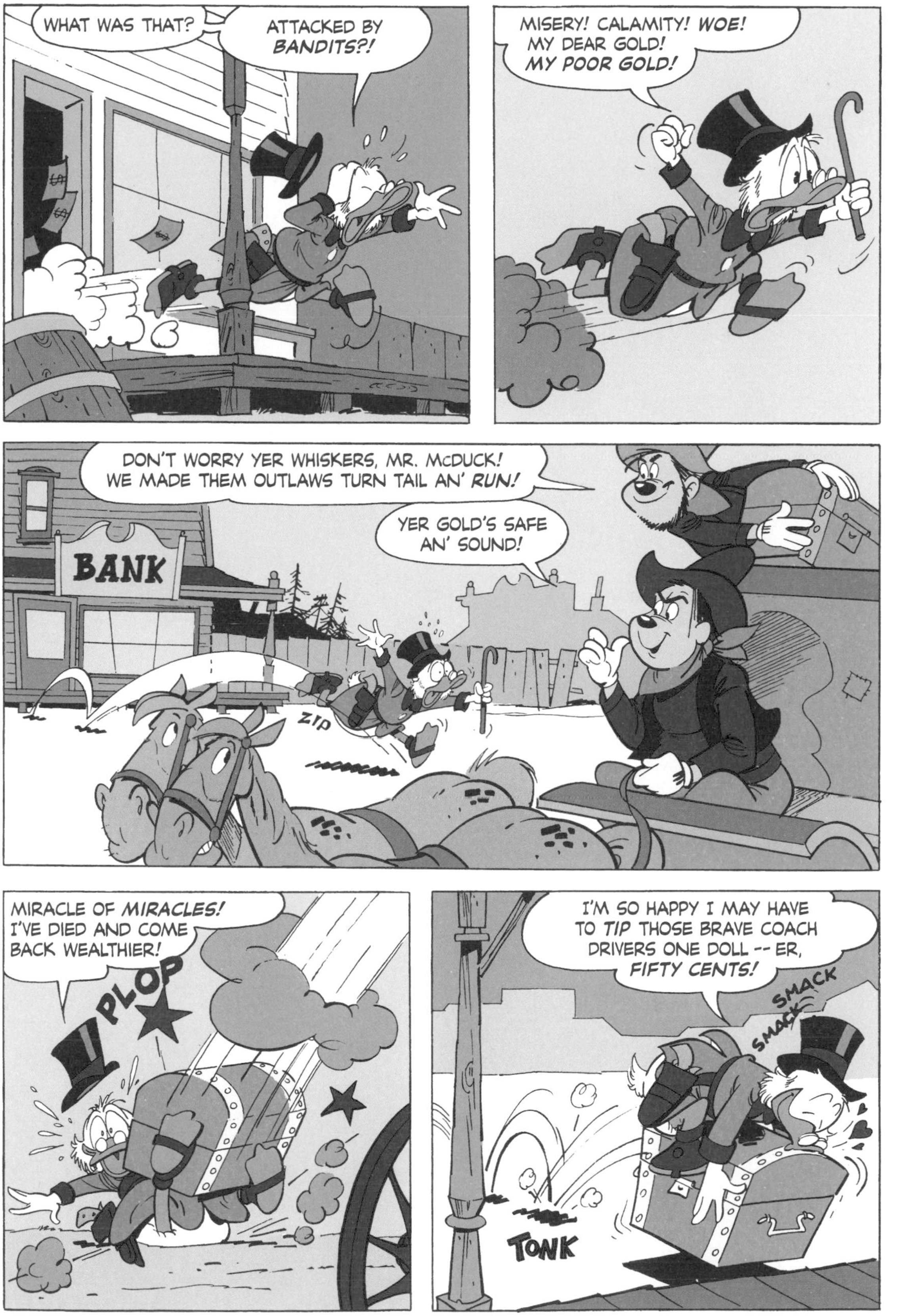

WHAT WAS THAT?
ATTACKED BY BANDITS?!
MISERY! CALAMITY! WOE! MY DEAR GOLD! MY POOR GOLD!
DON'T WORRY YER WHISKERS, MR. McDUCK! WE MADE THEM OUTLAWS TURN TAIL AN' RUN!
YER GOLD'S SAFE AN' SOUND!
BANK
ZIP
MIRACLE OF MIRACLES! I'VE DIED AND COME BACK WEALTHIER!
PLOP
I'M SO HAPPY I MAY HAVE TO TIP THOSE BRAVE COACH DRIVERS ONE DOLL -- ER, FIFTY CENTS!
SMACK
SMACK
TONK

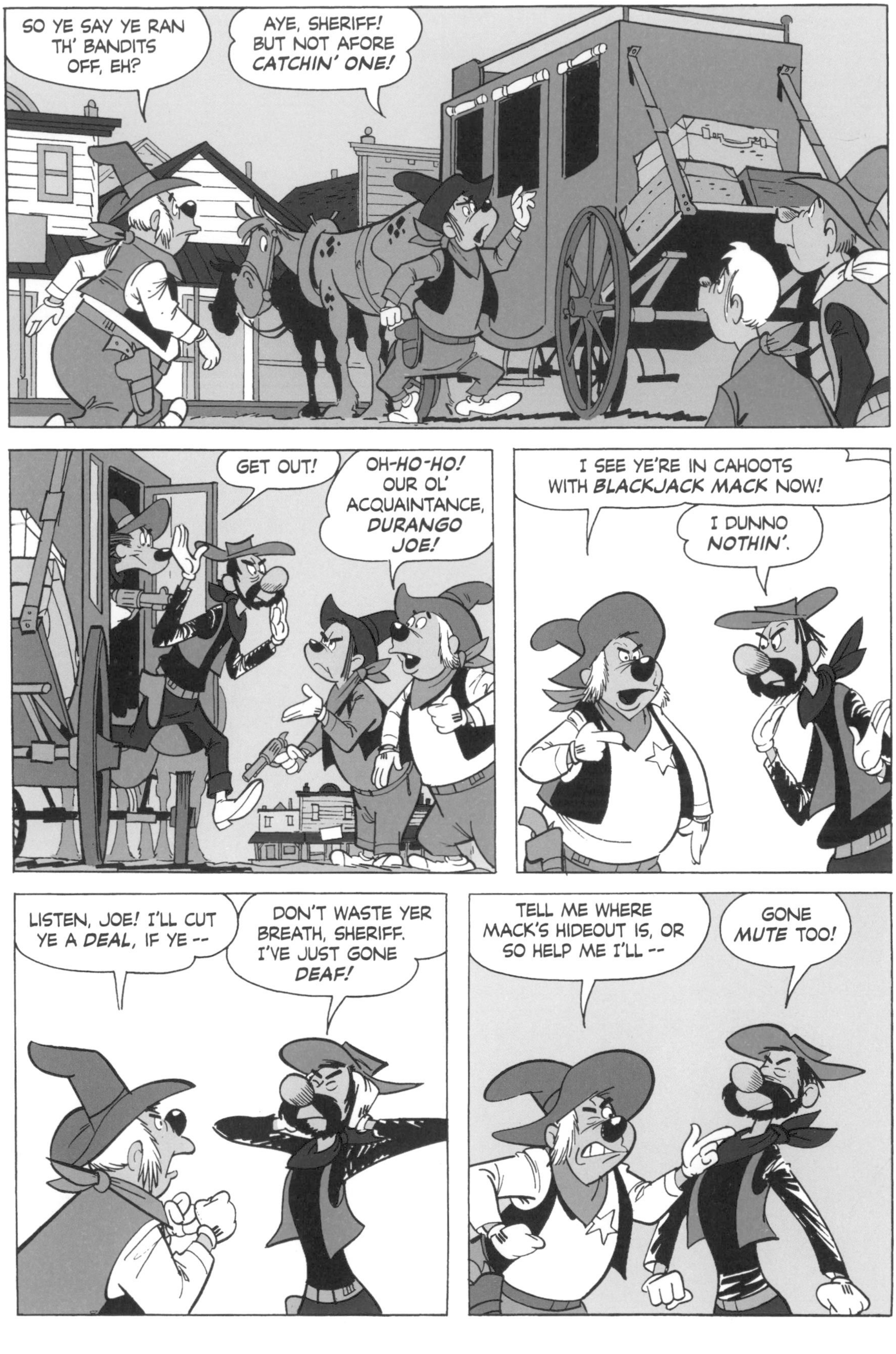
SO YE SAY YE RAN TH' BANDITS OFF, EH?
AYE, SHERIFF! BUT NOT AFORE *CATCHIN' ONE!*
GET OUT!
OH-*HO*-*HO!* OUR OL' ACQUAINTANCE, *DURANGO JOE!*
I SEE YE'RE IN CAHOOTS WITH *BLACKJACK MACK* NOW!
I DUNNO *NOTHIN'*.
LISTEN, JOE! I'LL CUT YE A *DEAL*, IF YE --
DON'T WASTE YER BREATH, SHERIFF. I'VE JUST GONE *DEAF!*
TELL ME WHERE MACK'S HIDEOUT IS, OR SO HELP ME I'LL --
GONE *MUTE* TOO!

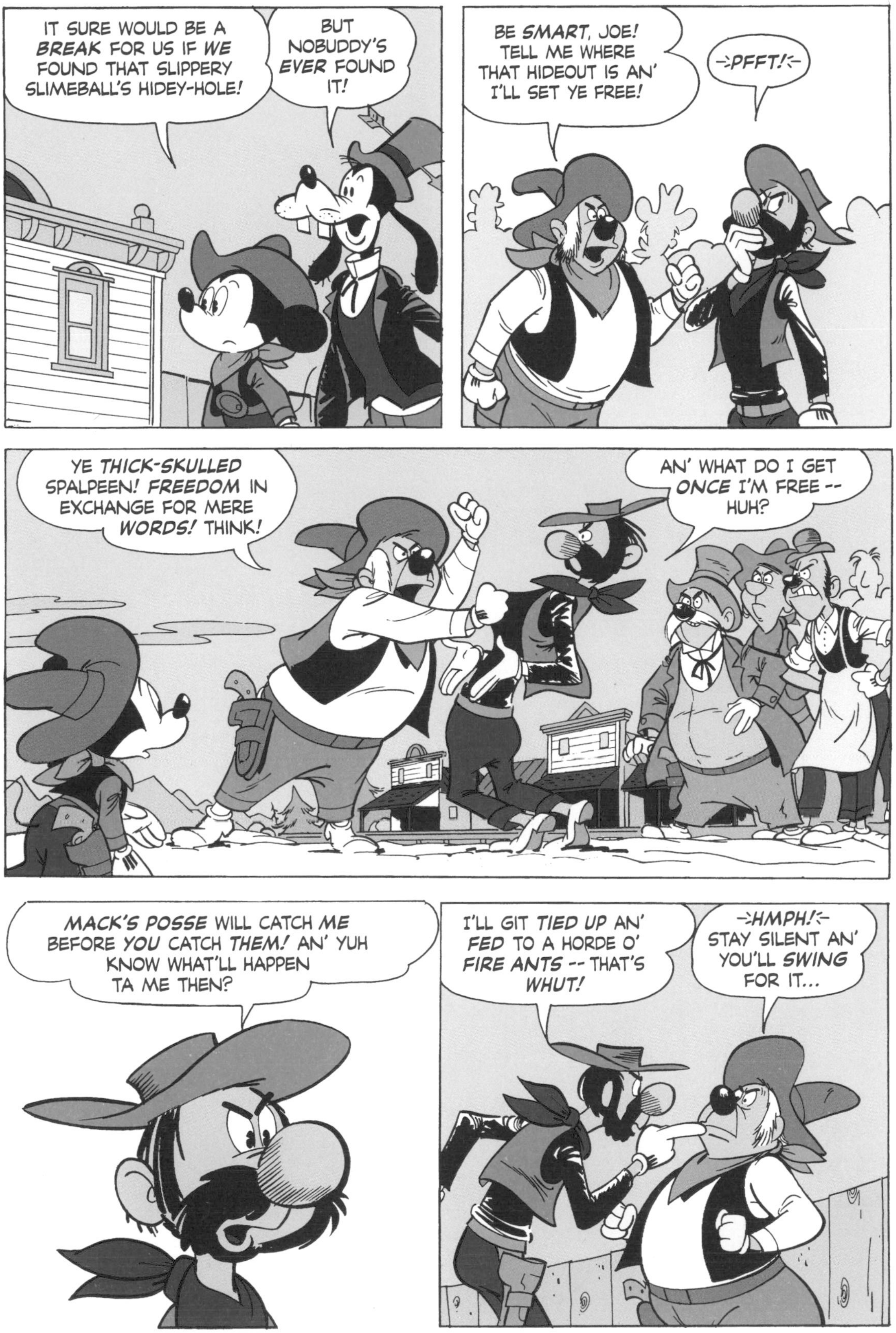
IT SURE WOULD BE A BREAK FOR US IF WE FOUND THAT SLIPPERY SLIMEBALL'S HIDEY-HOLE!
BUT NOBUDDY'S EVER FOUND IT!
BE SMART, JOE! TELL ME WHERE THAT HIDEOUT IS AN' I'LL SET YE FREE!
-PFFT!-
YE THICK-SKULLED SPALPEEN! FREEDOM IN EXCHANGE FOR MERE WORDS! THINK!
AN' WHAT DO I GET ONCE I'M FREE -- HUH?
MACK'S POSSE WILL CATCH ME BEFORE YOU CATCH THEM! AN' YUH KNOW WHAT'LL HAPPEN TA ME THEN?
I'LL GIT TIED UP AN' FED TO A HORDE O' FIRE ANTS -- THAT'S WHUT!
-HMPH!- STAY SILENT AN' YOU'LL SWING FOR IT...

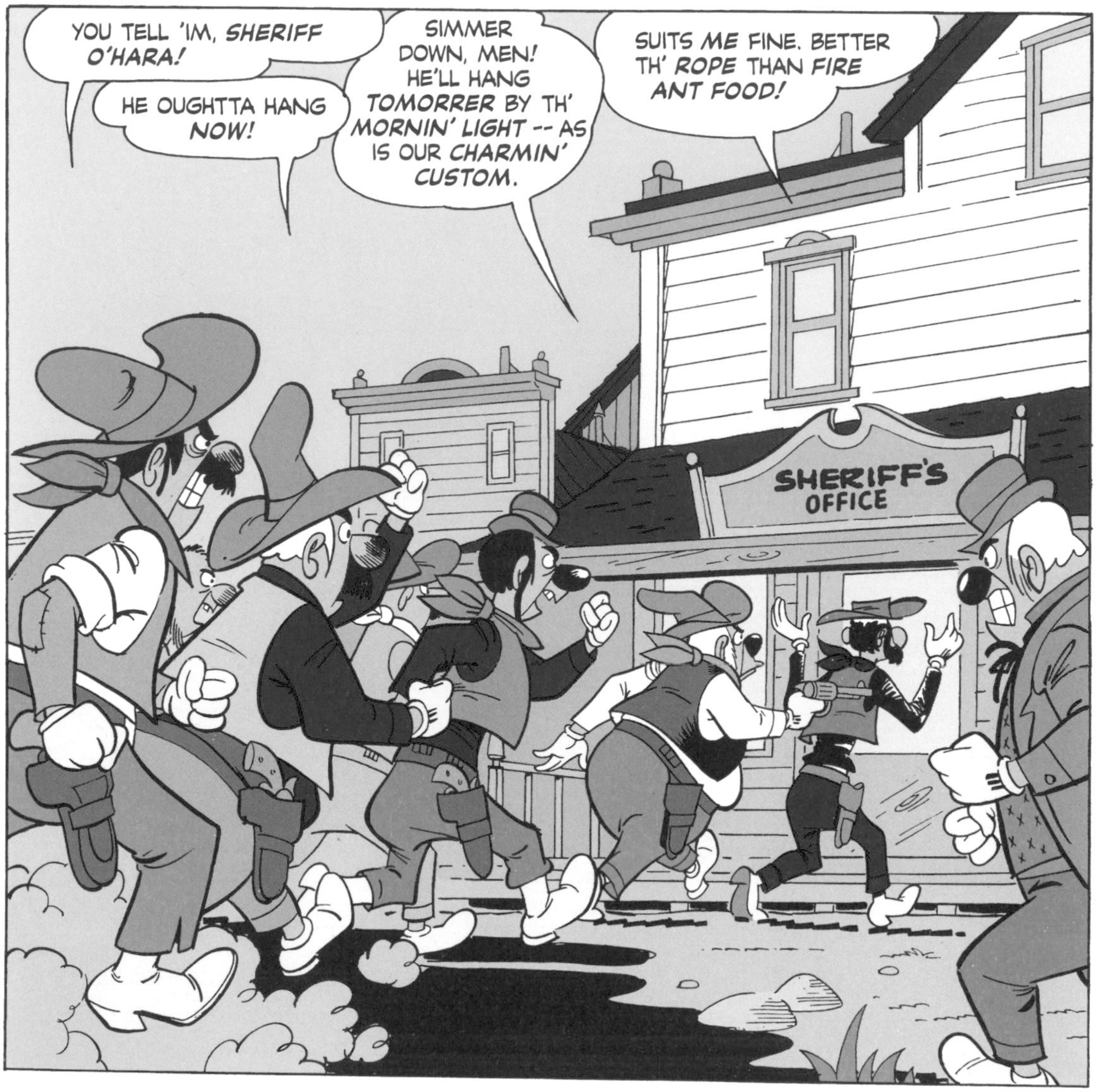
YOU TELL 'IM, *SHERIFF O'HARA!*
HE OUGHTTA HANG *NOW!*
SIMMER DOWN, MEN! HE'LL HANG *TOMORRER* BY TH' *MORNIN' LIGHT* -- AS IS OUR *CHARMIN' CUSTOM.*
SUITS *ME* FINE. BETTER TH' *ROPE* THAN *FIRE ANT FOOD!*
SHERIFF'S OFFICE

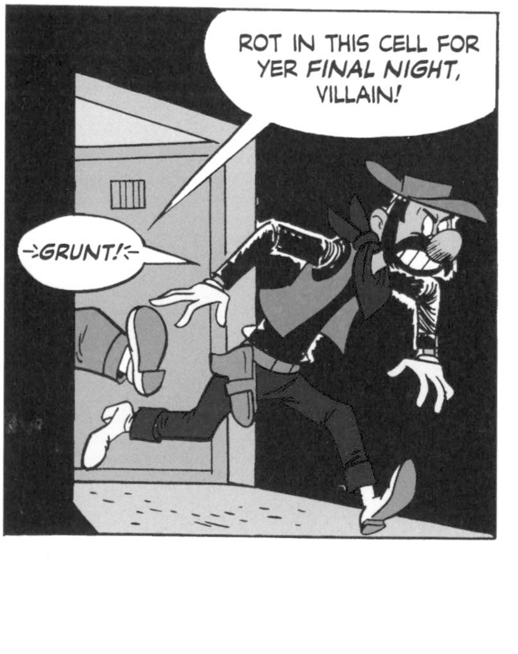
ROT IN THIS CELL FOR YER *FINAL NIGHT,* VILLAIN!
~GRUNT!~

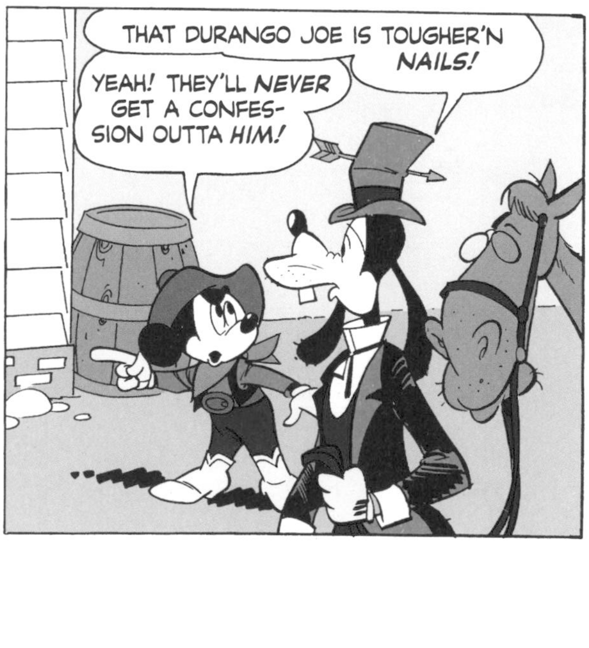
THAT DURANGO JOE IS TOUGHER'N *NAILS!*
YEAH! THEY'LL *NEVER* GET A CONFES-SION OUTTA *HIM!*

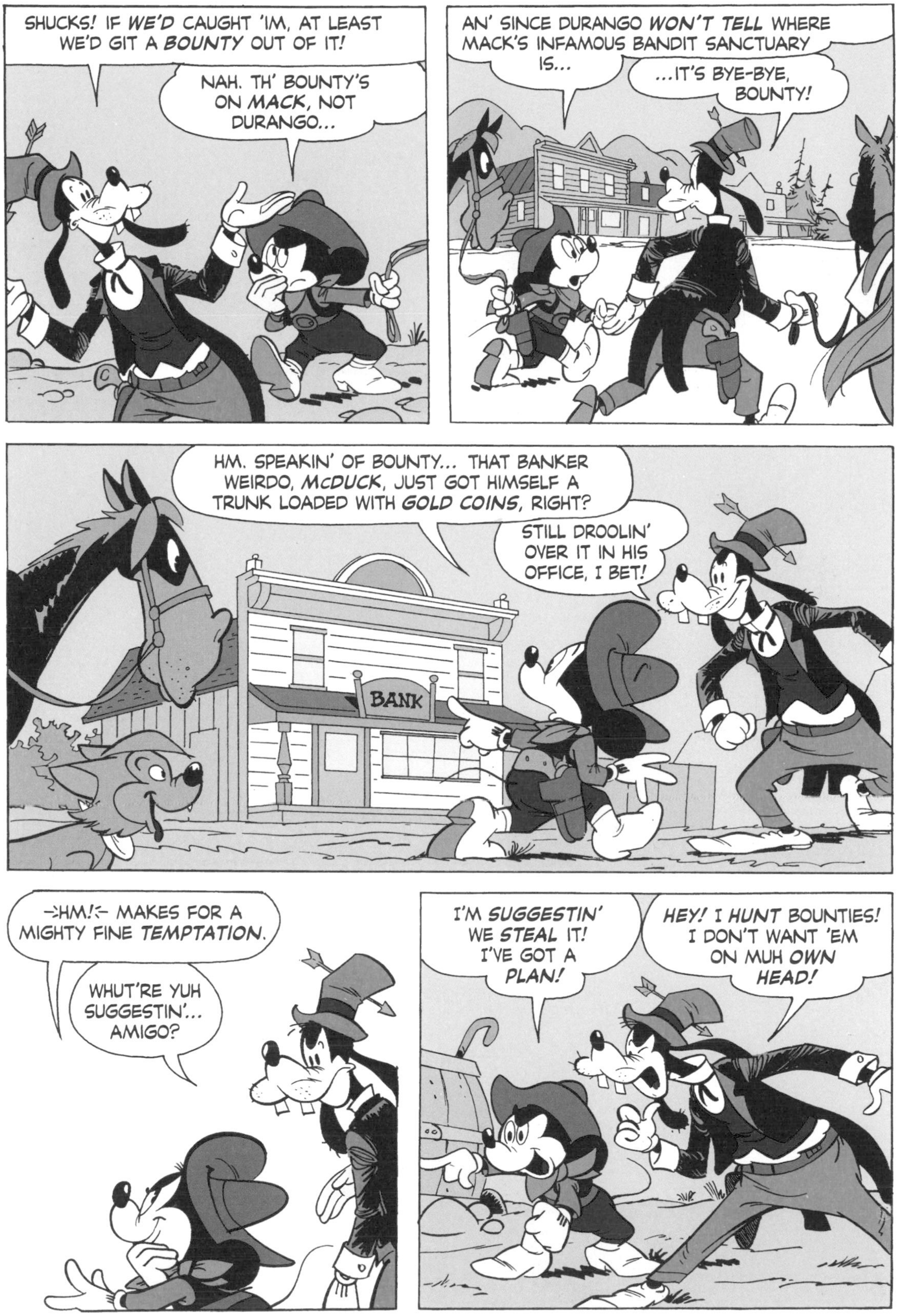
SHUCKS! IF WE'D CAUGHT 'IM, AT LEAST WE'D GIT A BOUNTY OUT OF IT!
NAH. TH' BOUNTY'S ON MACK, NOT DURANGO...
AN' SINCE DURANGO WON'T TELL WHERE MACK'S INFAMOUS BANDIT SANCTUARY IS...
...IT'S BYE-BYE, BOUNTY!
HM. SPEAKIN' OF BOUNTY... THAT BANKER WEIRDO, McDUCK, JUST GOT HIMSELF A TRUNK LOADED WITH GOLD COINS, RIGHT?
STILL DROOLIN' OVER IT IN HIS OFFICE, I BET!
BANK
–HM!– MAKES FOR A MIGHTY FINE TEMPTATION.
WHUT'RE YUH SUGGESTIN'... AMIGO?
I'M SUGGESTIN' WE STEAL IT! I'VE GOT A PLAN!
HEY! I HUNT BOUNTIES! I DON'T WANT 'EM ON MUH OWN HEAD!

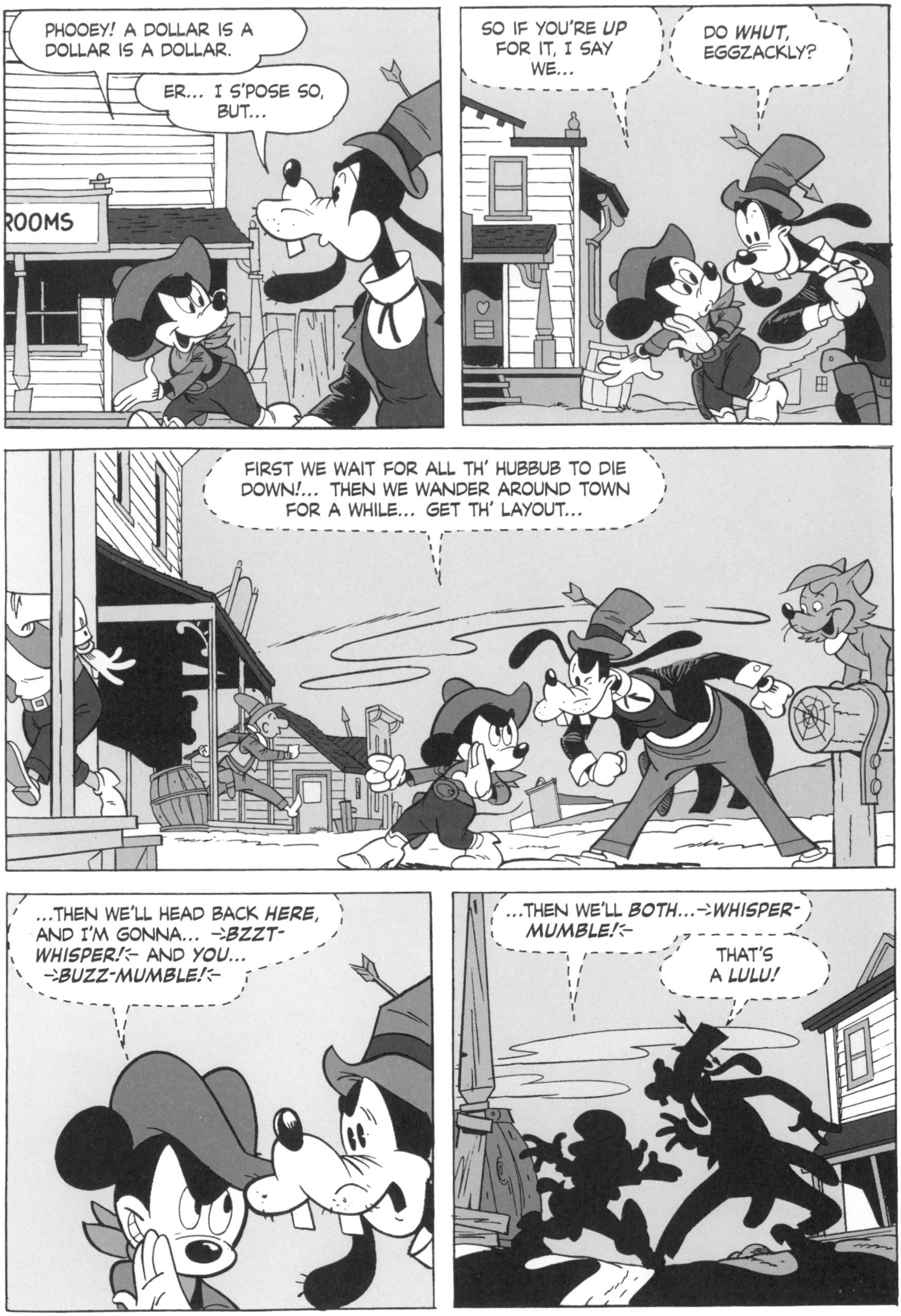
PHOOEY! A DOLLAR IS A DOLLAR IS A DOLLAR.
ER... I S'POSE SO, BUT...
ROOMS
SO IF YOU'RE UP FOR IT, I SAY WE...
DO WHUT, EGGZACKLY?
FIRST WE WAIT FOR ALL TH' HUBBUB TO DIE DOWN!... THEN WE WANDER AROUND TOWN FOR A WHILE... GET TH' LAYOUT...
...THEN WE'LL HEAD BACK HERE, AND I'M GONNA... BZZT-WHISPER! AND YOU... BUZZ-MUMBLE!
...THEN WE'LL BOTH... WHISPER-MUMBLE!
THAT'S A LULU!

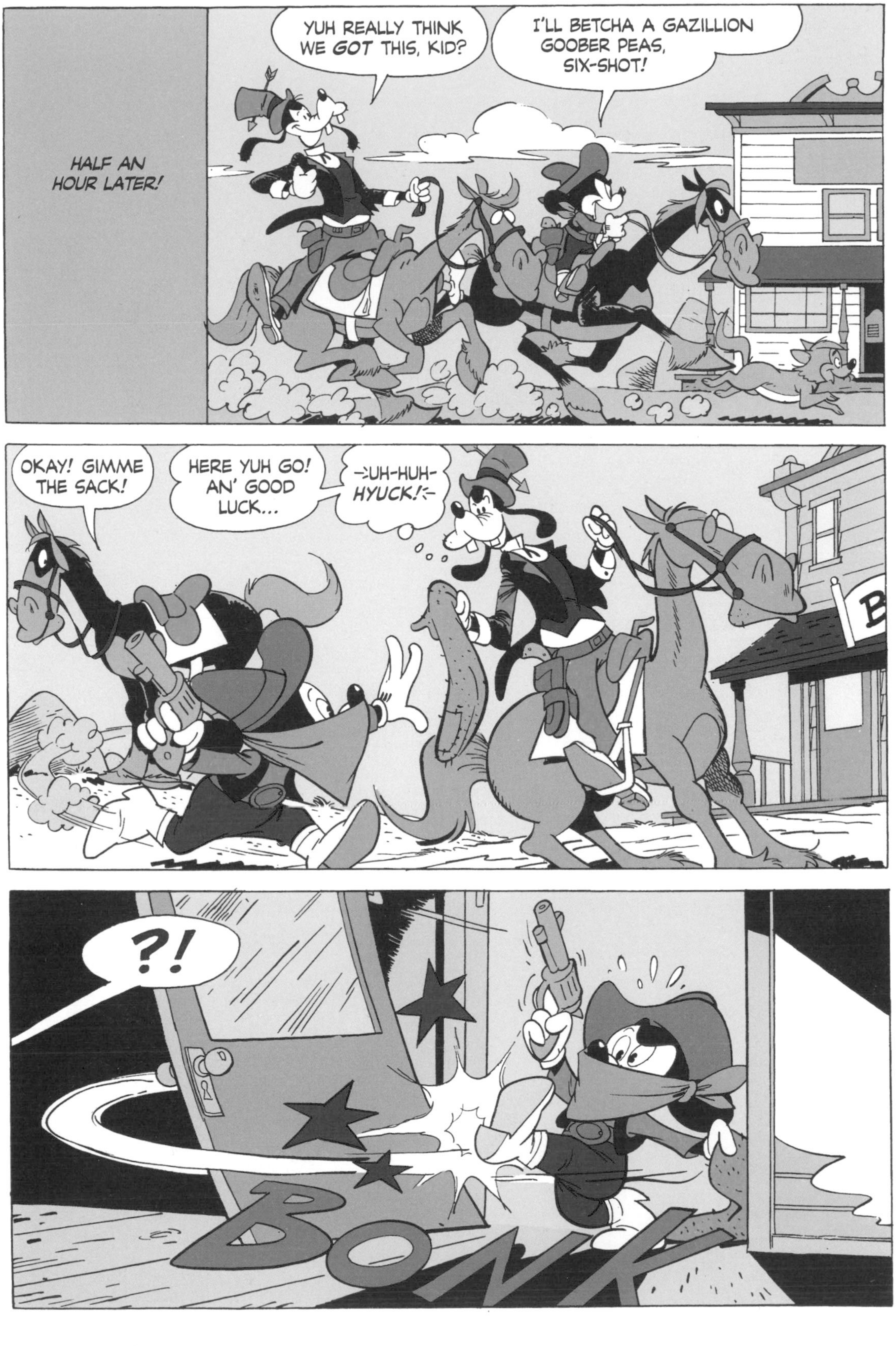
HALF AN HOUR LATER!
YUH REALLY THINK WE GOT THIS, KID?
I'LL BETCHA A GAZILLION GOOBER PEAS, SIX-SHOT!
OKAY! GIMME THE SACK!
HERE YUH GO! AN' GOOD LUCK...
UH-HUH-HYUCK!
?!
BONK

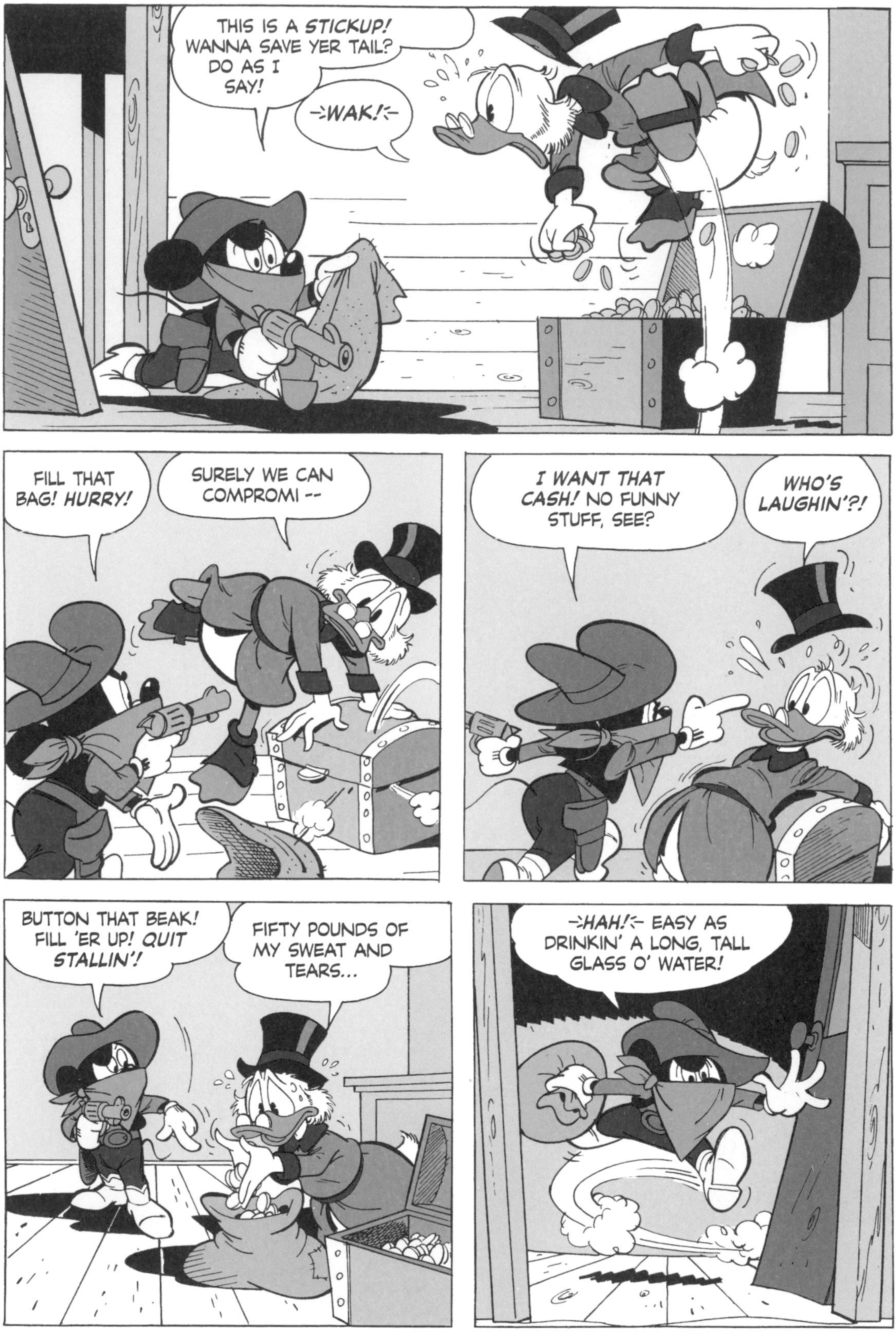

THIS IS A STICKUP! WANNA SAVE YER TAIL? DO AS I SAY!
-WAK!-
FILL THAT BAG! HURRY!
SURELY WE CAN COMPROMI --
I WANT THAT CASH! NO FUNNY STUFF, SEE?
WHO'S LAUGHIN'?!
BUTTON THAT BEAK! FILL 'ER UP! QUIT STALLIN'!
FIFTY POUNDS OF MY SWEAT AND TEARS...
-HAH!- EASY AS DRINKIN' A LONG, TALL GLASS O' WATER!

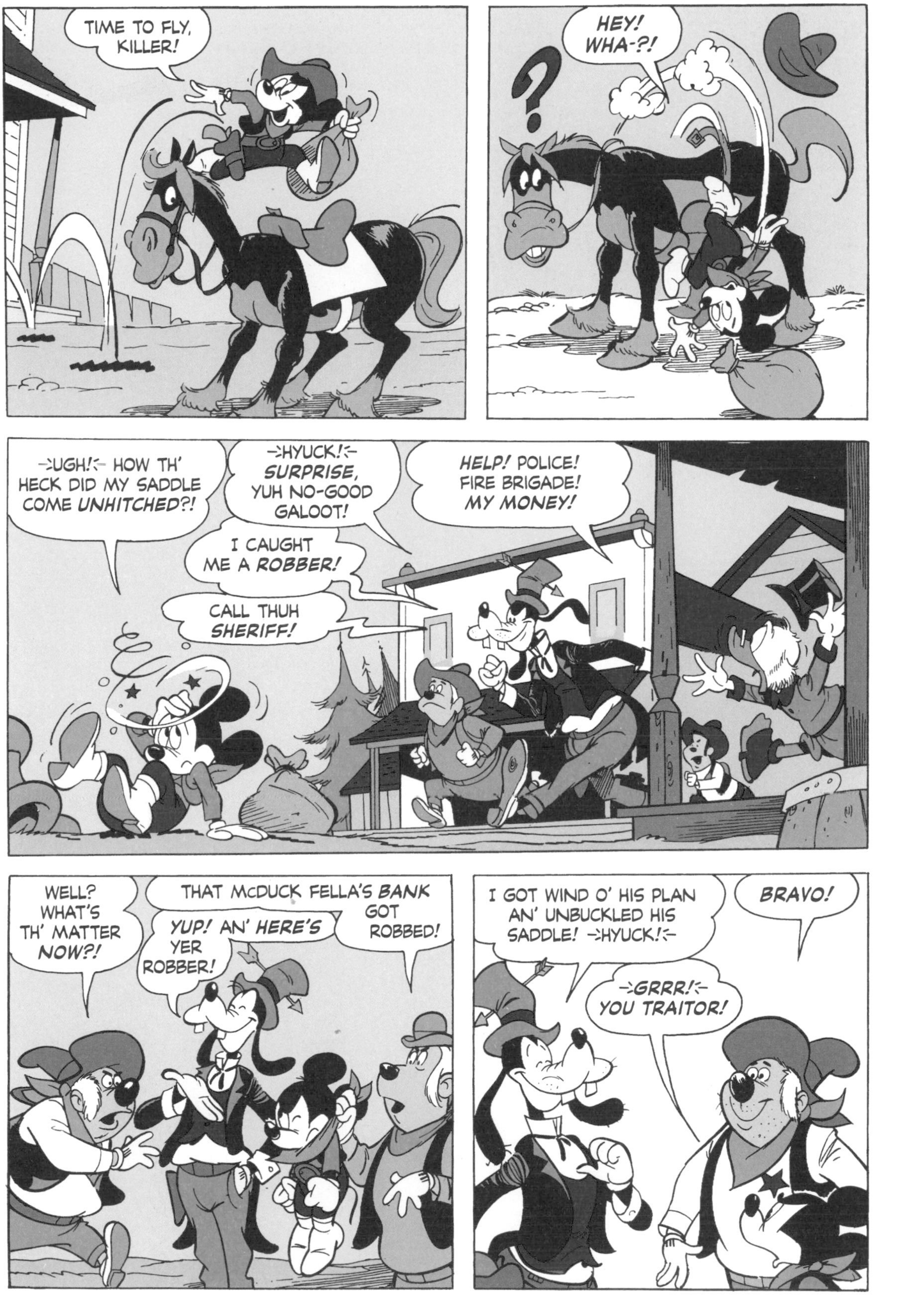
TIME TO FLY, KILLER!
HEY! WHA-?!
?
-UGH!- HOW TH' HECK DID MY SADDLE COME UNHITCHED?!
-HYUCK!- SURPRISE, YUH NO-GOOD GALOOT!
I CAUGHT ME A ROBBER!
CALL THUH SHERIFF!
HELP! POLICE! FIRE BRIGADE! MY MONEY!
WELL? WHAT'S TH' MATTER NOW?!
THAT McDUCK FELLA'S BANK GOT ROBBED!
YUP! AN' HERE'S YER ROBBER!
I GOT WIND O' HIS PLAN AN' UNBUCKLED HIS SADDLE! -HYUCK!-
BRAVO!
-GRRR!- YOU TRAITOR!

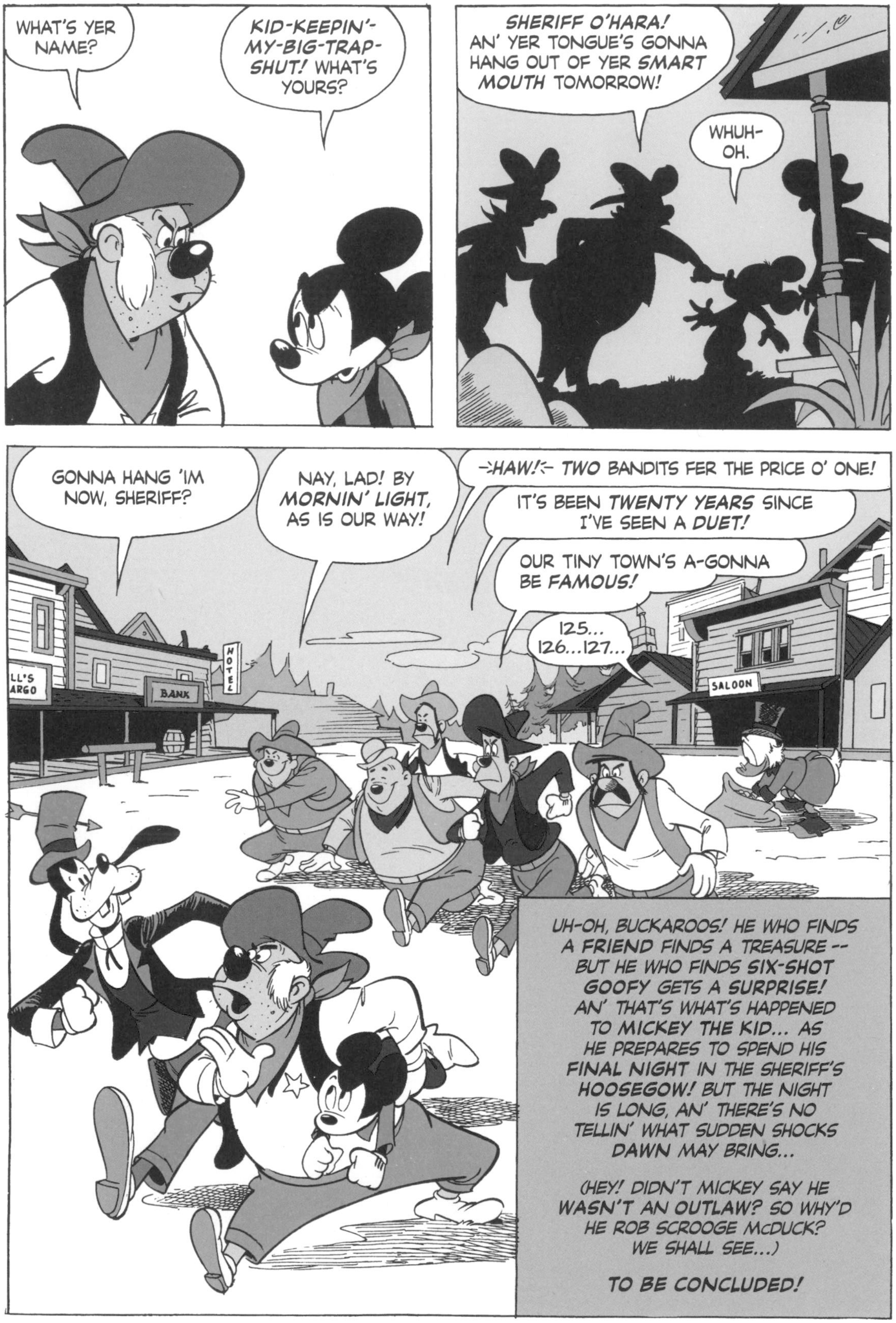
WHAT'S YER NAME?
KID-KEEPIN'-MY-BIG-TRAP-SHUT! WHAT'S YOURS?
SHERIFF O'HARA! AN' YER TONGUE'S GONNA HANG OUT OF YER SMART MOUTH TOMORROW!
WHUH-OH.
GONNA HANG 'IM NOW, SHERIFF?
NAY, LAD! BY MORNIN' LIGHT, AS IS OUR WAY!
-HAW!- TWO BANDITS FER THE PRICE O' ONE!
IT'S BEEN TWENTY YEARS SINCE I'VE SEEN A DUET!
OUR TINY TOWN'S A-GONNA BE FAMOUS!
125... 126...127...
BANK
HOTEL
SALOON
UH-OH, BUCKAROOS! HE WHO FINDS A FRIEND FINDS A TREASURE -- BUT HE WHO FINDS SIX-SHOT GOOFY GETS A SURPRISE! AN' THAT'S WHAT'S HAPPENED TO MICKEY THE KID... AS HE PREPARES TO SPEND HIS FINAL NIGHT IN THE SHERIFF'S HOOSEGOW! BUT THE NIGHT IS LONG, AN' THERE'S NO TELLIN' WHAT SUDDEN SHOCKS DAWN MAY BRING...
(HEY! DIDN'T MICKEY SAY HE WASN'T AN OUTLAW? SO WHY'D HE ROB SCROOGE McDUCK? WE SHALL SEE...)
TO BE CONCLUDED!

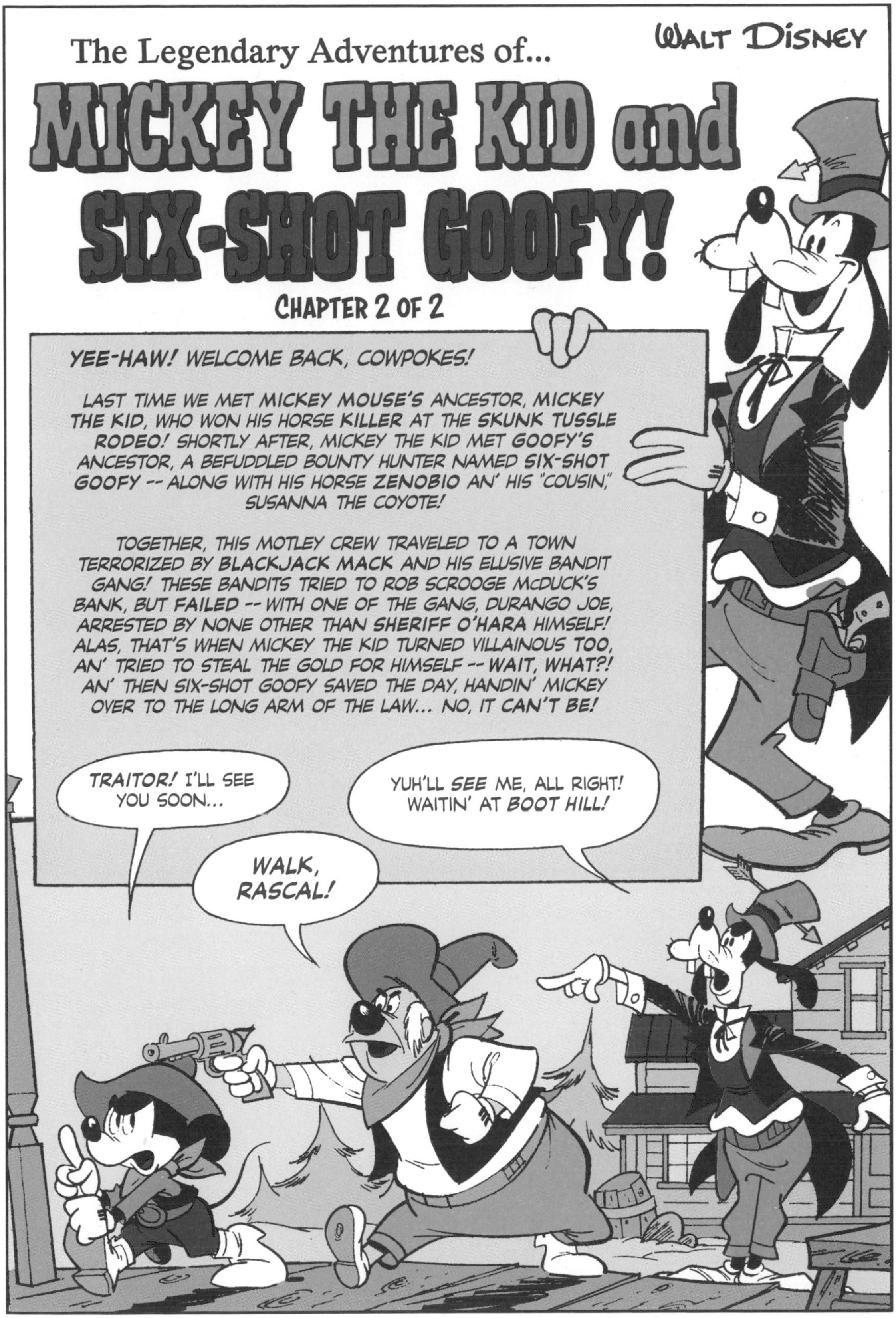
The Legendary Adventures of...
WALT DISNEY
MICKEY THE KID and SIX-SHOT GOOFY!
CHAPTER 2 OF 2
YEE-HAW! WELCOME BACK, COWPOKES!
LAST TIME WE MET MICKEY MOUSE'S ANCESTOR, MICKEY THE KID, WHO WON HIS HORSE KILLER AT THE SKUNK TUSSLE RODEO! SHORTLY AFTER, MICKEY THE KID MET GOOFY'S ANCESTOR, A BEFUDDLED BOUNTY HUNTER NAMED SIX-SHOT GOOFY -- ALONG WITH HIS HORSE ZENOBIO AN' HIS "COUSIN," SUSANNA THE COYOTE!
TOGETHER, THIS MOTLEY CREW TRAVELED TO A TOWN TERRORIZED BY BLACKJACK MACK AND HIS ELUSIVE BANDIT GANG! THESE BANDITS TRIED TO ROB SCROOGE McDUCK'S BANK, BUT FAILED -- WITH ONE OF THE GANG, DURANGO JOE, ARRESTED BY NONE OTHER THAN SHERIFF O'HARA HIMSELF! ALAS, THAT'S WHEN MICKEY THE KID TURNED VILLAINOUS TOO, AN' TRIED TO STEAL THE GOLD FOR HIMSELF -- WAIT, WHAT?! AN' THEN SIX-SHOT GOOFY SAVED THE DAY, HANDIN' MICKEY OVER TO THE LONG ARM OF THE LAW... NO, IT CAN'T BE!
TRAITOR! I'LL SEE YOU SOON...
YUH'LL SEE ME, ALL RIGHT! WAITIN' AT BOOT HILL!
WALK, RASCAL!

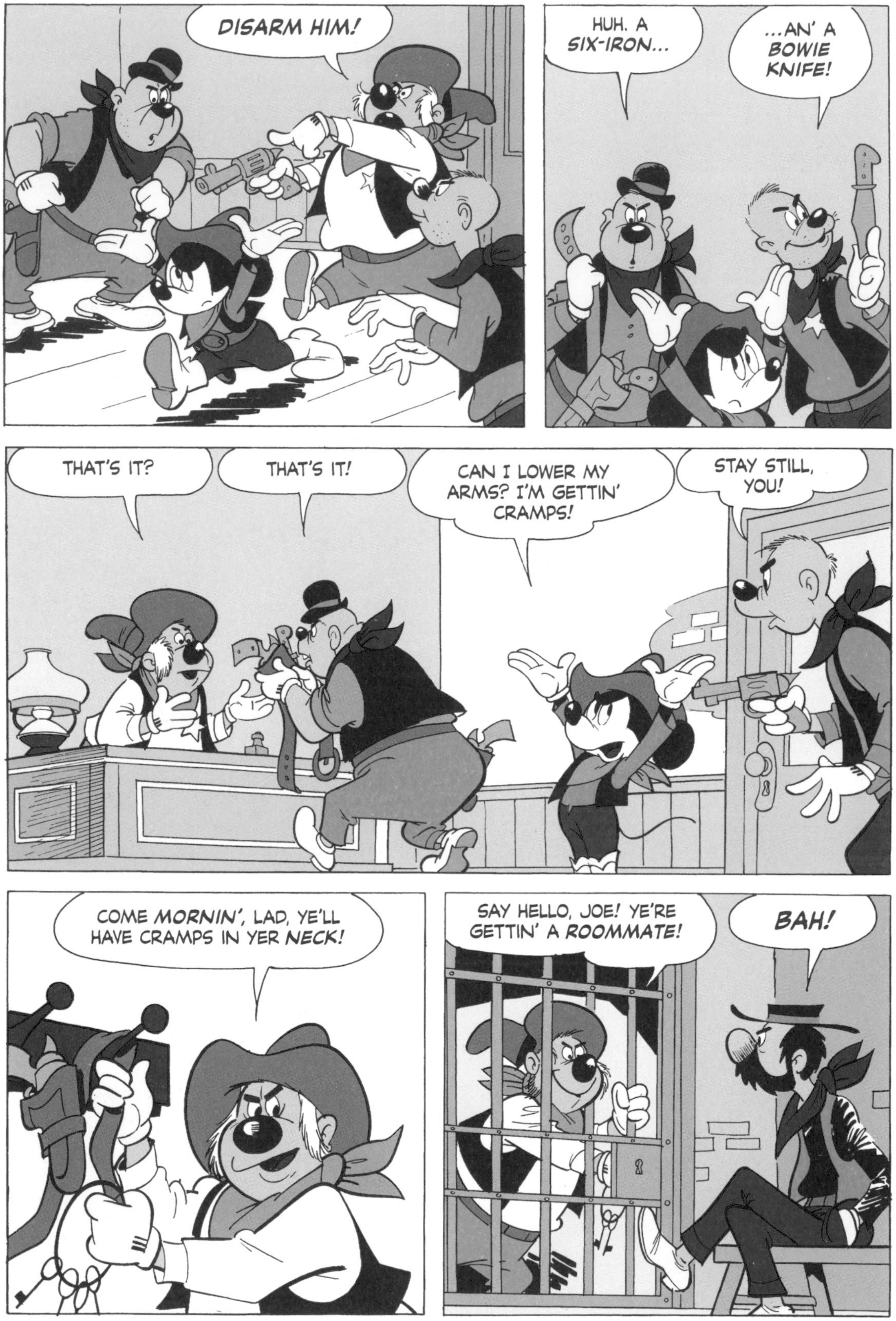
DISARM HIM!
HUH. A SIX-IRON...
...AN' A BOWIE KNIFE!
THAT'S IT?
THAT'S IT!
CAN I LOWER MY ARMS? I'M GETTIN' CRAMPS!
STAY STILL, YOU!
COME MORNIN', LAD, YE'LL HAVE CRAMPS IN YER NECK!
SAY HELLO, JOE! YE'RE GETTIN' A ROOMMATE!
BAH!

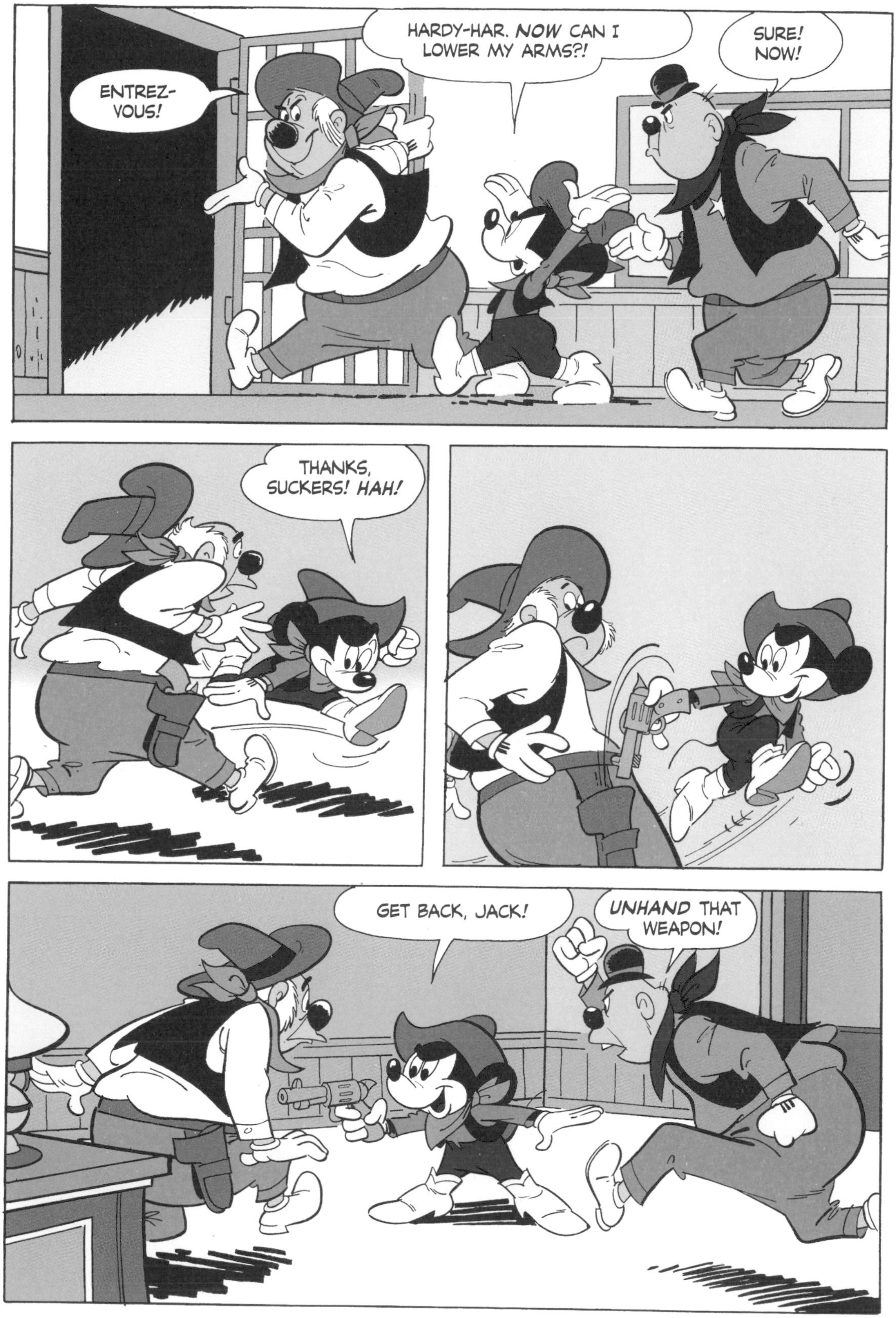
ENTREZ-VOUS!
HARDY-HAR. NOW CAN I LOWER MY ARMS?!
SURE! NOW!
THANKS, SUCKERS! HAH!
GET BACK, JACK!
UNHAND THAT WEAPON!

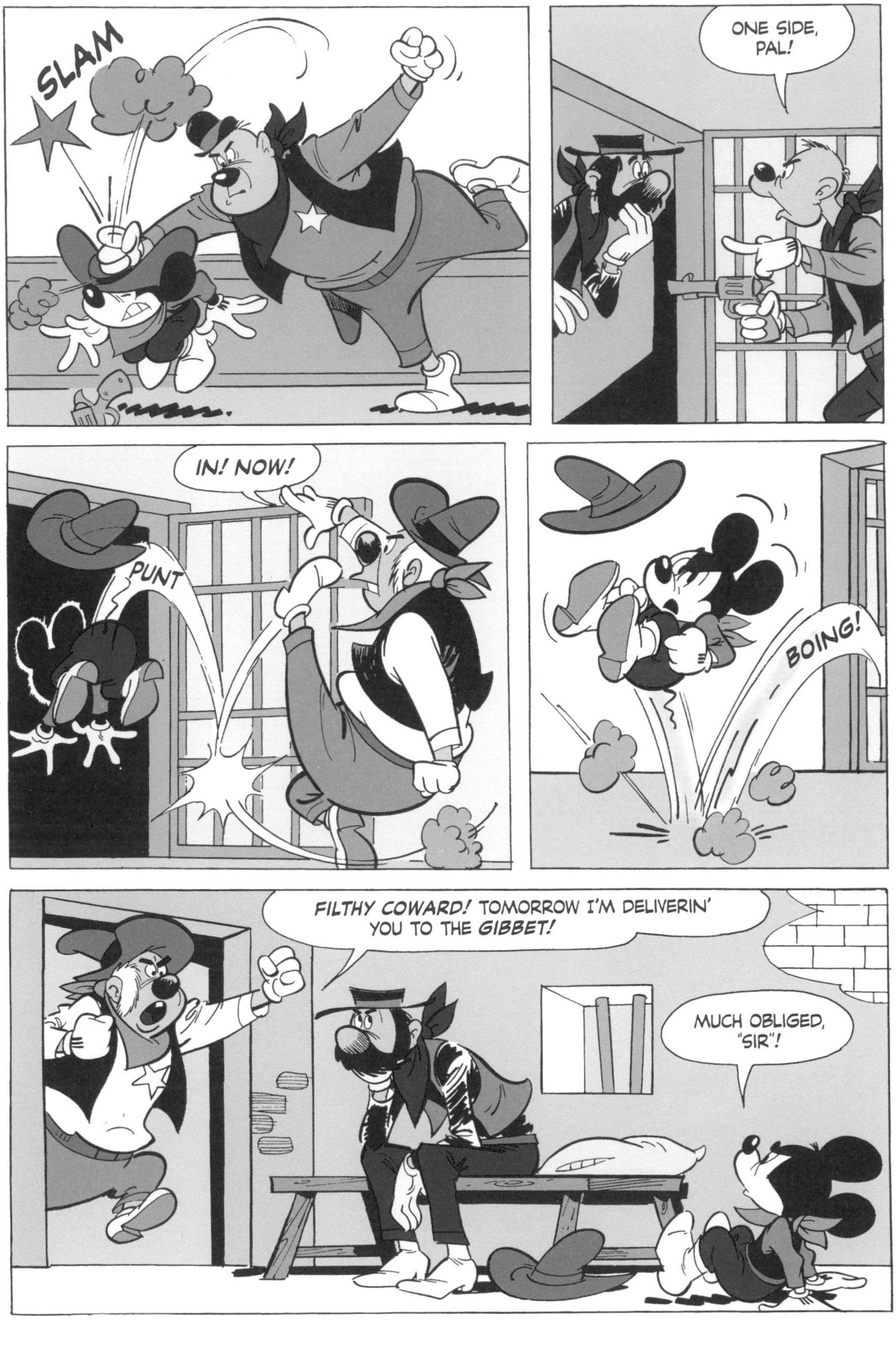
SLAM
ONE SIDE, PAL!
IN! NOW!
PUNT
BOING!
FILTHY COWARD! TOMORROW I'M DELIVERIN' YOU TO THE GIBBET!
MUCH OBLIGED, "SIR"!

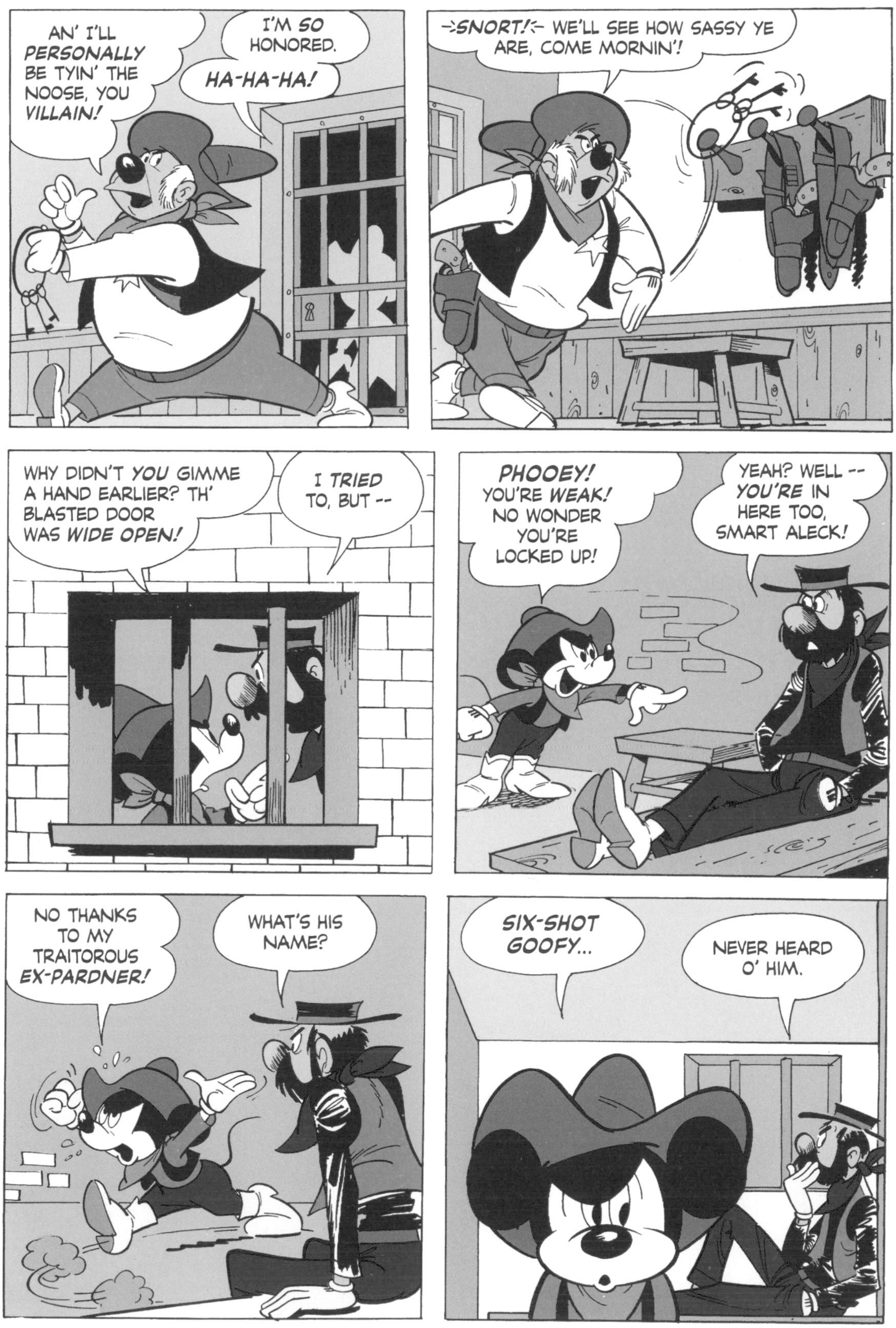
AN' I'LL PERSONALLY BE TYIN' THE NOOSE, YOU VILLAIN!
I'M SO HONORED.
HA-HA-HA!
-SNORT!- WE'LL SEE HOW SASSY YE ARE, COME MORNIN'!
WHY DIDN'T YOU GIMME A HAND EARLIER? TH' BLASTED DOOR WAS WIDE OPEN!
I TRIED TO, BUT --
PHOOEY! YOU'RE WEAK! NO WONDER YOU'RE LOCKED UP!
YEAH? WELL -- YOU'RE IN HERE TOO, SMART ALECK!
NO THANKS TO MY TRAITOROUS EX-PARDNER!
WHAT'S HIS NAME?
SIX-SHOT GOOFY...
NEVER HEARD O' HIM.

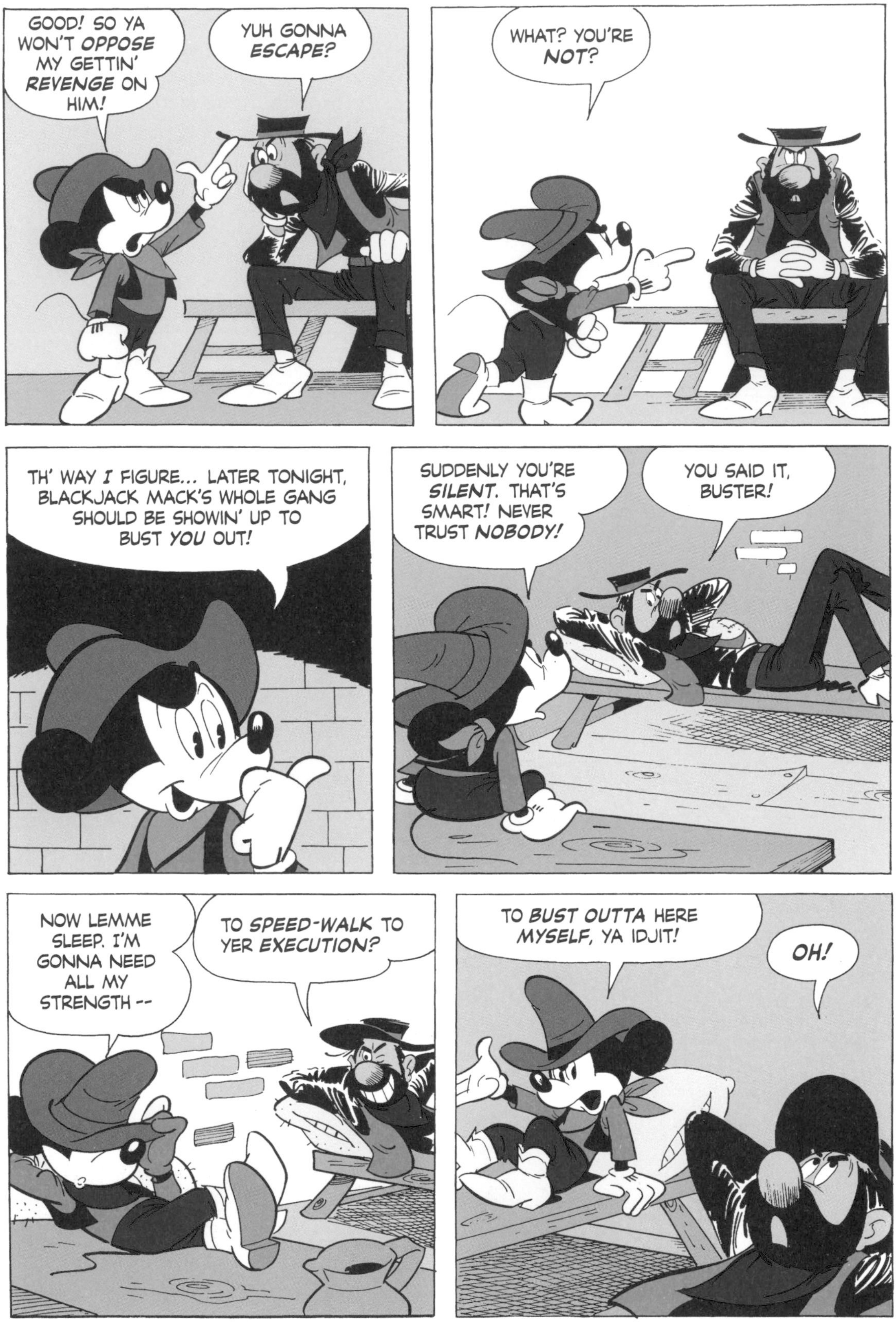
GOOD! SO YA WON'T OPPOSE MY GETTIN' REVENGE ON HIM!
YUH GONNA ESCAPE?
WHAT? YOU'RE NOT?
TH' WAY I FIGURE... LATER TONIGHT, BLACKJACK MACK'S WHOLE GANG SHOULD BE SHOWIN' UP TO BUST YOU OUT!
SUDDENLY YOU'RE SILENT. THAT'S SMART! NEVER TRUST NOBODY!
YOU SAID IT, BUSTER!
NOW LEMME SLEEP. I'M GONNA NEED ALL MY STRENGTH --
TO SPEED-WALK TO YER EXECUTION?
TO BUST OUTTA HERE MYSELF, YA IDJIT!
OH!

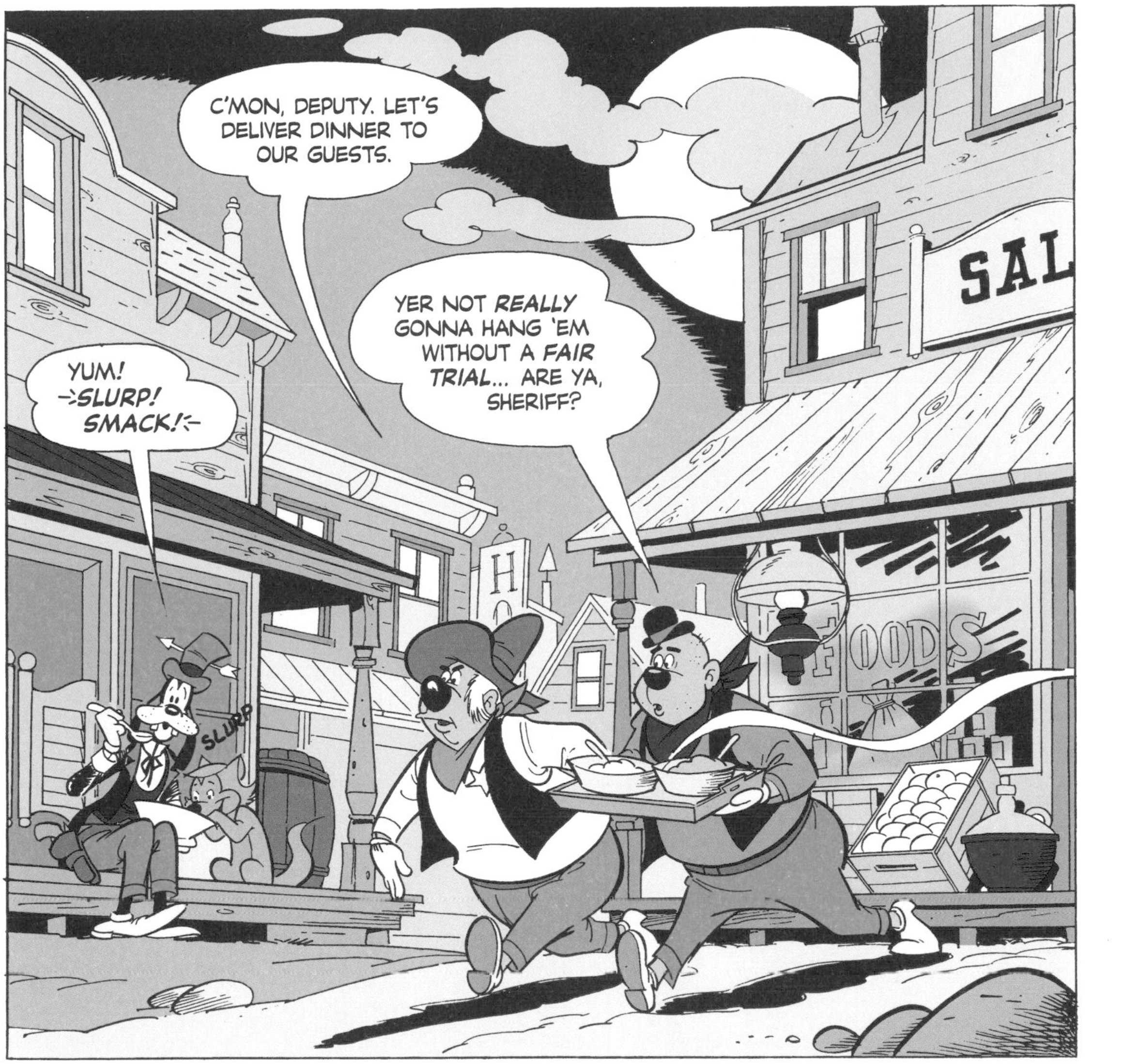
C'MON, DEPUTY. LET'S DELIVER DINNER TO OUR GUESTS.
YUM! -SLURP! SMACK!-
YER NOT REALLY GONNA HANG 'EM WITHOUT A FAIR TRIAL... ARE YA, SHERIFF?
SLURP
SAL
FOODS
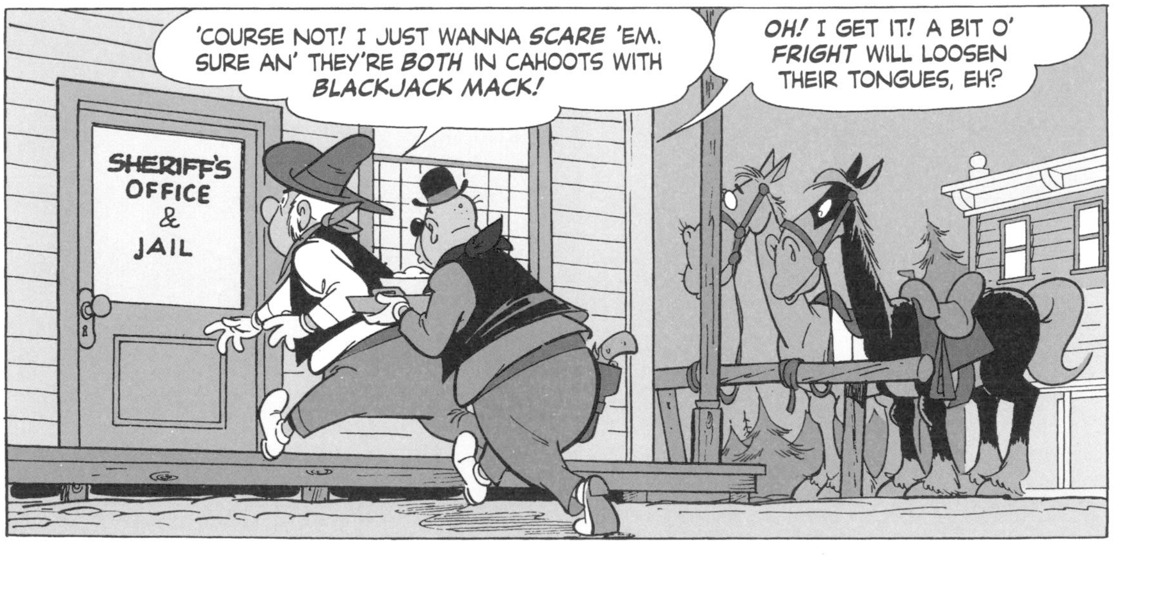
'COURSE NOT! I JUST WANNA SCARE 'EM. SURE AN' THEY'RE BOTH IN CAHOOTS WITH BLACKJACK MACK!
OH! I GET IT! A BIT O' FRIGHT WILL LOOSEN THEIR TONGUES, EH?
SHERIFF'S OFFICE & JAIL

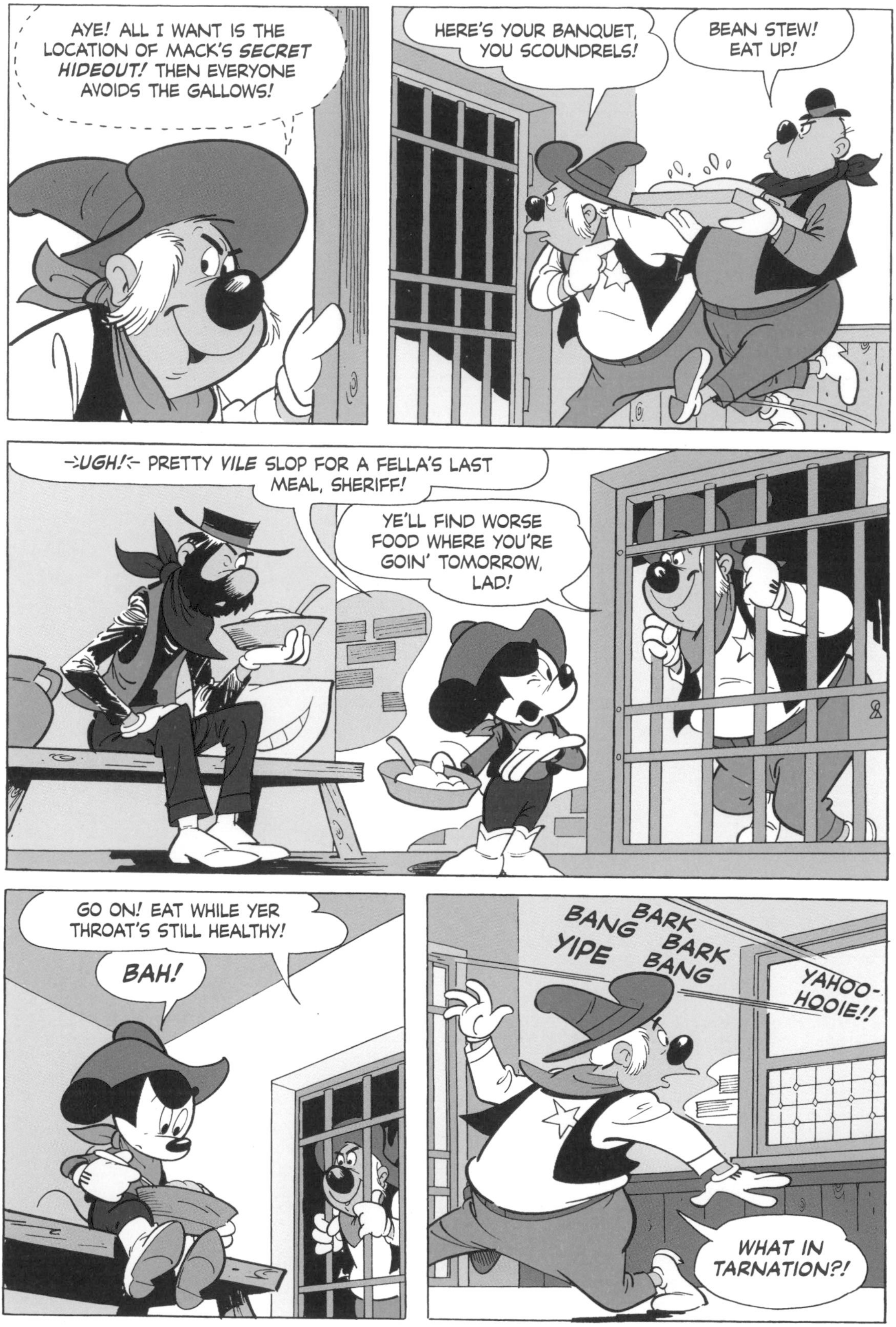
AYE! ALL I WANT IS THE LOCATION OF MACK'S SECRET HIDEOUT! THEN EVERYONE AVOIDS THE GALLOWS!
HERE'S YOUR BANQUET, YOU SCOUNDRELS!
BEAN STEW! EAT UP!
–UGH!– PRETTY VILE SLOP FOR A FELLA'S LAST MEAL, SHERIFF!
YE'LL FIND WORSE FOOD WHERE YOU'RE GOIN' TOMORROW, LAD!
GO ON! EAT WHILE YER THROAT'S STILL HEALTHY!
BAH!
BANG
BARK
YIPE
BARK
BANG
YAHOO-HOOIE!!
WHAT IN TARNATION?!

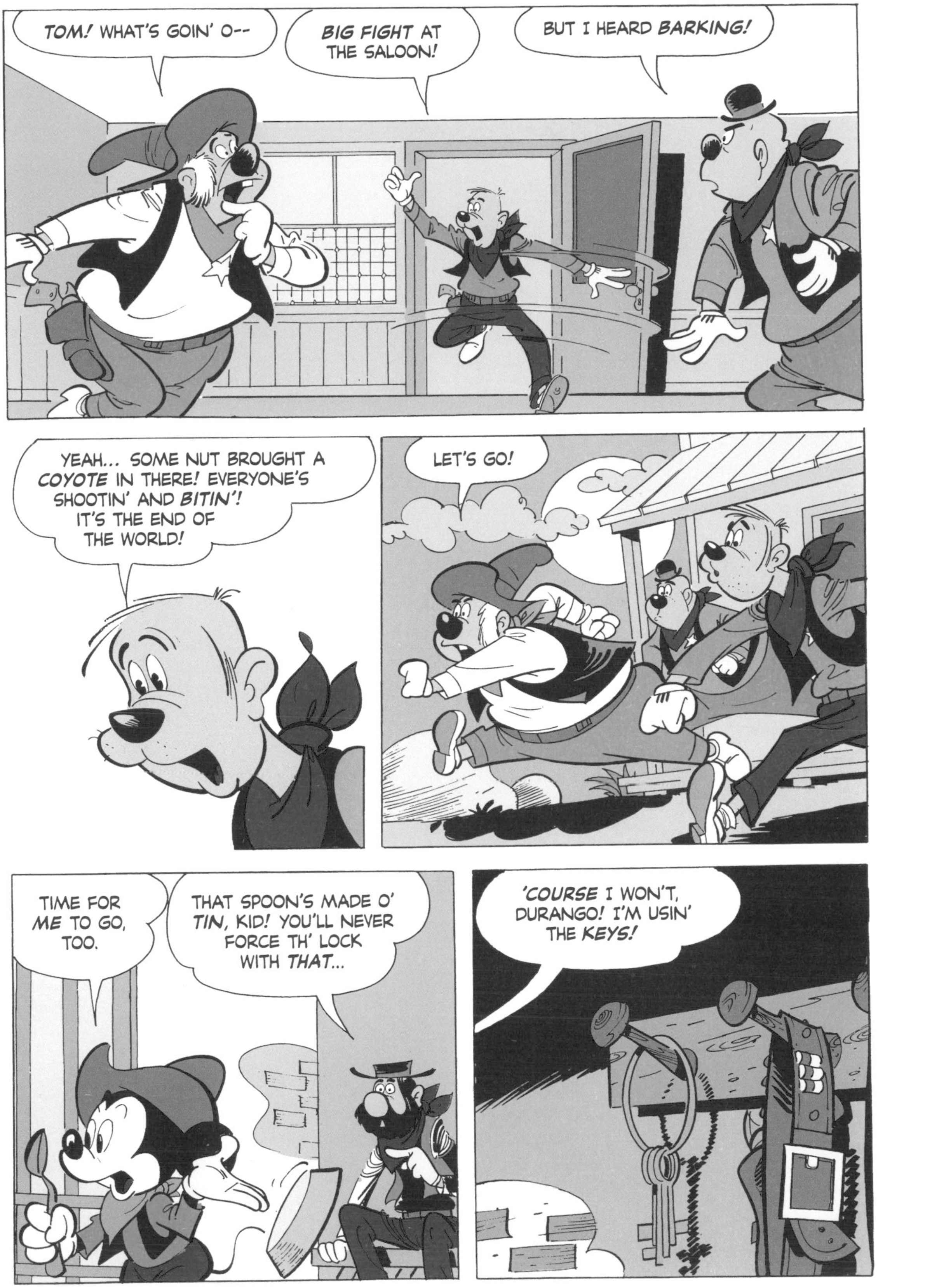
TOM! WHAT'S GOIN' O--
BIG FIGHT AT THE SALOON!
BUT I HEARD BARKING!
YEAH... SOME NUT BROUGHT A COYOTE IN THERE! EVERYONE'S SHOOTIN' AND BITIN'! IT'S THE END OF THE WORLD!
LET'S GO!
TIME FOR ME TO GO, TOO.
THAT SPOON'S MADE O' TIN, KID! YOU'LL NEVER FORCE TH' LOCK WITH THAT...
'COURSE I WON'T, DURANGO! I'M USIN' THE KEYS!

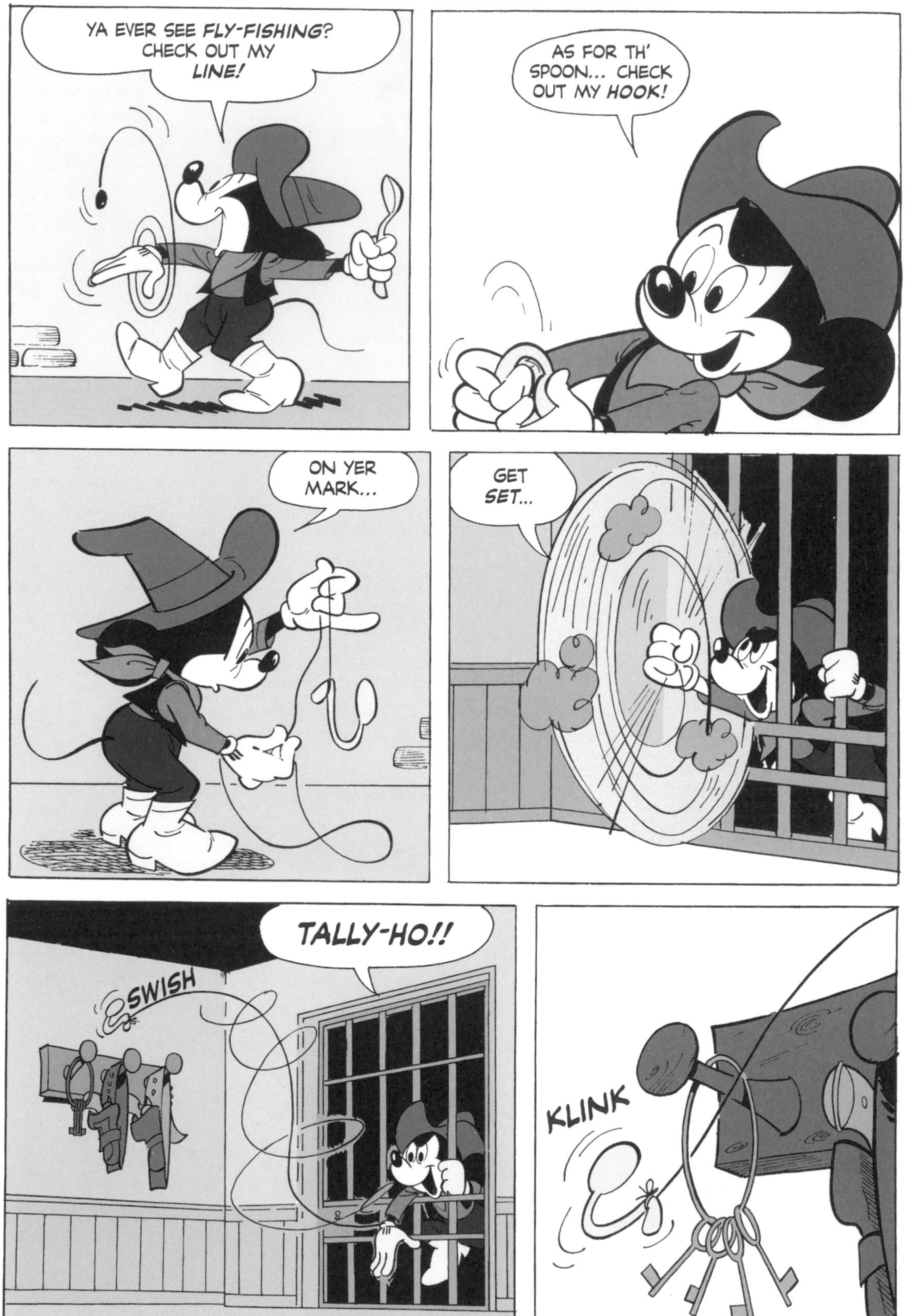
YA EVER SEE FLY-FISHING? CHECK OUT MY LINE!
AS FOR TH' SPOON... CHECK OUT MY HOOK!
ON YER MARK...
GET SET...
TALLY-HO!!
SWISH
KLINK

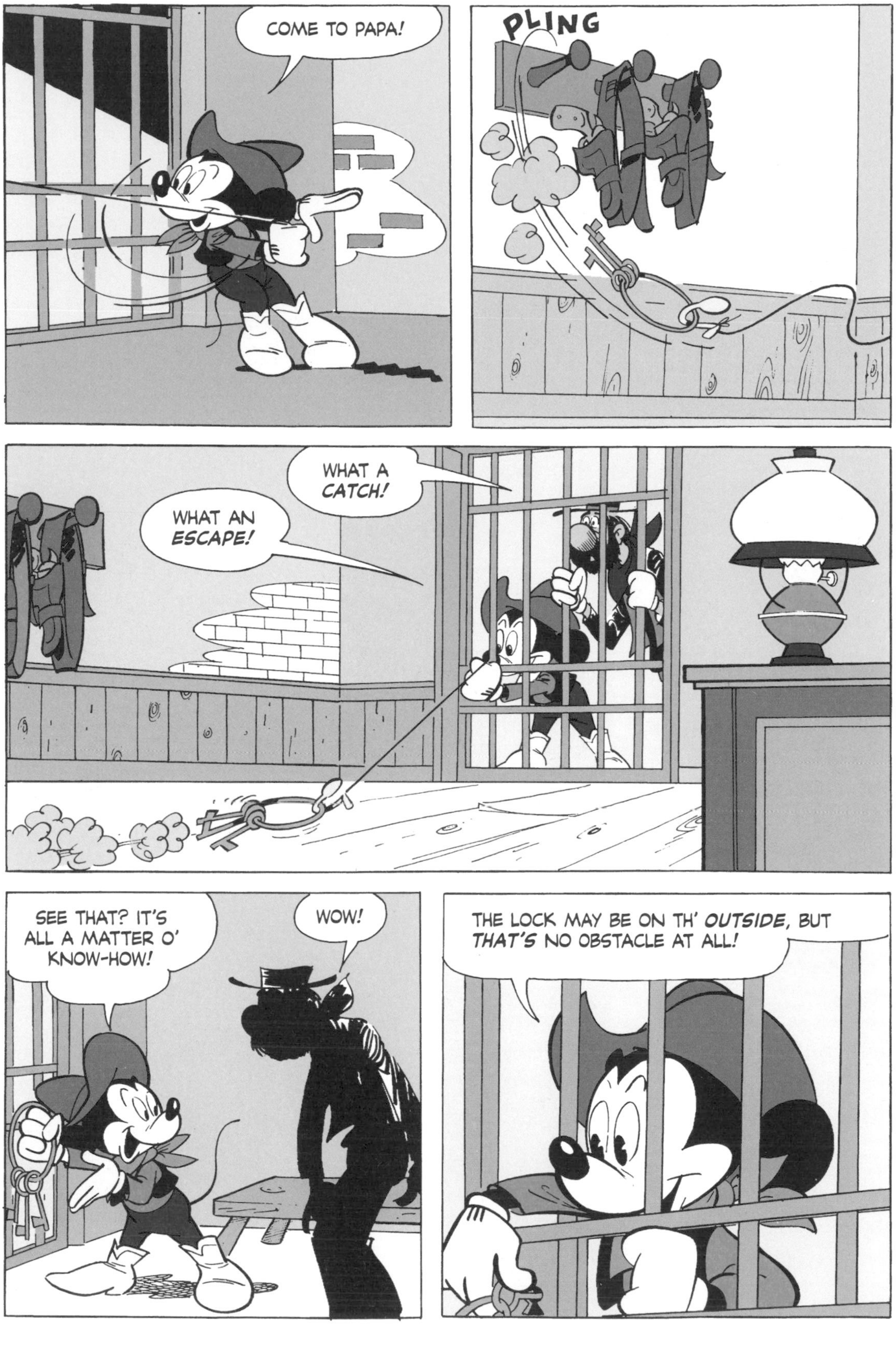
COME TO PAPA!
PLING
WHAT AN ESCAPE!
WHAT A CATCH!
SEE THAT? IT'S ALL A MATTER O' KNOW-HOW!
WOW!
THE LOCK MAY BE ON TH' OUTSIDE, BUT THAT'S NO OBSTACLE AT ALL!

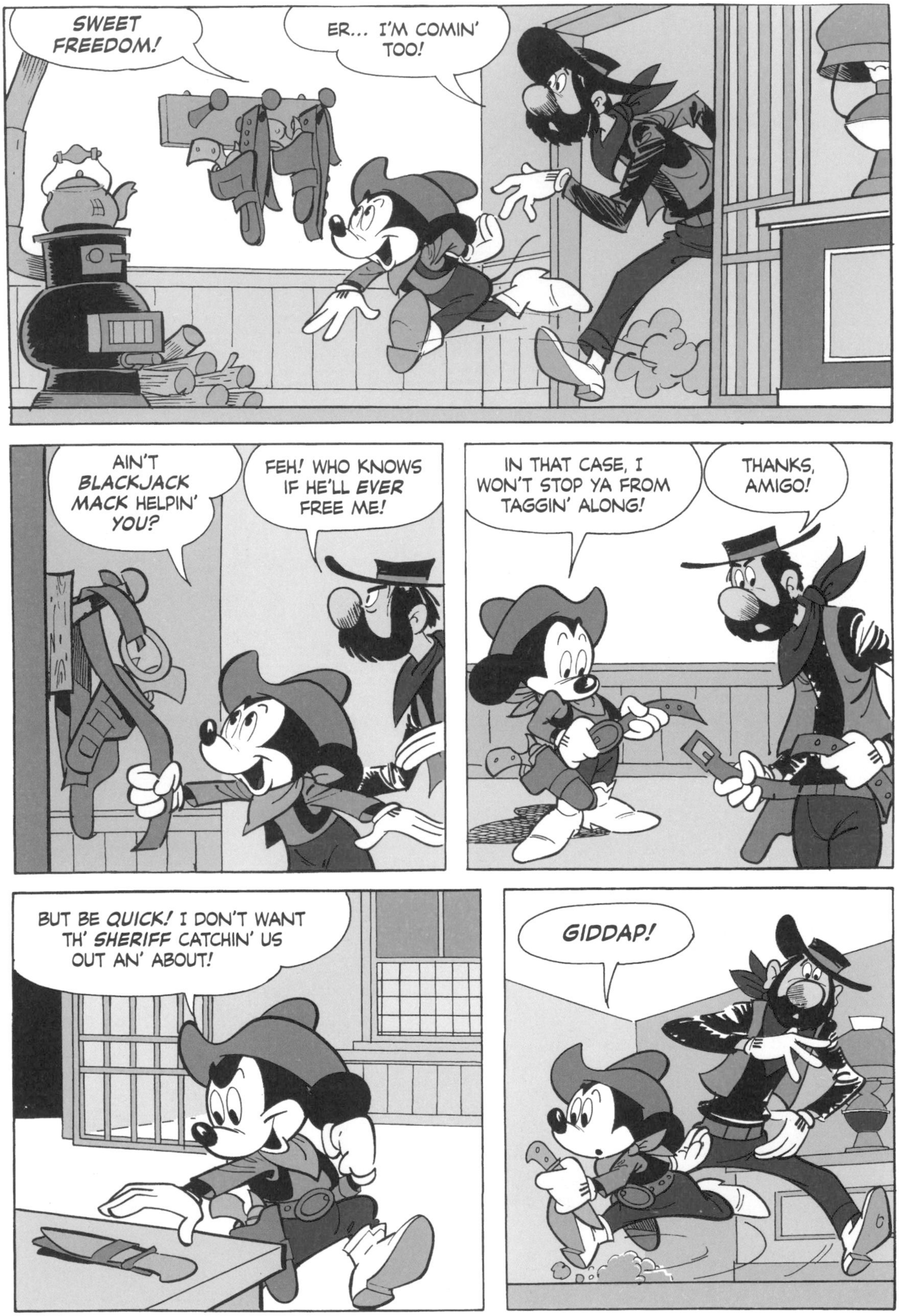
SWEET FREEDOM!
ER... I'M COMIN' TOO!
AIN'T BLACKJACK MACK HELPIN' YOU?
FEH! WHO KNOWS IF HE'LL EVER FREE ME!
IN THAT CASE, I WON'T STOP YA FROM TAGGIN' ALONG!
THANKS, AMIGO!
BUT BE QUICK! I DON'T WANT TH' SHERIFF CATCHIN' US OUT AN' ABOUT!
GIDDAP!

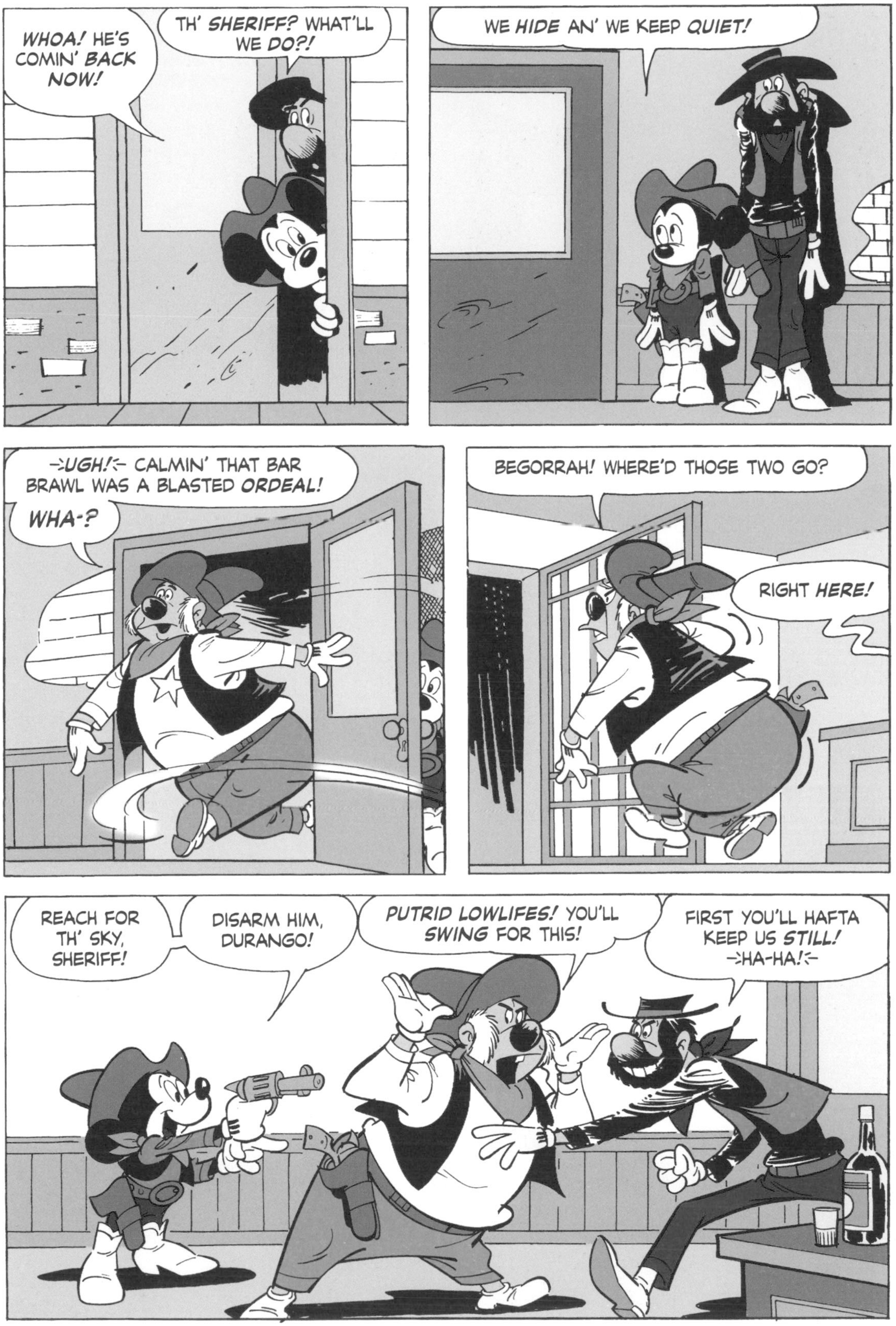

WHOA! HE'S COMIN' BACK NOW!
TH' SHERIFF? WHAT'LL WE DO?!
WE HIDE AN' WE KEEP QUIET!
-UGH!- CALMIN' THAT BAR BRAWL WAS A BLASTED ORDEAL!
WHA-?
BEGORRAH! WHERE'D THOSE TWO GO?
RIGHT HERE!
REACH FOR TH' SKY, SHERIFF!
DISARM HIM, DURANGO!
PUTRID LOWLIFES! YOU'LL SWING FOR THIS!
FIRST YOU'LL HAFTA KEEP US STILL! -HA-HA!-

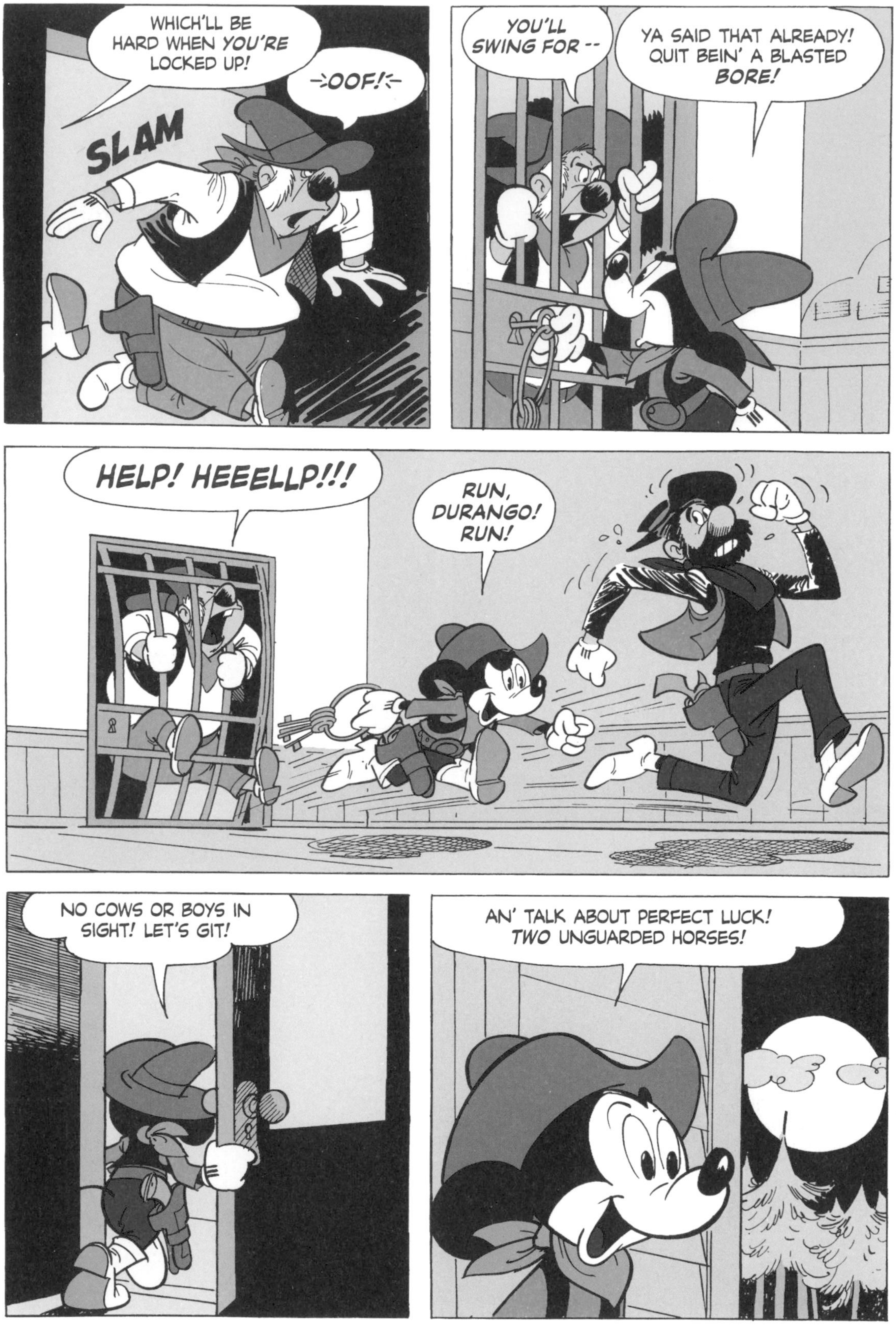
WHICH'LL BE HARD WHEN YOU'RE LOCKED UP!
SLAM
OOF!
YOU'LL SWING FOR --
YA SAID THAT ALREADY! QUIT BEIN' A BLASTED BORE!
HELP! HEEELLP!!!
RUN, DURANGO! RUN!
NO COWS OR BOYS IN SIGHT! LET'S GIT!
AN' TALK ABOUT PERFECT LUCK! TWO UNGUARDED HORSES!

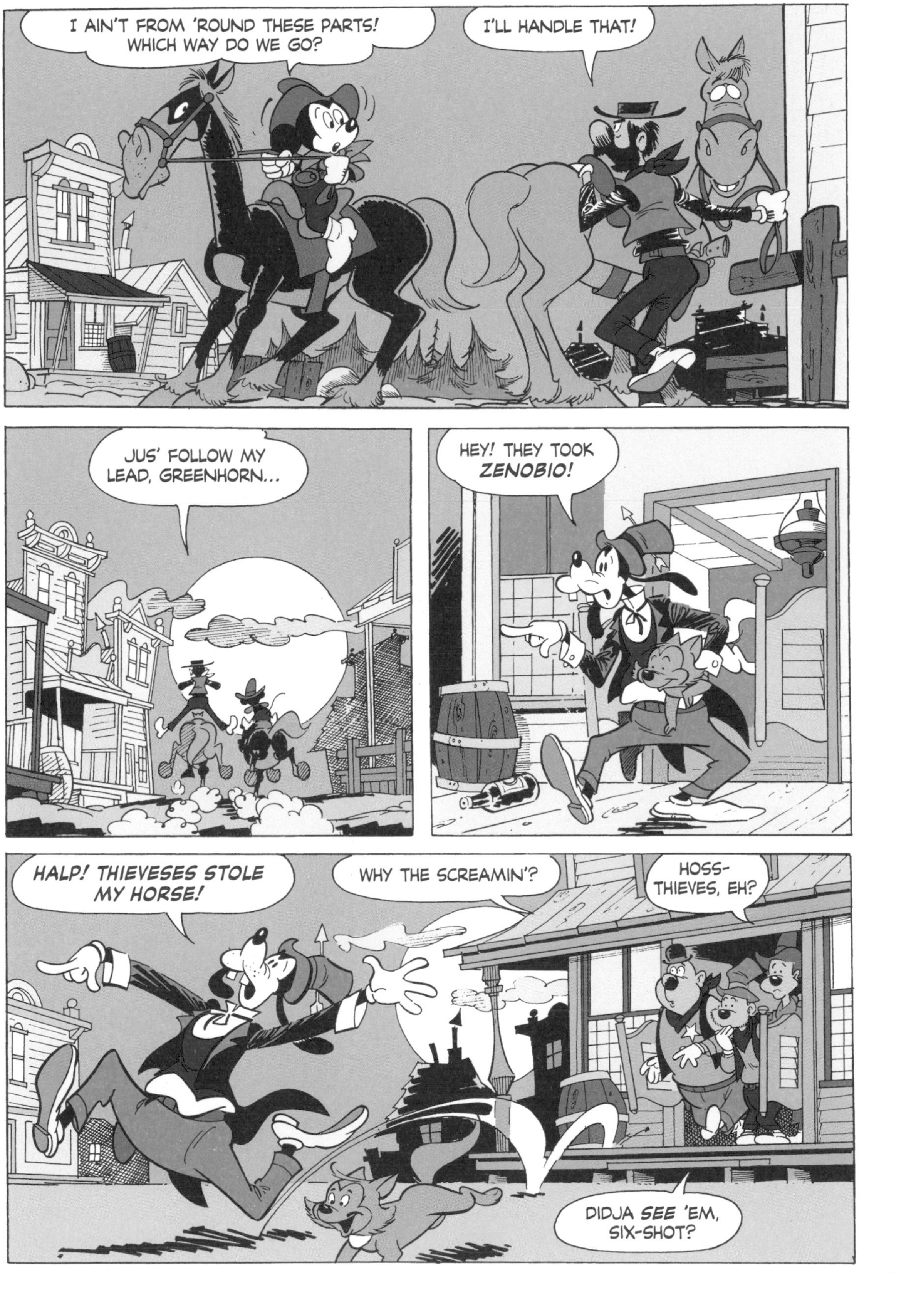
I AIN'T FROM 'ROUND THESE PARTS! WHICH WAY DO WE GO?
I'LL HANDLE THAT!
JUS' FOLLOW MY LEAD, GREENHORN...
HEY! THEY TOOK ZENOBIO!
HALP! THIEVESES STOLE MY HORSE!
WHY THE SCREAMIN'?
HOSS-THIEVES, EH?
DIDJA SEE 'EM, SIX-SHOT?

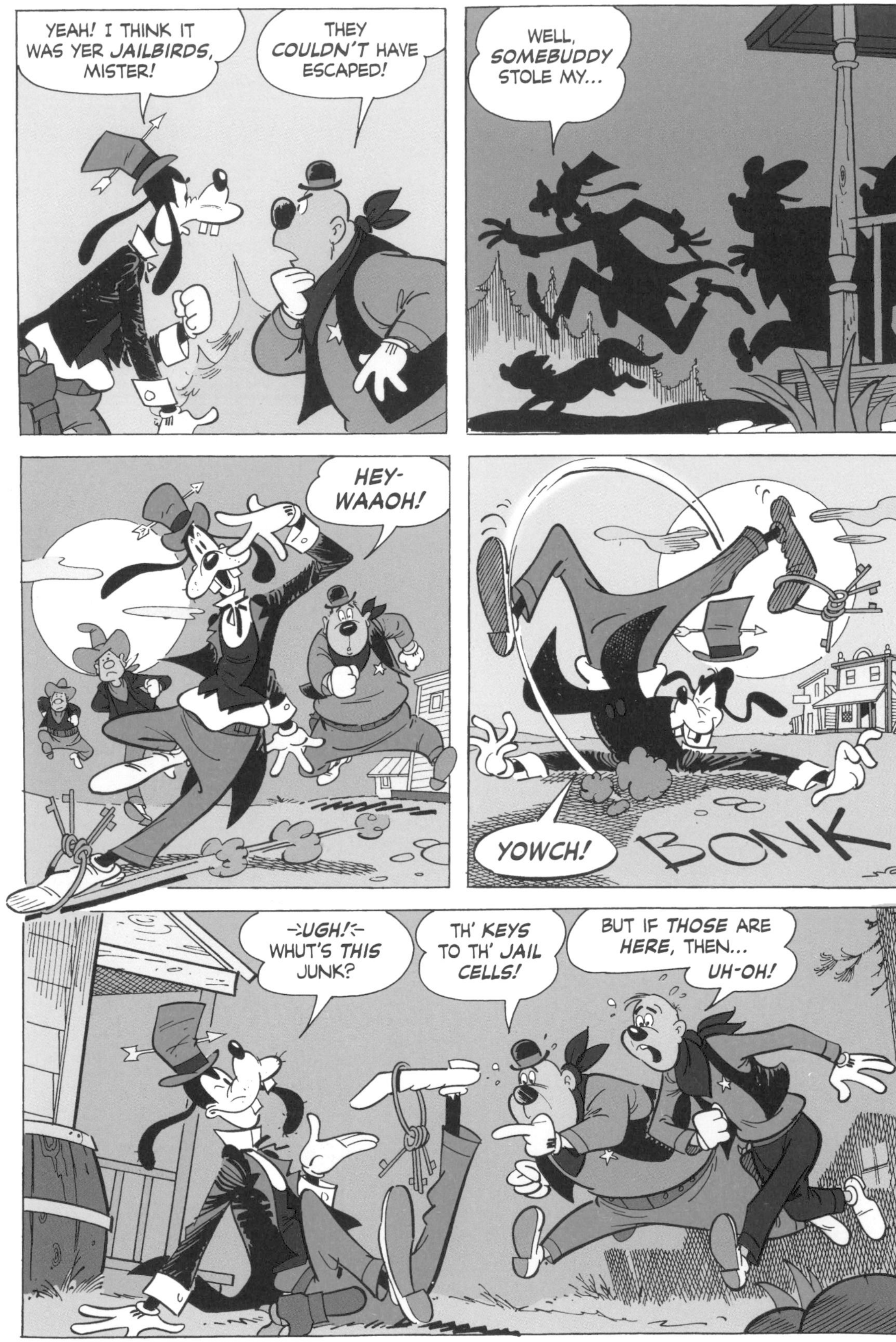
YEAH! I THINK IT WAS YER JAILBIRDS, MISTER!
THEY COULDN'T HAVE ESCAPED!
WELL, SOMEBUDDY STOLE MY...
HEY-WAAOH!
YOWCH!
BONK
-UGH!- WHUT'S THIS JUNK?
TH' KEYS TO TH' JAIL CELLS!
BUT IF THOSE ARE HERE, THEN... UH-OH!

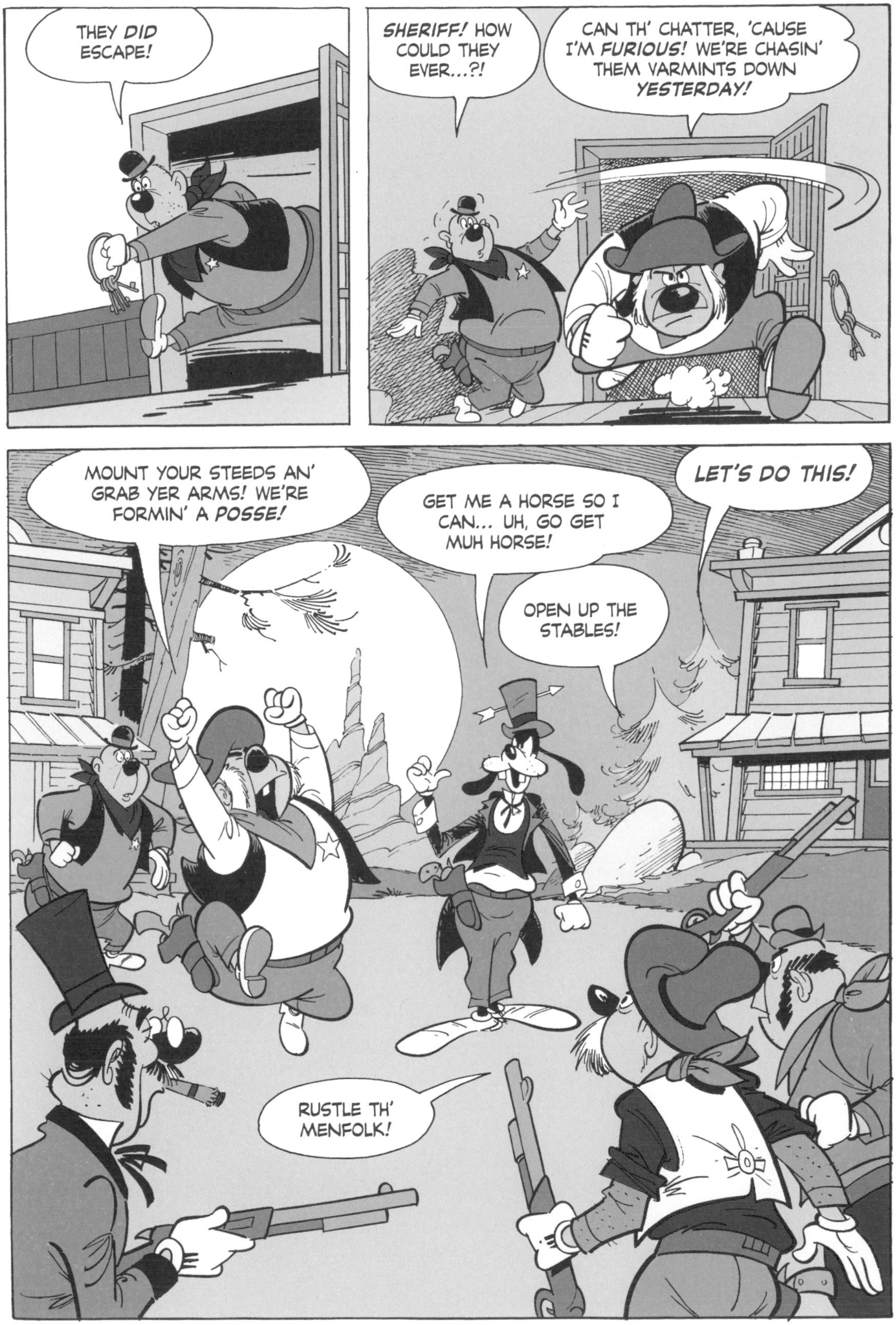
THEY DID ESCAPE!
SHERIFF! HOW COULD THEY EVER...?!
CAN TH' CHATTER, 'CAUSE I'M FURIOUS! WE'RE CHASIN' THEM VARMINTS DOWN YESTERDAY!
MOUNT YOUR STEEDS AN' GRAB YER ARMS! WE'RE FORMIN' A POSSE!
GET ME A HORSE SO I CAN... UH, GO GET MUH HORSE!
LET'S DO THIS!
OPEN UP THE STABLES!
RUSTLE TH' MENFOLK!

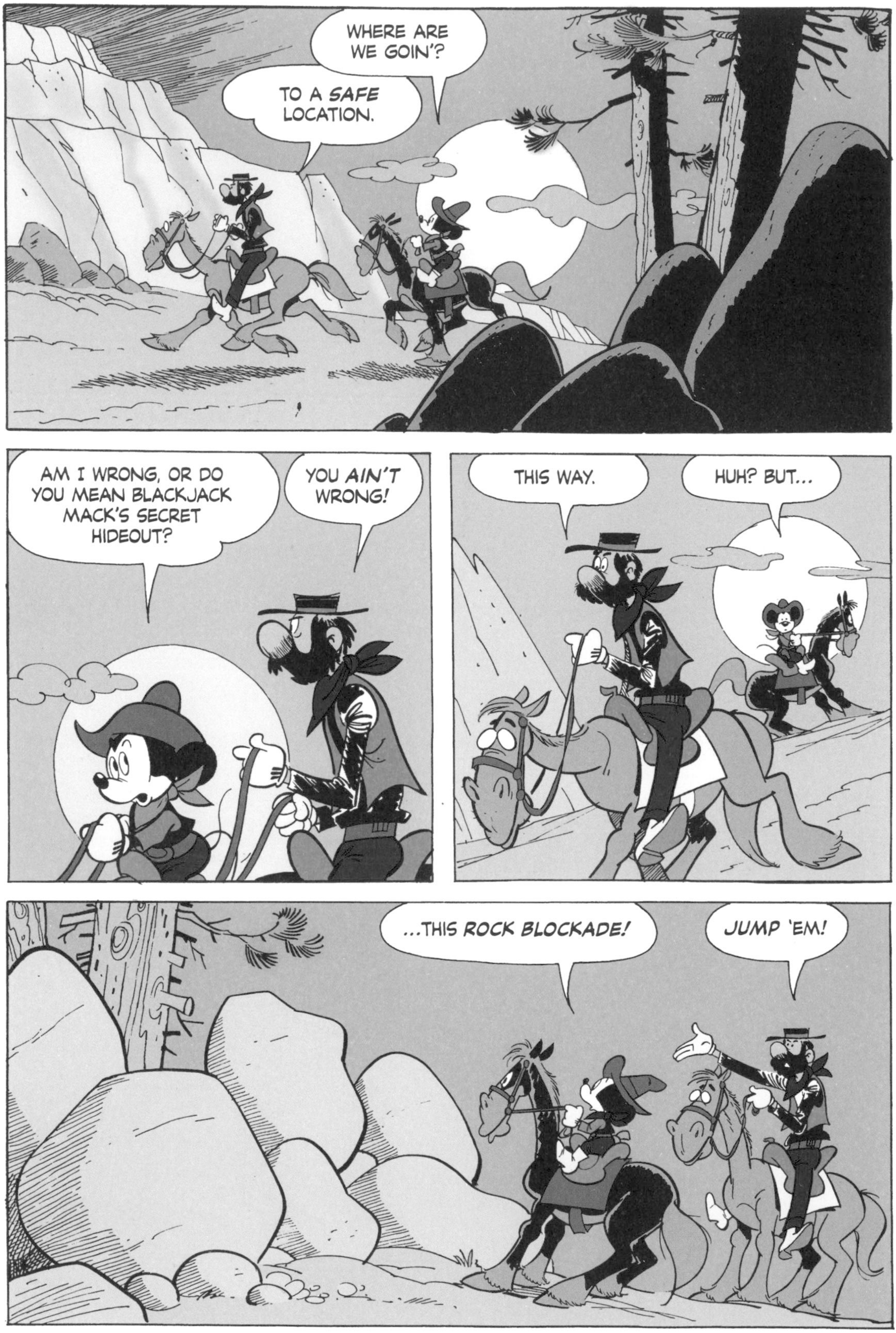
WHERE ARE WE GOIN'?
TO A SAFE LOCATION.
AM I WRONG, OR DO YOU MEAN BLACKJACK MACK'S SECRET HIDEOUT?
YOU AIN'T WRONG!
THIS WAY.
HUH? BUT...
...THIS ROCK BLOCKADE!
JUMP 'EM!

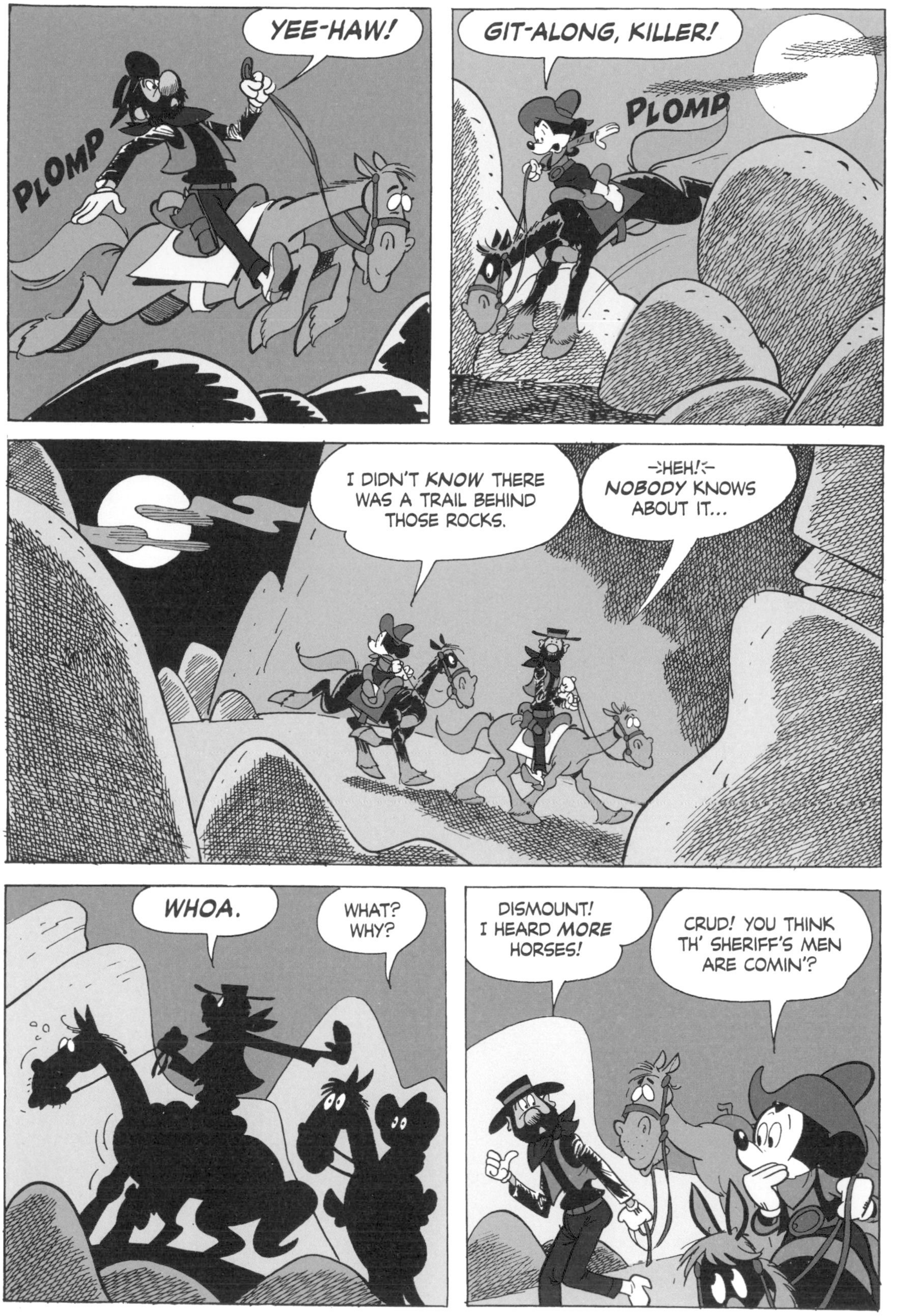
YEE-HAW!
PLOMP
GIT-ALONG, KILLER!
PLOMP
I DIDN'T KNOW THERE WAS A TRAIL BEHIND THOSE ROCKS.
–HEH!– NOBODY KNOWS ABOUT IT...
WHOA.
WHAT? WHY?
DISMOUNT! I HEARD MORE HORSES!
CRUD! YOU THINK TH' SHERIFF'S MEN ARE COMIN'?

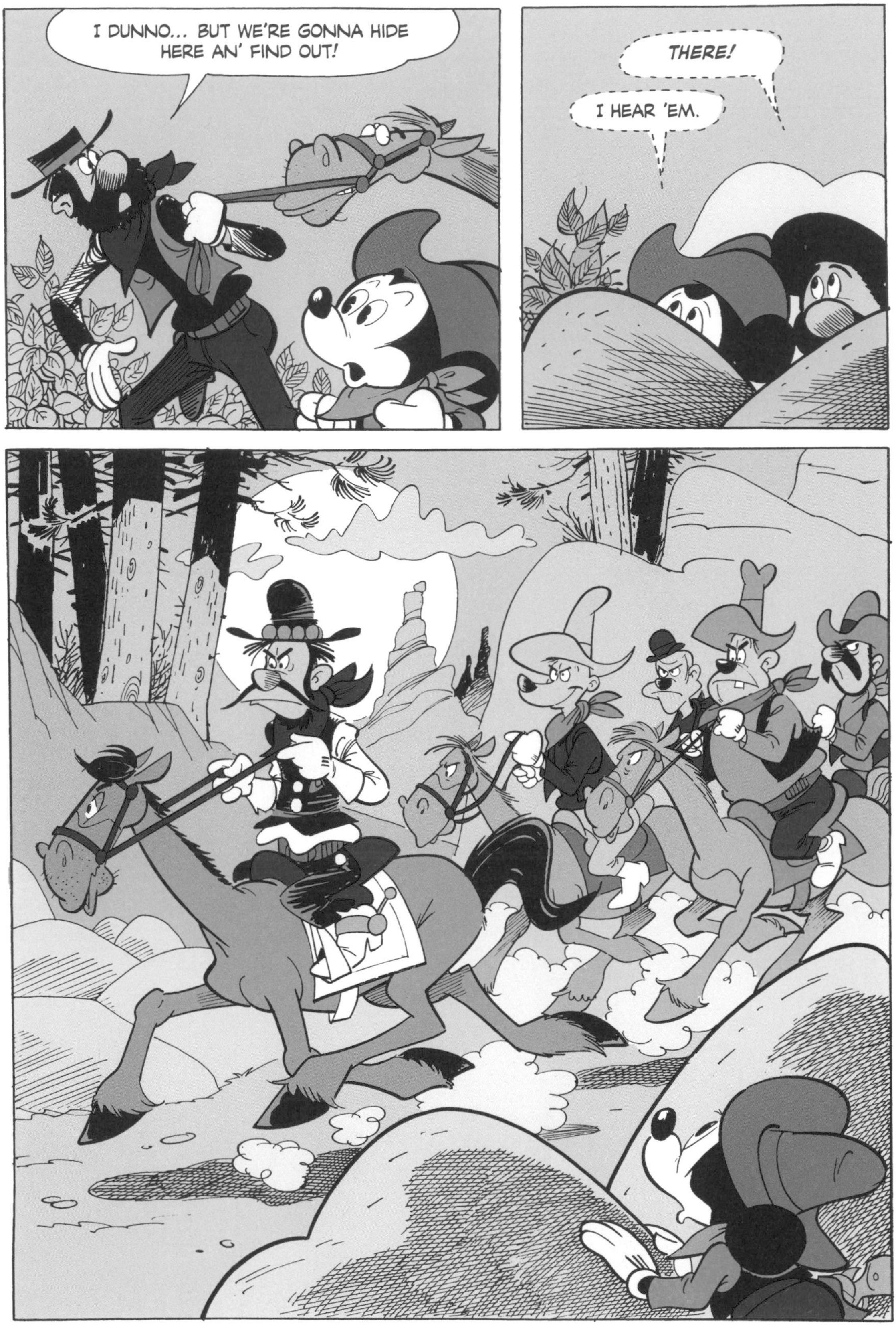
I DUNNO... BUT WE'RE GONNA HIDE HERE AN' FIND OUT!
THERE!
I HEAR 'EM.

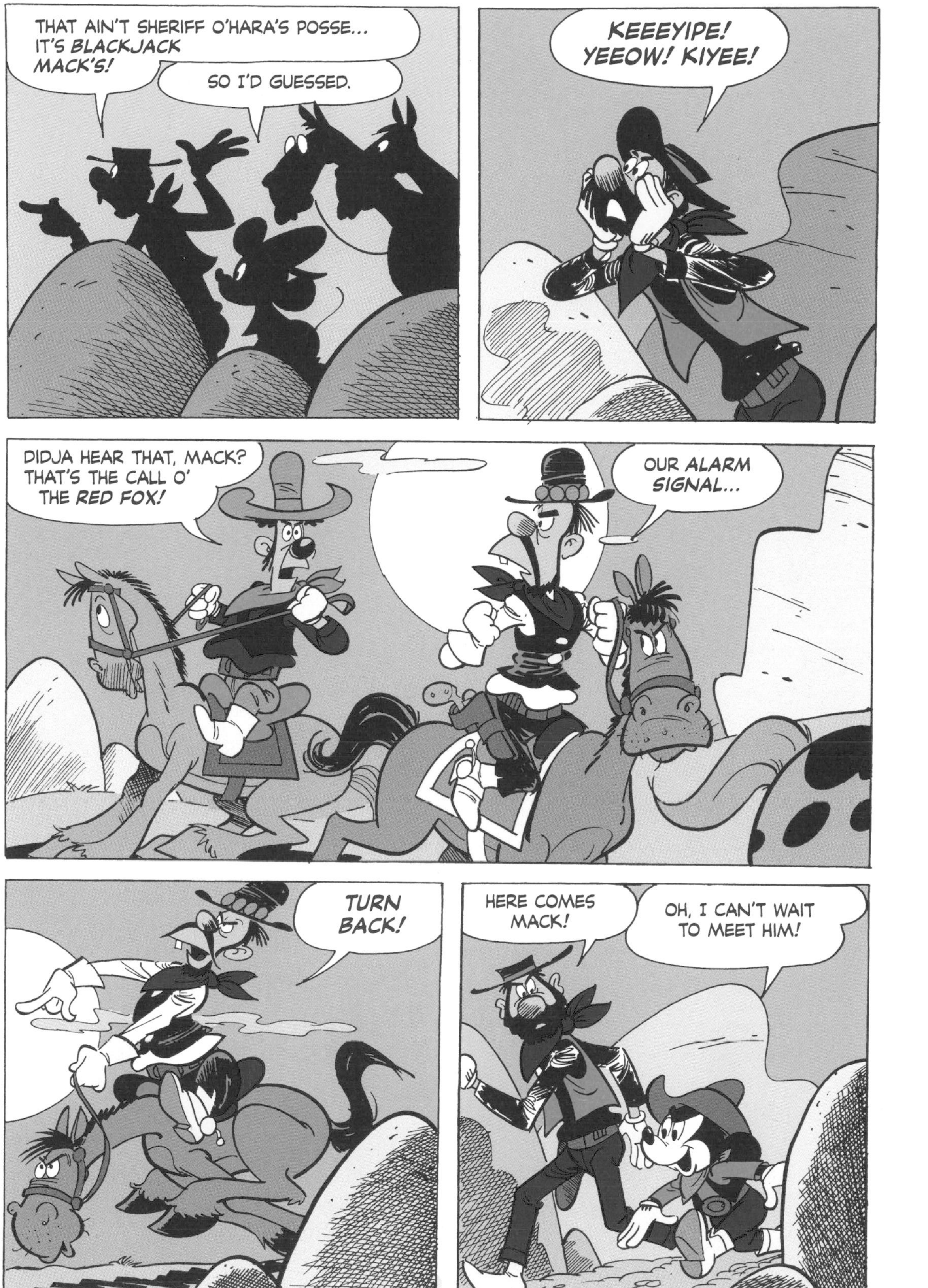
THAT AIN'T SHERIFF O'HARA'S POSSE... IT'S BLACKJACK MACK'S!
SO I'D GUESSED.
KEEEYIPE! YEEOW! KIYEE!
DIDJA HEAR THAT, MACK? THAT'S THE CALL O' THE RED FOX!
OUR ALARM SIGNAL...
TURN BACK!
HERE COMES MACK!
OH, I CAN'T WAIT TO MEET HIM!

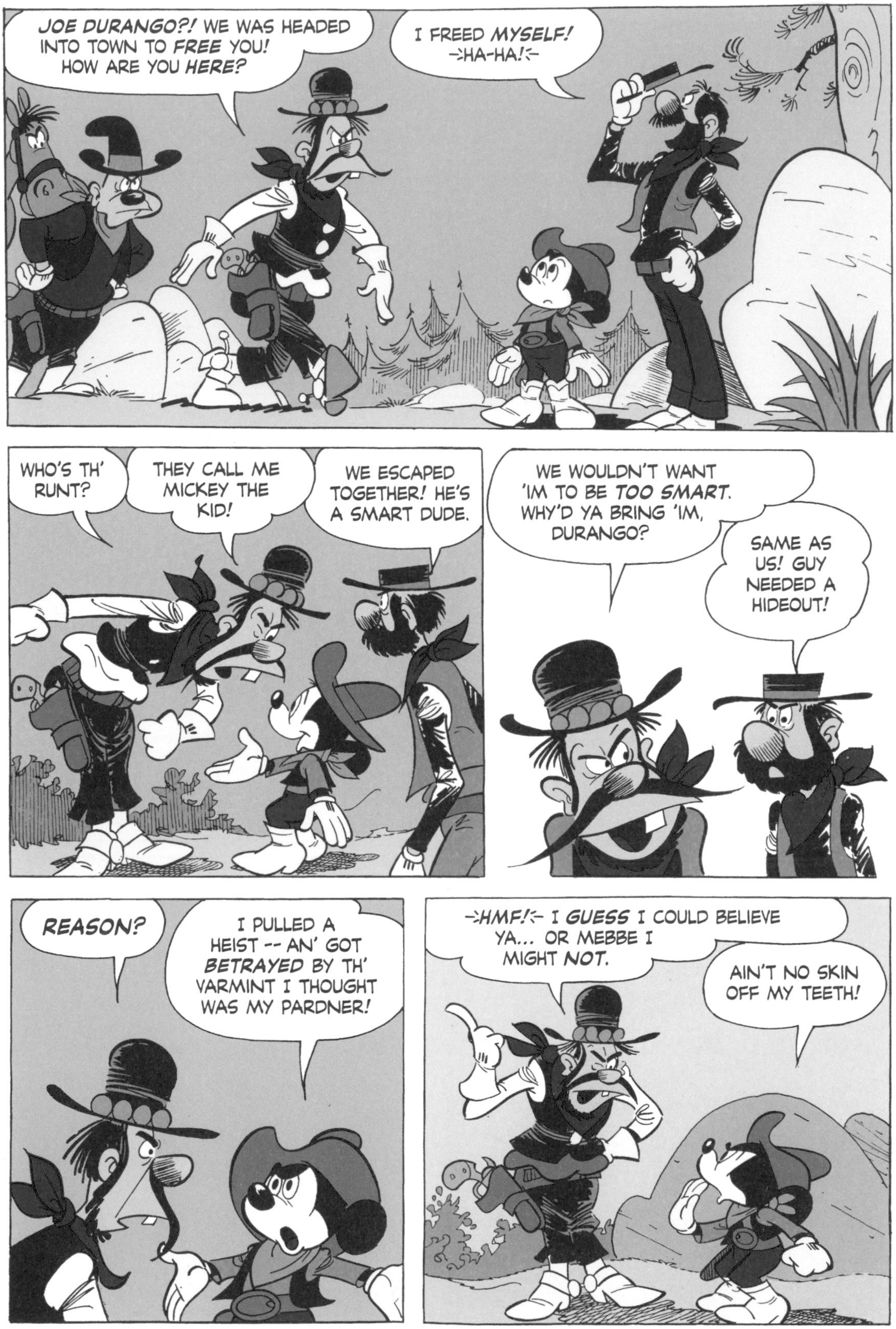
JOE DURANGO?! WE WAS HEADED INTO TOWN TO FREE YOU! HOW ARE YOU HERE?
I FREED MYSELF! -HA-HA!-
WHO'S TH' RUNT?
THEY CALL ME MICKEY THE KID!
WE ESCAPED TOGETHER! HE'S A SMART DUDE.
WE WOULDN'T WANT 'IM TO BE TOO SMART. WHY'D YA BRING 'IM, DURANGO?
SAME AS US! GUY NEEDED A HIDEOUT!
REASON?
I PULLED A HEIST -- AN' GOT BETRAYED BY TH' VARMINT I THOUGHT WAS MY PARDNER!
-HMF!- I GUESS I COULD BELIEVE YA... OR MEBBE I MIGHT NOT.
AIN'T NO SKIN OFF MY TEETH!

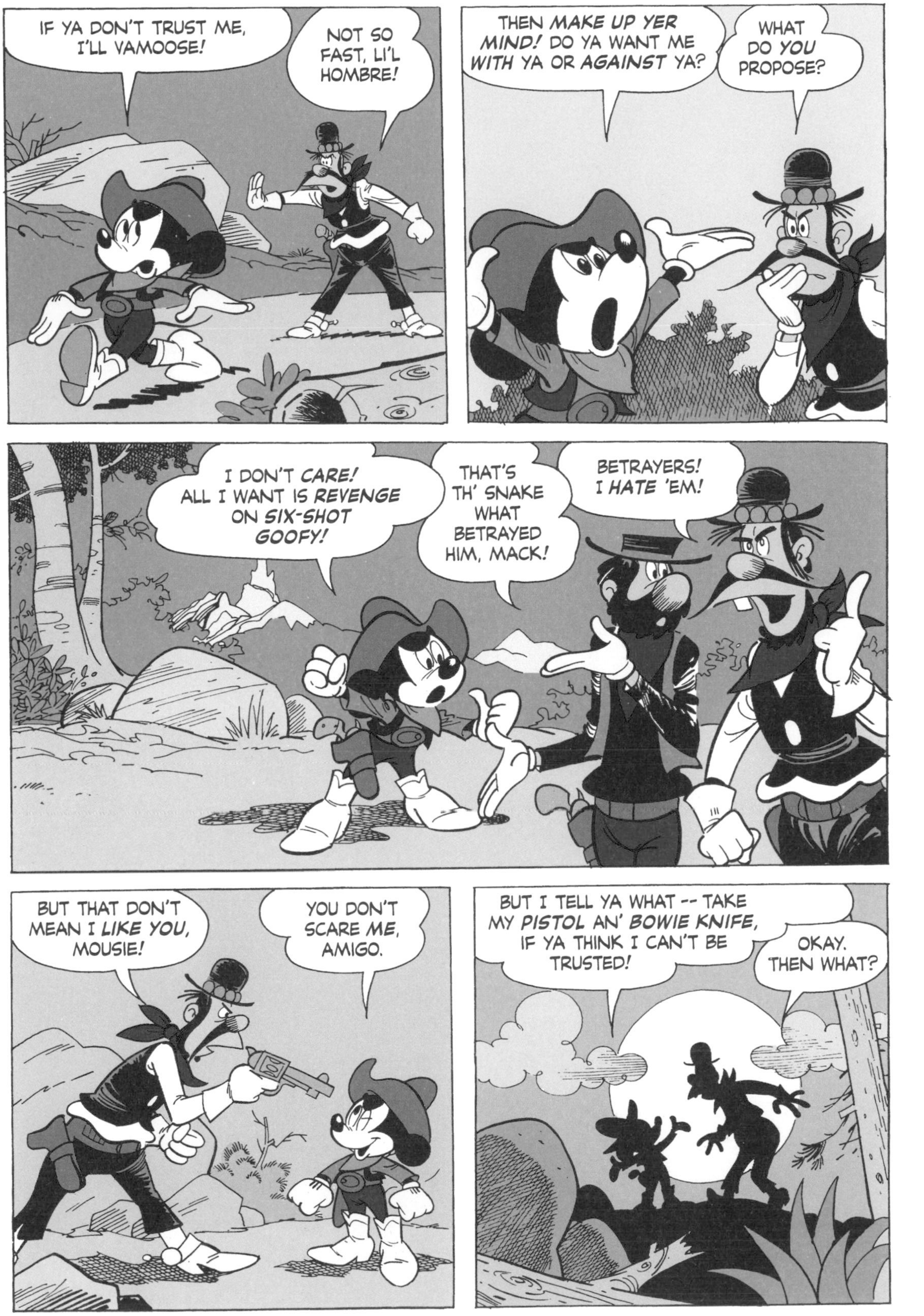
IF YA DON'T TRUST ME, I'LL VAMOOSE!
NOT SO FAST, LI'L HOMBRE!
THEN MAKE UP YER MIND! DO YA WANT ME WITH YA OR AGAINST YA?
WHAT DO YOU PROPOSE?
I DON'T CARE! ALL I WANT IS REVENGE ON SIX-SHOT GOOFY!
THAT'S TH' SNAKE WHAT BETRAYED HIM, MACK!
BETRAYERS! I HATE 'EM!
BUT THAT DON'T MEAN I LIKE YOU, MOUSIE!
YOU DON'T SCARE ME, AMIGO.
BUT I TELL YA WHAT -- TAKE MY PISTOL AN' BOWIE KNIFE, IF YA THINK I CAN'T BE TRUSTED!
OKAY. THEN WHAT?

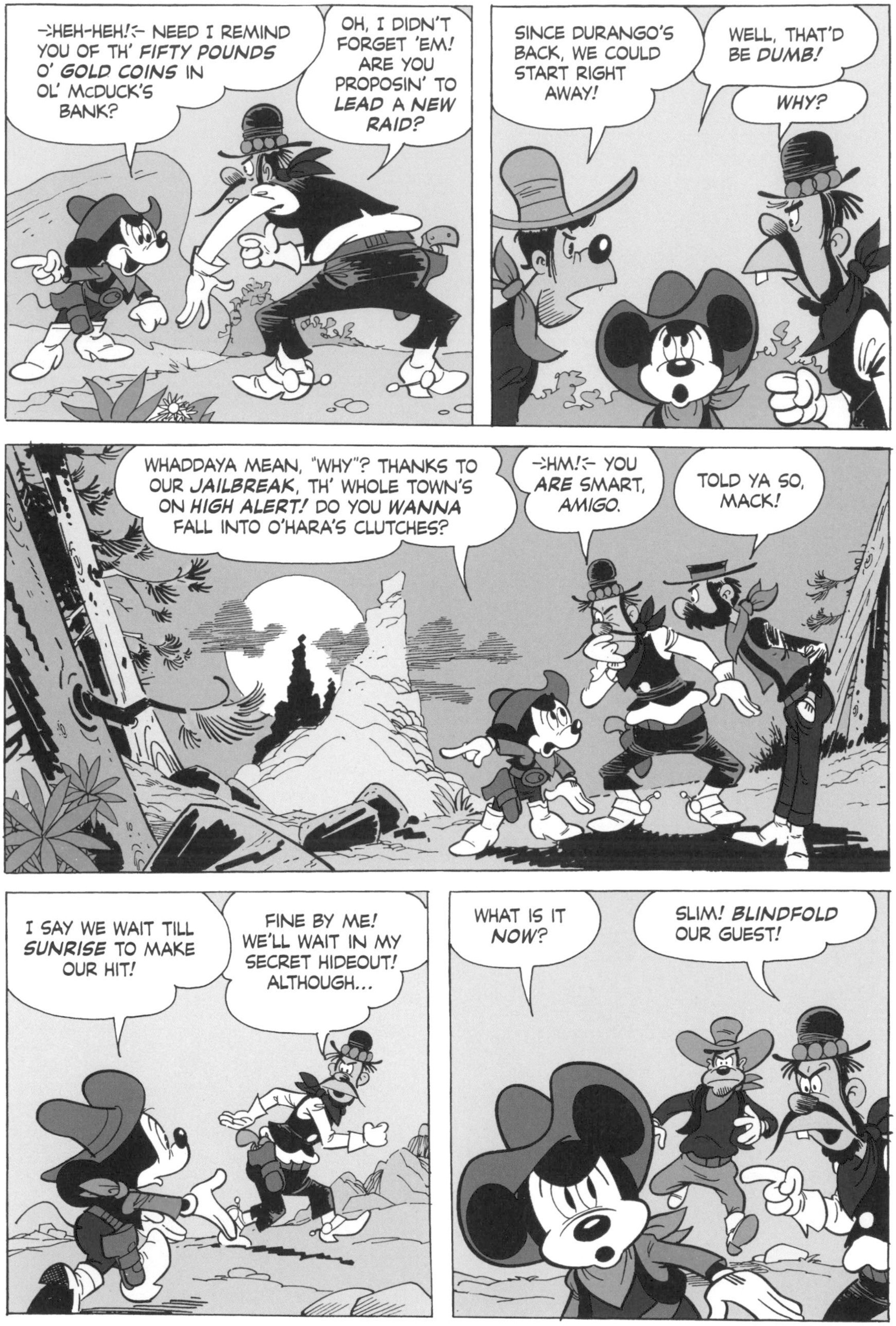
–HEH-HEH!– NEED I REMIND YOU OF TH' FIFTY POUNDS O' GOLD COINS IN OL' McDUCK'S BANK?
OH, I DIDN'T FORGET 'EM! ARE YOU PROPOSIN' TO LEAD A NEW RAID?
SINCE DURANGO'S BACK, WE COULD START RIGHT AWAY!
WELL, THAT'D BE DUMB!
WHY?
WHADDAYA MEAN, "WHY"? THANKS TO OUR JAILBREAK, TH' WHOLE TOWN'S ON HIGH ALERT! DO YOU WANNA FALL INTO O'HARA'S CLUTCHES?
–HM!– YOU ARE SMART, AMIGO.
TOLD YA SO, MACK!
I SAY WE WAIT TILL SUNRISE TO MAKE OUR HIT!
FINE BY ME! WE'LL WAIT IN MY SECRET HIDEOUT! ALTHOUGH...
WHAT IS IT NOW?
SLIM! BLINDFOLD OUR GUEST!

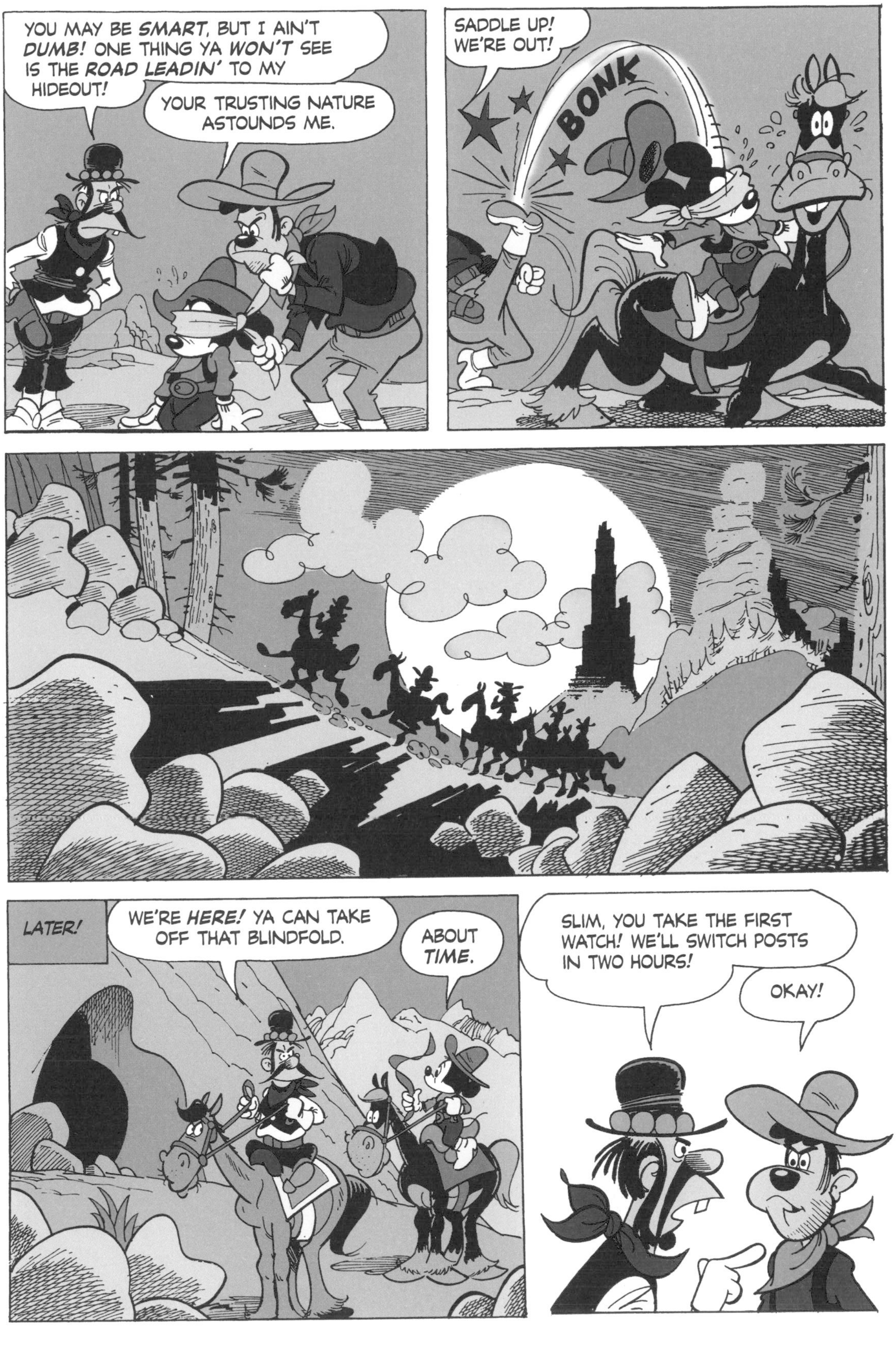
YOU MAY BE SMART, BUT I AIN'T DUMB! ONE THING YA WON'T SEE IS THE ROAD LEADIN' TO MY HIDEOUT!
YOUR TRUSTING NATURE ASTOUNDS ME.
SADDLE UP! WE'RE OUT!
BONK
LATER!
WE'RE HERE! YA CAN TAKE OFF THAT BLINDFOLD.
ABOUT TIME.
SLIM, YOU TAKE THE FIRST WATCH! WE'LL SWITCH POSTS IN TWO HOURS!
OKAY!

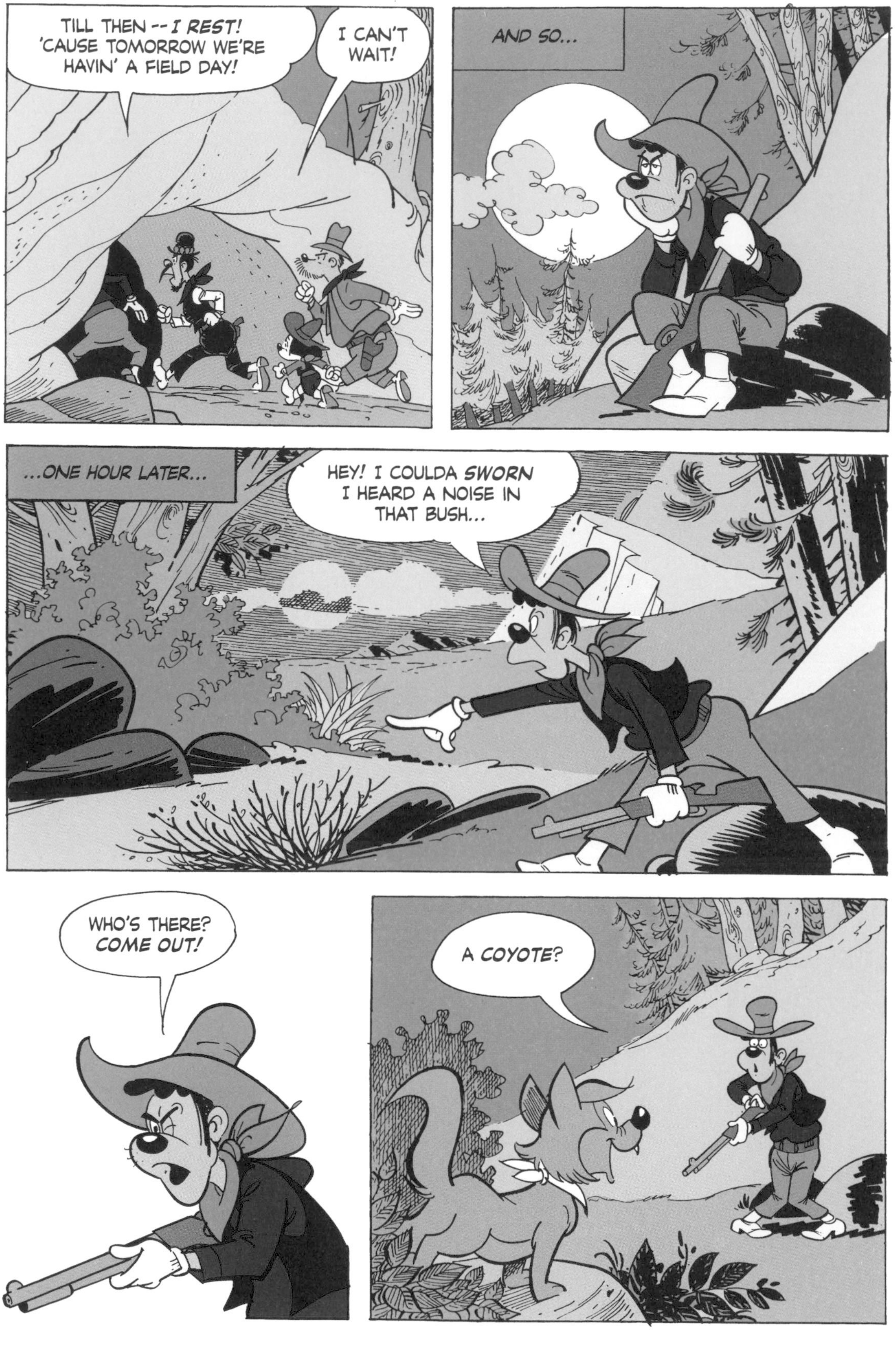
TILL THEN -- I REST! 'CAUSE TOMORROW WE'RE HAVIN' A FIELD DAY!
I CAN'T WAIT!
AND SO...
...ONE HOUR LATER...
HEY! I COULDA SWORN I HEARD A NOISE IN THAT BUSH...
WHO'S THERE? COME OUT!
A COYOTE?

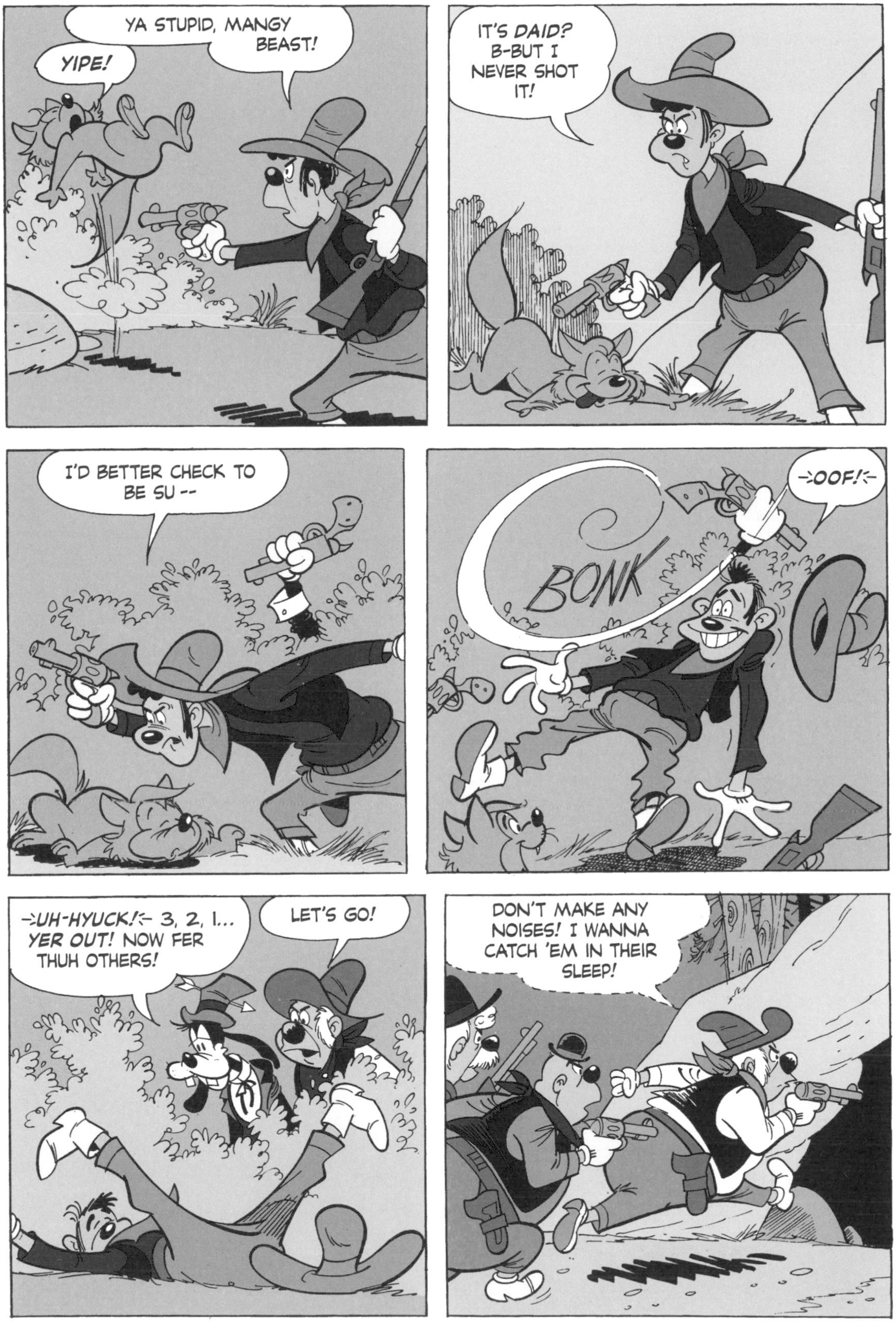
YA STUPID, MANGY BEAST!
YIPE!
IT'S DAID? B-BUT I NEVER SHOT IT!
I'D BETTER CHECK TO BE SU --
BONK
-OOF!-
-UH-HYUCK!- 3, 2, 1... YER OUT! NOW FER THUH OTHERS!
LET'S GO!
DON'T MAKE ANY NOISES! I WANNA CATCH 'EM IN THEIR SLEEP!

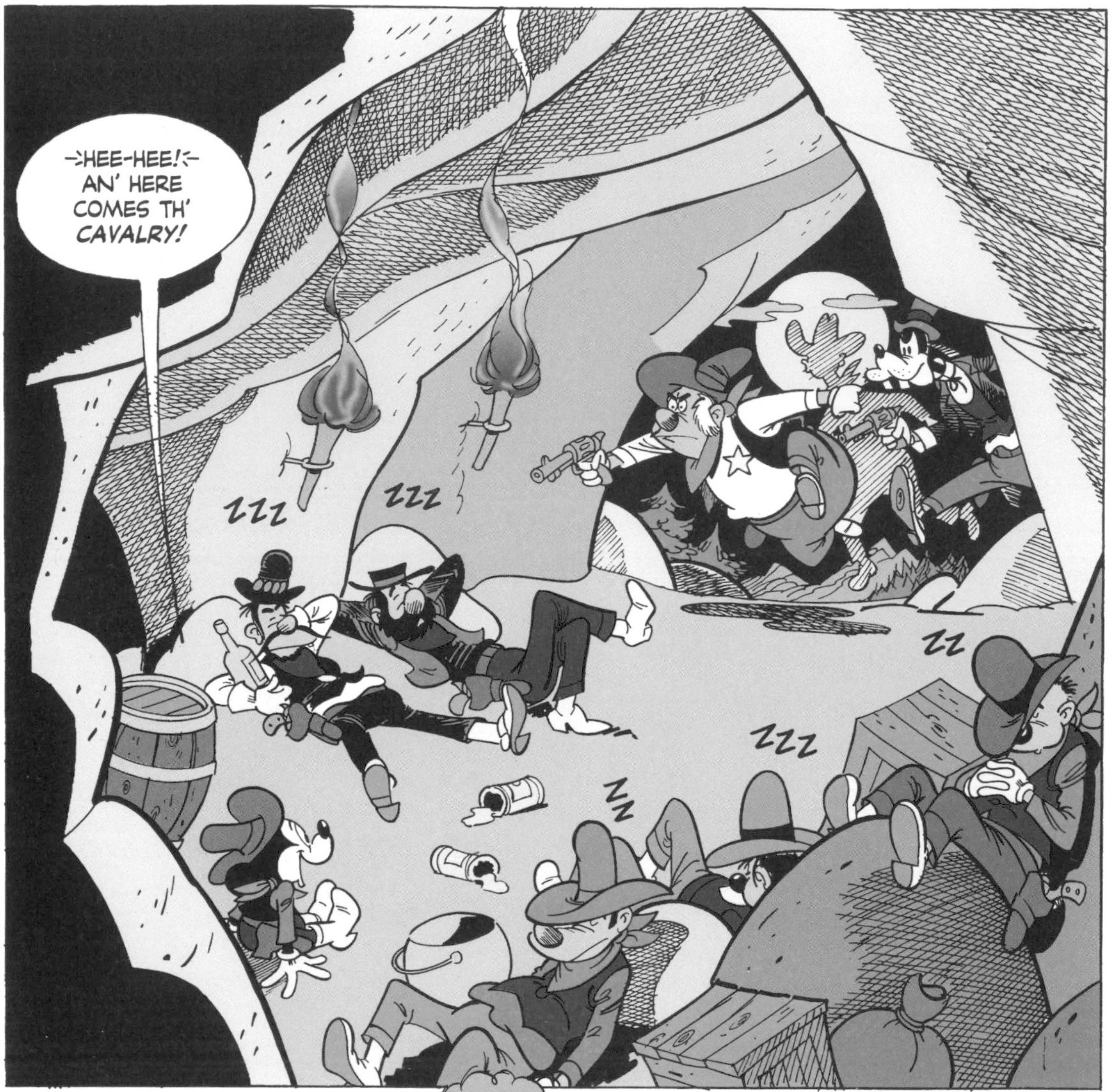
-HEE-HEE!- AN' HERE COMES TH' CAVALRY!
ZZZ
ZZZ
ZZ
ZZZ
ZZ

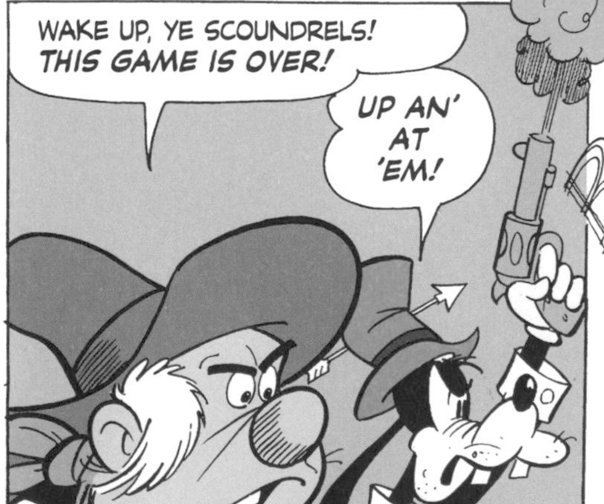
WAKE UP, YE SCOUNDRELS! THIS GAME IS OVER!
UP AN' AT 'EM!

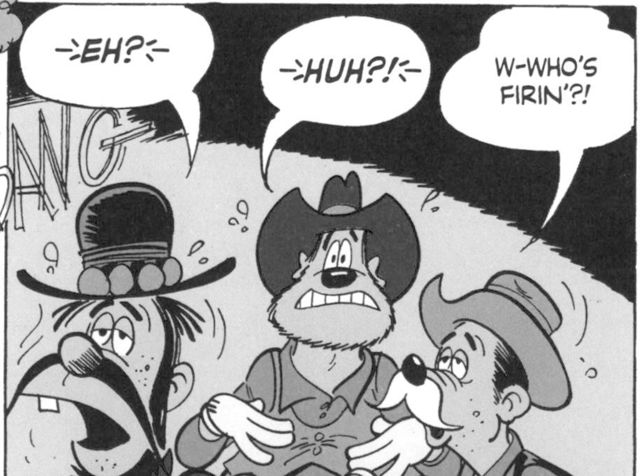
BANG
-EH?-
-HUH?!-
W-WHO'S FIRIN'?!

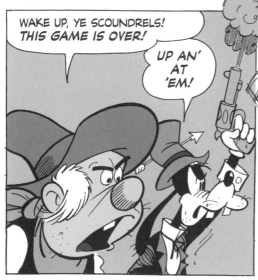

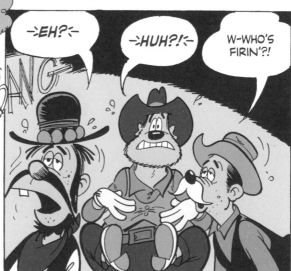

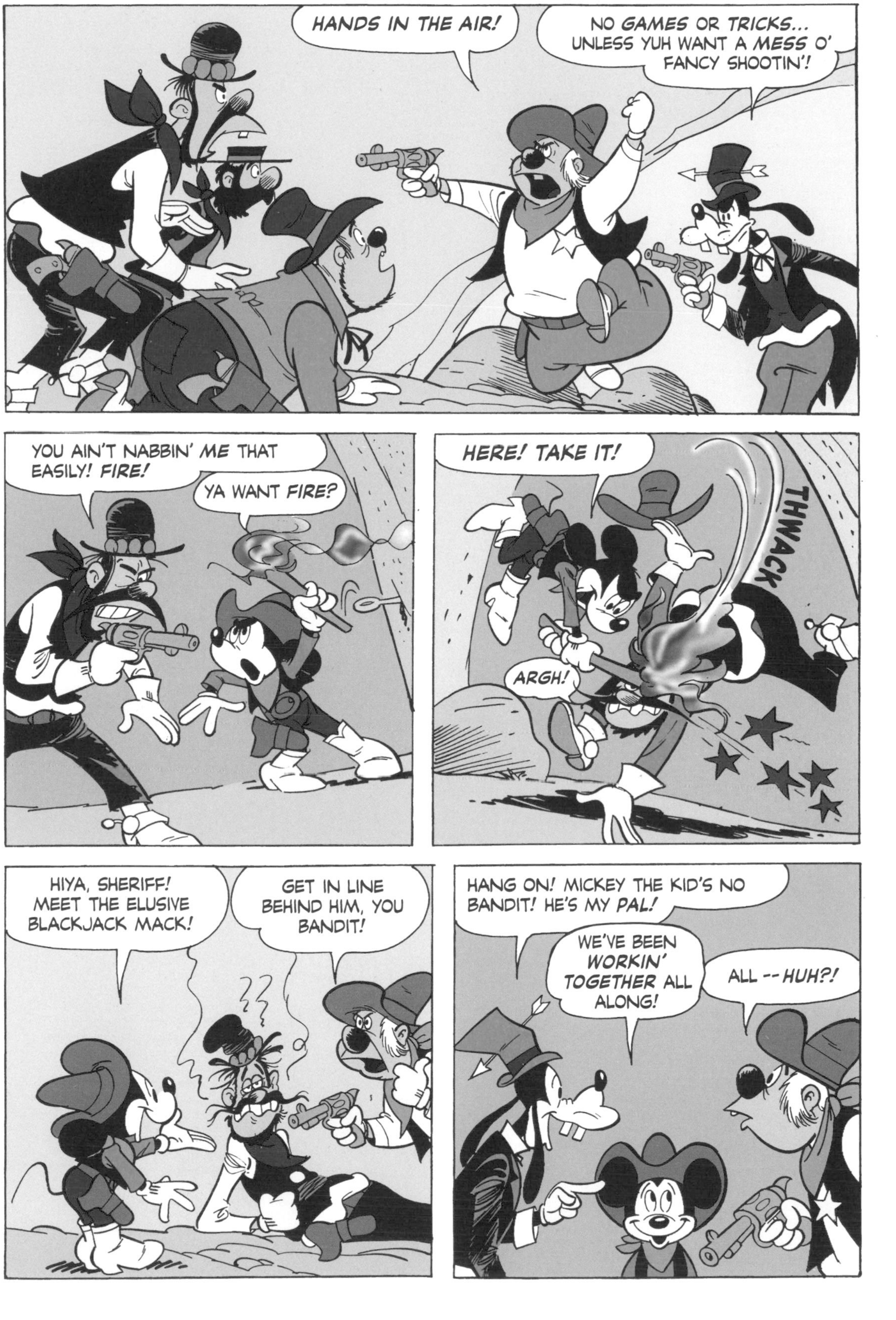
HANDS IN THE AIR!
NO GAMES OR TRICKS... UNLESS YUH WANT A MESS O' FANCY SHOOTIN'!
YOU AIN'T NABBIN' ME THAT EASILY! FIRE!
YA WANT FIRE?
HERE! TAKE IT!
THWACK
ARGH!
HIYA, SHERIFF! MEET THE ELUSIVE BLACKJACK MACK!
GET IN LINE BEHIND HIM, YOU BANDIT!
HANG ON! MICKEY THE KID'S NO BANDIT! HE'S MY PAL!
WE'VE BEEN WORKIN' TOGETHER ALL ALONG!
ALL -- HUH?!

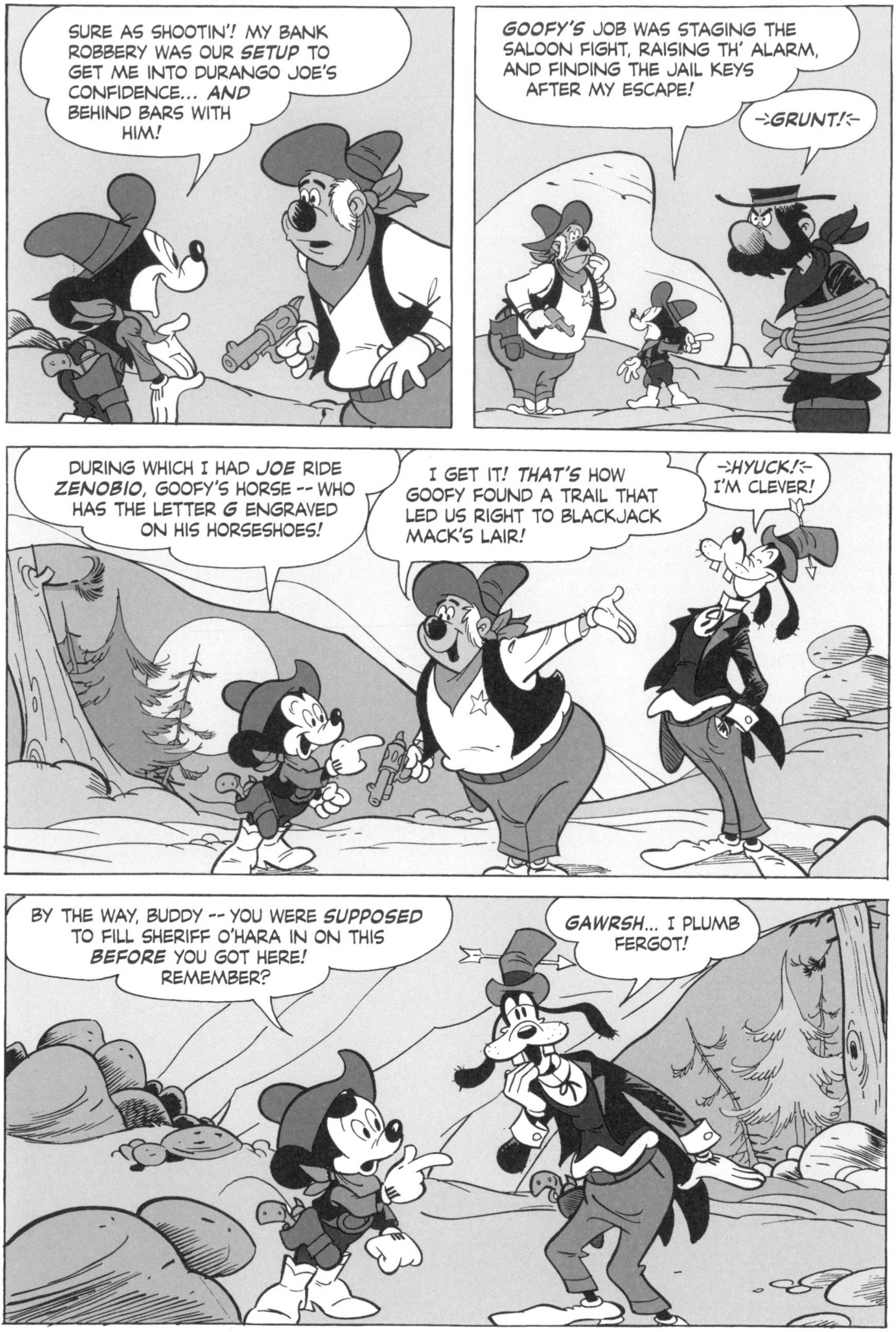
SURE AS SHOOTIN'! MY BANK ROBBERY WAS OUR SETUP TO GET ME INTO DURANGO JOE'S CONFIDENCE... AND BEHIND BARS WITH HIM!
GOOFY'S JOB WAS STAGING THE SALOON FIGHT, RAISING TH' ALARM, AND FINDING THE JAIL KEYS AFTER MY ESCAPE!
GRUNT!
DURING WHICH I HAD JOE RIDE ZENOBIO, GOOFY'S HORSE -- WHO HAS THE LETTER G ENGRAVED ON HIS HORSESHOES!
I GET IT! THAT'S HOW GOOFY FOUND A TRAIL THAT LED US RIGHT TO BLACKJACK MACK'S LAIR!
HYUCK! I'M CLEVER!
BY THE WAY, BUDDY -- YOU WERE SUPPOSED TO FILL SHERIFF O'HARA IN ON THIS BEFORE YOU GOT HERE! REMEMBER?
GAWRSH... I PLUMB FERGOT!

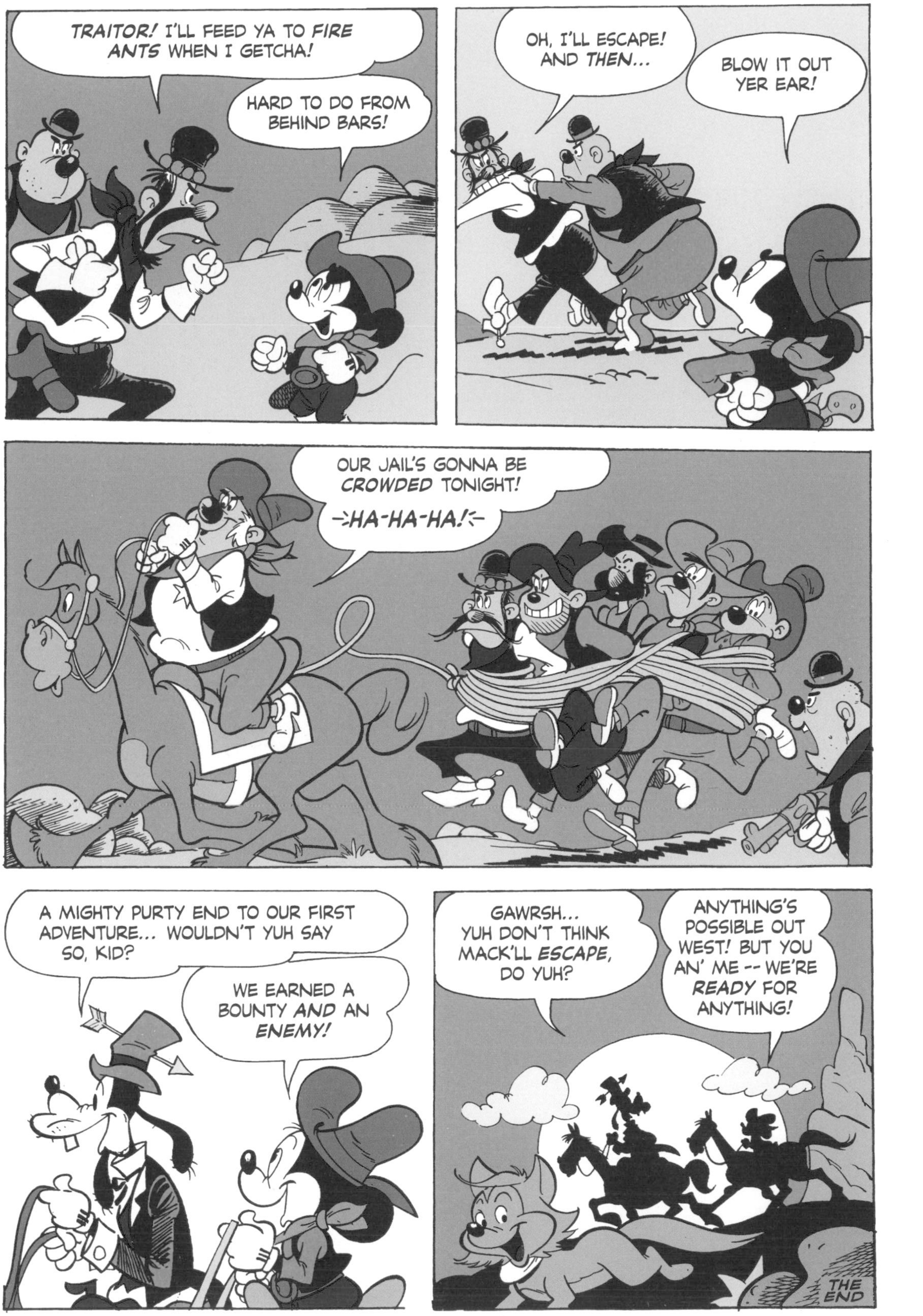
TRAITOR! I'LL FEED YA TO FIRE ANTS WHEN I GETCHA!
HARD TO DO FROM BEHIND BARS!
OH, I'LL ESCAPE! AND THEN...
BLOW IT OUT YER EAR!
OUR JAIL'S GONNA BE CROWDED TONIGHT!
HA-HA-HA!
A MIGHTY PURTY END TO OUR FIRST ADVENTURE... WOULDN'T YUH SAY SO, KID?
WE EARNED A BOUNTY AND AN ENEMY!
GAWRSH... YUH DON'T THINK MACK'LL ESCAPE, DO YUH?
ANYTHING'S POSSIBLE OUT WEST! BUT YOU AN' ME -- WE'RE READY FOR ANYTHING!
THE END

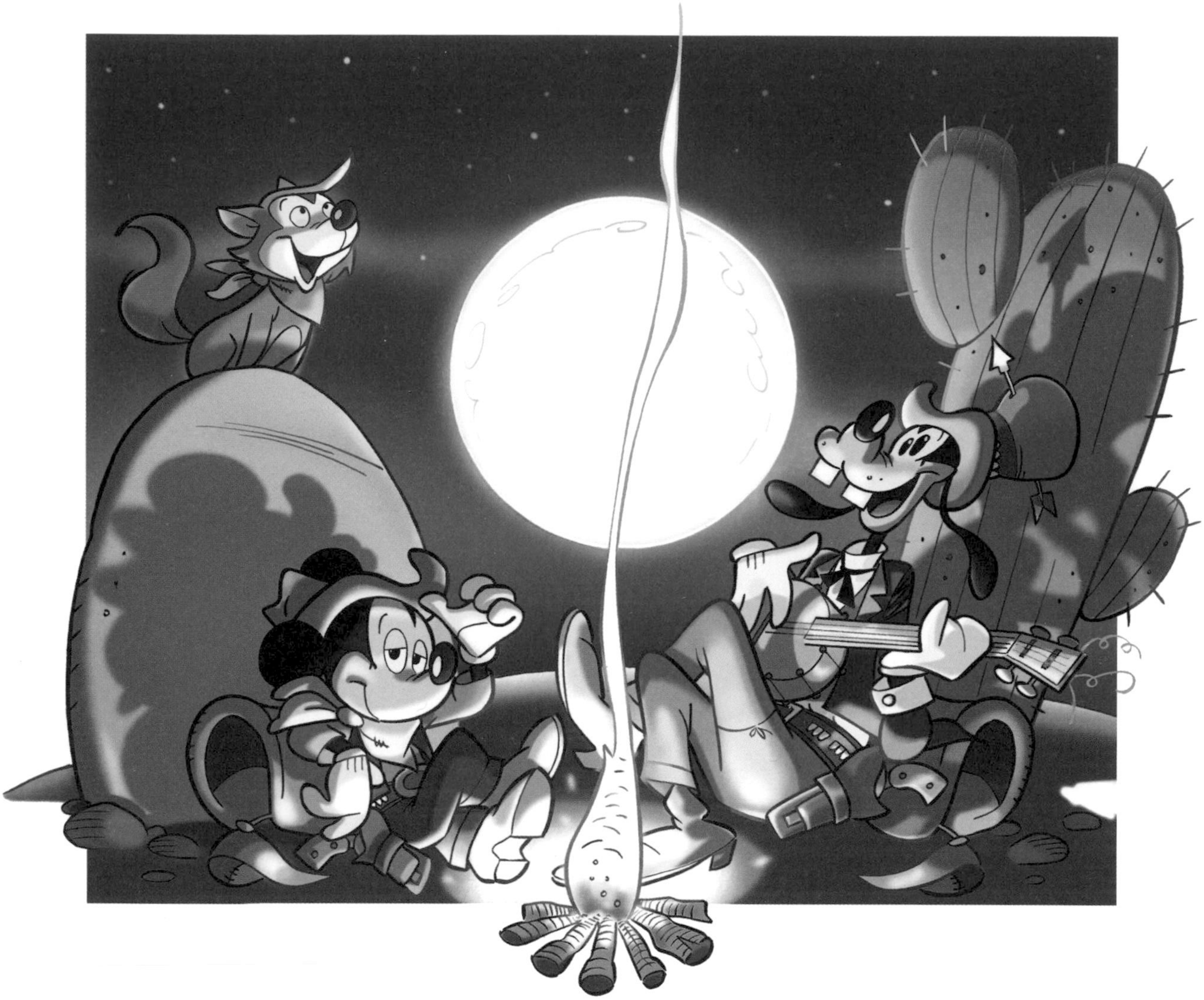

Giovan Battista Carpi's "Mickey the Kid" series has led to numerous sequels and covers by other famed talents over the years. Artist Marco Gervasio and colorist Stefano Intini created this image of the Kid, Six-Shot Goofy, and their faithful coyote pal for a 2010 Italian trade paperback collection.

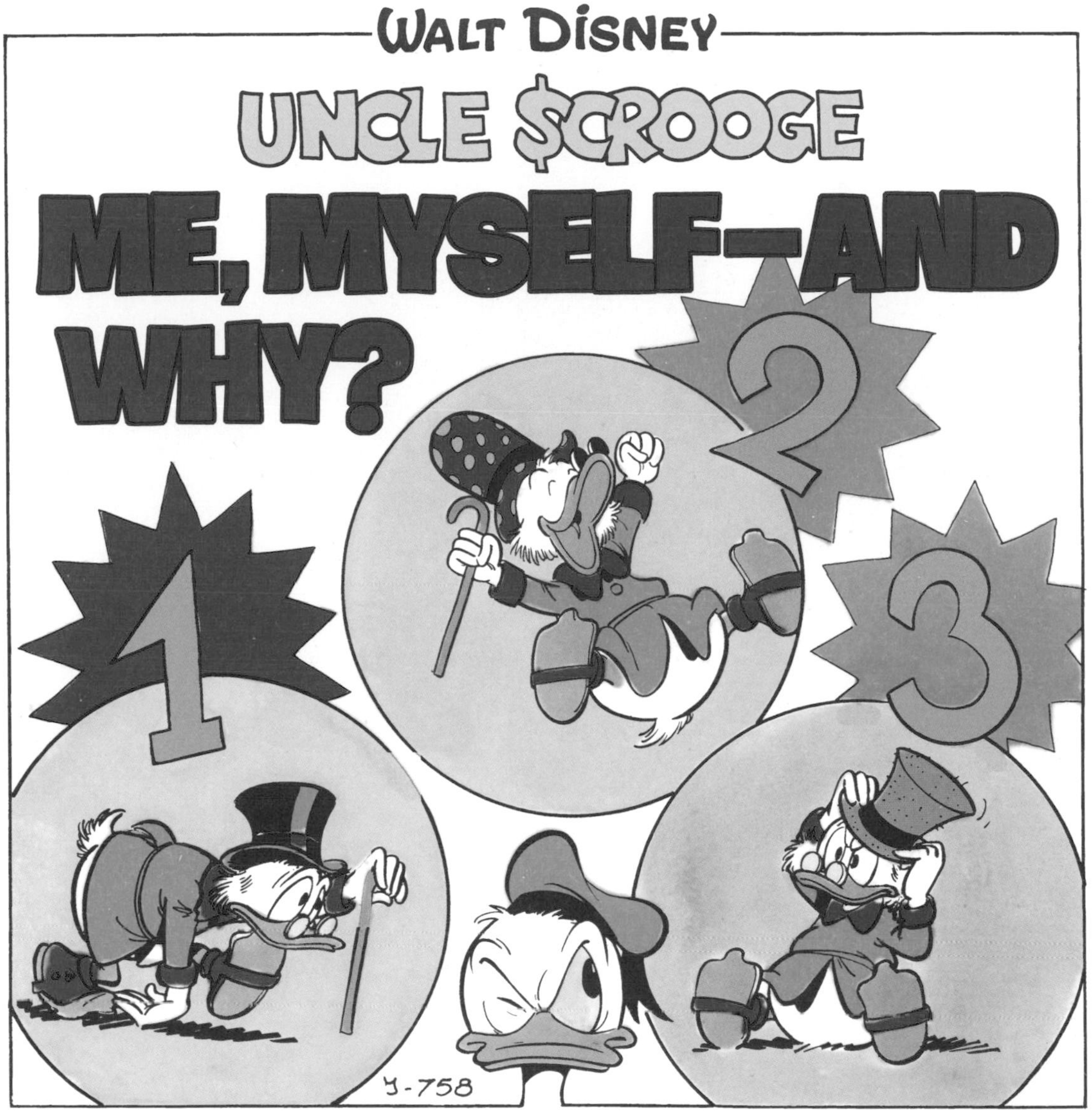
WALT DISNEY
UNCLE $CROOGE
ME, MYSELF—AND WHY?
1
2
3
Y-758

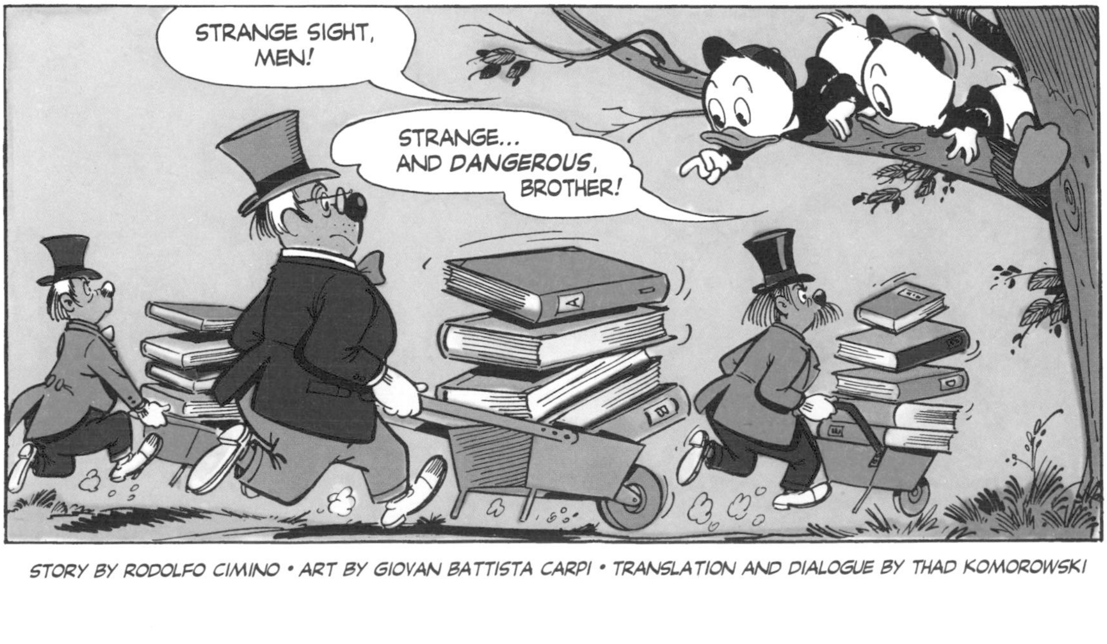
STRANGE SIGHT, MEN!
STRANGE... AND DANGEROUS, BROTHER!

STORY BY RODOLFO CIMINO • ART BY GIOVAN BATTISTA CARPI • TRANSLATION AND DIALOGUE BY THAD KOMOROWSKI

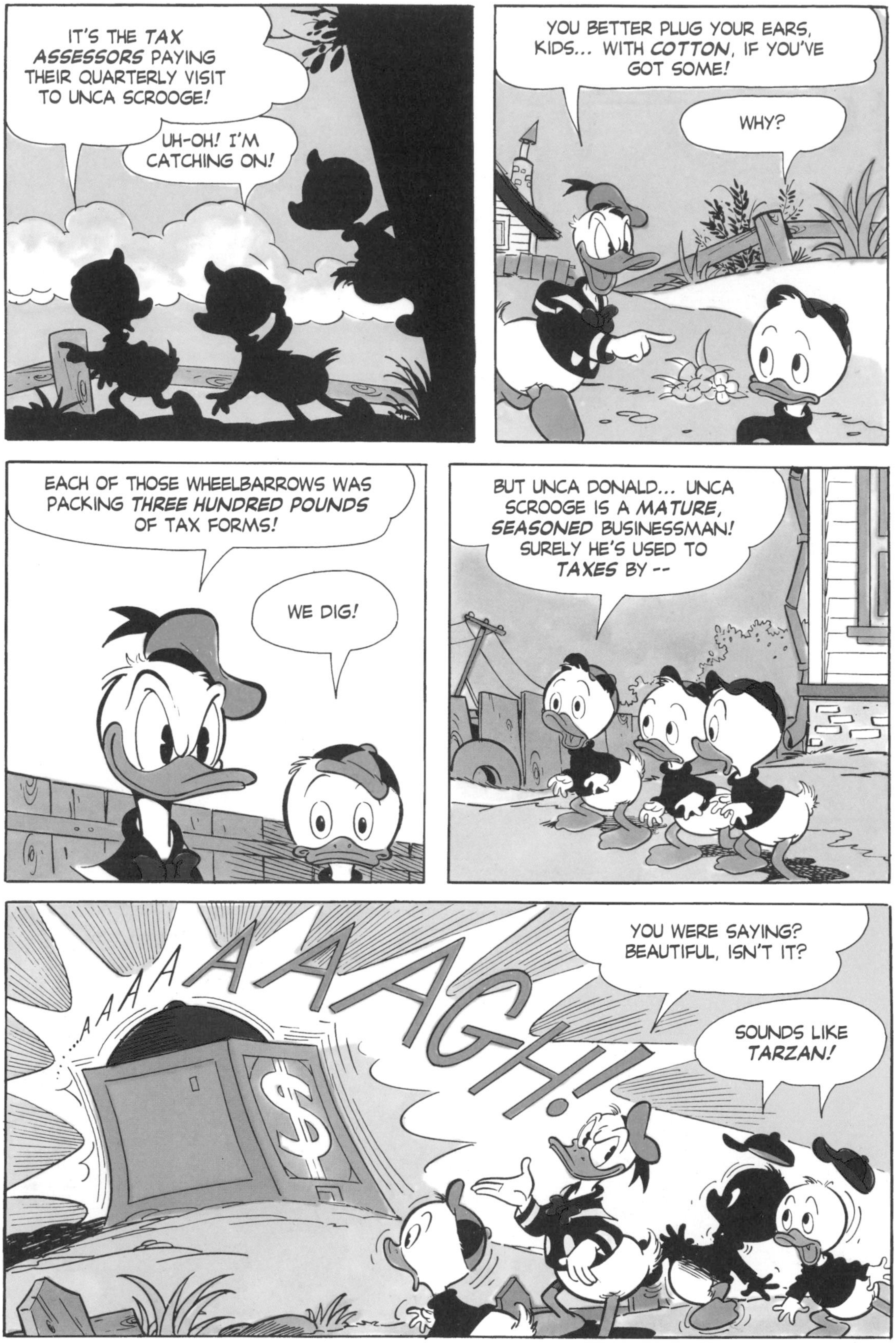
IT'S THE TAX ASSESSORS PAYING THEIR QUARTERLY VISIT TO UNCA SCROOGE!
UH-OH! I'M CATCHING ON!
YOU BETTER PLUG YOUR EARS, KIDS... WITH COTTON, IF YOU'VE GOT SOME!
WHY?
EACH OF THOSE WHEELBARROWS WAS PACKING THREE HUNDRED POUNDS OF TAX FORMS!
WE DIG!
BUT UNCA DONALD... UNCA SCROOGE IS A MATURE, SEASONED BUSINESSMAN! SURELY HE'S USED TO TAXES BY --
...AAAAAAAAAGH!
YOU WERE SAYING? BEAUTIFUL, ISN'T IT?
SOUNDS LIKE TARZAN!

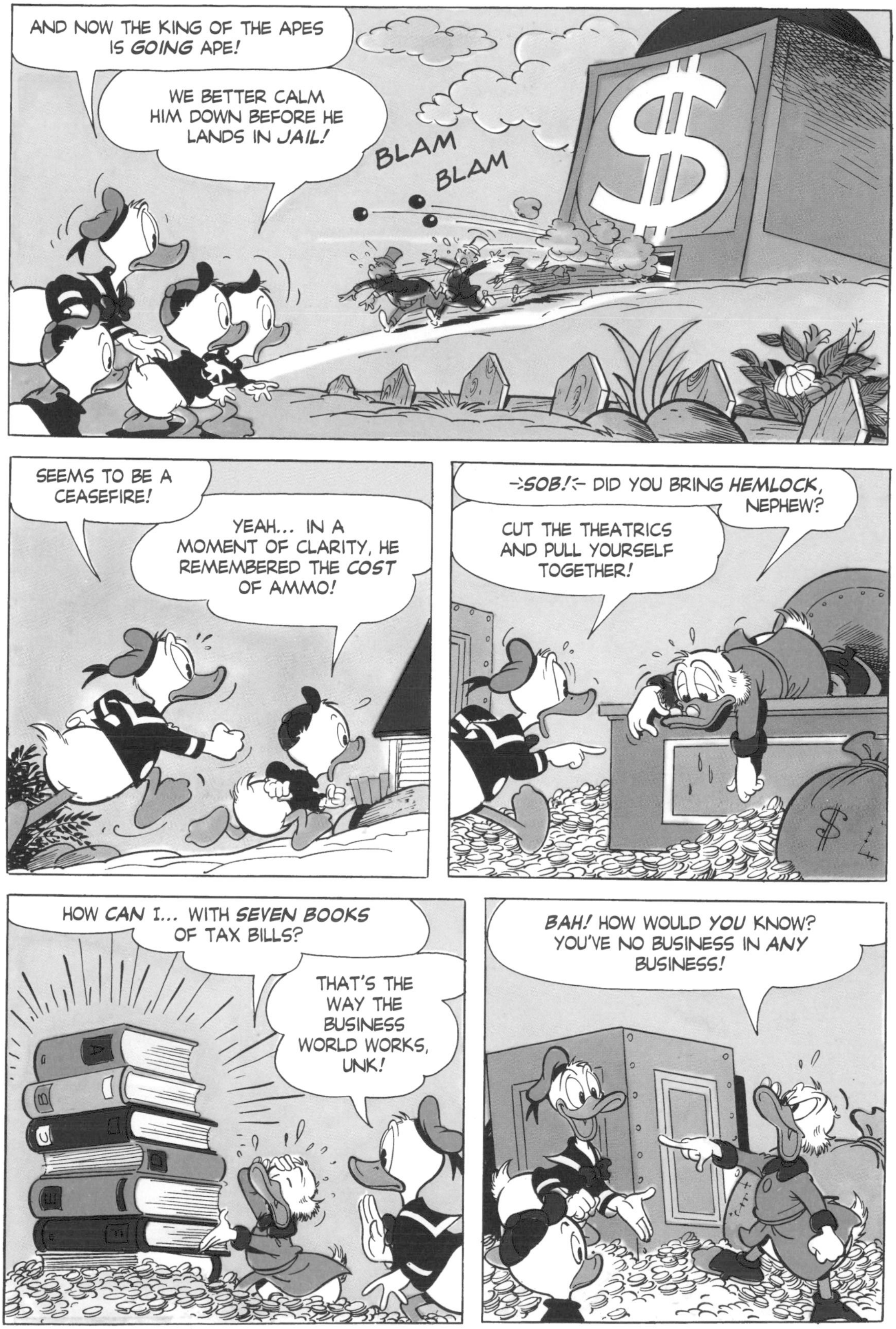
AND NOW THE KING OF THE APES IS GOING APE!
WE BETTER CALM HIM DOWN BEFORE HE LANDS IN JAIL!
BLAM
BLAM
SEEMS TO BE A CEASEFIRE!
YEAH... IN A MOMENT OF CLARITY, HE REMEMBERED THE COST OF AMMO!
SOB! DID YOU BRING HEMLOCK, NEPHEW?
CUT THE THEATRICS AND PULL YOURSELF TOGETHER!
HOW CAN I... WITH SEVEN BOOKS OF TAX BILLS?
THAT'S THE WAY THE BUSINESS WORLD WORKS, UNK!
BAH! HOW WOULD YOU KNOW? YOU'VE NO BUSINESS IN ANY BUSINESS!

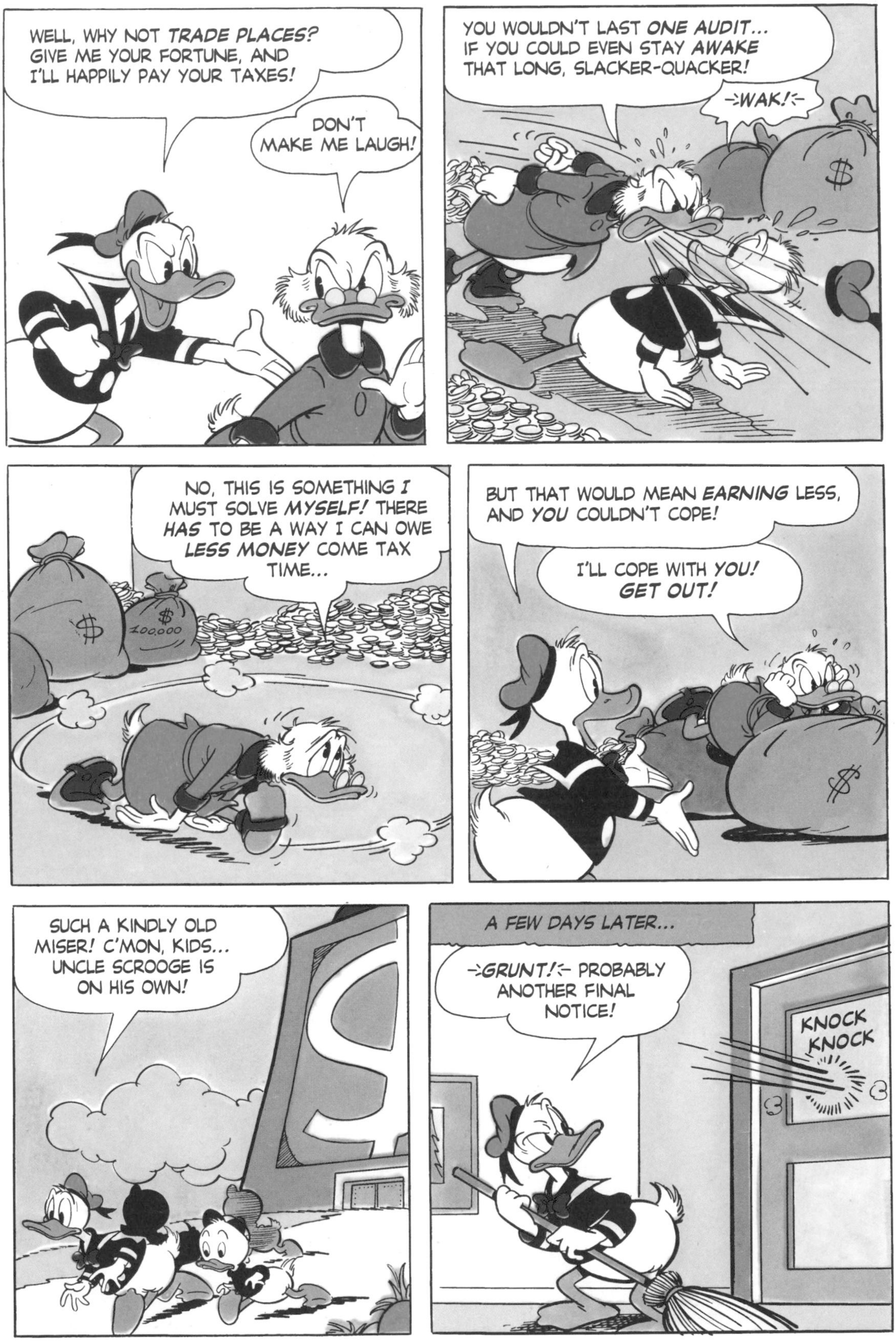
WELL, WHY NOT TRADE PLACES? GIVE ME YOUR FORTUNE, AND I'LL HAPPILY PAY YOUR TAXES!
DON'T MAKE ME LAUGH!
YOU WOULDN'T LAST ONE AUDIT... IF YOU COULD EVEN STAY AWAKE THAT LONG, SLACKER-QUACKER!
WAK!
NO, THIS IS SOMETHING I MUST SOLVE MYSELF! THERE HAS TO BE A WAY I CAN OWE LESS MONEY COME TAX TIME...
BUT THAT WOULD MEAN EARNING LESS, AND YOU COULDN'T COPE!
I'LL COPE WITH YOU! GET OUT!
SUCH A KINDLY OLD MISER! C'MON, KIDS... UNCLE SCROOGE IS ON HIS OWN!
A FEW DAYS LATER...
GRUNT! PROBABLY ANOTHER FINAL NOTICE!
KNOCK KNOCK

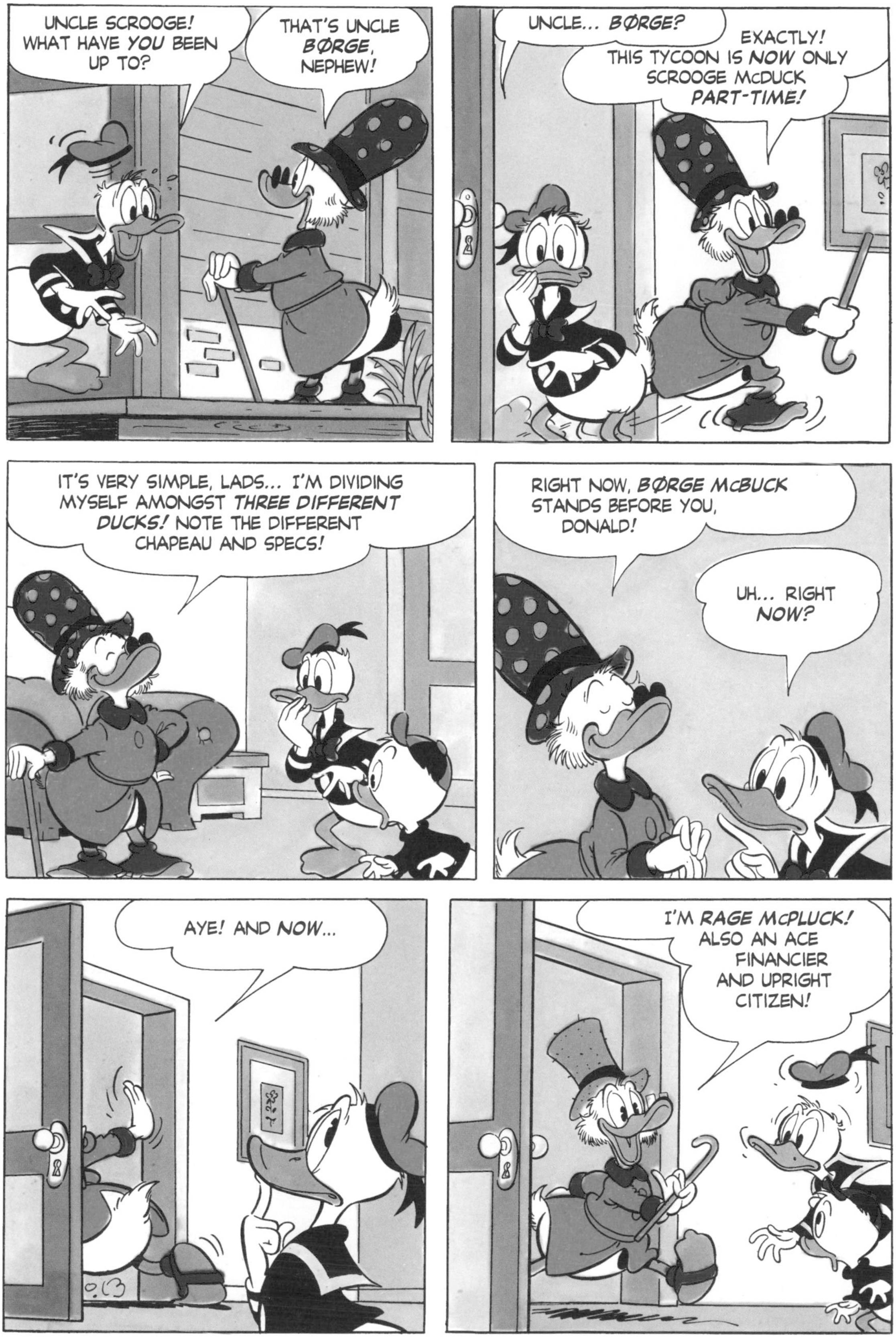
UNCLE SCROOGE! WHAT HAVE YOU BEEN UP TO?
THAT'S UNCLE BØRGE, NEPHEW!
UNCLE... BØRGE?
EXACTLY! THIS TYCOON IS NOW ONLY SCROOGE McDUCK PART-TIME!
IT'S VERY SIMPLE, LADS... I'M DIVIDING MYSELF AMONGST THREE DIFFERENT DUCKS! NOTE THE DIFFERENT CHAPEAU AND SPECS!
RIGHT NOW, BØRGE McBUCK STANDS BEFORE YOU, DONALD!
UH... RIGHT NOW?
AYE! AND NOW...
I'M RAGE McPLUCK! ALSO AN ACE FINANCIER AND UPRIGHT CITIZEN!

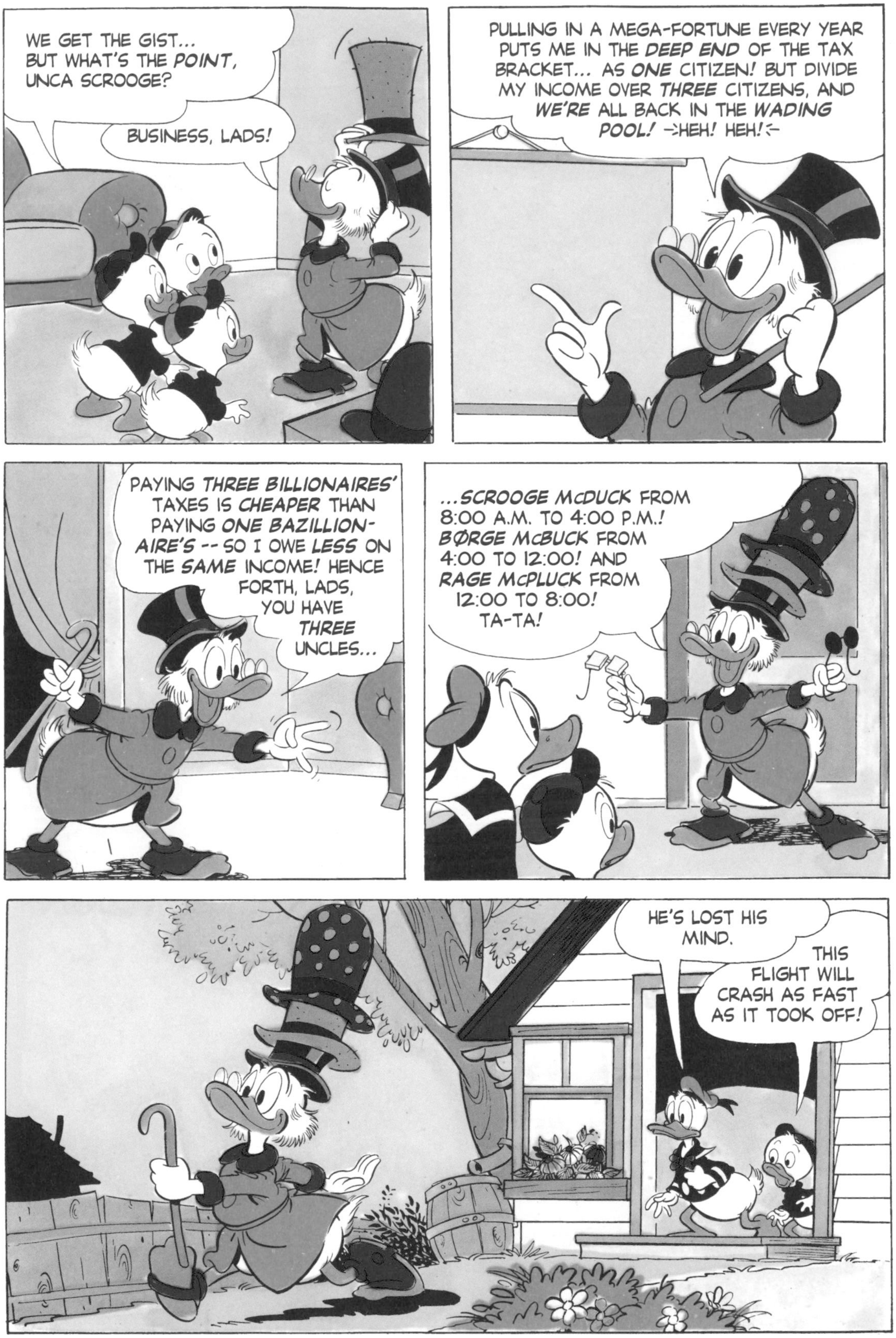
WE GET THE GIST... BUT WHAT'S THE POINT, UNCA SCROOGE?
BUSINESS, LADS!
PULLING IN A MEGA-FORTUNE EVERY YEAR PUTS ME IN THE DEEP END OF THE TAX BRACKET... AS ONE CITIZEN! BUT DIVIDE MY INCOME OVER THREE CITIZENS, AND WE'RE ALL BACK IN THE WADING POOL! HEH! HEH!
PAYING THREE BILLIONAIRES' TAXES IS CHEAPER THAN PAYING ONE BAZILLION-AIRE'S -- SO I OWE LESS ON THE SAME INCOME! HENCE FORTH, LADS, YOU HAVE THREE UNCLES...
...SCROOGE McDUCK FROM 8:00 A.M. TO 4:00 P.M.! BØRGE McBUCK FROM 4:00 TO 12:00! AND RAGE McPLUCK FROM 12:00 TO 8:00! TA-TA!
HE'S LOST HIS MIND.
THIS FLIGHT WILL CRASH AS FAST AS IT TOOK OFF!

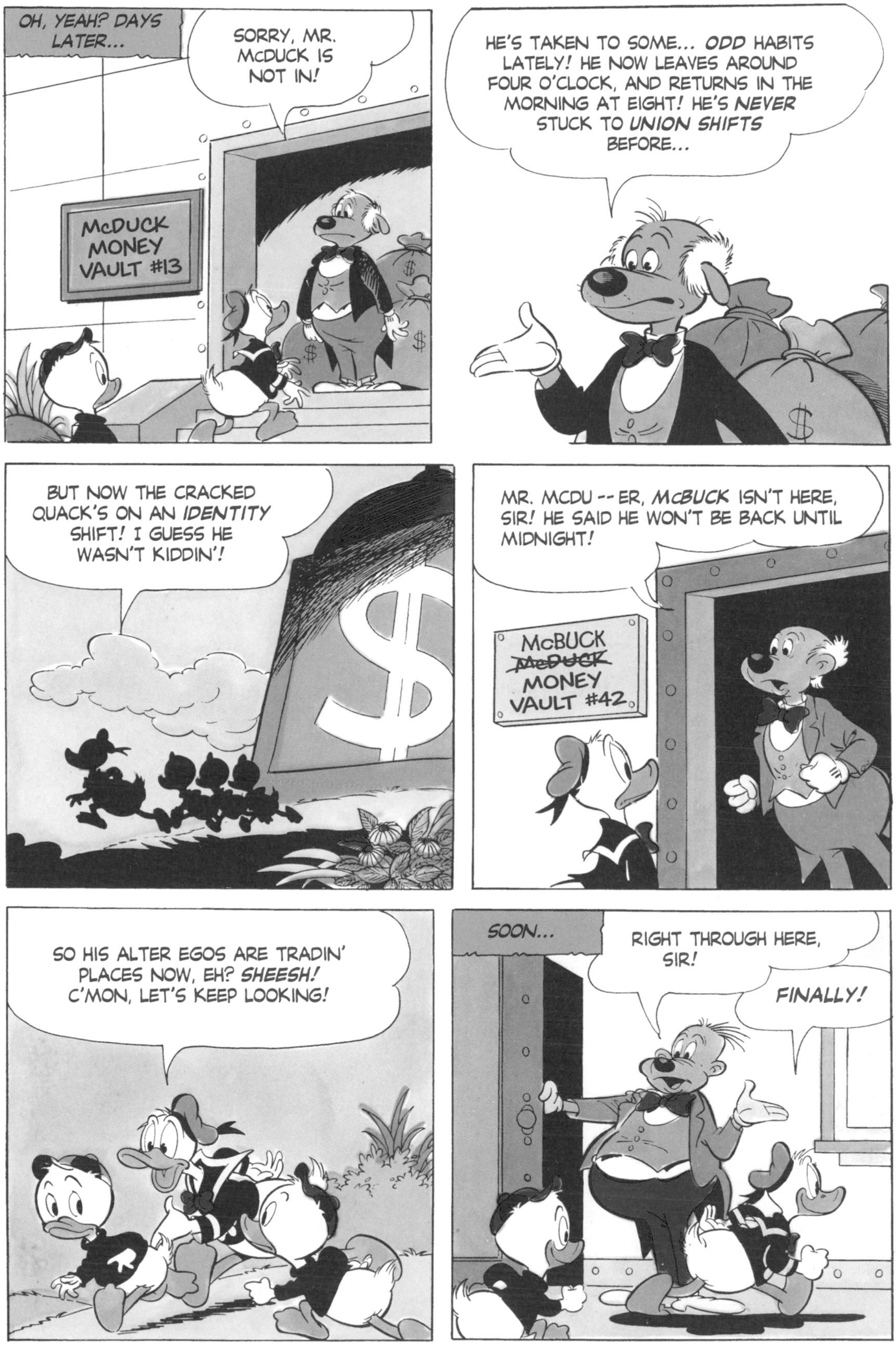
OH, YEAH? DAYS LATER...
SORRY, MR. McDUCK IS NOT IN!
McDUCK MONEY VAULT #13
HE'S TAKEN TO SOME... ODD HABITS LATELY! HE NOW LEAVES AROUND FOUR O'CLOCK, AND RETURNS IN THE MORNING AT EIGHT! HE'S NEVER STUCK TO UNION SHIFTS BEFORE...
BUT NOW THE CRACKED QUACK'S ON AN IDENTITY SHIFT! I GUESS HE WASN'T KIDDIN'!
MR. MCDU -- ER, McBUCK ISN'T HERE, SIR! HE SAID HE WON'T BE BACK UNTIL MIDNIGHT!
McBUCK McDUCK MONEY VAULT #42
SO HIS ALTER EGOS ARE TRADIN' PLACES NOW, EH? SHEESH! C'MON, LET'S KEEP LOOKING!
SOON...
RIGHT THROUGH HERE, SIR!
FINALLY!

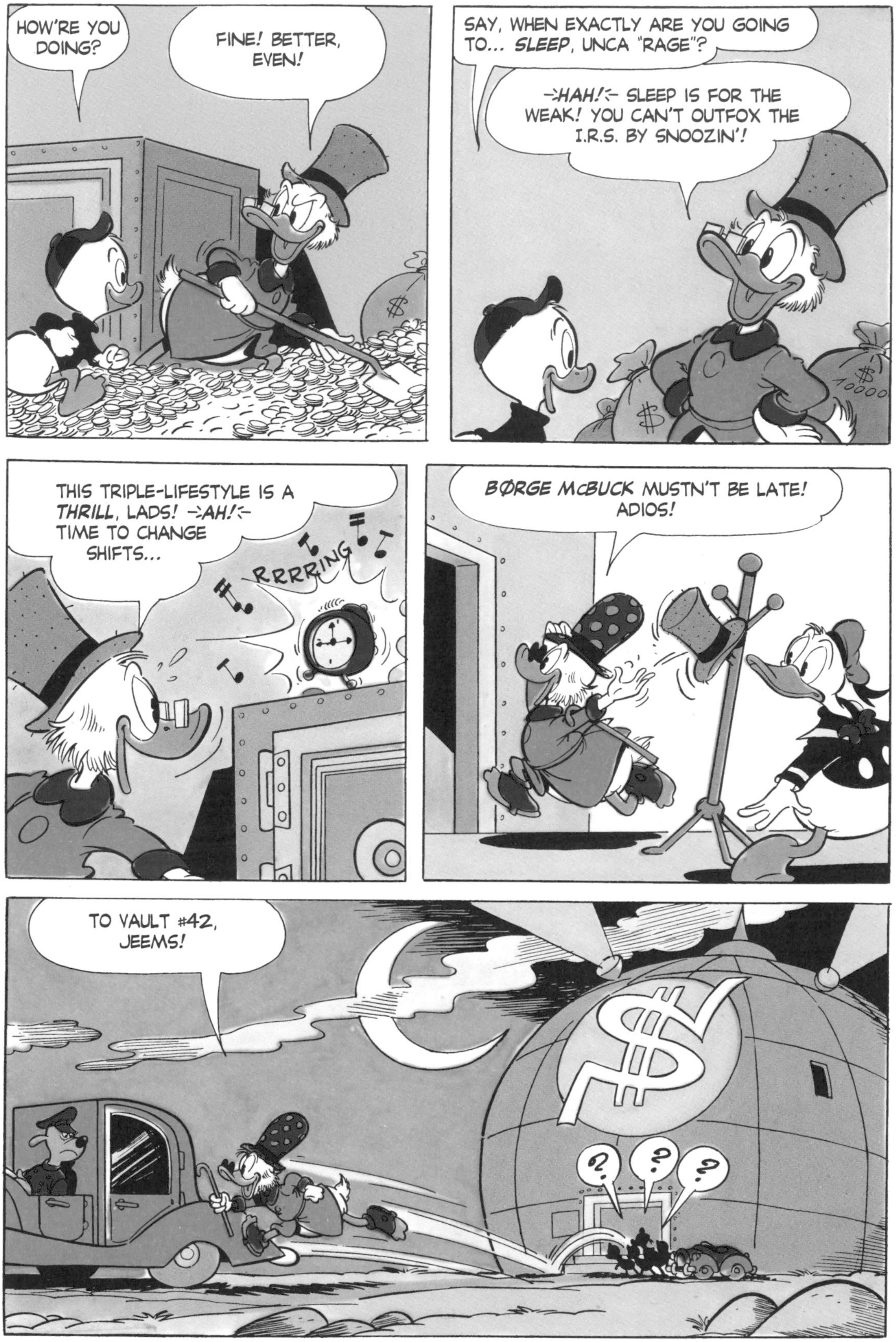

HOW'RE YOU DOING?
FINE! BETTER, EVEN!
SAY, WHEN EXACTLY ARE YOU GOING TO... SLEEP, UNCA "RAGE"?
–HAH!– SLEEP IS FOR THE WEAK! YOU CAN'T OUTFOX THE I.R.S. BY SNOOZIN'!
THIS TRIPLE-LIFESTYLE IS A THRILL, LADS! –AH!– TIME TO CHANGE SHIFTS...
RRRRING
BØRGE McBUCK MUSTN'T BE LATE! ADIOS!
TO VAULT #42, JEEMS!
$
?
?
?

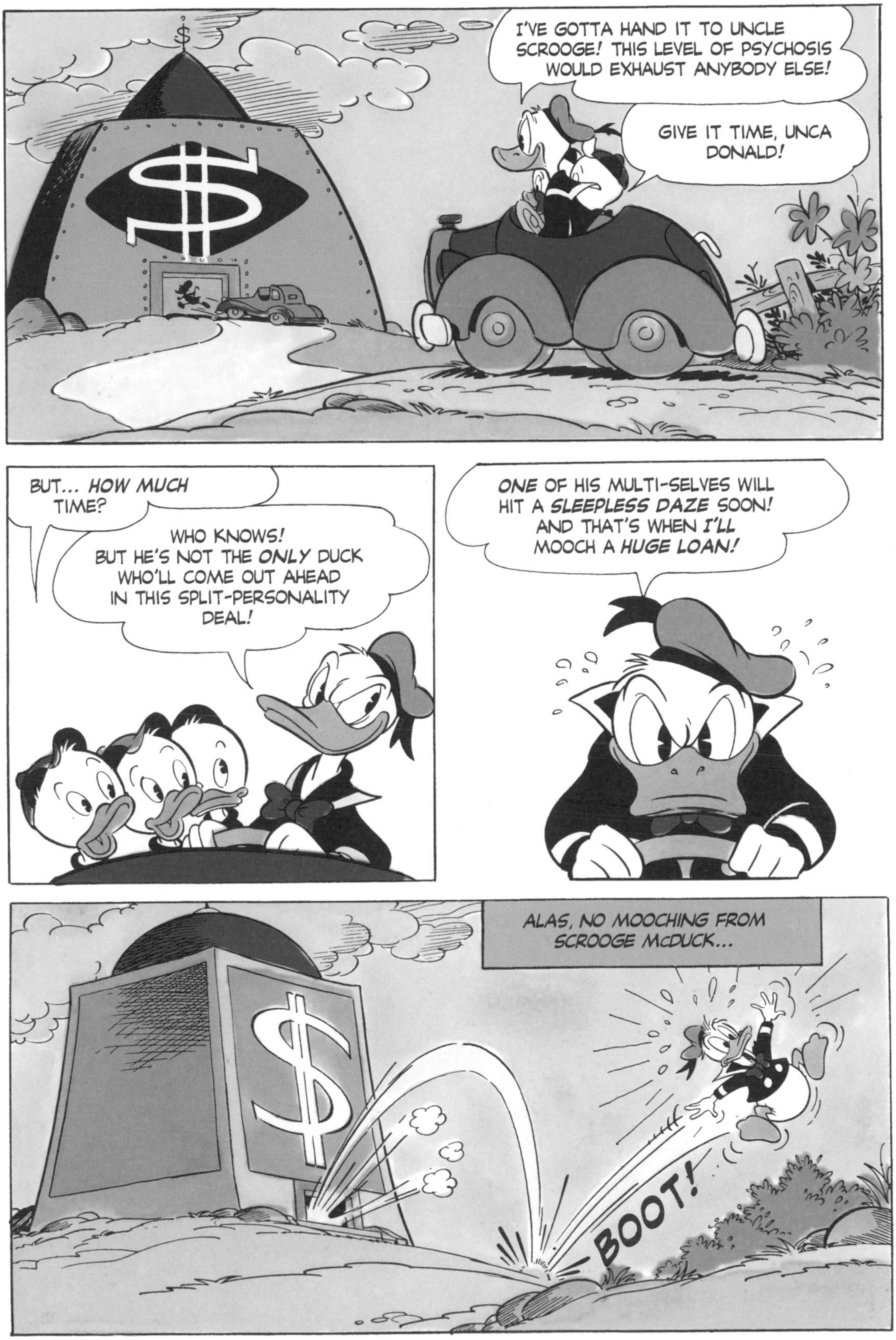
I'VE GOTTA HAND IT TO UNCLE SCROOGE! THIS LEVEL OF PSYCHOSIS WOULD EXHAUST ANYBODY ELSE!
GIVE IT TIME, UNCA DONALD!
BUT... HOW MUCH TIME?
WHO KNOWS! BUT HE'S NOT THE ONLY DUCK WHO'LL COME OUT AHEAD IN THIS SPLIT-PERSONALITY DEAL!
ONE OF HIS MULTI-SELVES WILL HIT A SLEEPLESS DAZE SOON! AND THAT'S WHEN I'LL MOOCH A HUGE LOAN!
ALAS, NO MOOCHING FROM SCROOGE McDUCK...
BOOT!

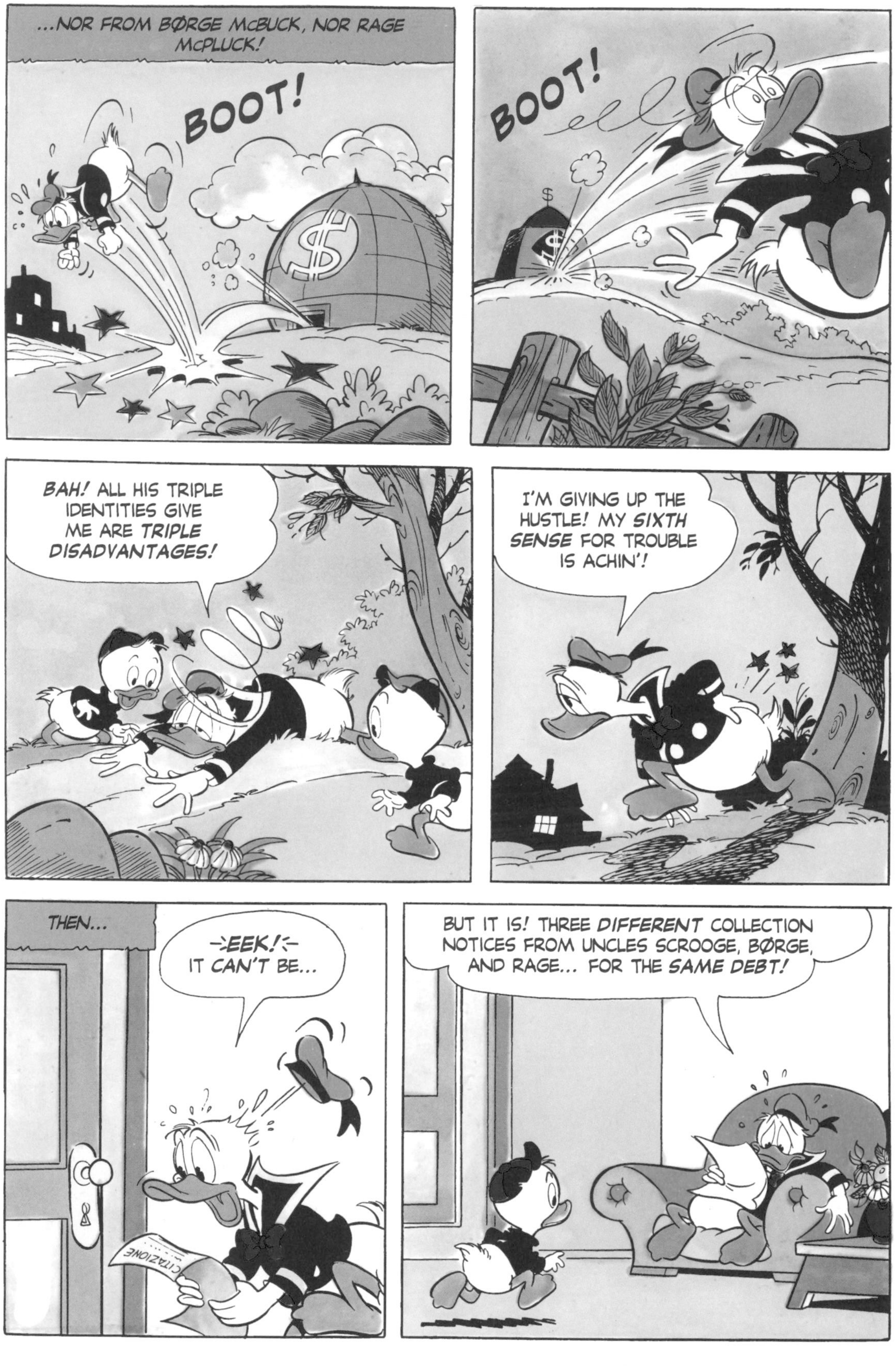
...NOR FROM BØRGE McBUCK, NOR RAGE McPLUCK!
BOOT!
BOOT!
BAH! ALL HIS TRIPLE IDENTITIES GIVE ME ARE TRIPLE DISADVANTAGES!
I'M GIVING UP THE HUSTLE! MY SIXTH SENSE FOR TROUBLE IS ACHIN'!
THEN...
-EEK!- IT CAN'T BE...
CITAZIONE
BUT IT IS! THREE DIFFERENT COLLECTION NOTICES FROM UNCLES SCROOGE, BØRGE, AND RAGE... FOR THE SAME DEBT!

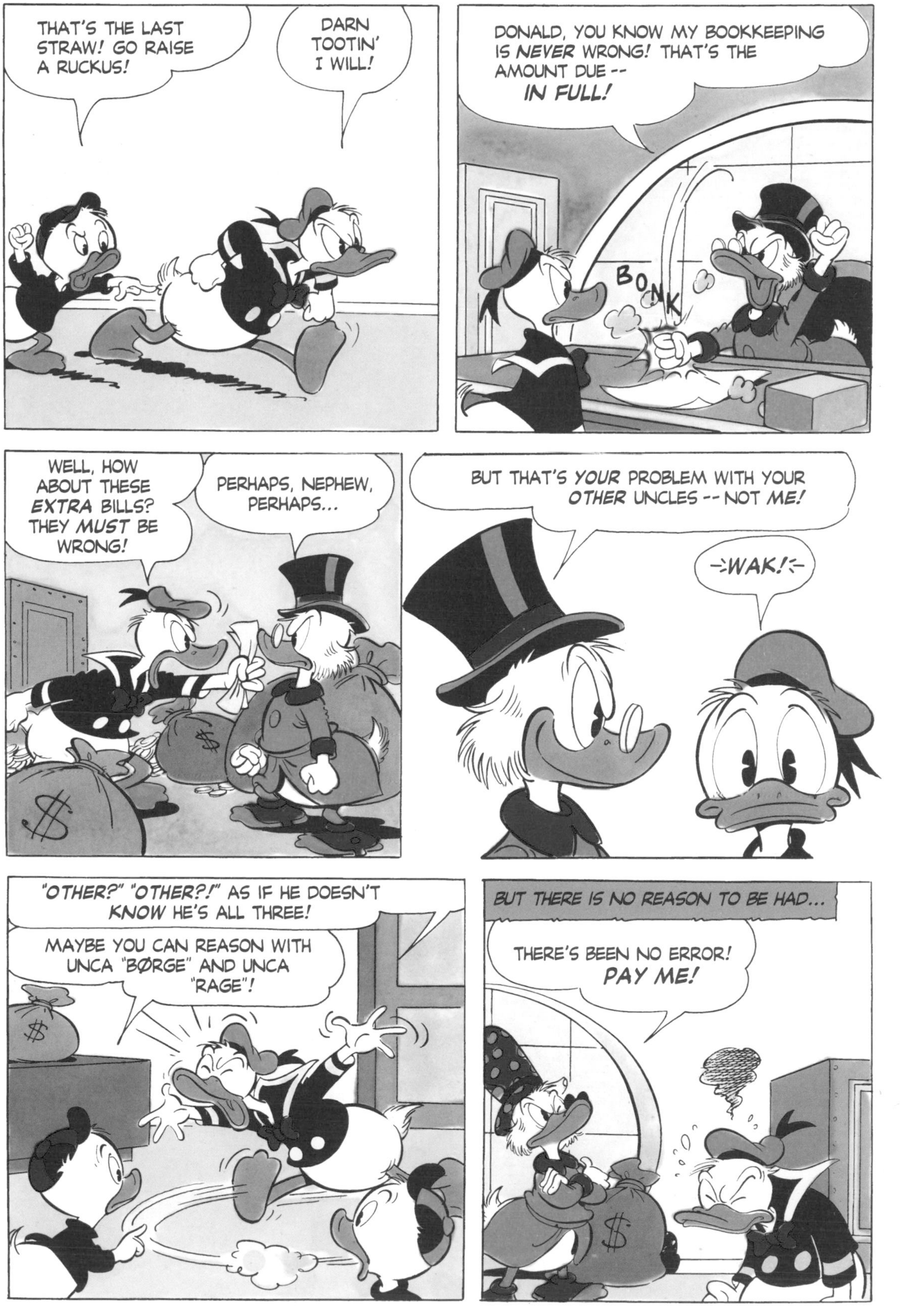
THAT'S THE LAST STRAW! GO RAISE A RUCKUS!
DARN TOOTIN' I WILL!
DONALD, YOU KNOW MY BOOKKEEPING IS NEVER WRONG! THAT'S THE AMOUNT DUE -- IN FULL!
BONK
WELL, HOW ABOUT THESE EXTRA BILLS? THEY MUST BE WRONG!
PERHAPS, NEPHEW, PERHAPS...
BUT THAT'S YOUR PROBLEM WITH YOUR OTHER UNCLES -- NOT ME!
WAK!
"OTHER?" "OTHER?!" AS IF HE DOESN'T KNOW HE'S ALL THREE!
MAYBE YOU CAN REASON WITH UNCA "BØRGE" AND UNCA "RAGE"!
BUT THERE IS NO REASON TO BE HAD...
THERE'S BEEN NO ERROR! PAY ME!

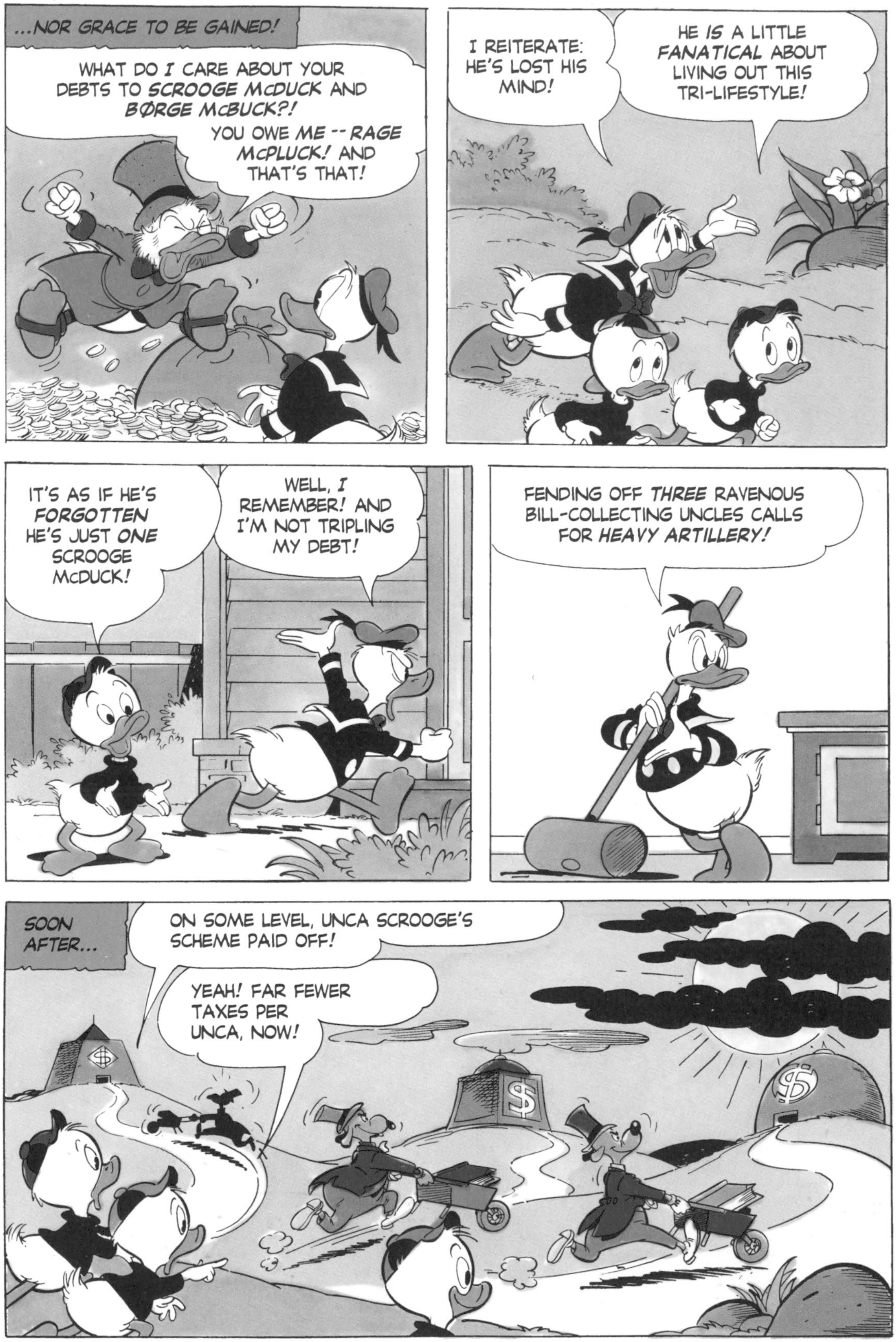
...NOR GRACE TO BE GAINED!
WHAT DO I CARE ABOUT YOUR DEBTS TO SCROOGE McDUCK AND BØRGE McBUCK?!
YOU OWE ME -- RAGE McPLUCK! AND THAT'S THAT!
I REITERATE: HE'S LOST HIS MIND!
HE IS A LITTLE FANATICAL ABOUT LIVING OUT THIS TRI-LIFESTYLE!
IT'S AS IF HE'S FORGOTTEN HE'S JUST ONE SCROOGE McDUCK!
WELL, I REMEMBER! AND I'M NOT TRIPLING MY DEBT!
FENDING OFF THREE RAVENOUS BILL-COLLECTING UNCLES CALLS FOR HEAVY ARTILLERY!
SOON AFTER...
ON SOME LEVEL, UNCA SCROOGE'S SCHEME PAID OFF!
YEAH! FAR FEWER TAXES PER UNCA, NOW!

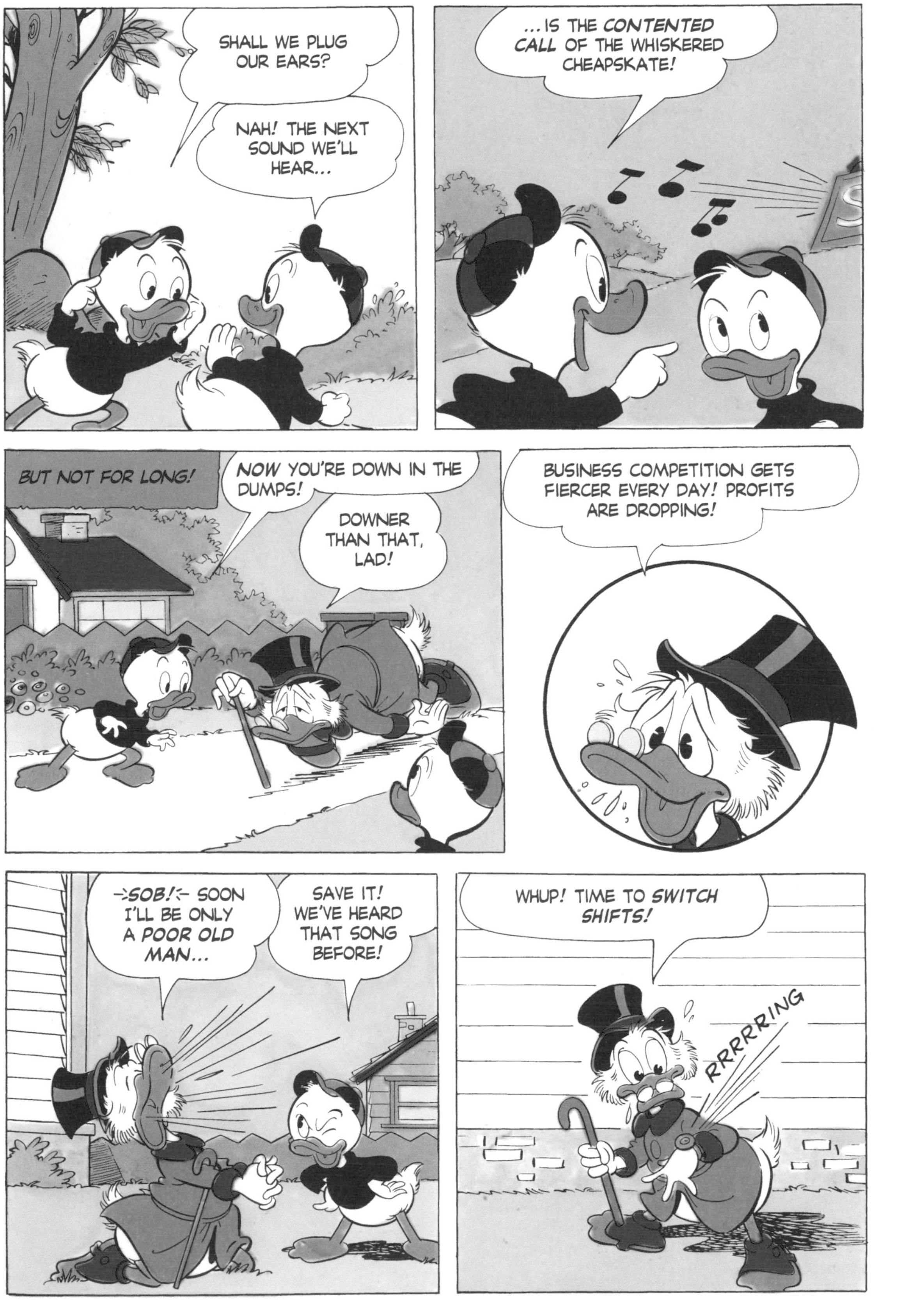
SHALL WE PLUG OUR EARS?
NAH! THE NEXT SOUND WE'LL HEAR...
...IS THE CONTENTED CALL OF THE WHISKERED CHEAPSKATE!
BUT NOT FOR LONG!
NOW YOU'RE DOWN IN THE DUMPS!
DOWNER THAN THAT, LAD!
BUSINESS COMPETITION GETS FIERCER EVERY DAY! PROFITS ARE DROPPING!
-SOB!- SOON I'LL BE ONLY A POOR OLD MAN...
SAVE IT! WE'VE HEARD THAT SONG BEFORE!
WHUP! TIME TO SWITCH SHIFTS!
RRRRRING

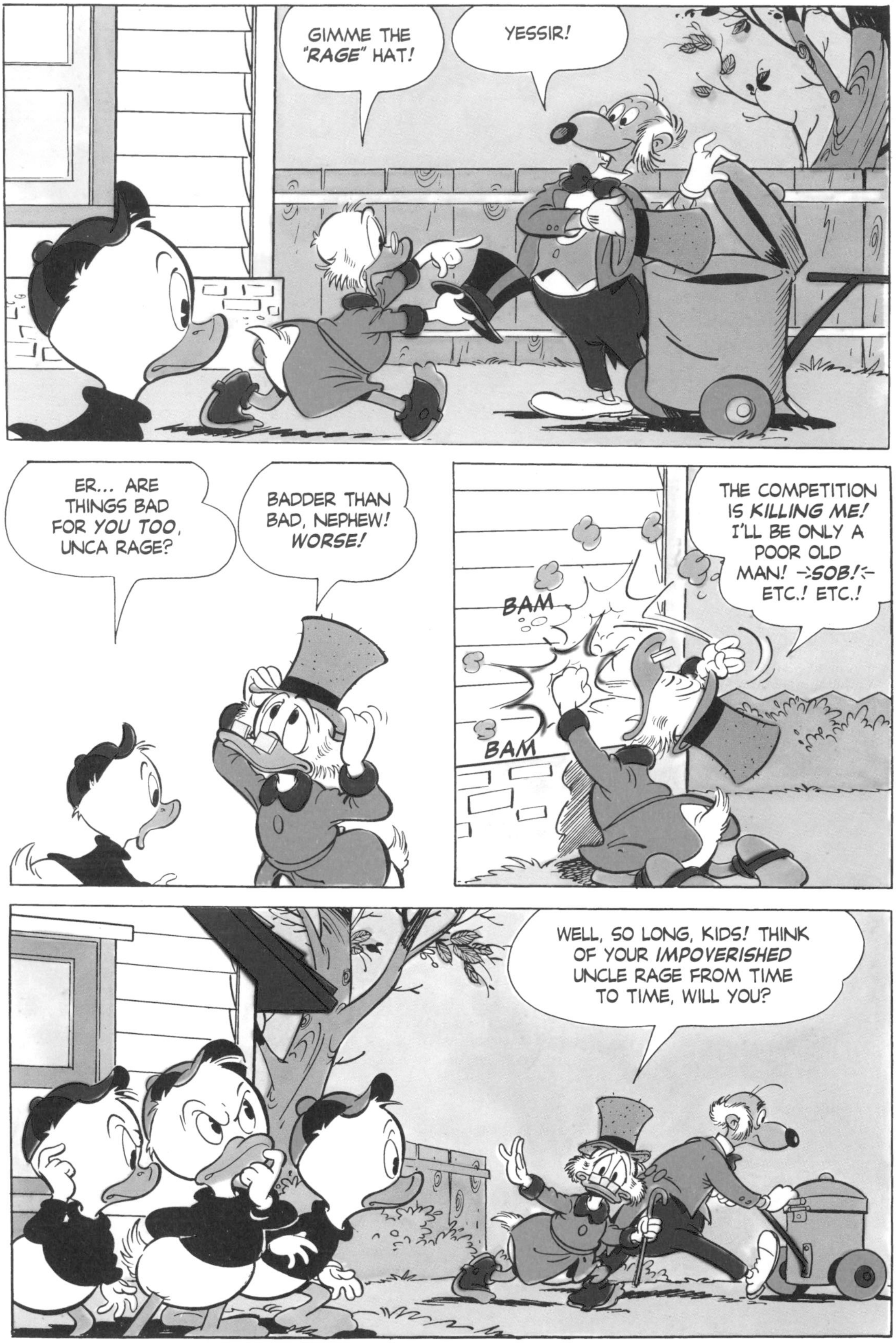
GIMME THE "RAGE" HAT!
YESSIR!
ER... ARE THINGS BAD FOR YOU TOO, UNCA RAGE?
BADDER THAN BAD, NEPHEW! WORSE!
BAM
BAM
THE COMPETITION IS KILLING ME! I'LL BE ONLY A POOR OLD MAN! -SOB!- ETC.! ETC.!
WELL, SO LONG, KIDS! THINK OF YOUR IMPOVERISHED UNCLE RAGE FROM TIME TO TIME, WILL YOU?

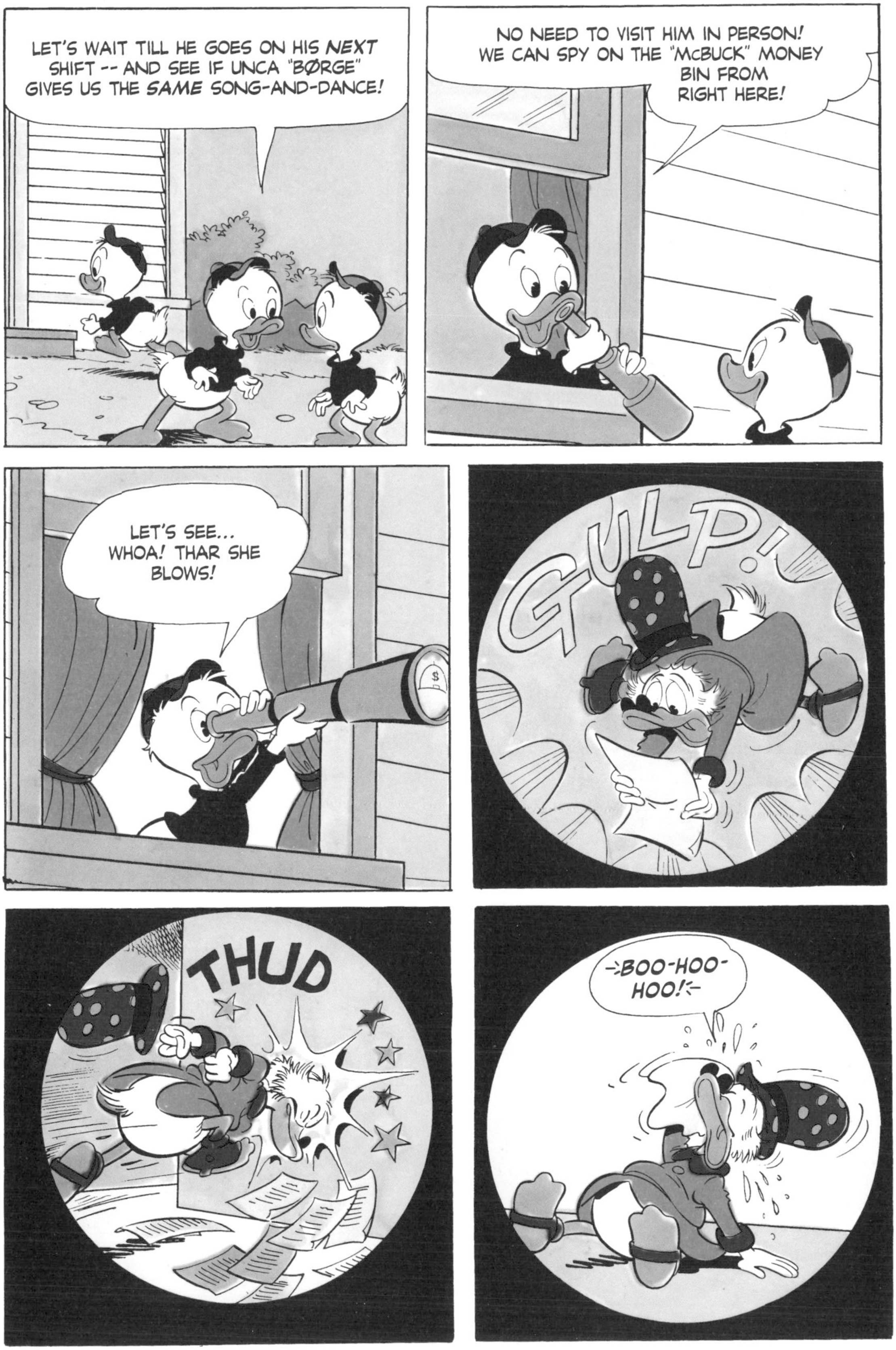
LET'S WAIT TILL HE GOES ON HIS NEXT SHIFT -- AND SEE IF UNCA "BØRGE" GIVES US THE SAME SONG-AND-DANCE!
NO NEED TO VISIT HIM IN PERSON! WE CAN SPY ON THE "McBUCK" MONEY BIN FROM RIGHT HERE!
LET'S SEE... WHOA! THAR SHE BLOWS!
GULP!
THUD
BOO-HOO-HOO!

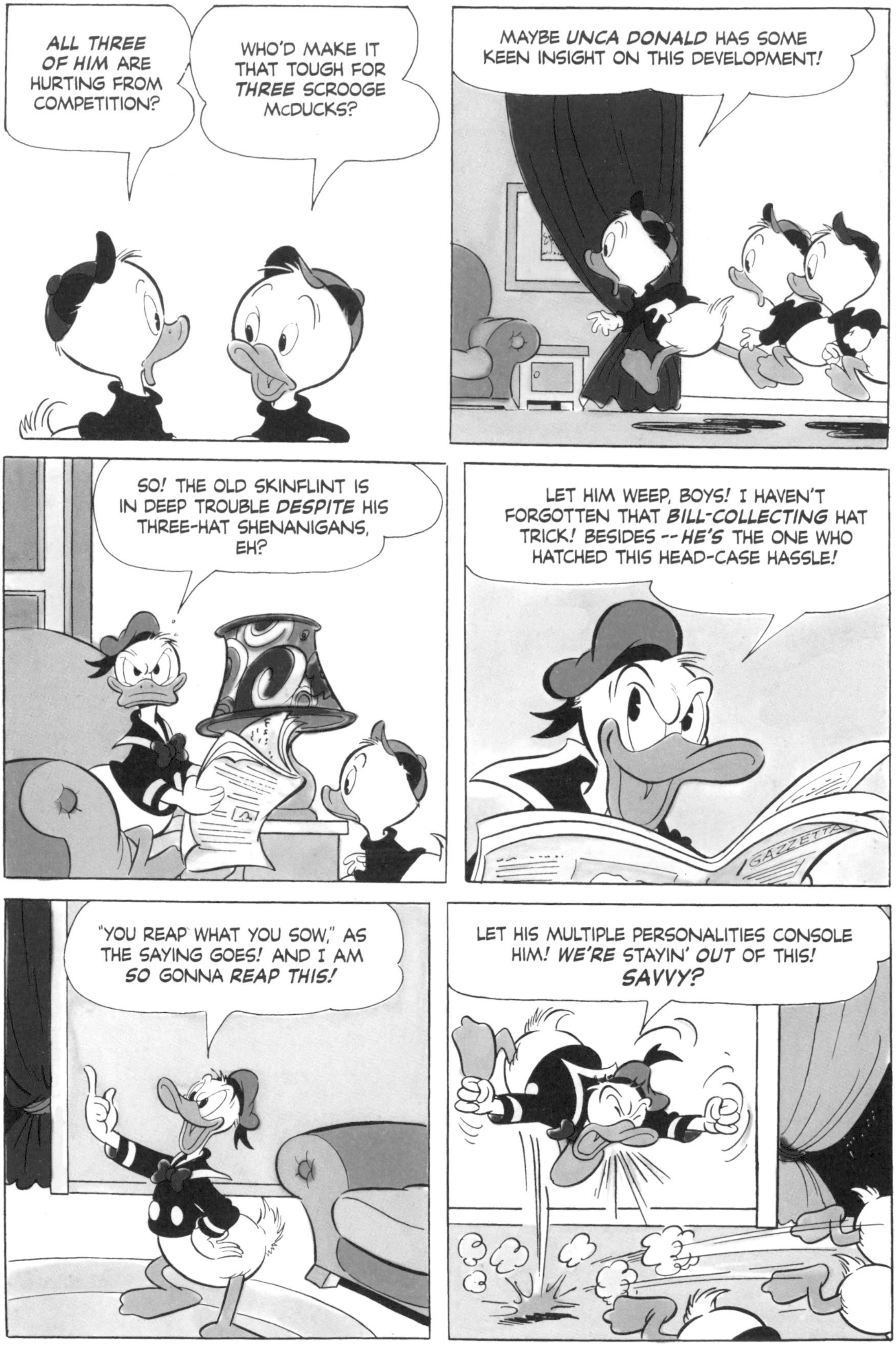
ALL THREE OF HIM ARE HURTING FROM COMPETITION?
WHO'D MAKE IT THAT TOUGH FOR THREE SCROOGE McDUCKS?
MAYBE UNCA DONALD HAS SOME KEEN INSIGHT ON THIS DEVELOPMENT!
SO! THE OLD SKINFLINT IS IN DEEP TROUBLE DESPITE HIS THREE-HAT SHENANIGANS, EH?
LET HIM WEEP, BOYS! I HAVEN'T FORGOTTEN THAT BILL-COLLECTING HAT TRICK! BESIDES -- HE'S THE ONE WHO HATCHED THIS HEAD-CASE HASSLE!
GAZZETTA
"YOU REAP WHAT YOU SOW," AS THE SAYING GOES! AND I AM SO GONNA REAP THIS!
LET HIS MULTIPLE PERSONALITIES CONSOLE HIM! WE'RE STAYIN' OUT OF THIS! SAVVY?

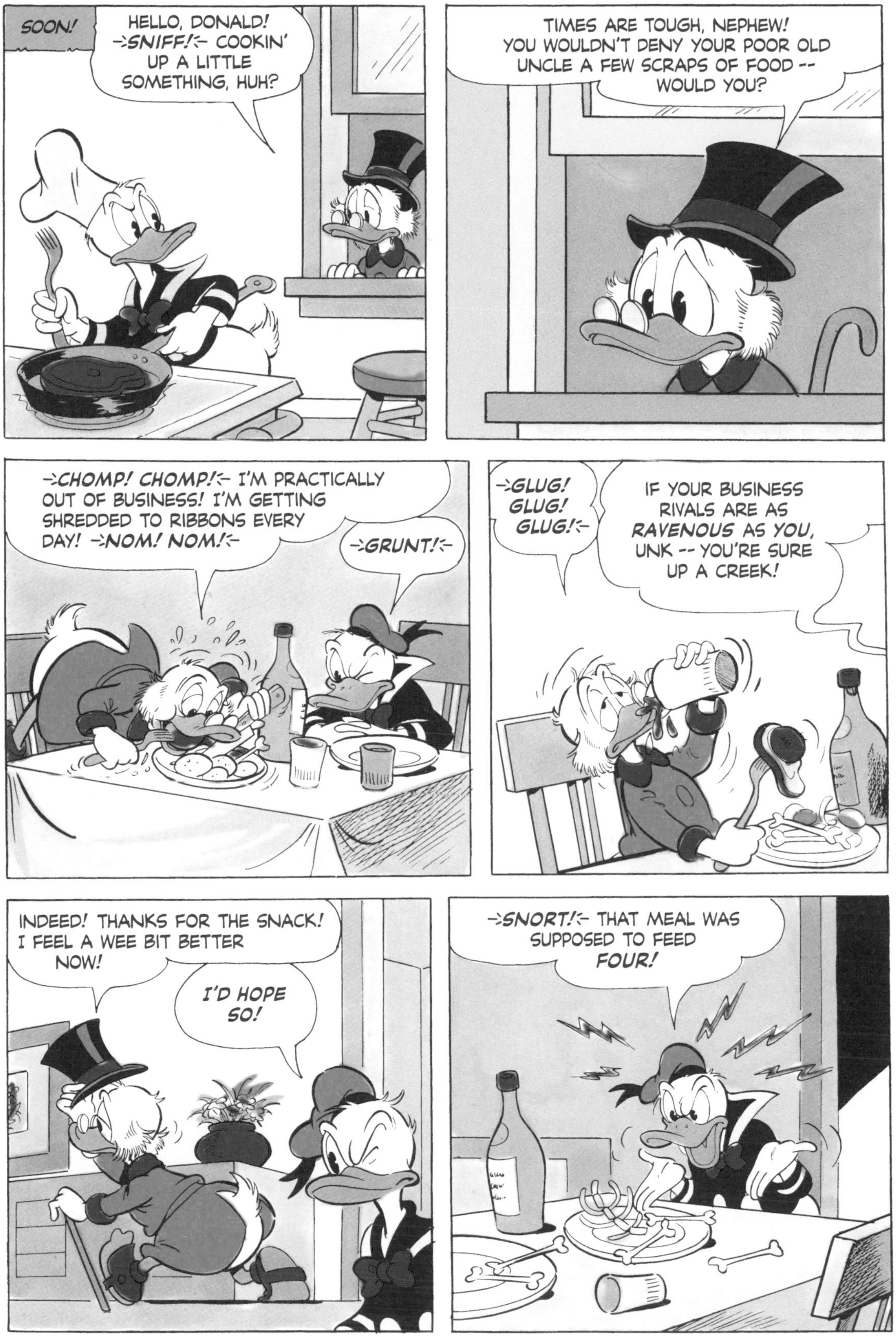
SOON!
HELLO, DONALD! -SNIFF!- COOKIN' UP A LITTLE SOMETHING, HUH?
TIMES ARE TOUGH, NEPHEW! YOU WOULDN'T DENY YOUR POOR OLD UNCLE A FEW SCRAPS OF FOOD -- WOULD YOU?
-CHOMP! CHOMP!- I'M PRACTICALLY OUT OF BUSINESS! I'M GETTING SHREDDED TO RIBBONS EVERY DAY! -NOM! NOM!-
-GRUNT!-
-GLUG! GLUG! GLUG!-
IF YOUR BUSINESS RIVALS ARE AS RAVENOUS AS YOU, UNK -- YOU'RE SURE UP A CREEK!
INDEED! THANKS FOR THE SNACK! I FEEL A WEE BIT BETTER NOW!
I'D HOPE SO!
-SNORT!- THAT MEAL WAS SUPPOSED TO FEED FOUR!

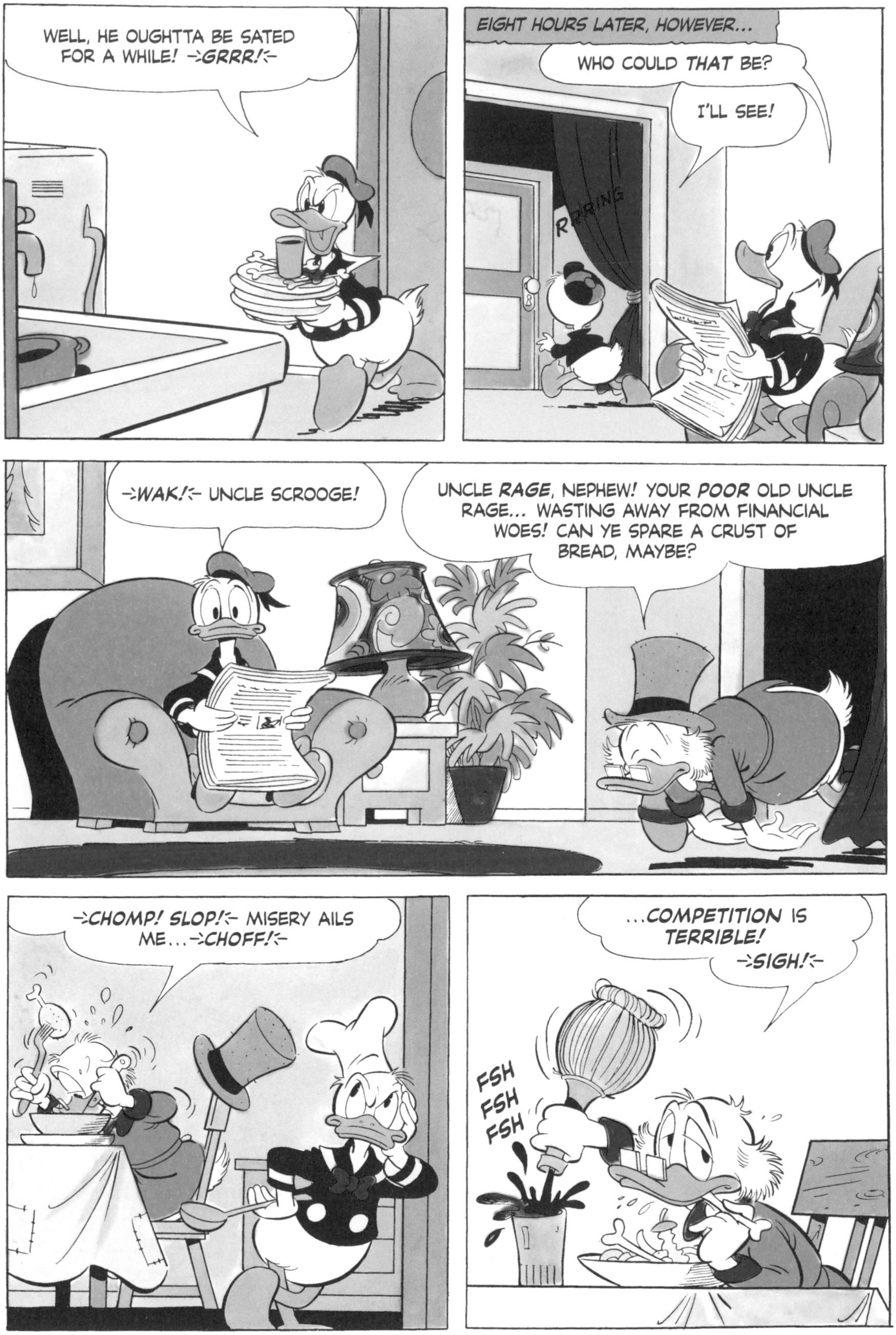

WELL, HE OUGHTTA BE SATED FOR A WHILE! -GRRR!-
EIGHT HOURS LATER, HOWEVER...
RRRING
WHO COULD THAT BE?
I'LL SEE!
-WAK!- UNCLE SCROOGE!
UNCLE RAGE, NEPHEW! YOUR POOR OLD UNCLE RAGE... WASTING AWAY FROM FINANCIAL WOES! CAN YE SPARE A CRUST OF BREAD, MAYBE?
-CHOMP! SLOP!- MISERY AILS ME... -CHOFF!-
...COMPETITION IS TERRIBLE! -SIGH!-
FSH FSH FSH

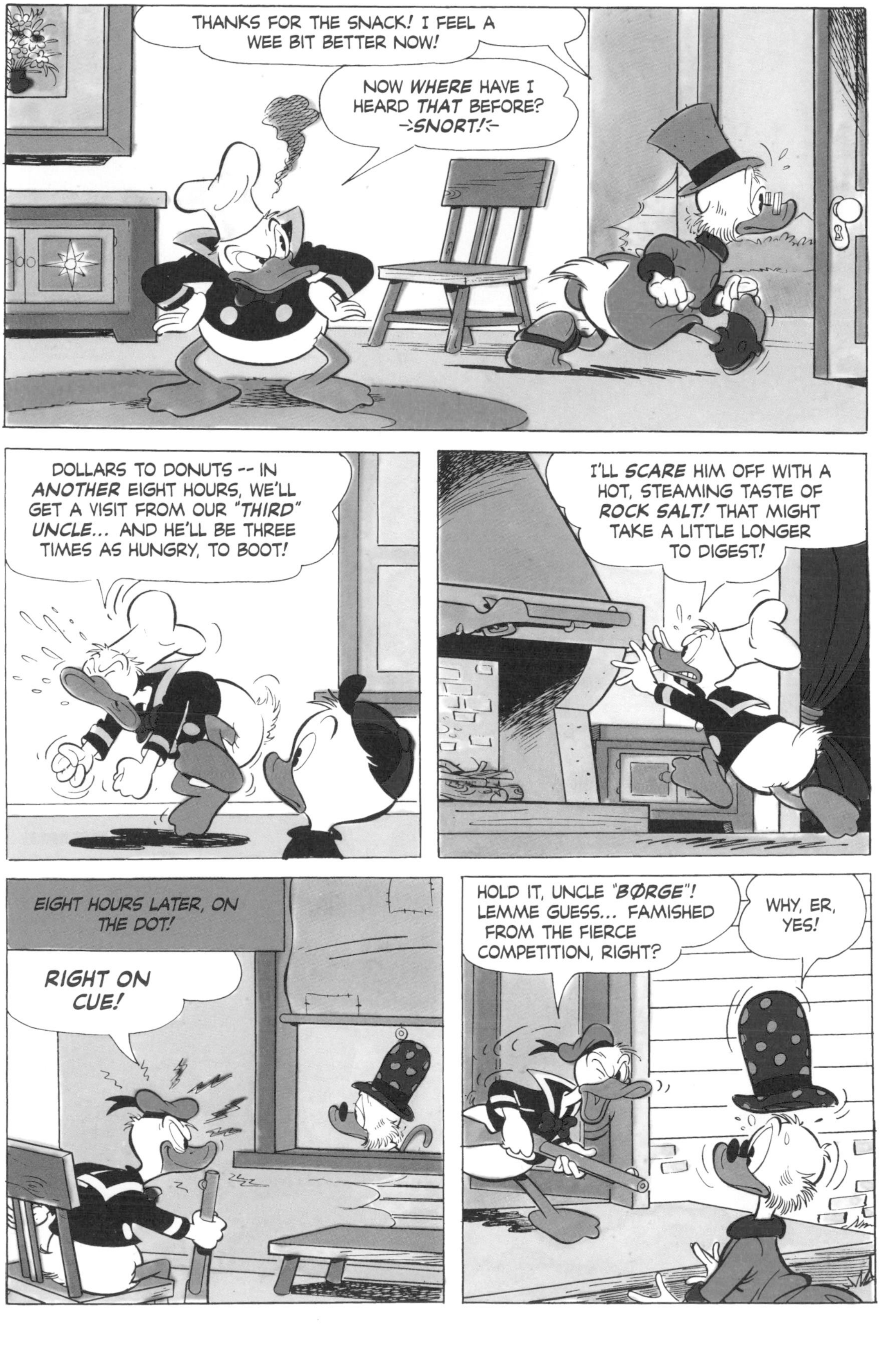
THANKS FOR THE SNACK! I FEEL A WEE BIT BETTER NOW!
NOW WHERE HAVE I HEARD THAT BEFORE? -SNORT!-
DOLLARS TO DONUTS -- IN ANOTHER EIGHT HOURS, WE'LL GET A VISIT FROM OUR "THIRD" UNCLE... AND HE'LL BE THREE TIMES AS HUNGRY, TO BOOT!
I'LL SCARE HIM OFF WITH A HOT, STEAMING TASTE OF ROCK SALT! THAT MIGHT TAKE A LITTLE LONGER TO DIGEST!
EIGHT HOURS LATER, ON THE DOT!
RIGHT ON CUE!
HOLD IT, UNCLE "BØRGE"! LEMME GUESS... FAMISHED FROM THE FIERCE COMPETITION, RIGHT?
WHY, ER, YES!

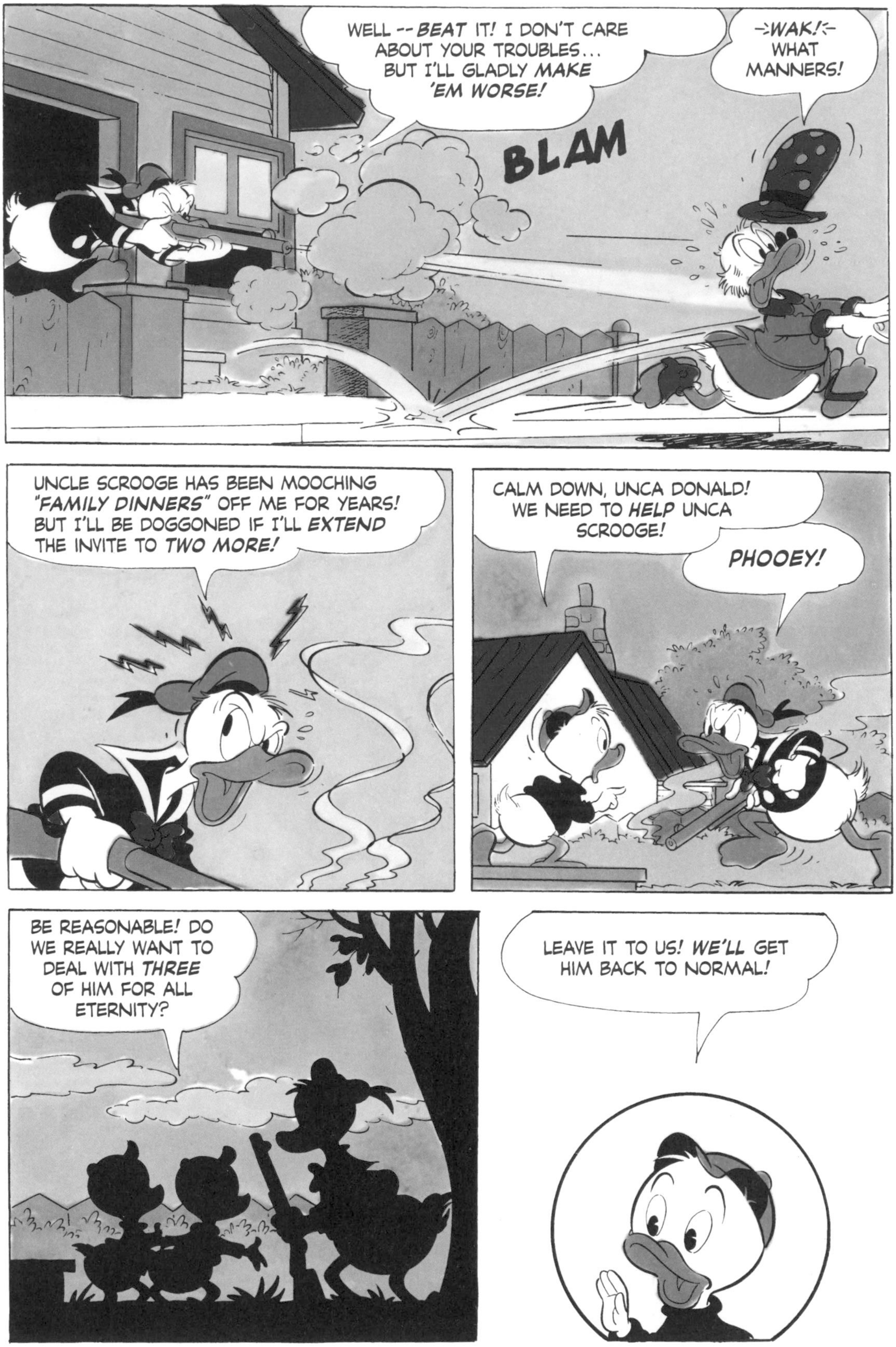
WELL -- BEAT IT! I DON'T CARE ABOUT YOUR TROUBLES... BUT I'LL GLADLY MAKE 'EM WORSE!
BLAM
-WAK!- WHAT MANNERS!
UNCLE SCROOGE HAS BEEN MOOCHING "FAMILY DINNERS" OFF ME FOR YEARS! BUT I'LL BE DOGGONED IF I'LL EXTEND THE INVITE TO TWO MORE!
CALM DOWN, UNCA DONALD! WE NEED TO HELP UNCA SCROOGE!
PHOOEY!
BE REASONABLE! DO WE REALLY WANT TO DEAL WITH THREE OF HIM FOR ALL ETERNITY?
LEAVE IT TO US! WE'LL GET HIM BACK TO NORMAL!

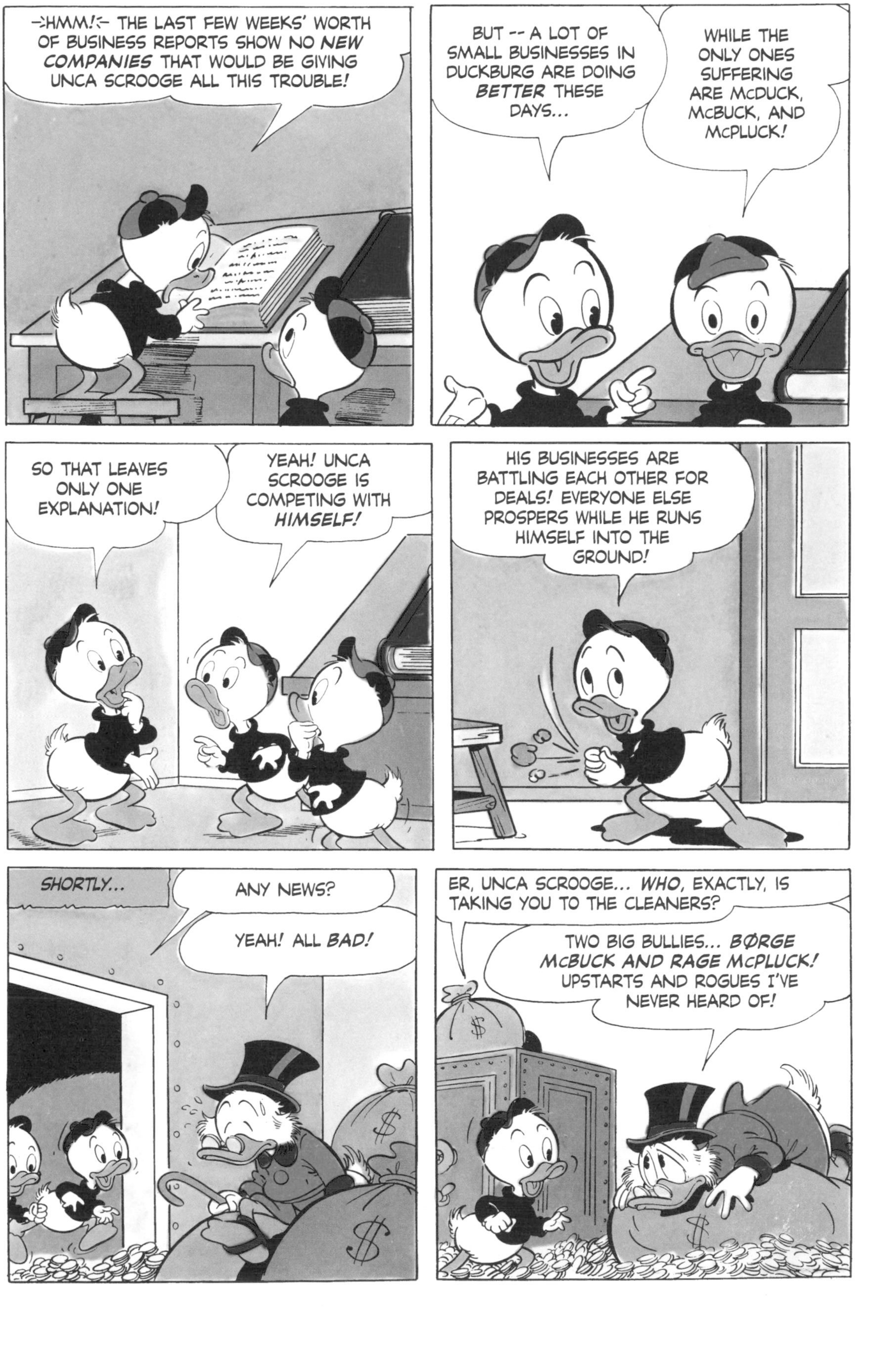
-HMM!- THE LAST FEW WEEKS' WORTH OF BUSINESS REPORTS SHOW NO NEW COMPANIES THAT WOULD BE GIVING UNCA SCROOGE ALL THIS TROUBLE!
BUT -- A LOT OF SMALL BUSINESSES IN DUCKBURG ARE DOING BETTER THESE DAYS...
WHILE THE ONLY ONES SUFFERING ARE McDUCK, McBUCK, AND McPLUCK!
SO THAT LEAVES ONLY ONE EXPLANATION!
YEAH! UNCA SCROOGE IS COMPETING WITH HIMSELF!
HIS BUSINESSES ARE BATTLING EACH OTHER FOR DEALS! EVERYONE ELSE PROSPERS WHILE HE RUNS HIMSELF INTO THE GROUND!
SHORTLY...
ANY NEWS?
YEAH! ALL BAD!
ER, UNCA SCROOGE... WHO, EXACTLY, IS TAKING YOU TO THE CLEANERS?
TWO BIG BULLIES... BØRGE McBUCK AND RAGE McPLUCK! UPSTARTS AND ROGUES I'VE NEVER HEARD OF!

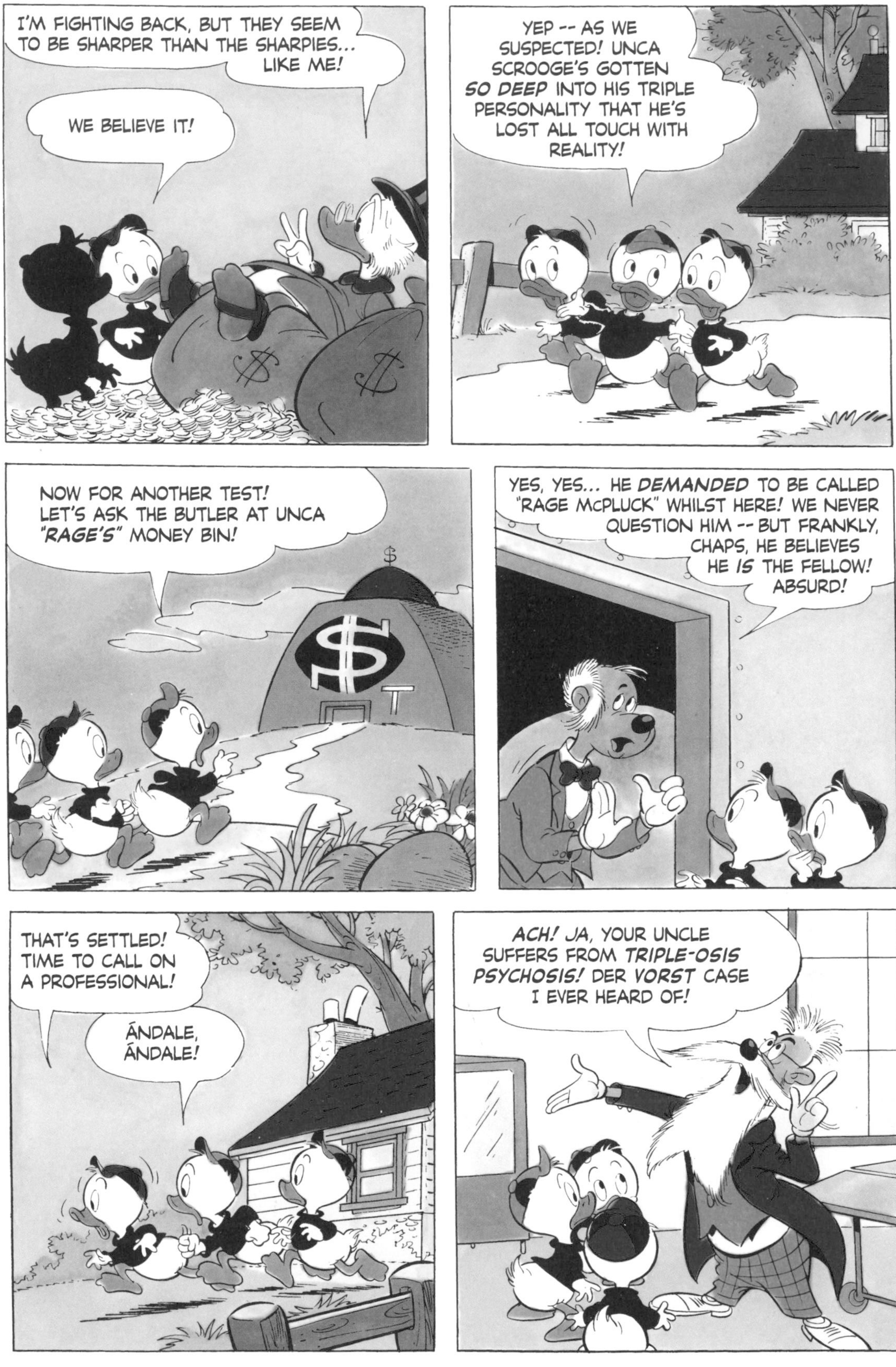
I'M FIGHTING BACK, BUT THEY SEEM TO BE SHARPER THAN THE SHARPIES... LIKE ME!
WE BELIEVE IT!
YEP -- AS WE SUSPECTED! UNCA SCROOGE'S GOTTEN SO DEEP INTO HIS TRIPLE PERSONALITY THAT HE'S LOST ALL TOUCH WITH REALITY!
NOW FOR ANOTHER TEST! LET'S ASK THE BUTLER AT UNCA "RAGE'S" MONEY BIN!
YES, YES... HE DEMANDED TO BE CALLED "RAGE McPLUCK" WHILST HERE! WE NEVER QUESTION HIM -- BUT FRANKLY, CHAPS, HE BELIEVES HE IS THE FELLOW! ABSURD!
THAT'S SETTLED! TIME TO CALL ON A PROFESSIONAL!
ÁNDALE, ÁNDALE!
ACH! JA, YOUR UNCLE SUFFERS FROM TRIPLE-OSIS PSYCHOSIS! DER VORST CASE I EVER HEARD OF!

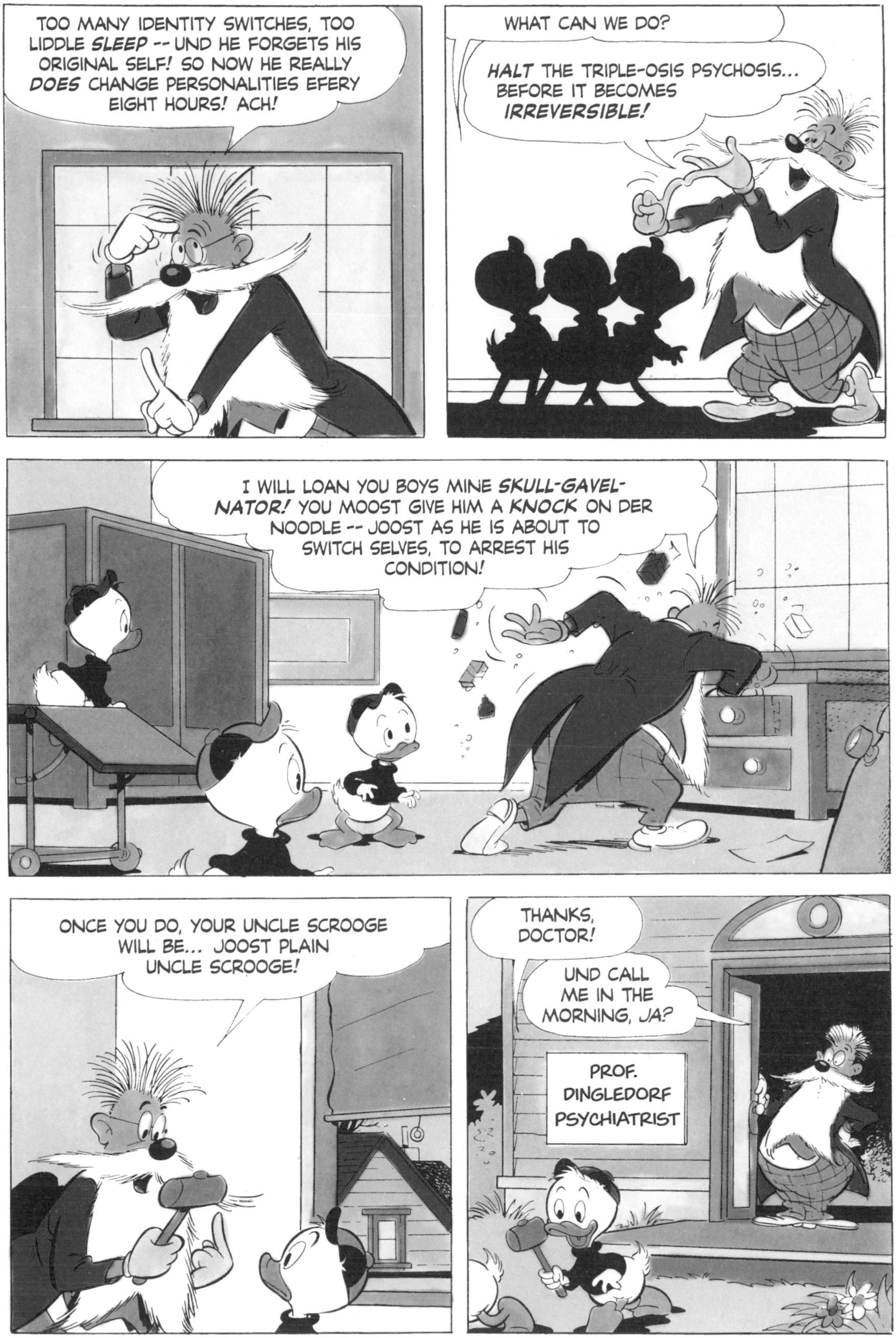

TOO MANY IDENTITY SWITCHES, TOO LIDDLE SLEEP -- UND HE FORGETS HIS ORIGINAL SELF! SO NOW HE REALLY DOES CHANGE PERSONALITIES EFERY EIGHT HOURS! ACH!
WHAT CAN WE DO?
HALT THE TRIPLE-OSIS PSYCHOSIS... BEFORE IT BECOMES IRREVERSIBLE!
I WILL LOAN YOU BOYS MINE SKULL-GAVEL-NATOR! YOU MOOST GIVE HIM A KNOCK ON DER NOODLE -- JOOST AS HE IS ABOUT TO SWITCH SELVES, TO ARREST HIS CONDITION!
ONCE YOU DO, YOUR UNCLE SCROOGE WILL BE... JOOST PLAIN UNCLE SCROOGE!
THANKS, DOCTOR!
UND CALL ME IN THE MORNING, JA?
PROF. DINGLEDORF PSYCHIATRIST

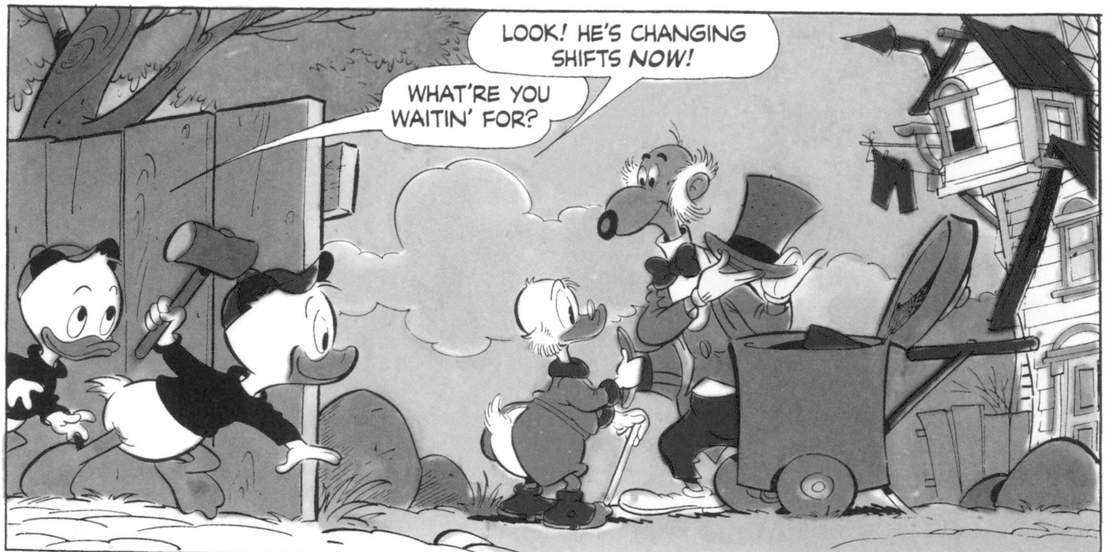

WHAT'RE YOU WAITIN' FOR?
LOOK! HE'S CHANGING SHIFTS NOW!

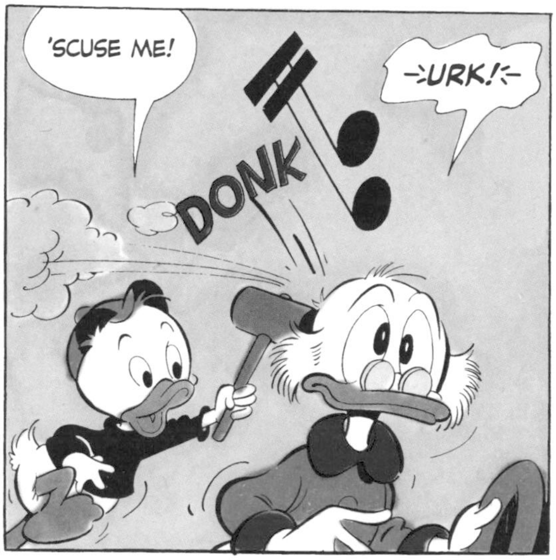

'SCUSE ME!
DONK
-URK!-

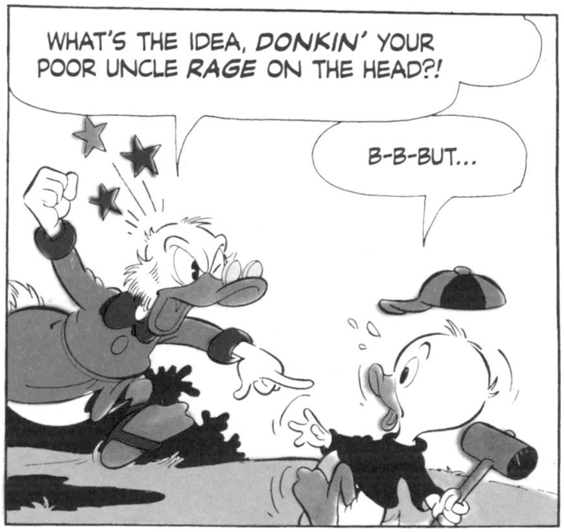

WHAT'S THE IDEA, DONKIN' YOUR POOR UNCLE RAGE ON THE HEAD?!
B-B-BUT...

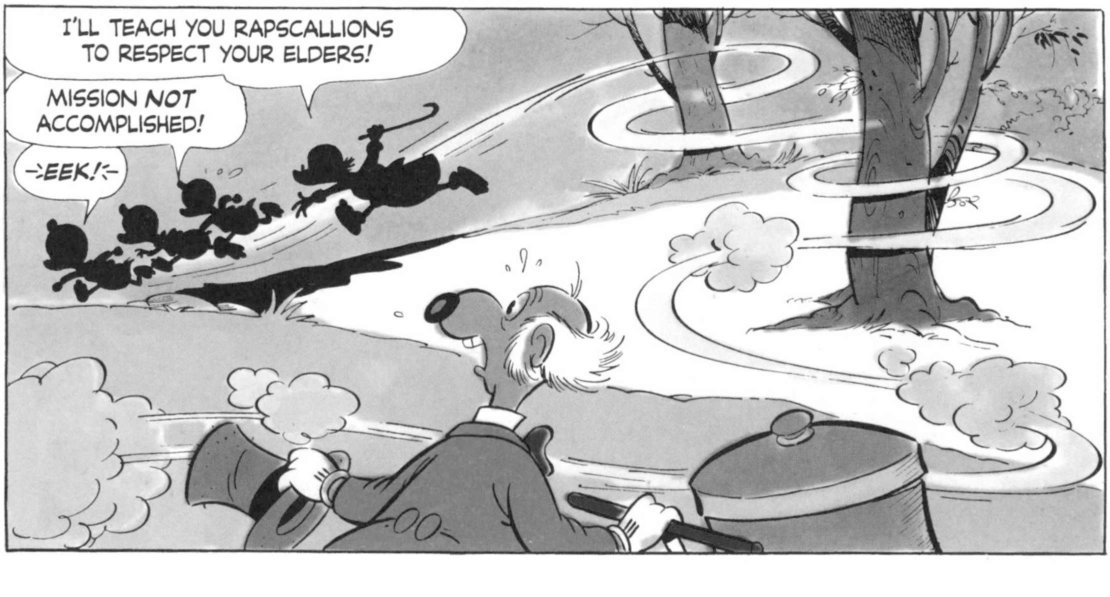

I'LL TEACH YOU RAPSCALLIONS TO RESPECT YOUR ELDERS!
MISSION NOT ACCOMPLISHED!
-EEK!-

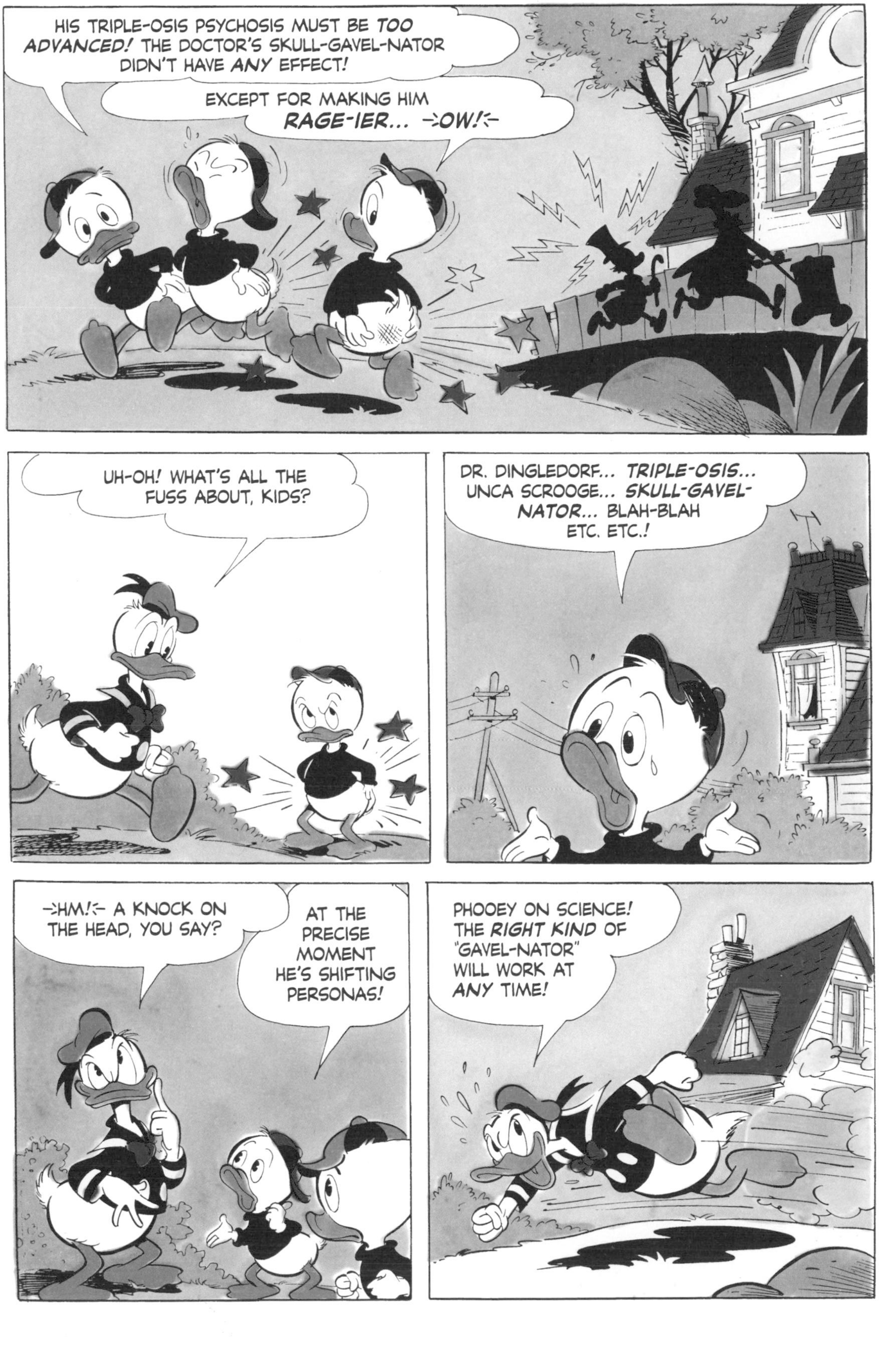
HIS TRIPLE-OSIS PSYCHOSIS MUST BE *TOO ADVANCED!* THE DOCTOR'S SKULL-GAVEL-NATOR DIDN'T HAVE *ANY* EFFECT!
EXCEPT FOR MAKING HIM *RAGE-IER... -OW!-*
UH-OH! WHAT'S ALL THE FUSS ABOUT, KIDS?
DR. DINGLEDORF... *TRIPLE-OSIS...* UNCA SCROOGE... *SKULL-GAVEL-NATOR...* BLAH-BLAH ETC. ETC.!
-HM!- A KNOCK ON THE HEAD, YOU SAY?
AT THE PRECISE MOMENT HE'S SHIFTING PERSONAS!
PHOOEY ON SCIENCE! THE *RIGHT KIND* OF "GAVEL-NATOR" WILL WORK AT *ANY* TIME!

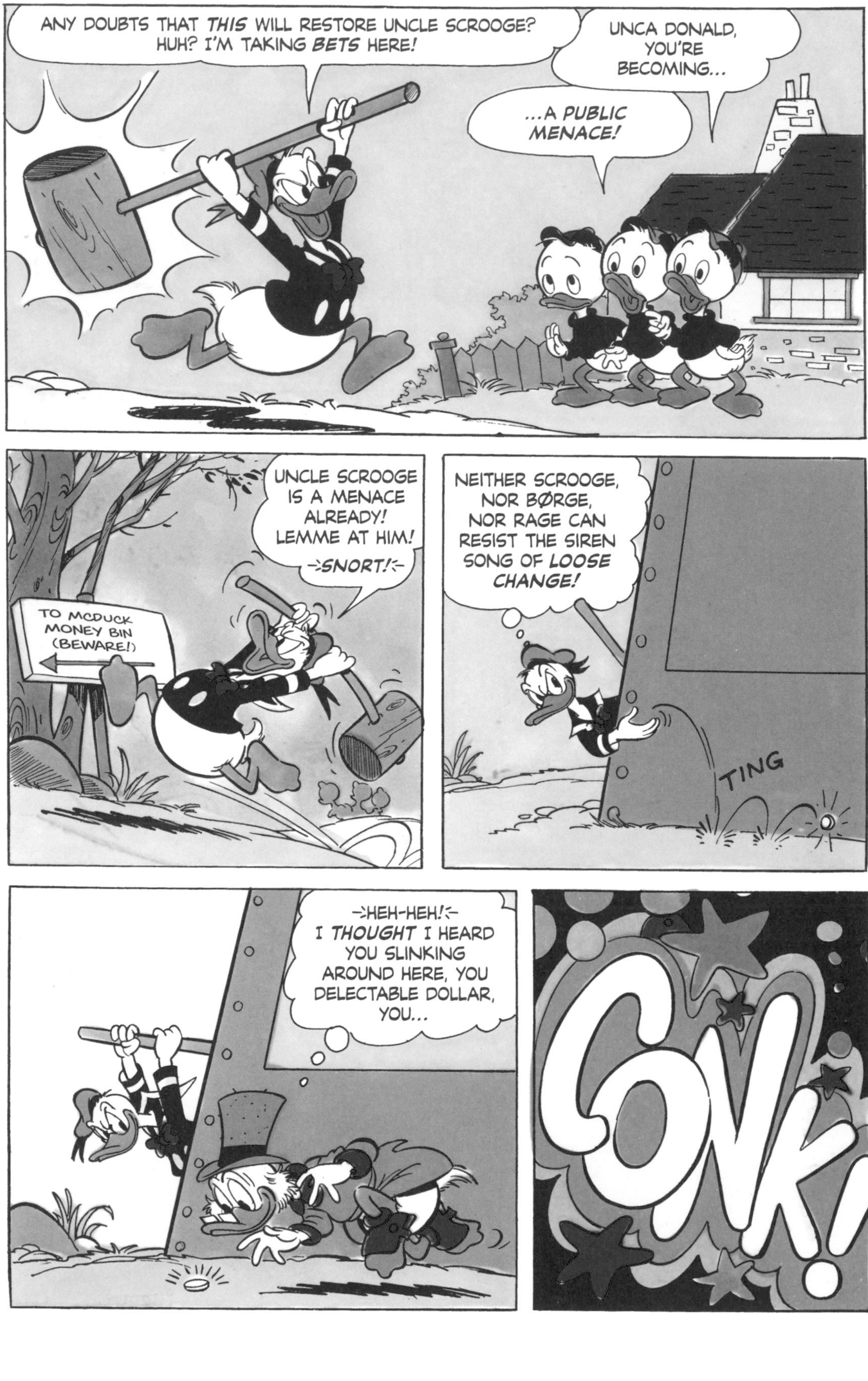
ANY DOUBTS THAT THIS WILL RESTORE UNCLE SCROOGE? HUH? I'M TAKING BETS HERE!
UNCA DONALD, YOU'RE BECOMING...
...A PUBLIC MENACE!
UNCLE SCROOGE IS A MENACE ALREADY! LEMME AT HIM! -SNORT!-
TO McDUCK MONEY BIN (BEWARE!)
NEITHER SCROOGE, NOR BØRGE, NOR RAGE CAN RESIST THE SIREN SONG OF LOOSE CHANGE!
TING
-HEH-HEH!- I THOUGHT I HEARD YOU SLINKING AROUND HERE, YOU DELECTABLE DOLLAR, YOU...
CONK!

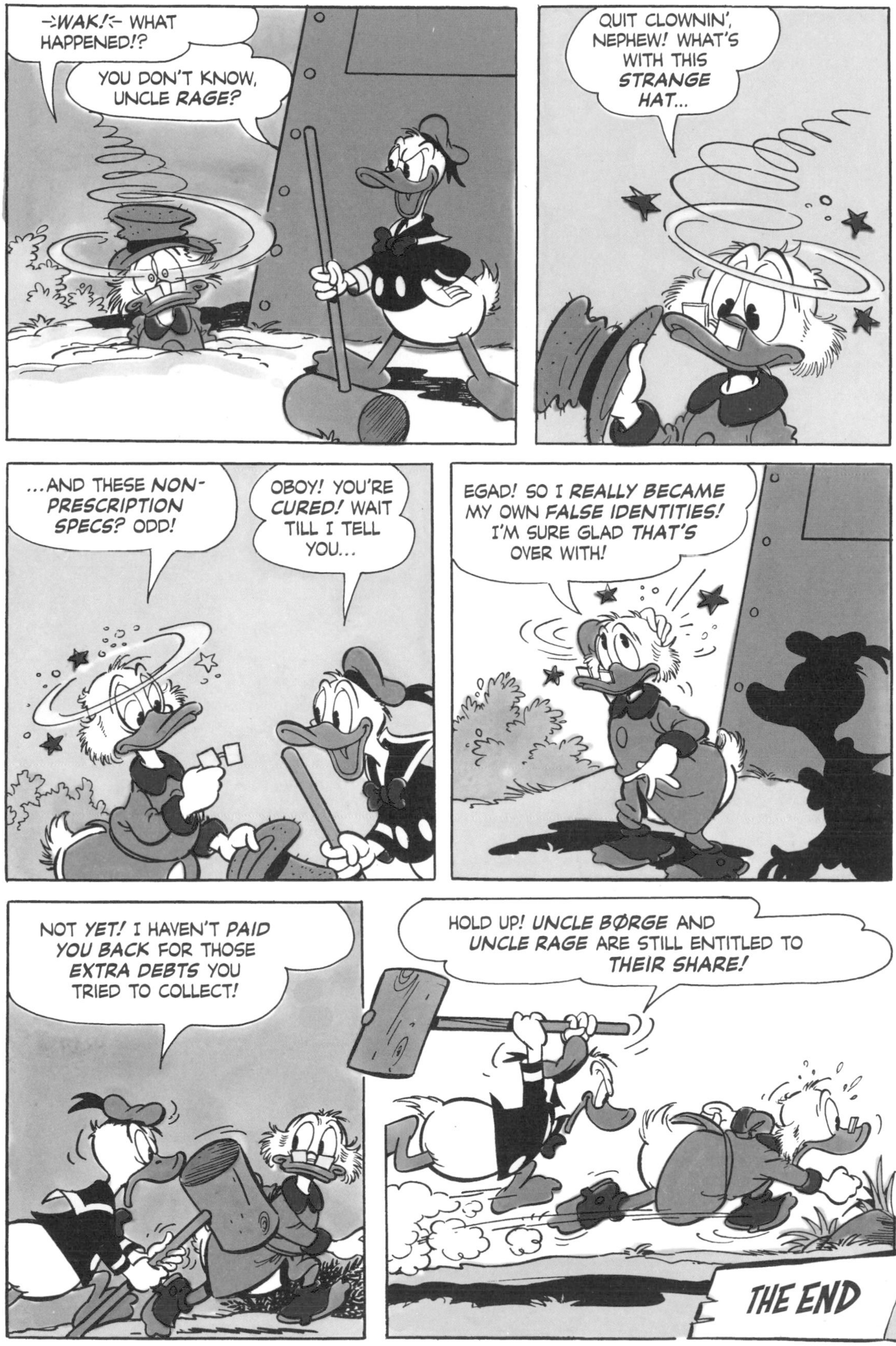
-WAK!- WHAT HAPPENED!?
YOU DON'T KNOW, UNCLE RAGE?
QUIT CLOWNIN', NEPHEW! WHAT'S WITH THIS STRANGE HAT...
...AND THESE NON-PRESCRIPTION SPECS? ODD!
OBOY! YOU'RE CURED! WAIT TILL I TELL YOU...
EGAD! SO I REALLY BECAME MY OWN FALSE IDENTITIES! I'M SURE GLAD THAT'S OVER WITH!
NOT YET! I HAVEN'T PAID YOU BACK FOR THOSE EXTRA DEBTS YOU TRIED TO COLLECT!
HOLD UP! UNCLE BØRGE AND UNCLE RAGE ARE STILL ENTITLED TO THEIR SHARE!
THE END

Giovan Battista Carpi

by LUCA BOSCHI

Translation by David Gerstein

GIOVAN BATTISTA CARPI and a European Disney master better known in the United States, Romano Scarpa, are often given shared billing in their home country of Italy. Carpi and Scarpa divided up the honors in a watershed 1968 episode of the TV program *Canzonissima*, which presented them as the Italian Disney comics school's twin leading lights. And Carpi and Scarpa shared art credits in the watershed miniseries "Storia a gloria della dinastia dei paperi" ("Duck Family Stories of Glory"), the first Disney comics effort to chronicle the Ducks' and McDucks' illustrious ancestors in detail.

But while Carpi's career might have converged with Scarpa's at several critical points, Carpi himself came to comics from a different point of origin, with work in illustration and painting preceding his work in the funnies. An accomplished draftsman and artist whose achievements were recognized in 1996 with an honorary doctorate from the University of Bologna, Carpi was born in Genoa on November 16, 1927. After attending the Accademia Ligustica di Belle Arti (Academy of Fine Arts) in his hometown and working as an assistant to the famed painter Giacomo Picollo, the young Carpi made his comics debut in 1945, when the magazine *Faville* (*Sparks*) gave him his break drawing the family sitcom strip *La famiglia Serafina*. In 1946 Carpi began contributing material to the educational journal *Lo Scolaro* (*The Schoolboy*), as well as drawing the character of Sparagrosso, a safari hunter, for *Gazzetta dei Piccoli*, the weekly children's supplement to the major newspaper *La Gazzetta del Popolo*. The young cartoonist had arrived.

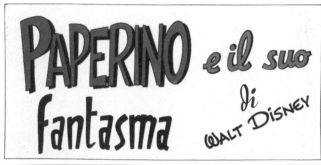

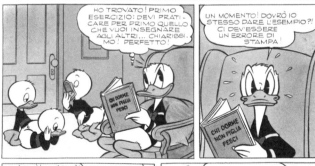

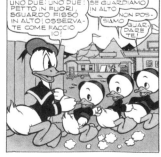

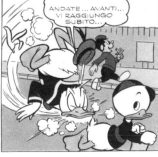

From there to Disney was a short step. In 1947, Carpi launched *Celestino al centro della Terra* ("Celestino at the Center of the Earth"), the first comics feature he singlehandedly created, wrote, and drew, this time for the children's magazine *Giornalino di Carroccio*. Moving to Milan that same year, Carpi began working as an in-betweener for the animation studio of Nino and Toni Pagot, then hard at work on *The Dynamite Brothers* (1949), Italy's first feature-length animated film in color. It was while working for the Pagots, several years later, that Carpi met Scarpa, who put a bug in his ear about the production of new Italian comics starring Mickey Mouse and Donald Duck.

PAPERINO e il suo fantasma
di WALT DISNEY
HO TROVATO! PRIMO ESERCIZIO: DEVI PRATI-CARE PER PRIMO QUELLO CHE VUOI INSEGNARE AGLI ALTRI... CHIARISSI-MO! PERFETTO!
CHI DORME NON PIGLIA PESCI
UN MOMENTO! DOVRÒ IO STESSO DARE L'ESEMPIO?! CI DEV'ESSERE UN ERRORE DI STAMPA!
CHI DORME NON PIGLIA PESCI
UNÒ DUÈ! UNÒ DUÈ! PETTO IN FUORI, SGUARDO FISSO IN ALTO! OSSERVA-TE COME FACCIO IO!
SE GUARDIAMO IN ALTO
NON POS-SIAMO
GUAR-DARE TE!
ANDATE... AVANTI... VI RAGGIUNGO SUBITO...
"Donald's Garrulous Ghost" (1953), drawn in a style inspired by Disney newspaper strips, marked Carpi's debut on the Duck comics scene.

Carpi joined up with publisher Mondadori and became a Disney comics artist, initially collaborating on stories with animator colleague Giulio Chierchini. "Paperino e il suo fantasma" ("Donald's Garrulous Ghost"), written for Carpi and Chierchini by Guido Martina, was the first of these collaborations—and also the second-ever European Disney story to feature the Beagle Boys.

Unlike many talents who jumped into Disney comics in this period, Carpi continued his independent projects at full strength. The 1950s saw Carpi contributing tempura-painted art for an edition of *Pinocchio* by the publisher Edizioni dell'Aquilone. For the Milan printing house of Renato Bianconi, with and without Chierchini's assistance, Carpi drew comics featuring such characters as the junior cowboy Raviolo Kid, the Eskimo hunter Nino, the medieval minstrels Salvatore and Chitarrone, the penguins Orazio and Arturo, the middle-aged grump Veleno, and Chico Cornacchia, a sort of Donald Duck-surrogate crow with two nephews instead of three. For the digest *Volpetto*, Carpi created the good little devil Geppo, his pal Torneo, and the feisty grande dame Nonna Abelarda. Beginning in 1957, Abelarda became a permanent fixture in another title, *Soldino*, in which she featured as the adoptive grandmother of the title character, the boy king of Bancarotta ("Bankruptia").

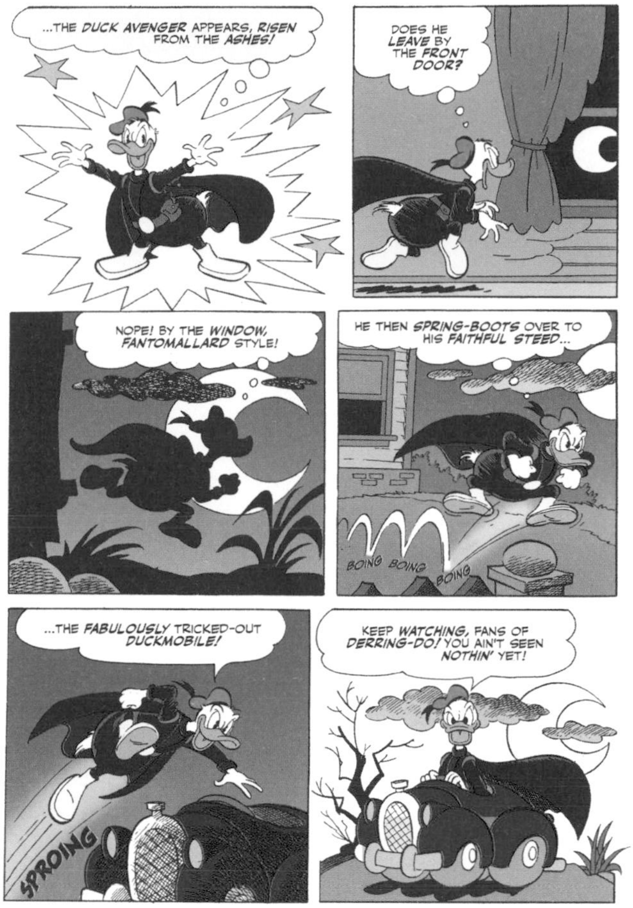

...THE DUCK AVENGER APPEARS, RISEN FROM THE ASHES!
DOES HE LEAVE BY THE FRONT DOOR?
NOPE! BY THE WINDOW, FANTOMALLARD STYLE!
HE THEN SPRING-BOOTS OVER TO HIS FAITHFUL STEED...
BOING BOING BOING
...THE FABULOUSLY TRICKED-OUT DUCKMOBILE!
SPROING
KEEP WATCHING, FANS OF DERRING-DO! YOU AIN'T SEEN NOTHIN' YET!

Donald's baptism of fire as the Carpi-drawn "Diabolical Duck Avenger" (1969) finds him famously talking in the third person and breaking the fourth wall.

As well-remembered as Carpi might be for Abelarda—not to mention later Italian comics stars like Beniamino Clorofilla, Zero, Gargantua, and the Dodo—he remains perhaps most famous for being the first to draw another Disney creation, Donald's feisty secret identity of Duck Avenger. The exploits of Duckburg's super-antihero began in 1969 with a concept from *Topolino* editor-in-chief Elisa Penna and a script by Guido Martina: rather than the cocky good guy he later became, the "diabolical" Avenger was initially inspired by Fantomas, a popular villain of public domain fiction. Duck Avenger's super gadgetry was provided by "Fantomius" (Fantomallard), a steampunk-era gentleman thief. Duck Avenger's motivating drive was less to fight crime and corruption, and more to get even with Uncle Scrooge and lucky cousin Gladstone for years of bullying. While Carpi drew few vintage Duck Avenger stories after the first, the Avenger's iconic, defiant look was designed to thrill anyone who'd taken pity on Donald over the years—and succeeded in a run that continues to date.

Yet many would argue that Carpi's greatest Disney triumphs lay elsewhere. Italy's ongoing *Grandi Parodie* (*Great Parodies*) comics subseries, continuing to date, is a decades-long tradition of Mouseton and Duckburg costume dramas, both retelling famous literary works and spoofing modern cinema. The series has long proven a constant canvas for Italian Disney talents at their best. From the Shakespeare-inspired "Hamlet, Prince of Duckmark" (1960) to "Sandodon and the Pearl of Labuan" (1976), based on Emilio

SETTIMANALE SPED. ABB. GR. 2/70 · *Walt Disney* · N. 1044 ★ LIRE 300 30 NOVEMBRE 1975

TOPOLINO

ARNOLDO MONDADORI EDITORE

Carpi's cover for *Topolino* #1044 (1975) illustrates "Jack the Steamer," a later tale of Mickey the Kid that pitted him against a steampunkish robot horse.

Salgari's 19th century novels, Carpi made his mark in this area, with Donald- and Scrooge-themed spoofs of *War and Peace* (1986) and *Les Miserables* ("That Missing Candelabra," 1989) perhaps the most famous. Beyond parodies of existing stories, Carpi created original costume dramas in the same vein: this volume's "Mickey the Kid and Six-Shot Goofy" (1974) inaugurated a popular series chronicling Mickey's and Goofy's cowboy-era ancestors—with occasional supporting roles for longtime stars, including Scrooge McDuck, who in earlier stories had been portrayed as living his younger days in the Wild West.

Carpi finished his career by turning from student—of Barks, of great artists and literature—to teacher. At the urging of longtime *Topolino* editor Gaudenzio Capelli, in 1988 Carpi became the director of the Scuolo Disney ("Disney school"), the Walt Disney Company's own Italian engine for comics artist training and supervision. Renamed the Accademia Disney in 1993, the program is still run today by a Carpi pupil, Roberto Santillo.

Carpi's storied life produced enough highlights to fill a new chapter of Huey, Dewey, and Louie's legendary Junior Woodchuck Guidebook. Is it any surprise that in 1969, Carpi also illustrated a local Italian edition of the Guidebook? Until his passing in 1999, this longtime master surged from strength to strength. 🦆